I0677778

Thicker

Than

Water

By: Matthew Daniels

Aka

TheRealBookWorm

Chapter 1

Before the couple could even make it to the door of their hotel room, Shonda threw herself on Abdul in a fit of passion. As she proceeded to grope his growing manhood through his black G-Unit jeans and shove her tongue down his throat, Abdul did little to stop her. His only response, which involved groping's of his own, was one of encouragement.

The man sitting alone inside of his black 2007 Cavalier watched them intensely. The sight of a man and woman preparing for a long night of sexual bliss at the Economy Lodge Hotel was a regular thing. As the man watched Abdul and Shonda go as far as they cared to go in public, he thought about how long it had been since he had gotten laid himself.

The bulge in his pants told him that it had been far too long. Allowing fantasies of the dark-skinned Shonda to enter his mind, he reached inside of his pants, pulled out his rock-hard penis, and began to slowly massage his member. Completely oblivious to their stalker, Abdul extended his arms and pressed Shonda's back up against the door to their hotel room.

"You gone make me bend you over and fuck you right here." Abdul declared, looking down at Shonda.

She squealed with glee.

"Oh, please do, daddy!" she begged seductively, biting her lower lip with fiery passion in her eyes. "I like that rough shit. If you think you're man enough to take it, by all means... take it."

Abdul grinned at the challenge, as he glanced left and right to see if they were alone. It was probably 11:30pm and the foot traffic had died down. Most, if not all of the guest, were already locked up in their rooms doing exactly what Abdul and Shonda would be doing shortly. Many of the lights lining the building were either broken or burned out, so it was indeed nice and dark. However, someone could easily exit their room at any given moment and catch them in the act.

Exhibitionism was indeed an exhilarating drug, but it took a special kind of freak to actually go all the way out in the open. After careful consideration of the pros and cons, Abdul decided he was freaky, but not that freaky. He figured it would be better to wait until they were inside the hotel room to satisfy the burning desires within him.

Releasing her from his grasp, Abdul fished the room key out of his pocket and slid the card through the lock. Just as he was opening the door, Shonda spun him around.

"Nu-uh scary." She said, reaching for his zipper. "You not gone get off that easy."

With that, she dropped down to her knees and skillfully unbuckled his pants. Before Abdul could even protest, Shonda had inserted his entire dick into her mouth. Her nose pressed hard up against his pubic hairs and his shaft crept deep into her waiting throat like a long black snake slithering into its lair. Gagging only slightly, she began to suck him off right there in the doorway as if she were auditioning for a job with Pornhub. Shonda made sure to gently massage his testicles as she sucked. It was a somewhat cold outside and she wanted his little friends to stay nice and warm.

"Mmmm!" She moaned, obviously enjoying her late-night meal.

Abdul quickly forgot about possible spectators and placed his hand on the back of Shonda's head.

Closing his eyes and grabbing a fist full of hair, he growled.

"You, nasty… little… bitch! Suck on it baby. Suck that dick."

Shonda didn't mind being called a bitch. It actually sort of turned her on. The vulgarity was like motivation. Shonda used her tongue to lick every inch of Abdul's thick black shaft as she bobbed her head up and down on his tool. Abdul wasn't sure exactly what she was doing, but whatever it was, he liked it. He slowly began to back up into the room with Shonda crawling in front of him not stopping at all from servicing him.

The man in the Cavalier noticed them entering the room, so he put his penis back inside of his pants and hurried out of the car. It was time to move. Rushing to get to them before they could close the door, he crouched down and began to slightly jog. Confident that he would make it to them in time, he reached inside of his long black trench coat and pulled out a .380 hand pistol with a silencer attached to it.

The gap between predator and prey quickly disappeared. The man wasted no time with pointless conversation. Standing behind a kneeling Shonda, and in front of an unaware Abdul, he quickly released two shots from his pistol and struck Abdul in both of his shoulders.

"Auugghh!" Abdul cried out in pain, as his body rocked backwards from the force of the bullets.

Shonda barely heard the shots, but the removal of Abdul's dick from her mouth, coupled with his loud scream, confirmed to her what had just happened. The man stepped inside of the room with them and shut the door. The two late-night lovers were now locked inside with the armed man in the trench coat.

Abdul collapsed onto the floor.

"Fuck!" He hollered, wincing in pain.

He attempted to grab his wounds, but the shots to his shoulders had severely compromised his ability to move his arms.

Gritting his teeth, he looked up at his assailant, but didn't recognize him.

Shonda jumped to her feet.

"It's about time, Squeak." She said, turning to the man with the gun and wiping her mouth off at the same time. "I thought this nigga was gonna nut before you stepped in. You know I don't like to make nobody cum but you."

"Better late than never." Squeak responded, walking around her and pointing the gun directly at Abdul's head.

Abdul grimaced in pain, but he was still conscious of the things going on around him.

"What the fuck is this?" He asked through clenched teeth, as he watched his attacker and the whore, he had paid top dollar for, stand side by side.

"You fucking slut!" He spat out. "You set me up."

Shonda laughed out loud.

"Naw lil daddy." She responded, pointing towards his waist. "Yo' dick set you up, not me. Niggas always wanna get that nut out."

Turning his attention to Squeak, he asked, "So what do you want? Money? Drugs? Both? What the fuck is this about?"

Squeak reached inside of his pocket and pulled out a wad of 100-dollar bills. He had close to $5,000 in cash.

"Money? I don't want your fucking money." He informed him coldly.

"I want your last breath. I want your life. I want to be the last thing you see in this world. Infamous sent me. Does that name ring a bell? He sends his regards."

Abdul's eyes got huge as silver dollars at the mention of Infamous. Infamous was one of the most powerful gang leaders in Texas City, Tx.

"You're lying." Abdul accused.

"The Southlane Villains and the Dramaside Hooligans have a truce. Infamous can't kill me. You must not know who I am? You can't kill me."

Squeak let an evil grin form across his lips.

"Wrong, wrong, and wrong my friend. The Villains and The Hooligans 'HAD' a truce, Infamous 'CAN' kill you, and I 'DO' know who you are. I just don't give a fuck."

Then, with no more words, he shot Abdul one more time in the forehead, execution style. Abdul died instantly. Looking down at his now motionless victim, Squeak thought about the ramifications of his actions. Murdering the second in command of the Dramaside Hooligans in cold blood, and for no apparent reason, would no doubt start a war. Coincidentally, that's exactly what his boss Infamous had in mind.

"Go wipe down his car and clean off your fingerprints." Squeak instructed Shonda, as he knelt beside Abduls' body.

Obediently, Shonda headed out of the room. Knowing that he needed to work fast, Squeak pulled a pocket knife out of his pocket and began to cut down the middle of Abdul's shirt, effectively splitting it down the middle.

"This should get their attention." He mumbled under his breath as he began carving into the dead man's torso.

Back in the parking lot, Shonda was happy to see that the commotion going on in their room didn't alert anyone to what was happening. She tugged on the hem of her skirt to keep it from riding up as she made her way to the Chrysler 300 that her and Abdul had arrived in. Removing the handkerchief that Squeak told her to carry in her bra, she used that to open the car door on the passenger side of the vehicle and climbed in. Doing her best to remember what all she had touched, she decided to simply wipe off everything that could be reached from where she was sitting. She wiped off the steering wheel, the dashboard, the middle console, and both of the front doors.

Shonda finished just in time, because as she was getting out of the car, she saw Squeak emerging from the hotel room. Noticing that she was finished cleaning the vehicle, Squeak motioned with his head for her to make her way over to the Cavalier. Squeak, on the other hand, headed towards the Chrysler. As they passed each other, Squeak gave Shonda the keys to the Cavalier, and Shonda gave Squeak the handkerchief.

Hopping into the Cavalier and starting it up, she looked over at Squeak. He was stuffing the handkerchief into the gas tank of Abdul's car. Shonda backed out of the parking space and drove around to the back of the hotel. By the time she had made it to the designated spot, Squeak was already running full speed through the center of the building towards the car. She leaned over and opened the passenger side door for him.

Diving in, he shouted, "Go!" just as a large explosion rocked the entire vehicle.

A fireball mingled with thick black smoke shot straight up above the roof of the hotel. Several car alarms went off simultaneously creating an almost musical tune of beeps, honks, and wails. Everyone inside of the hotel heard the explosion and exited their rooms to investigate. Instinct caused all eyes to gravitate towards the car engulfed in flames in the front, and just as Squeak had planned, no one noticed the black Cavalier making a slow getaway in the back.

Chapter Two

The savory aroma of eggs, bacon, biscuits, and sausage seemed to drift effortlessly through the entire 8-bedroom mansion. In the kitchen, Silvia worked diligently to prepare breakfast for herself, her husband, and her twin sons DeShawn and DeAnte. She knew that her husband Sticks could easily afford to hire a maid, but she didn't like the idea of another woman taking care of her man and her family. Silvia was one of those old-fashioned women who enjoyed playing the role of a traditional housewife. In her opinion, as long as Sticks provided for the household, she would take care of all the chores.

Silvia sang some old school TLC to herself as she swayed her hips back and forth.

"I'll give you the red... light... speeeeeciallllll, alllll through the night. Baby it's yoursssssss. I'm yoursssss. If you want it tooooonight." She sang.

Standing over the stove in a metallic gray robe that she had received as a birthday present from Sticks the year before, she looked like a model. Silvia Trenice Wayne stood 5"10 and weighed around 150 lbs. She was tall and slim, but she had curves in all the places a woman was expected to have them. From head to toe, her skin was an even paper sack brown, and her jet-black hair, which she had pulled back into a ponytail, extended 2 inches passed her shoulders.

Everyone always told her that because of her height and her husband's height, DeShawn and DeAnte would probably grow up to be professional basketball players. Sticks, her husband, stood 6"4 and he was slim just like his wife. The two of them even had a similar skin tone. Their relationship was crushing to the old adage that opposites attract. Silvia and Sticks could pass for brother and sister.

Without warning, Silvia's serenade to herself was cut short when her two four-year-old sons came charging into the kitchen.

"Mommiiee!" They screeched, as they raced to see who could get to her first.

Silvia started to scold them about running in the house but hearing their gleeful laughter as they attached themselves to her legs softened her up. Looking down at her two little blessings in their superhero pajamas, she couldn't help but to smile. Their resemblance never ceased to amaze her. As a mother, she could tell them apart, but for purposes of quick recognition, each child had his own style. DeShawn liked Spiderman and his favorite color was blue. DeAnte liked the Incredible Hulk and his favorite color was green.

Silvia sat the spatula down and lowered the heat on the stove.

Kneeling down, she hugged her boys and said, "Heeeey baby. How's mama's big boys doing today?"

They squirmed and continued to laugh as she kissed them all over their faces over and over again.

"Stop mama." They playfully protested, trying in vain to escape her grasp.

Once she felt satisfied with the number of kisses she had given them, she released them and stood back up. Happy to be free, both boys turned and headed full speed out of the kitchen.

"Go wake up your daddy!" She shouted after them, as she went back to cooking breakfast.

The boys loved it when they got permission to wake up their daddy. They would do it without permission all the time but to them it seemed better when they were told specifically to do it. Wasting no time whatsoever, they climbed the stairs and burst into the master bedroom. Sticks was still sound asleep and stretched out across the center of his king-sized bed. Everything inside of his room was black and gold, so even with the light from the hallway filtering in, it was still somewhat dark.

That did nothing to slow the boys down though. They had chased each other through every room of the house so much that they could probably run full speed through the house with blindfolds on and not stumble or trip so much as one time. Crossing the threshold of the room, they both stopped running when they got to the edge of the bed. Lowering their laughter to a light giggle, they eased their way onto the bed, and stood on either side of Sticks. DeAnte could hardly contain himself, so he covered his mouth with one of his hands to muffle the noise. DeShawn was excited too, but he was better at maintaining his composure. So as usual, DeShawn whispered the countdown.

Both boys got ready to pounce as soon as DeShawn whispered, "5...4...3...2..."

Just as he was about to say 'one', Sticks sat straight up in the bed and yelled at the top of his lungs.

"Aaaauuuggghhh!" He screamed, grabbing both of them by their pajama tops.

Instantly being gripped with fear, the boys began to screech like a banshee. Sticks shook them and continued to yell as the boys twisted and squirmed trying to get free. When Sticks finally let them go, both boys tumbled off the sides of the bed and hit the floor with a loud "THUD." As the two boys began to cry, Sticks erupted in laughter. The boys rushed out of the room, one holding his head, the other clutching his elbow, and both crying for their mother.

"Lil bad asses." Sticks called after them as he slid to the edge of the bed and swung his legs off. "Always fucking with me."

Getting a good stretch in, Sticks turned his attention to the nightstand next to his bed. Sitting on top of it, there was an alabaster jewelry box with hieroglyphics carved into it. His jewelry box did not contain jewelry, but it did house something just as valuable. His jewelry box held his weed stash. Stick's had a habit of starting every day off by smoking an apple flavored mini-blunt re-rolled with the best hydro Texas City had to offer inside of it. He had been doing it for so long, the act became almost ritualistic to a degree and Stick's felt that if he missed his breakfast blunt his day would not go right.

As he went through the motions of lighting the blunt and inhaling his first puff of the day, he reveled in the fact that he had finally gotten Deuce and Bear, his nicknames for his sons, back for all the times they woke him up by using him as a human trampoline. Lucky for him, he was awakened earlier by the scent of Silvia working her magic downstairs in the kitchen. He knew that it wouldn't be long before his boys came looking for him, so he played sleep and waited for them. Replaying the event in his mind caused him to laugh out loud all over again. Unfortunately, the sweet taste of victory was only short lived.

"Kenneth Baker Wayne!" He heard Silvia shout-out. "What did you do to my babies?"

Not surprisingly, they had told on him. Sticks hit the blunt hard again and mentally prepared for the chastisement from his wife.

....

On the other side of town, at the Texas City Police Department Headquarters, Detective Derrick Rose was going over his papers one more time while sipping a hot cup of coffee before going to question his only possible lead. He already had a person of interest that his instincts told him would know something about his homicide victim from last night. The same victim that was found shot dead and carved up in a hotel room at the Economy Lodge.

Detective Rose had worked plenty of murder cases in his career. Texas City was a small town of only about 60,000 people, but the murder rate was high. The local newspapers and media outlets tried to portray Texas City as an All-American City, but crime ran rampant in the streets. The gangs and drug dealers had just as much power and influence as the police and politicians. Rose had been dealing with the filth so long, he could always tell when the case that came across his desk was going to be difficult to crack.

Most murder cases were difficult to crack anyway. The whole no snitch rule was law in Texas City. If the dirtbags found out that someone was working with law enforcement, their entire family was in jeopardy. Rose could recall a time he had to investigate the murder of two women who were working with the TCPD. They were drug addicts, so they knew a lot of valuable information about what was going on in the underworld. Rose could still remember the day he was called out to a bloody scene on the back road 197. Either the local gangs or the crooked police on the force had found out that they were snitching, and so they decapitated both women and dumped their remains on the side of road. It was eventually blamed on a Hispanic drifter from out of town, but everybody, including Rose knew the truth. The real killer was from Texas City and still roaming the Texas City streets.

Rose knew that this was definitely going to be one of those cases. Detective Rose operated on one fundamental premise though. He understood that all murders could be solved. Why? Because all killers left clues. No killer was perfect. Some of them were highly intelligent, extremely sophisticated, and very crafty, but none of them were perfect. They all made mistakes. He had seen cases blown wide open by something as small as a single strand of hair, or something as seemingly insignificant as a discarded piece of chewing gum.

The victim in his most recent homicide case was named Abdul Mustaf. Abdul was a 32-year-old African native from Nigeria with an arrest record as long as Interstate Highway 45. It was common knowledge amongst the TCPD that he was a high-ranking member of the Texas City street gang known as The Dramaside Hooligans. He had been arrested several times, but no official charges had been able to stick since he had rose in the ranks of the Hooligans. Everyone in their organization was dirty, but they were so disciplined and feared that they were virtually untouchable.

The thing that Rose couldn't understand was, first, how did someone manage to get close enough to Abdul to murder him, and secondly, why. Knowing that there was only one way to find the answers to his questions, Rose gathered all of his files and photographs, and then headed to his unmarked Crown Victoria.

As he loaded up his things inside of his vehicle, Rose thought back to a night two weeks prior to last night. He was eating dinner with his wife and complaining about how boring his job had become. There was more than enough work for the narcotics department, but ever since the Hooligans and the Villains made their truce, the murder rate in Texas City had dropped dramatically. He told his wife that he couldn't help but to wish he had more to do on a daily basis. He didn't necessarily want innocent people to start getting killed, he just wanted a little action. He wanted to feel the exhilaration of combing through a crime scene. He wanted the thrill of chasing down bad guys in dark alleys. He wanted to interrogate some tough guys and brake down some thugs. Rose wasn't ready to sit behind a desk and push papers. He wanted action. Shoot-outs, car chases, the whole nine. Now that he seemed to be about to receive it, his wife's warning replayed over and over in his mind.

"Be careful what you wish for, Derrick. You might just get it."

As Rose made his way over to the West Side of Texas City, to the Amburn Oaks subdivision, he racked his brain trying to unravel the mystery. Nothing about the murder made any sense. His victim was shot 3 times. Once in each shoulder and once in the forehead. The shots in the shoulders seemed to imply that the shooter wanted to immobilize Abdul before killing him, but why? Robbery was ruled out as the motivating factor of the murder, because when the forensics unit searched his clothes, the victim still had over $3,000 in his pockets.

Another mystery was the purpose the killer had for blowing up Abdul's car. Was it meant to destroy evidence? Could the vehicle have somehow been used to link the killer to the murder? Was something removed from the vehicle, prior to its destruction? It would've been great if the hotel had some useable camera footage, but they only had cameras situated inside the lobby and facing the cash registers. It was confirmed that Abdul paid for the room himself, but they were blind to what went on outside of the lobby in the parking lot. This was probably the only time Rose had wished the hotel owner was one of those perverts who placed hidden cameras inside of their rooms so they could masturbate to the activities of their guests. Maybe then he would have some solid evidence.

Detective Rose brought his car to a halt at the red light. While waiting on the light to turn back green, he sifted through the photographs he had of the crime scene lying in the passenger seat. Coming to the photo of Abdul's body, his right eye twitched slightly. Picking it up so that he could examine it better, he was once again made aware of just how desensitized his job had made him. The average person would probably become queasy at the sight of a contorted dead body lying in a pool of blood. Rose, however, wasn't too shaken up by it. True, this murder was different from the ones he had encountered in the past, but a murder was a murder. A dead body was a dead body.

Rose brought the picture up to his face. He noticed that Abdul had died with his eyes open. Staring deep into Abdul's glazed over expression, Rose wondered what he saw right before he was killed. He peered into the dead man's pupils, as if through some stroke of luck, the image of his killer would be imprinted somewhere within them. It was his job to unlock the secrets of the deceased, but something was telling him that this one would be a hard one to crack.

"What happened to you?" Rose whispered to the photograph. "Did your lifestyle finally catch up to you? After years of living above the law and beyond consequences, did you finally have to answer for your sins?"

Half waiting for an answer, and half wishing for a revelation, he closed his eyes and massaged the brim of his nose. Come on Rose, think. What are you missing here? There has to be something. There's always something.

Rose began to walk through the crime scene in his mind.

Hmmm. The bed was still made, so the room had not been used. Over on the sink, the towels were still folded, and the complimentary bars of soap were still neatly wrapped. The free coffee had not been opened and the TV was turned off. It was common knowledge that the Economy Lodge was used for Johns and their prostitutes, but nothing about the scene made Rose think that Abdul was there having sex. He didn't even have a condom in his pocket. Well, that didn't really mean much.

Texas City was an industrial town. It had about just as many refineries as it did city parks. This dynamic kept a steady flow of outsiders commuting to Texas City daily for work. Some of those workers would be chasing shutdowns and so they would need a place to live for a few months while they worked their 12 hour shifts 7 days per week. A lot of the hotels were filled with refinery workers just passing through. Refinery workers who had left wives and children hundreds of miles away back in their hometowns.

Refinery workers who still had needs. Sexual needs. Local prostitutes made a killing in hotels like the Economy Lodge.

Wait a minute. Rose scanned the room in his minds eye. Abdul's pants. They're unzipped. His pants are unzipped. There was a woman there with him.

Honk! Honk! Honk!

Rose jumped in his seat and his eyes sprang back open.

He was brought back to the here and now by the sound of the cars behind him honking their horns. He took his foot off the brake and pressed the gas pedal. He wondered how long the light had been green. Driving for a few more blocks down FM 1765, he made a right turn onto Amburn Road and then turned right again into the subdivision known as Amburn Oaks. The house he was looking for was toward the back. Reading the numbers on the mailboxes as he crept down the streets, he realized he was getting closer. When he pulled in front of the house labeled 916, he stopped.

He retrieved his notepad from the pocket of his shirt and flipped it open. Double checking the address he had written down, and the address on the mailbox, he knew that he had the right house. Sliding on his shoulder holster with his chrome .45 in it, he checked his weapon to make sure it was ready to fire. Then, he placed all of his loose paperwork and photographs into a small briefcase, climbed out of his vehicle, and put on his jacket. Rose was wearing a blue 3-piece suit with black alligator skin Stacy Adams shoes on.

Before dawning his sunglasses, he quickly observed the residence. The dwelling was a two-story red brick home with a two-car garage attached to it. Parked in the driveway was a candy blue H3 sitting on 26-inch chrome rims. The lawn was healthy and appeared to be tended to regularly. Glancing up and down the block, Rose made a mental note that this was one of the largest homes in all of Amburn Oaks.

As he walked up the driveway towards the front door, he had a fleeting thought. He had held a job ever since he turned 16 and he had never been in any trouble, yet, he still couldn't afford to live in the luxurious style of a man who had never worked a day in his life and had made a career out of criminal activity.

"Maybe I'm in the wrong line of work." He said to himself.

Pausing momentarily to look at the flower bed to the left of the door, he just shook his head. Rose loved his line of work, but anything that paid good enough to have a person living like this was worth fantasizing about.

Returning his attention back to the task at hand, he grabbed his badge out of his back pocket and knocked on the front door. Doing his best to listen to what was going on inside, he leaned in closer to the door. After a couple of minutes, he heard footsteps approaching.

"Who is it?" A male voice called from inside the home.

Rose shifted his weight from one foot to the other nervously. This was one of the few times he wished he had allowed the department to assign him a partner.

"Detective Rose." He answered.

"Detective?" The voice questioned. "How do I know you're really a detective?"

"Well," Rose responded, trying to place his face directly in front of the peephole. "If you would just open the door, sir, I could show you my badge."

The man inside chuckled.

"Well, sir." He said sarcastically, doing his best to mimic Rose's voice. "If you would just hold your badge up and to the left, I might decide to open the door."

Rose was confused. He looked up and to the left, and for the first time, he noticed a small surveillance camera mounted just above one of the windows. He wondered how he had missed that earlier. Police officers are trained to recognize everything. In police work, to be aware is to be alive. Then, he looked directly under where the camera was placed, and it hit him. The beauty of the flowerbed had drawn his attention when he examined that side of the home. That little distraction was obviously intentional. Rose couldn't help but to smile as he held his badge up to the camera.

After a few moments, the voice spoke again.

"Alright. Now that we've established you are who you say you are... what are you here for?"

Rose sighed. "Sir." He began. "If you don't mind, I would like to ask you a few questions about a homicide that took place around 11:45pm last night."

"Homicide?" The voice repeated. "I don't know anything about a homicide. You'd be wasting your time questioning me."

Rose had anticipated his hesitation to talk to him. Returning his badge to his pocket, Rose opened his briefcase and fished out one of the photographs. Holding it up to the camera, he wondered what type of effect it was having on the man inside the house. When he heard the door being unlocked, he knew that it served its purpose.

When the door opened, Rose found himself face to face with one of the most notorious gang leaders in his Texas City. He wasn't at all what he expected. Rose had seen pictures of him before, but seeing the tall, slim, brown skinned man in person was different. The individual known as Sticks was standing there in a blue bathrobe, blue house shoes, and he was holding a lit cigar in his right hand.

Reaching for the picture that Rose was holding, Sticks said, "Let me see that."

Rose studied his expression as he looked over the photograph. Strangely, he appeared genuinely surprised to see his right-hand man stretched out dead. Rose thought for sure that Sticks had ordered the hit because of some form of disloyalty on Abduls part. Many times, when a high ranking official of some gang came up dead, the people responsible were their fellow gang members themselves. There wasn't much honor amongst thieves. One false move or one disobeyed command could be deadly for even the most loyal soldier. It was how the leaders maintained control. Love was a strong motivator but fear trumped love. Even the God of the bible understood that concept. Hence hell, the lake of fire, and eternal torment.

As he looked at his top lieutenant, Sticks anger was mixed with mourning. Over the years he had formed a strong bond with Abdul. No matter how many friends one lost in the streets, one never really got used to it. Sure, you could get somewhat numb to the pain, but that was only because your brain had taught itself to bury the hurt. The hurt was definitely there, it was just buried deep. What shocked him more than the fact that someone had murdered Abdul, was the fact that whoever did it had crudely carved the letters D.S.H. into his torso. D.S.H. stood for Dramaside Hooligans, but Sticks knew that no one in his organization was responsible for Abduls' death.

As Sticks tried to make heads or tails of what he was seeing, the scent from his cigar filtered up to the nose of Rose. He instantly recognized the smell as marijuana. Rose wondered how Sticks could feel comfortable enough to smoke marijuana right in front of a police officer. Possession of marijuana was a misdemeanor, so maybe that's why it didn't faze him. Rose still found it to be arrogant and disrespectful. Either way, Rose was there to investigate a homicide, not arrest a possible millionaire for a misdemeanor marijuana possession. Ironically, Sticks' arrogance somewhat impressed him.

"Who did this?" Sticks demanded, not looking up from the photo.

"That's funny." Rose answered. "I was just about to ask you the exact same thing."

Sticks looked up. "How the fuck should I know?" He asked, shoving the picture into Rose's chest.

"Well," Rose began. "The letters on his chest..."

Sticks cut him off.

"Yeah, I see the letters. But come on man. Do you really think I would have Abdul killed and leave evidence that points directly back to me?" Sticks rubbed his face. "This is obviously a set-up." He added.

Rose glanced at the photo once more.

"A set-up?" He thought, mulling over the idea in his mind.

He kicked himself for not thinking of that before, but now that Sticks had mentioned it, it did seem to be very plausible. The Detective scratched his head.

"Who would want to set-up the Hooligans?" He wondered. "If it was indeed a set-up, who would stand to gain the most?"

As Rose and Sticks stood face to face in the doorway, both of their minds were working overtime trying to piece together the puzzle. Each man knew that justice must be served. However, each man had a totally different concept of justice. By justice, Rose meant that the person responsible should stand before a jury of their peers and be sentenced to hard time in the Texas Department of Criminal Justice. For Sticks, justice meant simply, death. An eye for an eye. A tooth for a tooth. A life for a life. Hell, considering how he felt about his close companion, Abdul, several people might have to pay for this with their lives.

"Baby." Silvia called from inside the home.

They both looked up simultaneously. Silvia was holding a cordless telephone in her hand. Without saying anything, Sticks turned around and approached his wife, leaving the door open and Rose watching. Rose figured that the caller may have been one of Sticks workers calling to inform him about Abdul's murder since he obviously didn't know about it prior to Rose visit. As he watched Sticks talk on the phone, his own cellphone started to ring. Fishing it out of his pocket, he answered it.

"This is Detective Rose." He answered.

The person on the opposite end of the line was talking quickly.

"Detective Rose." They said. "This is Officer Stanton. There's been another homicide. Two more actually. This time in broad daylight. We need you to get over here as soon as possible. We think this has something to do with the homicide you're investigating at the Economy Lodge. I'm texting you the address now."

"What? Are you serious? What the hell is going on?" Rose told them.

"We're not sure, sir." Officer Stanton replied. "But something about this thing just doesn't seem right. A lot of us have a bad feeling about this one. My gut tells me that this thing, whatever it is, is only getting started."

Rubbing his head, Rose added, "I have the exact same feeling, Stanton. You know we've both been around long enough to understand when something big is brewing in the underworld. Abdul wasn't just a random murder. People like that just don't get murdered without something deeper going on. Now, if you have two more homicides that are possibly connected to Abdul's murder, I'm convinced that things are about to get messy. Go ahead and send me that address. I'll head right over."

When Rose hung up, Sticks was walking back towards the front door.

"I have to go." He said calmly. "It was nice speaking with you, but please, don't come to my home anymore."

Then, he shut the door in Rose face.

Rose wondered why after the phone call he suddenly had to go, but he had more important things to tend to. He would run across Sticks again. It was just a matter of time. So instead of giving it too much thought, he simply walked back over to his Crown Vic, and sped off in the direction of The Chelseas over on 12st.

What the heck was happening? Another homicide? In broad daylight? Rose crossed his fingers and hoped like hell that this new homicide wasn't connected to Abdul's murder like Officer Stanton had suggested it was. If it were, things were getting real serious real fast.

Back over at the home in Amburn Oaks, Silvia noticed rage written across her husband's face. She seen that look plenty of times in their marriage. Sticks was a level-headed man in general, but one didn't reach the level in the streets of Texas City that he reached by simply being levelheaded. It took an enormous amount of savagery as well. Silvia witnessed countless men and women beaten within an inch of their lives right there in her own living room.

She knew firsthand what that expression on his face meant. It meant that people were about to get hurt.

"What's going on, baby?" She asked with concern in her voice.

Walking passed her and dialing another number on the phone, he said, "Someone is going out of their way to get my attention. I don't know who they are or what their ultimate goal is, but I'll promise you one thing; now that they have it, I'm going to make them regret their decision to seek it."

As he walked up the stairs, Sticks considered the possibilities. He might not have spoken much to Detective Rose about who he thought was responsible for the death of Abdul, but that didn't mean he didn't have his suspicions. In his mind, there was only one person in Texas City that would dare to attack his organization in such a way. He had no proof of his assumption, but he knew that he had to respond. Soon, the entire city would know about what happened to Abdul. He had to either strike back fast and hard, or risk appearing weak. The street game in Texas City was played one way. Blood for blood and life for life. There was no way in hell that his second in command would be the only death the streets would be talking about.

Sticks had dialed a number that he knew well. It was a number that he used often. A number that he used when things got messy. A number that he knew was the perfect number to call at a time like this.

He didn't have to let the phone ring long before a man with a deep raspy voice answered it.

"What's crackin', Hooligan?" The raspy voice asked, in classic Dramaside Hooligan fashion.

"Shiiit, I ain't doin' nothing but cracking heads and bringing drama!" Sticks responded.

"Fa sho, cuzz. Dramaside up."

Making a gang sign with his hand out of habit, Sticks replied, "Dramaside up!"

The man with the raspy voice rubbed the long scar on his throat. "What you need, boss? Talk to me."

"I got a job for you, Shock" Sticks told him, getting straight down to business. "A big job. I don't know if you've heard, but somebody killed Abdul last night. You know we can't just let that shit slide."

There were a few seconds of silence while Shock processed what he had just been told. He wasn't extremely close to Abdul, but Abdul was still family though. Dramaside was Dramaside whether they spoke daily or not. An attack against one was an attack against all.

Finally, Shock said, "I'm listening boss."

Sticks quickly filled Shock in on what was going on and what was specifically required of him. He listened to every detail.

After Sticks was finished explaining the specifics of the job, he asked, "Do you think you can handle that, or will it be a problem?"

"Come on, boss. You know me. Consider it done." Shock replied with confidence. "Dramaside."

"Dramaside." Sticks repeated.

With that, they both hung up the phone.

After Shock had placed his cellphone down on the bed beside him, he looked around his efficiency apartment. As it had done countless times before, his gaze came to rest on the picture of his mother. Shock lived alone inside of the Rancho Santa-Maria apartments, and he existed off of the bare minimum of necessities. The entire apartment complex was run down and dirty, but Shock didn't mind. He never been too flashy. He preferred being low key and virtually undetectable.

Rancho Santa-Maria was a block shaped apartment complex that sat off of Texas Ave. and 16th street. There was a raggedy lot of grass with about two palm trees planted on it, in the center of the structure, and there were some units that faced inside towards the grass and some that faced outside towards the street.

Rancho Santa-Maria was one of the cheapest places to live in Texas City and it was also drug infested. If you were to walk down the alley that lined the back of the complex you would be sure to find used needles, broken crack pipes, discarded beer cans, and empty packages of swisher sweet blunts filled up with tobacco instead of the cigars. Things were so bad out there, that if anyone called the police to report a crime in the area, they'd be lucky if anyone showed up. One time, a racist white supremacist stabbed an elderly black to death inside of one of the units and the police didn't even do anything about it. It took a handful of street savvy vigilantes to go out and get justice for the old man.

Shock didn't choose to live there because he couldn't afford to live lavish somewhere else. Not at all. Shock had money; he was just more at home in that type of an environment. Everyone wasn't meant for champagne and chandeliers. Some people were more comfortable with Olde English 40's and ceiling fans. In fact, Shock had close to $350,000 stashed away inside a safe in his apartment. You would never know it by looking at him. His daily attire was blue jeans and a t-shirt. He rarely even shaved his face.

Shock didn't remember much about his life before being adopted, but there were things that his foster parents did tell him. Shock knew, for instance, that he had come from humble beginnings. He was born into a family that already had two children that they could barely afford to take care of, and his parents had chosen to put him up for adoption at the age of 5. Since he was the youngest of the 3 children, they assumed he had the best chance of getting placed into a loving and caring home. Their assumption however, proved wrong. Very wrong. He did eventually get adopted, but his adoptive mother was anything but loving and kind.

Shock, whose real name was LaQuincy Allen, stayed in foster care until he was 16 years old. At the age of 16, he had enough of the abuse, and he ran away from his foster home and started living on the streets. The streets of Texas City were rough, but so was his home life. It wasn't all bad, but it was definitely more bad going on than good. Considering how his life turned out, it was actually a blessing that his childhood made him as hard as it did. It took a special kind of individual to swim in those waters of Texas City and not drown. Luckily, Shock was just heartless enough to not only survive but to also thrive. He was willing to do anything to keep his head above the water. He was willing to lie, cheat, steal, kill, and sell drugs.

The drug game in Texas City was cutthroat. Everyone was trying to get a piece of the same pie, and more often than not, disputes over territory and sales led to violence. Shock didn't have the patience of most drug dealers. His brain wasn't designed for it. At times, drug dealers were expected to simply accept a loss and charge it to the game. Shock, on the other hand, wasn't accepting anything. If you crossed him, he was coming for you. If you owed him money and didn't pay, he was coming for you. If you sold him bad dope, he was coming for you. If you begged him to 'bless your game', he was coming for you. Pretty much, if you just breathed to hard in his direction, he was coming for you.

With an attitude like his, selling drugs always led to beef. Beef always led to violence. Violence would then lead to more violence, and Shock quickly earned a reputation that made his name both respected and feared. It wasn't long before his aptitude for cracking heads came on the radar of Sticks. Sticks was always looking for the most ruthless Hooligans in his entourage. The one thing a boss could not have too much of was young aggressive muscle.

Eventually, cracking heads for Sticks, turned into burying people for Sticks. He turned out to be so good at it, Sticks began to pay him good money to exclusively carry out hits. That turned out to be a pretty lucrative occupation. More lucrative in fact, then selling drugs. Plenty of people in Texas City needed to be taken care of it, but not many people had the heart to carry it out themselves. That made people like Shock valuable. It was all about supply and demand. The streets often demanded the head of a motherfucker, and Shock had no problem supplying the metaphorical blade.

When he wasn't actively engaged in gang activity, Shock spent most of his free time sitting at home and wondering what life would've been like if he had stayed with his biological family. Would he still have become so ruthless? Would he still have become so heartless? Maybe, in another world, he would've become a doctor or a lawyer. A scientist maybe. Maybe he would've been more functional in society. As it stood though, his only connection to his real family was an old picture of his mother that he kept with him since his days in foster care. A picture and scattered fragments of cloudy memories that he really couldn't make heads or tails of. He had no name to go along with the photo. It was only a distant memory from his past that he felt like he would never fully be able to appreciate. Still, he kept the picture in its original frame sitting on the nightstand next to his bed. He looked at it several times per day and fantasized about the life he never knew.

Forcing himself to stop staring at the picture, he put his mind back on the task at hand. Reaching into the drawer on the nightstand, he pulled out a pen and a piece of paper. With it, he wrote down the information that Sticks had given him. It wasn't anything too in-depth. It was only a name. The name of the person that Sticks was going to pay him to kill. Shock wrote down the name and stared at it.

He didn't write it down to help himself remember it; he had a totally different reason. It was the same process with all his jobs. Shock laid the paper with the name on it out in front of himself. Then, he started to stare at it. Before long, he was able to picture his victim. Not the actual person, but a silhouette that represented them. Then, he began fantasizing about different ways he could kill them.

Death. Death could come a thousand and one different ways. There was stabbing death, shooting death, and death by strangulation. The was death by fire, death by drowning, and death by falling from a very high place. There was poison, torture, and even car wrecks. A person's death could come fast and unexpected or slow and drawn out. Shock was a connoisseur of death. He loved killing as much as other men loved sex.

As he sat and daydreamed about the actual murder, he smiled from ear to ear. There were only two occasions when he wasn't focused on his internal pain and when he was genuinely happy. One of those occasions was when he was planning a job, and the other occasion was when he was executing a job.

"This is gonna be fun." He mumbled, as he closed his eyes and lost himself in the murderous fantasies.

Chapter 3

"That's what I'm talking about bro!" Shonda exclaimed, grinning from ear to ear.

Squeak glanced over at her and smiled as he pulled the Cavalier into the rock driveway of their two-bedroom home on Anderson St.

"You like that shit, sis?" He asked, putting the vehicle in park and turning off the ignition.

The pair lived in a quiet neighborhood on the westside of Texas City. The house they lived in was nice but modest. It was a one-story white and green house with a chain link fence surrounding it. They had a nice sized backyard and their lawn was well kept. Nothing about the house made it stand out, and that's exactly how they liked it. The nature of their lifestyle required them to be able to blend in with their surroundings. They enjoyed being able to come and go as they pleased without anyone paying too much attention to their activities.

The street that they lived on was inhabited by a lot of elderly people that tended to mind their own business. If there wasn't a lot of traffic, loud music, or weed smoking in the front yard, Squeak and Shonda had nothing to worry about with their neighbors.

Climbing out of the Cavalier, Shonda began twisting her hips hard, as she led the way inside. Squeak walked up the driveway behind her, slightly mesmerized by the motion of her hips. The back and forth movements were tantalizing indeed. Like the ebb and flow of a great oceans' waves crashing upon the shores of land. Deep down, Squeak was extremely attracted to his older sister, Shonda. He knew it was wrong, that's why he never acted on it, but it was a constant struggle. Her smooth chocolate skin and her womanly curves were like a buffet of delicacies calling out to him, imploring him to toss all caution to the wind and fully indulge his gluttonous lust.

Shonda was beautiful. Thick thigs, full lips, nice voluptuous breasts, and perfectly symmetrical facial features. It was a proven fact that the more symmetrical a person's face was, the more attractive they were to others. In addition to beauty, Shonda was loyal. If you were her family or friend, she would do anything for you. She would even kill for those closes to her. Shonda had an attitude problem though. The side effect of having a strong, confident, ride or die female around, was having to deal with her attitude. It wasn't that she went out of her way to be annoying or argumentative, she was just the type of person who spoke her mind. Good, bad, or ugly. If something you said or did made her feel a certain type of way, best believe you were going to hear about it.

Once they were inside the house, Shonda turned around and caught Squeak staring at her firm butt. In response, she grinned mischievously and slapped herself hard on the side of her left butt cheek. Her ass was so round that it was able to jiggle even inside of the skintight blue jeans she was wearing.

"You like what you see, daddy?" She asked seductively, as she sashayed over to him and stood with her breast thrust out in front of her.

Squeak shook his head and maneuvered around her. "Come on, Shonda." He said with a little pleading in his voice. "I don't feel like going through this right now. You know that shit ain't right. Just leave it alone."

"What ain't right about it?" She snapped. "Because we family?!? That ain't never stop daddy from fucking me! And that ain't stop you from fucking me when we were growing up."

Squeak quickly turned down the hallway that led to his room, and tried to walk away from her, but she followed close on his heels. He knew what was coming next, and he was not looking forward to it. Squeak knew that they were going to argue back and forth about right, wrong, and their childhood. The two of them came from what the majority of psychologist would call a textbook dysfunctional family.

The term is defined like this. A "**Dysfunctional Family**" – *is a family in which conflict, misbehavior, and often child neglect or abuse on the part of individual parents occur continuously and regularly, leading other members to accommodate such actions. Children sometimes grow up in such families with the understanding that such a situation is normal. Dysfunctional families are primarily a result of two adults,*

one typically overtly abusive and the other codependent,
and may also be affected by addictions (such as substance
abuse – e.g. drugs, including alcohol), or sometimes by an
untreated mental illness.

The household that Shonda and Squeak were raised in fit that definition to the letter. The pair came from an extremely poor environment, so all the kids they went to school with use to tease them. They would make fun of their clothes, their shoes, their haircuts, and even the vehicles that their parents drove. Consequently, neither Shonda nor Squeak had many friends. To be honest, they didn't have any friends at all. The only friend they had was each other.

To make matters worse, both of them were molested almost daily. Their father, Tune, was one sick son of a bitch. He was the lowest of the low. A real scum of the earth, dirtbag type of dude. Tune had no moral code whatsoever. He was vile, vulgar, aggressive, and his heart was as cold as ice. The only person he cared about was himself. If there ever was a man who was better of rotting in a grave or burning in hell, believe me, Tune was that man.

He was so sadistic and mentally twisted, that he would have sex with Shonda, his own damn daughter, and he would force his wife, Laina, to have sex with Squeak, her own damn son. Tune would rape Shonda for his own sick sexual pleasure, and in his twisted mind, having Squeak fuck his mother would make a man out of him. Really, their mother Laina, was just as much of a victim as they were. The entire household was held captive to the whims of a certified madman.

Eventually, Shonda and Squeak began to turn to each other for the comfort, love, and security that all human beings intrinsically craved. They were searching for a way to escape from the confines of the mental and physical cage they were trapped in and find some form of solitude and peace. Unfortunately, due to years and years of the most horrid expressions of abuse, the only way they knew how to express themselves was the way that they were taught. The pair eventually began to form an unhealthy incestual relationship amongst themselves. The way they saw it, at least they were choosing to be together as opposed to being forced. In their home, no one had a choice. Their father was a merciless tyrant. The only choice was to obey their father or suffer the consequences. There was no middle ground.

"Look sis!" Squeak said, turning to face Shonda, who had followed him into his bedroom. "When we were young, we ain't know no better. But now that we're grown, we know that that shit ain't right. It's incest, sis. It's not normal for us to be doing that. Family members aren't supposed to do that with each other."

Shonda folded her arms and pouted. The years of continued physical, mental, and sexual abuse left her more messed up in the head than her brother. In her mind, her brother was the only man she loved, trusted, and cared about, so she felt like she should be allowed to be in a relationship with him. Who cares what the rest of the world says or thinks? She sure didn't. The rest of the world never came to her aid as a child. As far as Shonda was concerned, they could all go to hell.

Squeak knew that once his sister began her rants about how much she didn't give a damn about what other people thought, he resolved to do what he always did when these disputes started up. While listening to Shonda voice her opinion, he made his way over to his walk-in closet, and searched around for his red Nike shoebox. Finding it on the floor in the corner, underneath a pile of discarded dirty shirts, he opened it up and fished out a sandwich bag full of coke. Emerging from his closet, he then made his way to his bed and picked up a black porcelain plate off the floor. Shonda watched as he dumped the white powder out onto the plate and almost instantly her attention shifted.

"You wanna hit this?" Squeak asked her, using his pinky finger to form about 4 short parallel lines out of the substance.

He had about a quarter ounce of coke in the sandwich bag, so it made a nice sized pile on the plate. Shonda placed her hands on her curvaceous hips and smacked her teeth.

"You know I want some." She said. "Stop playing."

Squeak knew that the only way to change the subject was to either break out the powder pack or roll up the weed. Over the years he had dealt with this issue countless times, and every time he did, it was getting harder and harder to tell Shonda no. Truth be told, he probably wanted her just as bad as she wanted him, but he felt like he would be taking advantage of her if he acted on his impulses. He was mentally affected by their upbringing, but he could tell that his sisters scars were far deeper than his were.

As he prepared the lines that they were going to snort, he did his best to console his sister.

"I feel where you be coming from, sis." He began. "Trust me I do. I told you numerous times how I feel about you. But now is not the time for us to get sidetracked on all of that. We done pulled off two jobs, but we ain't finished yet. We gotta stay focused, Shonda."

He passed her the plate. Shonda knew that Squeak was telling the truth. Any slip up in their line of work could be fatal. She pressed one of her nostrils closed with her index finger and bent over with her head hovering over the plate. Then, in one quick motion, she swung her head from left to right, inhaling the line that Squeak set aside for her.

"Mmmm." She moaned, as she felt the initial rush of the drug entering her system and causing her nostril to tingle.

Handing the plate back to Squeak, she plopped down on the bed next to him. "How much longer we have to live like this?" She asked, putting an arm around his waist while he sniffed one of the lines.

Squeak wiped the excess coke off the tip of his nose and looked at her. He was always amazed at how quickly his sister's mood could change. She could go from zero to one hundred in 2 seconds flat and from one hundred back to zero just as fast.

"Not too much longer." He told her, caressing her head. "Not much longer at all." Squeak inhaled another line of coke and laid back next to Shonda and let the drugs work their magic.

Back when they were only 14 and 15, they moved out of their parents' house and got an apartment together. Squeak was selling dope in the streets and supporting the both of them while Shonda was taking care of the things at home. Squeak always told her that he would only hustle long enough to get them right financially and then they would move out of the state of Texas completely and start all over. Unfortunately, things rarely ever go as planned.

Squeak quickly built a reputation in the streets for his fighting skills. It may have been the years of fighting his father or just natural born ability, but Squeak had hands like a certified prize fighter. He was strong, quick, agile, and accurate. If you made the mistake of swinging at him and missing, the fight was over. Squeak once beat a boy at school from one end of the hallway to the other. Literally. The fight began next to the homeroom class and ended up by the science room. At the age of 13 he was embarrassing dudes that were 25.

It was no way that a normal man was going to whip him hand to hand, so the best option for his opponents was to grab the great equalizer. He was so good with his feet work that a knife wasn't much help either. Nope. You needed a gun. Squeak didn't mind gun play neither. He made a name for himself on the Southside of Texas City as a ruthless individual who would never hesitate to pull the trigger. He shot his first man over $15. To Squeak, it wasn't about the money, it was about the respect.

He absolutely detested his father, but nevertheless, he still learned life lessons from the man. His father always told him that it didn't matter if it was the top to his beer bottle, it was his and didn't nobody else have any business putting their hands on it. Squeak lived by that. Some of his most violent encounters were over things that most people would consider insignificant. Squeak often had nightmares of one such incident. He always heard that if you look into the eyes of a man that you kill, you will be haunted by that man's spirit if it doesn't find rest in the afterlife. Squeak was a firm believer in that. Life and experience made him a believer.

He thought back to a time when he was only 15 years old. Growing up on the Southside of Texas City, he had gotten initiated into the Southlane Villains at a young age, but he wasn't a full-fledged member yet. He was just a young tag along. For as long as he could remember, the Villains were at war with the Hooligans. In Texas City, if you were any kind of street person, your only hope at becoming an actual factor in the underworld was to become either a Villain or a Hooligan. The only catch to that was that you would eventually have to prove yourself to the gang.

The process was known as "putting in work". The order would come down from Infamous, the top man himself, to go on a mission for the sole purpose of proving yourself. Most of the new members were ready to put in work, but they were still a bit apprehensive about the idea. Squeak, on the other hand, was overly eager. He found a satisfying peace in random acts of violence. All he would do is picture his father's face on his victim, and he would experience pleasure from the actual murder. One night, as he sat inside of one of the Villains dope houses with his big homies, he decided to take some initiative and put in some work on his own.

The Villains had him assigned to a brown shotgun style house over on 3rd Ave. It was a dope house they called the snake pit. He was working with two older cats. Suko and Tao. Suko and Tao were brothers. Twin brothers. They were half black and half Vietnamese. Suko and Tao did everything together. If you saw one, you were guaranteed to see the other one close by.

Squeak sat on the dingy leather couch in the living room of the snake pit, passed the blunt to Tao, and stood up. "Man, I'm sick of this shit, Villain!" He declared, pacing around the small room.

The brothers just looked at him. Tao took a long drag on the marijuana.

"Sick of what?" Tao finally asked, after he exhaled the smoke.

"I'm sick of waiting." Squeak told him. "Shit. I'm a real nigga. I ain't never been scared to get down, but Infamous got a nigga 'round this bitch waiting on the order to go and prove I got heart. Like... like I'm one of these other young cats. I go hard, Villain. I deserve my flag. You feel me?"

He stopped circling the room. "Fuck that shit." He added.

"Man," Suko told him, "Everybody gotta do that. Not just you. Me and Tao did it too. You gone be aiight. Quit trippin' lil homie."

Squeak stared menacingly at Suko. "Naw nigga, you ain't hearin' me." He informed him. "I ain't trippin' on bustin' that heat. That's my type of shit. I'm just sick of waiting. I wanna go do it right now, Villain. You feel me? I wanna go let that thang loose right now. Like, tonight type shit."

The brothers looked at each other and rolled their eyes. They had encountered youngsters like this before. They want everybody to respect them so bad that they pretend to be extra super-duper hard. They knew how to handle youngsters like that. You just called their bluff.

Suko reached in his waistband and pulled out a chrome .32 revolver. Then, trying to call Squeak's bluff, he handed him the gun.

"Well fuck it, Villain." Suko said. "You the man. Don't wait on the order. You know where them Hooligans be at. Pull up and handle your business."

Squeak looked down at the gun in his hands and then back up at the brothers. "You ain't said nothin'!" He told them, as he turned around and headed for the door.

Suko and Tao watched him wondering how long it would take him to renege. They thought for sure that he didn't have enough guts to stroll into Hooligan territory by himself and get into a gun fight.

Squeak walked out into the night and felt the chill of the air caress his skin. He was wearing only a red muscle shirt and a pair of blue jeans, and it was the month of December.

"They got me fucked up." He said to himself as he headed in the direction of the Eastside.

With the pistol tucked away in his back pocket, he stuffed his hands in his side pockets and pulled his arms in close, attempting to stay warm. On foot it took him every bit of 45 minutes to make it from the Southside to the Eastside, and he was pumping himself up the whole way. He knew that he was completely out of bounds and in danger of being killed, but strangely, he wasn't afraid. He was so focused on what he was going to do to someone else that thoughts of what someone might do to him didn't have room to linger in his mind. Once Squeak made it to 5th Avenue he knew that he was now at the point of no return. He had no specific plan of attack; he was just going to find someone wearing blue and then let them have it. Squeak made his way up and down the streets on the Eastside until he saw a corner store about four blocks up.

"Paks." He said, reading the name of the convenience store off the front of the building.

There were plenty of slabbed out cars and people in front of the store, so his instincts told him that this was one of the hood stores where the Hooligans congregated. Patting his back pocket to reassure himself that he still had his pistol on him, he calculated what he would do once he got to the store. He didn't want to walk up to the actual store, but if he had to, he would.

When he got within two blocks of the parking lot however, he noticed an all-white dodge dynasty pulling away from Paks, turning onto the street he was walking down, and heading in his direction.

Realizing the potential of the situation, he told himself, "Now or never, Villain."

With that, he pretended to be injured and limped from the sidewalk into the middle of the street, blocking the cars path. As expected, they brought the car to a halt to avoid hitting him. Looking inside the car through the windshield, he counted 3 people. He couldn't kill them all with only 6 shots, but he could kill one and wound another. Limping around to the driver's side of the vehicle, he pulled his .32 out of his back pocket, and pointed his gun at the driver before anyone in the car could react.

"Southlane Villains!" Squeak shouted. "Big Squeak!"

Then, he pulled the trigger. The first bullet struck the driver in the side of his head causing his entire body to jerk to one side. The other two occupants yelled and tried to duck. Squeak assumed they were reaching for guns of their own, so he rushed closer to the driver side window and let off two more shots intended for the passenger. He knew that he hit him when the Hooligan sat back up screaming and trying to grab his own back. His action presented Squeak with the perfect opportunity to do more than just injure him.

He shot the passenger two more times in the head. To his surprise, the dude in the back seat jumped out of the car and ran full speed in the opposite direction. Squeak pointed his pistol at him, but he thought twice. He only had one shot left. Why waste it? It might come in handy if he hoped to escape. Back at the store, the rest of the Hooligans had heard the shots, seen the commotion going on up the street, and they were all frantically jumping into their cars.

Squeak knew that he needed to get the hell out of there.

Doing the first thing that came to his mind, he opened the driver side door and drug the driver's lifeless body out. Tossing his limp body in the middle of the street, he hopped in the car and pressed down on the gas pedal as hard as he could. The tires of the Dodge Dynasty squealed as he peeled out. Looking in the rearview mirror, he saw that he had a nice head start on the pursuing vehicles. That didn't stop them from shooting though. Shots rang out in the background as Squeak sped off in the direction of the Southside. He knew that if he could make it back to his side of town, he would be safe.

Squeak made a hard, left turn onto 12th street, and the dead Hooligan in the passenger seat fell slumped over into his lap. He didn't have time to move the dead corpse, so he just did his best to maintain control of the vehicle with the body bouncing up and down. To his surprise, the Dynasty was going pretty fast. Squeak knew that if they caught up to him, all he had was one bullet left in the revolver. One bullet was not enough. Not by a long shot.

Having enough common sense to use his head start to an advantage, Squeak made another turn every one or two blocks. That way, the people chasing him would not be able to see which way he went. From 12th St he turned left down 4th Ave and then turned right again on 11th St. He flew straight up 11th St and blazed across Texas Ave. After crossing Texas Ave, he weaved up and down more blocks trying desperately to make it back to the snake pit.

By the time he made it back to the Southside, he had lost them all. Still, he didn't slow down until he was back in the driveway of the house on 3rd. When he made it there, he was exhausted. Both mentally and physically. He yoked the car into the rock covered driveway and hit the brakes hard. The Dynasty came to a halt with a loud screech and skidded into the grass on the side of the house.

Covered in sweat and blood, and taking really deep breaths, he put the car into park and pushed the dead body off his lap. The Hooligan slumped over in the seat with the back of his head on the window. Squeak noticed that his eyes were still open. For a moment, he got lost in the man's lifeless expression. The realization that he had taken a life hit him hard. Like a ton of bricks. True, he shot people before, but he never actually killed a man. Let alone had to ride around with his victim in the car with him. This was an entirely new experience. One that the young Squeak could tell would stick for him for the rest of his life.

The mans' mouth hung open and he had blood oozing out of several holes in his body. The stench was getting stronger now that Squeak actually had time to slow down and smell it. Still staring at the dead body, Squeak wiped his face off with the palm of his hand and took another deep breath.

"Damn." He said.

Squeak probably would've stared at the dude forever if Suko and Tao wouldn't have come outside with their guns drawn to see who the hell was speeding into the driveway of the snake pit. They rushed the Dodge Dynasty and found Squeak smeared with the blood of Hooligans.

Word of what he had done spread like wildfire. It even earned him a face to face meeting with Infamous himself. Infamous was so impressed by his style that he took him in under his wing. Eventually, he became the go-to guy when someone specific needed to get touched. It was obvious that Squeak wasn't afraid to die, and he wasn't afraid to kill. That combination traits made Squeak very valuable to Infamous and it made him a force to be reckoned with amongst the Villains.

"Squeak." Shonda called out, shaking his shoulder, trying to get his attention. "Squeak."

Squeak blinked a few times and brought himself back to the present.

"Huh?" He asked.

Looking into his eyes with concern, she asked, "What do you be thinking about when you drift off like that? What is going on in that head of your?"

Squeak sat up straight and straightened out his shirt with the palm of his hand.

"Nothing". He lied, rising to his feet. "Look," he added. "We got Abdul and we got them young niggas over in The Chelseas, so now we only have one more to go."

Walking over to his closet, he began to change clothes. "I'm gone do this next one by myself." He told her. "I just need you to hold the spot down. If Infamous calls, give him an update."

Shonda followed him inside the closet. "Be careful, bro." She urged him. "This one ain't nothin' like the last two. It's not going to be as easy."

Squeak put on an all blue outfit trying to disguise himself like one of the Hooligans. "Yeah, I know." He said, giving her a hug. "But, if anybody can pull it off, I can. You and I both know that I'm the best to ever do it."

Then he gave her a brotherly kiss and smiled arrogantly.

"You think you the shit." She said, smiling back at him.

"No, I don't." He responded, exiting the room. "You do!"

....

Detective Rose pulled up to the house in The Chelseas off of 12st. There were 3 police cruisers already on the scene and nosey neighbors crowded around the yellow police tape with cellphones in hand trying to record what was going on. The forensics van was there also, so the onlookers knew that someone inside the home had been killed, but they didn't know exactly what was happening. Self-proclaimed neighborhood reporter, a brown skinned woman named Nana, was standing off to the side recording everything for Facebook live. Many people from Texas City preferred her impromptu, no holds barred, style of reporting. They would watch her live Facebook videos before they watched the mainstream videos of pages like I45 Now, ran by TJ Aulds. In fact, that was her competition. She prided herself on getting to the scene before TJ.

Parking his Crown Victoria, Rose climbed out of the car, and approached the uniformed officers.

"So, what do we know?" He asked the two officers standing in the front yard.

"Not much." Officer Stanton responded. "All we know for sure is that we have two dead on the inside. Possibly gang related."

Rose turned and watched the train of police officers file in and out of the residence. The Chelseas were a name used to refer to neighborhood that spanned several city blocks. It ran all the way from Texas Ave down to 9th Ave. Many of the homes inside of The Chelseas were duplex style homes. There was family that lived in the upstairs house and another family that lived in the bottom half.

The house Rose was standing in front of was no different. It was an off-white color with visible structural damage to the sides and the roof. The City would no doubt be condemning the house in a few years if the owners didn't fix it up. This particular house was only occupied on the bottom half. No one lived upstairs.

"Detective Rose!" A female police officer called out.

Looking around, Rose spotted Officer Sierra Martin waving him over to her.

"Excuse me." He said to the other two officers as he made his way over towards Sierra.

"I'm glad you made it so quickly." She informed him as he got close to her.

"Well," He responded. "The tone of Officer Stanton's voice made me think that this was something important. He intimated that it could possibly be connected to another case I'm working on."

Sierra's face lit up as if what he said caused her to remember something.

"Oh, but it is important." She said. "And it is directly connected to that case you started working on last night. I'm sure of it."

Rose tilted his head down and looked at her over the top of his sunglasses. "Annnd, just how do you know that?" He asked, somewhat skeptical of her assertion.

Sierra smiled like she was about to reveal some long-lost secret. "Come see for yourself." She said, turning to lead him into the house. "I want to show you something."

Following her towards the house, Rose silently prayed that this was not just another unwarranted attempt to get his approval. Rose was well aware of the fact that Sierra aspired to make detective one day, and not only that, she wanted to be his partner. She had made several attempts during her short time on the force to prove herself to him. Rose understood the dynamic. Here she was, a new face to the Texas City Police Department, with dreams of rising through the ranks and becoming a detective like the actors from her favorite television programs and movies.

She had no doubt heard the stories about Derrick Rose when she first entered the academy. He wasn't the best cop to ever be on the force, but he was damn sure a legend in his own right. Some of his arrests were epic. He had busted bank robbers, he had been in shoot-outs, he had been in car chases, the whole nine. When the Hooligans and the Villains had made their truce, and homicide was on the decline in the city, Detective Rose single handedly solved multiple cold cases that many officers thought would never be solved. He brought closure to families that had lost hope decades ago, and he brought justice to individuals who thought they had successfully gotten away with murder.

Sierra wasn't the first cop who tried to get in close to him, and she wouldn't be the last. She was wasting her time though. Rose was a loner. Ever since his last partner got killed in the line of duty right in front of him, he had vowed not to ever have another partner again. Sierra felt as if she could make him change his mind. She felt like she had a skillset that not many other officers had. If anybody deserved to be partnered with the great Detective Derrick Rose, she did.

When Rose stepped inside of the house, he was not prepared for what he saw. There were forensics specialist everywhere. They were dusting for prints, collecting evidence, and taking pictures. Immediately to his left, Rose saw his two homicide victims slumped over on a brown couch. Both men were wearing blue, so it was safe to assume that they were Hooligans just like Abdul was. Not to mention The Chelseas were Hooligan territory and this particular house was obviously used to house and sell marijuana for the gang.

Directly in front of the two homicide victims was a small wooden table with about a quarter pound of weed spread across it. There were plastic sandwich bags on the table and also lying on the floor. It was clear that the men were bagging up sacks to sell when they were attacked. Rose made a mental note that whoever murdered these men did not bother to rob them as well. The motive appeared to be murder only. Just like Abdul's murder. Someone was killing Hooligans.

That isn't what shocked him though. What shocked him was the way that the killer had staged the crime scene. On all four walls of the living room, the killer had spray painted the letters D.S.H. in red. Rose knew that D.S.H. stood for Dramaside Hooligans. Something about the manner in which the letters were written made Rose think about the letters D.S.H. that the killer had carved into the chest of Abdul.

Sticks had suggested that someone was trying to set-up his organization, and Rose had to admit that that did seem plausible, but what if the killer was actually a Hooligan? He couldn't rule that scenario out just yet. Gangs had internal conflicts all the time. His killer, or killers, could very well be disgruntled Dramaside Hooligans. Fortunately, whoever had murdered these two men had left another clue. Rose had no idea what it meant, but it was clue none the less. Directly below each spray painted D.S.H., the killer had also spray painted a Bible verse.

"Genesis 4: 23-24". Rose recited the verse slowly. Then, speaking more to himself then to anyone else, he added, "Great. I bet there are no Bibles in here, and I bet there aren't any pastors on this block either."

"Oh, we don't need one." Sierra told him. "The verses say, 'And Lamech said unto his wives, Adah and Zillah, Hear my voice; ye wives of Lamech, hearken unto my speech: for I have slain a man to my wounding, and a young man to my hurt. If Cain shall be avenged sevenfold, truly Lamech seventy and sevenfold."

Once she finished reciting the verse, Rose just stared at her bewildered. Noticing the confused look on his face, she offered an explanation.

"My father is a preacher." She began. "I don't know the whole Bible by heart, but I do know a lot."

Rose thought about the verse in his head. It didn't make sense to him. "But why would our killer leave those particular verses? What does it mean? What the heck does that have to do with the Hooligans?"

"Well," Sierra began, "I can't say for sure yet, but I have a theory that I'm about 95% sure about. My father preached a sermon on that story one Sunday. You have to look at the reference in context in order to understand what why the killer chose those verses. According to the Bible, after Adam and Eve were kicked out of the garden of Eden, they had two sons. One named Cain and one named Abel. Cain ended up getting into a dispute with his brother Abel and he murdered him. After he murdered his brother Abel, God banished Cain from the land where he was raised and forced him to go live in an area known as the land of Nod."

"Cain was afraid that the people who lived in Nod would murder him when he got there, so he begged God for mercy. God heard his cries and placed a mark upon Cain and stated that if anyone in Nod would dare to kill Cain, then God Himself would take vengeance on them seven-fold. Lamech, the man mentioned in this verse, was one of the descendants of Cain who was born in the land of Nod."

"Apparently what Lamech was saying was that he had killed two people. Not because he wanted to, but as self-defense. That's why he says he has slain a man to his wounding and a young man to his hurt. He is claiming that the two men he murdered had attacked him first. Then Lamech goes on to say that if Cain, who killed his brother for an unjust reason would be avenged seven-fold, then surely, he who had killed for a just reason would be avenged seventy-seven fold. So, it seems like the killer is saying that he is justified like Lamech in the murder of these two men because they had attacked him first."

Rose looked over at the two young men positioned next to each other on the couch. Both shot 3 times each. One bullet in each shoulder and one bullet, the kill shot, in their foreheads. Just like Abdul.

"I doubt," Sierra added, "that the killer was accusing these two dudes of attacking him personally though. I feel like it goes deeper than this incident right here. I mean, look at them. They were shot dead while sitting on this couch, and Abdul was gunned down inside of The Economy Lodge Hotel. Both attacks seem premediated and unprovoked. There's no signs of a struggle at either location. To me, this implies the killer is saying that the Hooligans offended or attacked him some way and these homicides are his response."

"Revenge killings?" Rose thought about the theory. "Could someone be targeting the Hooligans in response to the Hooligans targeting them first?"

Suddenly, Rose had a revelation. He had seen something similar to this before in the past. He wondered why some of this seemed oddly familiar. Now it was beginning to dawn on him. He had indeed seen something like this take shape on the streets of Texas City. He slapped his forehead.

"How could I be so blind?" He asked out loud. "The answer is right in front of me."

Sierra studied his expression. "What?" She questioned, trying to get some insight into what Rose was thinking. "What's right in front of you?"

Rose looked at the red spray paint on the walls. He thought about the letters carved into Abdul's chest, and made visible by his red blood. Both letters were symbolically written in blood at both crime scenes. Sticks had suggested that the letters were written as a set-up. He implied that maybe the killer was not a Hooligan, and they were just leaving those letters at the scene to trick the police into believing that the killer was a Hooligan. Sticks was half right. The killer was not a Hooligan, but the letters were not meant as a set-up neither. It was a message. A message from the only people in Texas City that would dare to take on the Dramaside Hooligans.

"It's the Southlane Villains." Rose declared out loud. "They are starting another gang war with the Hooligans."

The revelation caused his stomach to twist and turn. If his hunch was correct, which it most likely was, there would be a lot more bodies in the coming days. The Villains and The Hooligans had gone to war before. The two gangs were the biggest and most notorious gangs in Texas City. The last time they went to war, violence erupted on the streets so intensely that the TCPD were overwhelmed with calls. At times they felt powerless to stop the carnage.

The two leaders of the gangs, Sticks and Infamous, had enough money and drugs to throw around that they would never run out of soldiers to fight for them. The same poverty that the city officials forced the majority of the population to live in was the same poverty that pushed the great majority of citizens into crime. The youngsters in Texas City figured that if they couldn't depend on Mayor Matt Doyle to make a way for them to feed themselves, then Sticks or Infamous would.

Sierra thought about what Rose had just said. That's why she had so much respect for him. He was damn good at his job. A war between The Hooligans and The Villains did make the most sense. The only question was what did The Villains think The Hooligans did to break the truce. Why were they attacking them?

"But what did the Hooligans do to provoke them?" She asked. "The Bible verse implies this is a reaction to something."

Rose took off his shades and rubbed the brim of his nose. He racked his brain trying to make a connection with a past crime and these recent homicides.

"Maybe something happened that the police force knows nothing about?" He thought to himself. "Maybe a business deal went bad. Maybe a disagreement went too far. Hell, for all he knew, this could all be over a woman. Maybe Sticks and Infamous both had eyes for the same lady. Many a war had been fought over love. Well, love and lust."

Rose was indeed making progress in his case, but the progress he was making was discouraging. If a full-blown war was about to erupt on the streets of Texas City, they would go through hell trying to stop it once it got going. Rose knew that his best hope was to stop the war before it erupted. To do that, he needed to find out why it was being started, who was doing the killing, and then and only then could he begin to set things right.

"I need to talk to Chief Burby." He decided. "Face to face. He needs to know what is going on."

Walking fast out of the house towards his car, Rose knew that there was only one way to prevent a war. The police would have to act before the Hooligans caught on to what was going on and retaliate. Hopping into the driver's side of his car, he was shocked to see Sierra getting in on the passenger side.

"What are you doing?" He questioned, as he started up the car.

"I'm going with you." She told him, buckling her seat belt.

"Sierra, I don't have time for this right now." He said, raising his hands in the air. "I have to try and stop this war from starting."

"Well," Sierra responded calmly, folding her arms. "If you don't have time, I suggest you do less talking and more driving."

Rose glared at her through his shades, but he didn't feel like arguing. Letting out an exasperated sigh, he reluctantly pulled off with Sierra in the car with him. Turning off of 12st, Rose used his cellphone to call the station. Inquiring where Chief Burby was at, he was informed that the Chief had went home early.

Chief Robert Burby lived in Alvin, Tx. Alvin was about a 40-minute drive from Texas City. Rose knew that only Burby could call the shot to be proactive in this matter, so he needed to speak with him face to face. Rose turned on his emergency lights and began speeding as fast as he could in the direction of Alvin, Tx. He tried calling Chief Burby's cellphone to let him know that he was on the way, but the Chief didn't pick up. It was very unprofessional, but Chief Burby rarely answered his phone when he was of duty.

Unfortunately for Rose and Sierra, someone else had arrived at Chief Burby's house before they could get there.

………………..

Chief Robert Burby peered through the peephole on his front door. Seeing a man dressed in all blue, he relaxed a bit. Burby opened the door.

"Do you have it?" Burby asked, with his hand outstretched and his palm open.

"Yeah." Squeak answered, looking Burby in his eyes. "I got it."

Then he pulled his trusty .380 with the silencer attached out, and quickly shot the Police Chief once in each shoulder and once in each kneecap. As the Chief stumbled backwards and collapsed to the floor, Squeak entered the home and closed the door behind himself. Squeak relieved the Chief of the pistol on his ankle and searched him to make sure he was unarmed. Burby groaned in pain and spat out a few curse words. Squeak stood over him and pointed the pistol at his head.

"Infamous sent me." He told him.

"Wait... wait. Please." The Chief begged. "What's going on? Infamous?"

"Yeah. Infamous motherfucka."

Then, Squeak delivered the kill shot to his forehead.

Infamous had given Squeak explicit instructions to let all of his victims know who had ordered the hit before they died. Squeak turned around and peered through the window. He didn't park his car in front of the Chief's house, but he still didn't want to be seen leaving the residence.

Satisfied that no one was watching, he reached for the doorknob. He had already been inside for too long. The killing of a police officer was not something to be taken lightly. Just as he began to turn the knob, he heard something that froze him in his tracks.

"Daddy!" A little boy screeched.

Squeak turned around and aimed his weapon in the direction of the voice. He was shocked to see a young boy, about 10 years old, standing in the hallway. He wasn't expecting to encounter a child on the job. No one told him that Burby didn't live alone. He was supposed to be home alone.

"Fuck!" Squeak thought.

In one instant Squeak analyzed his dilemma. He had been seen. On one hand, he didn't want to hurt a child. On the other hand, the child was old enough to give a description of him to the police. He was quite capable of identifying him. One of the rules of his trade that helped him to last this long was that you never leave a witness. Especially a witness that has seen your face up close.

Seemingly unaware of the danger he was in, the boy rushed to Chief Burby's side.

"What did you do to my daddy?" He screamed, as he lifted his father's head and cried profusely. "Daddy! Daddy!"

Squeak actually felt compassion for the boy, as he sat there calling to his father while blood oozed out of the wound in his forehead.

"Daddy!" The boy said to his dad's dead body. "Daddy! Are you ok? Daddy! Wake up daddy! Get up. What did you do to my daddy? Why did you shoot him? Daddy!"

The boy buried his face into his father's blood-stained shirt and begged in vain for his father to get up. Squeak swallowed the lump in his throat. He didn't want to do it, but he knew what had to be done. Looking down at the boy, begging in vain for his father to come back, Squeak slowly aimed his pistol at the back of the boy's head.

"I'm sorry." He whispered, as he pulled the trigger.

The bullet penetrated the back of the boys' skull and lodged in his brain. His death was quick and painless. He didn't even see it coming. For the first time in years, Squeak actually wanted to cry. He stared at the two bodies for a few moments more and then he shook his head.

"Stay focused, Squeak. What's done is done."

Not allowing himself to dwell on what he had just done, he made a quick sweep around the entire home to make sure there were no more people inside anywhere. He didn't want to waste time searching the home, but he had to. Just to be safe. Squeak searched every room, closet, nook and cranny. After he was sure that the Police Chief and his son were the only people inside of the home, he rushed out the front door and jogged around the back of the house towards the alley. It was time to get the hell up out of Alvin.

Chapter 4

Just as Squeak was exiting the home of Chief Burby, Detective Rose was turning onto the street.

"Who is that? Rose asked, when he saw a man dressed in all blue leaving the Chief's house and running around toward the back.

"I don't know." Sierra answered, leaning forward in her seat and squinting her eyes. "Looks like one of the Hooligans though."

"Why would a Hooligan be running away fr…"

Rose voice trailed off as he pulled up in front of the Chief's house. The first thing that he noticed was that the front door was left wide open. His police instincts told him that something was wrong. Very wrong.

"Something isn't right, here." Rose asserted, removing his sidearm from his shoulder holster. "Be ready for anything. There may be more people here. You check the house. I'll go check around back and see where that guy just ran off too."

Sierra nodded her head to let him know that she understood. Rose got out of the car, placed his finger on the trigger of his .45, and sprinted around the house in the direction he saw the man in all blue go. His adrenaline had already started pumping through him. He didn't know why, but his gut was telling him that he had stumbled up on a break in his case. Whoever this mystery man was, he knew something. Rose could feel it.

Holding his firearm out directly in front of him, Rose reached the edge of the house and stopped. Taking two deep breaths, he stepped around the corner and scanned the backyard. There was a barbeque pit and a lawn mower, but there was no man in sight. Rose looked left toward the alley.

"Could it be?" He wondered, as he took off toward the alley.

Jumping the chain link fence that surrounded Chief Burby's backyard, Rose ran into the alley and scanned the area in both directions. By the time he made it to the alley, however, the man in blue was nowhere to be found. Slightly disappointed, he made his way back around to the front of the home and found Sierra still standing in the doorway with a horrified expression on her face.

Approaching her, he asked, "Sierra, what's wr…."

His question was cut short when he saw what she was looking at. The Chief of Police was lying there in a pool of blood, just 6 feet inside the door, and his son's lifeless body was sprawled across his chest. Rose heart dropped. Both bodies had bullet holes in their heads. The child's wound was in the back of his skull. Whoever had done this had murdered the boy as he kneeled down over his father. Whoever had done this was a monster.

It appeared that this wasn't just a war between rival Texas City street gangs. This was something that even a veteran like Rose had never witnessed before. This was a war between rival street gangs and also the Texas City Police. Somebody wanted total control of Texas City, and they had proven that they were willing to go to any lengths to get it.

"Sierra." Rose called, placing a hand on her shoulder. "I have to clear the house. Get on the phone and call this in with the Alvin Police Department, immediately. Tell them we saw a suspect dressed in all blue running towards the alley behind the home. They need to set up a perimeter, a.s.a.p. We can't let that guy get away."

Sierra stood stone faced still in mild shock from the scene.

"Sierra." Rose called a little more forcefully, shaking her shoulder. "Do you hear me? Snap out of it. I need you here with me."

Sierra blinked a few times and began to come back to her senses. "Yeah. Yeah. I hear you. Call it in."

"Ok." Rose said. "Good. Call it in, and then contact the TCPD headquarters and tell them what's going on. I'm going to go inside and clear the house. There may be more victims or suspects inside."

Pushing pass Sierra and entering the home, Rose carefully stepped over the two new homicide victims and headed towards the hallway in front of him. Not waiting to oversee the actual call, Rose searched the house. His gut told him that no one was still there, but it wouldn't hurt to check the premises anyway. There might be more dead bodies inside.

As Rose searched, he noted that the entire home smelled like death. One of the two victims, probably the small boy, relieved his bowels when he was murdered, and the scent was wafting through the hallways contaminating Rose's nostrils with a foul stench. After he was satisfied that they were the only ones in the house, Rose made his way back into the living room. Sierra was still standing in the same place he had left her in. She was frozen inside of the doorway staring at the two bodies lying in a pool of their own blood. In her hand was her cellphone, so at least she was able to call the paramedics.

Approaching her slowly, Rose felt sorry for her. He knew that she had seen dead bodies before but seeing a 10-year-old boy murdered in his home with his Police Chief father was obviously too much.

"Are you alright?" He asked, placing his hands on her shoulders.

Sierra's mouth quivered when she tried to speak. "He's... he's just a little boy." She managed to stammer out. "What kind of person would do that to a child?"

Then she fell into Rose arms and started to sob. Deciding that she had seen enough, Rose led her back over to his car and sat her down in the passenger seat.

"It's going to be alright." He assured her. "We are going to find the people responsible for this and make them pay."

Sierra just sat in the car with her chin buried in her chest. Rose had been through enough to know that she would be alright. It was just going to take a little time. He kicked himself for bringing her along with him. She had pretty much forced his hand though. She left him with no choice. Fishing a pack of Newport shorts out of his pocket, he lit a cigarette and went and stood in the front yard. He couldn't help but to wonder what would have happened if they would've arrived before the killer was fleeing the scene. Rose didn't want to consider the possibilities, but he was never able to fight off his pessimistic thoughts. He already lost one partner in the line of duty. His conscious couldn't handle another Officer losing their life on his watch.

As Rose took a long drag on his cigarette, he glanced over at Sierra. She looked so fragile, innocent, and exposed. Suddenly, the feelings of protectiveness started to filter into his heart. With those feelings came the memories. Rose shook his head and tried to stay focused on the here and now, but as usual, he couldn't win the battle against the demons of his past. In his mind's eye, his Crown Victoria transformed into a regular black and white police cruiser, Officer Sierra Martin became Office Tameka Stevens, and Detective Rose regressed into the rookie Officer Rose that he been so many years ago.

Rose, and his partner Tameka had received a tip from a confidential informant that a murder suspect that they had been looking for was at a residence on 3rd Ave. Rose, eager to make a name for himself within the department, was speeding towards the address with determination in his eyes.

"You don't think we should call for back-up?" Tameka asked.

Rose didn't take his eyes off the road. "We don't need any back-up." He told her. "We can handle this one on our own."

Tameka was nervous. Neither her nor Rose had been on the force long, and they were going after a guy who had just killed 2 people in cold-blood 3 days earlier. She didn't want to get on bad terms with her partner, but she felt compelled to voice her opinion.

"This guy is a stone-cold killer, Rose." She began. "What if he's armed? What if he's not alone? What if we get into trouble?"

Becoming upset with his partners whining, Rose pulled the police cruiser over.

"Look." He said, making eye contact with Tameka. "This partnership thing won't work if we don't have complete trust in one another. I know this guy is a murderer, but that comes with the job. We're police officers. We go after the bad guys. True, it's dangerous, but I got your back and you got mine. We'll be alright. We took an oath, Tameka. We are sworn to protect and serve. Even if it's dangerous, we the first line of defense. Yes, this guy has murdered two people. That's exactly why we have to get him off the streets. If you're afraid... if you don't want to go... if that's what's you're saying, I won't hold it against you. If that's how you feel, you can get out of the car right now, but as for me... I'm going to get this dirtbag."

Rose was not about to let this opportunity slip through his fingers. If he could nab this guy, he knew he would rise in the police ranks in no time. His ultimate goal was to make Detective, and no one, not even Tameka was going to stand in his way. Rose waited patiently as Tameka mulled over his little speech. He had already told himself that if she didn't want to go, he would put her out of the car and then go at it alone. He refused to not get credit for this arrest.

Everyone on the police force was looking for this guy. The tip came to him directly. In his mind, that was fate. It was his destiny to arrest this guy. He didn't care if there were 20 gangbangers at the address. That just meant he was going to be arresting 20 gangbangers instead of just one. Rose felt like Superman.

Tameka thought it over. She still didn't like the idea, but she didn't want to let her partner down. The bond between partners was supposed to be sacred. One of the things they taught them in the academy was that you never leave your partner hanging. Every cop in the TCPD police force that had abandoned their partner in the field, was looked upon as scum. Lower than low. No one trusted them after they committed that sacrilegious act. Tameka was loyal to Rose. She didn't want to let him down and she didn't want to ruin her name within the department.

Reluctantly, Tameka said, "Alright partner. I trust you. Let's do this."

Rose smiled. Not because Tameka had decided to go, but because he could almost taste the recognition and glory; and to him, the recognition tasted good. Rose put the cruiser back into drive and continued in the direction of 3rd Ave.

"Wooo! Wooo! Wooo! Wooo!"

The sound of the approaching police cars and E.M.S. trucks caused Rose's unwanted ride down memory lane to cease abruptly. He was extremely happy. He never liked to relive that night, but those demons didn't care much about what he liked. They haunted him in his dreams and daydreams alike.

Turning his attention to Sierra, he could tell that she was trying to regain her composure before the Alvin police officers arrived on the scene. For the first time since Rose had met Sierra, he noticed how pretty she actually was. Sitting there, slightly vulnerable, helped him to see her in a whole new light. He noticed the actual woman instead of the annoying rookie trying to make a name for herself.

Officer Sierra Martin was a light skinned black woman who only stood about 5'3. She had a petite build, but she was very thick in the thighs for her size. When she smiled, her already chubby cheeks would cause her eyes to squint up. Picturing her smiling in his head, Rose concluded that it was extremely cute. Sierra always kept her hair pulled back in a ponytail when she was at work.

Rose wondered why he had never noticed how attractive she was before just then. He figured it must be because he seen too much of his younger self in her.

Her eagerness to prove her merit was reminiscent of his own attitude as a new boot on the force. It wasn't that he didn't like her, it was just he knew firsthand where that type of approach to police work could lead. Not a day went by that he wished he did not know. Oh God, how he wished he did not know.

Doing his best to get back in the right frame of mind, he flicked away his half-smoked cigarette and lit a fresh one. The initial rush of nicotine was welcome in his waiting lungs. Rose knew he would have to be calm and thinking clearly if he was going to get a handle on this situation that now seemed to be spiraling out of control. The only good thing that he could see was the fact that the Hooligans had not yet retaliated on the Villains. It was possible that Sticks had not yet figured out who it was that launched the assault on his organization.

Pulling up in front of the residence and all hopping out at once, a total of 4 Alvin Police Officers came running up to Rose while the medical personnel entered the home. Rose had already withdrew his badge and he was holding it up for the officers to see.

"Detective Derrick Rose of the Texas City Police Department." He stated calmly. "The two vic's in there are Police Chief Robert Burby of the TCPD and his 10-year-old son. Both were D.O.A. when we arrived."

"Police Chief?" One of the other officers repeated. "What's going on here?"

Rose took a drag of his Newport. "Honestly gentleman," he began. "I have absolutely no idea, but I can fill you in on what I think is happening."

The 4 officers listened to every word that came out of Rose mouth. The crime rate in Alvin, Tx was almost non-existent, so all of this talk about gang lords and old vendettas sounded like something straight out of the movies. They were more intrigued than anything else. They never had action like the type of action Rose was describing.

Sierra got out of the car and joined Rose while he explained what they saw when they pulled up. One of the officers immediately put out an A.P.B. on a black male wearing an all blue outfit. Rose didn't say anything, but he was 100% positive that the killer was no longer in Alvin. He had come down here specifically to kill the police chief. By now, he was halfway back to Texas City. After he finished telling them everything that he knew, the officers let them go and went to investigate the crime scene. Rose decided to head back to Texas City.

Sierra saw Rose headed to his vehicle and tried to think fast. She didn't want to leave Police Chief Burby's house without getting a good look around.

"Wait a minute." Sierra said. "I think we should search the house too."

Rose looked at her. "Why do you think that?" He asked. "Our killer is back in Texas City by now. I highly doubt he left any real clues behind, but if he did, the Alvin PD will find it and let us know. This is out of our jurisdiction. Let's just let them do their jobs."

Sierra eyes shifted back and forth. There were things inside of the Chief's house that she needed to see. Things that she couldn't mention to Rose.

"I know that." She answered. "But don't you remember the Bible verse?"

Rose thought about it. "The one about Lamech?" He asked, not knowing where she was going. "Yeah. What about it?"

"Yeah." She told him. "That's the one. The whole concept of the killer leaving that verse was to inform us that his murders were not random. He is only targeting those people that he feels has somehow wronged him. Now, I'm not 100% sure, but based on your theory about the Villains waging war on the Hooligans, I'm willing to bet you that Burby has a connection to the Hooligans somehow."

Rose let her words tumble around in his brain. He had no evidence about Police Chief Burby working with the Hooligans, but he knew all too well that there were plenty of dirty cops working the Department. He did not want Burby to be a part of that cesspool, but at this point, he couldn't rule anything out. Sierra had more snap then he gave her credit for. He didn't want to admit it, but with a little more self-discipline, she would make one hell of a detective. Sierra watched as Rose processed her opinion through his mental computer. She knew that the two of them working together could figure this thing out. Sierra felt like this might be her big chance to prove that she had what it took to be a detective.

Paying attention to every expression that Rose made, Sierra noticed a hint of understanding cross his face. "What is it?" She asked, anticipating what he was thinking.

"Well," Rose started, puffing on his cigarette again. "It may not be anything, but then again, it may be everything."

Then, heading towards the front door of the house, he said, "Distract them for me."

Sierra had no idea what was going on, but she wanted to be of some type of assistance, so she just did what he said to do. They both entered the house. The Alvin police were still inside the living room making absolutely no progress. Sierra walked up to them and just started talking.

"You want to know what I think?" She asked.

The officers, who were left scratching their heads, were more than willing to hear someone else's point of view. While they indulged in Sierra's ramblings, Rose slid off into the back room. Upon his initial search of the house when they had first arrived, he saw something that had no meaning at first, but after taking into consideration what

Sierra had just said, he figured it was worthy of a second look.

Whoever had murdered Burby was dressed like a Hooligan, but Rose was sure that was just a rouge. Everything about this case said that the killer was a Villain, and he had most likely worn blue so that he could impersonate a Hooligan. But the question was this, why would a Villain feel as if he dressed like a Hooligan, Police Chief Burby would have his guard down when he showed up? Sierra's assessment that Burby had some kind of a connection to the Hooligans was most likely accurate.

Entering the master bedroom, Rose made his way to the nightstand next to the bed. Sitting on top of the nightstand was a little black address book and a small notepad. Rose picked up the address book and flipped through the pages. Nothing stood out until he got to a name with no address underneath it. All it was, was a name, a cellphone number, and what appeared to be a 9-digit number that he couldn't guess what it represented. None of that is what made the entry standout, though. It was the four-stars next to the name. It was the only name marked like that.

The entry read "Abdul ****".

"What the hell are you doing with Abdul's name in your address book, Chief?" He asked.

Feeling like he had gotten what he was looking for, he placed the address book, as well as the notepad, into his pocket and left the room. Seeing Rose walking with determination, Sierra knew that it was time to go.

"So," she said, clapping her hands together, "the killer probably came in, thought 'oh my God' someone is home, shot them both and then ran away. The end."

Praying that they wouldn't ask any questions, Sierra walked out of the front door close on the heels of Rose. The Alvin Police Officers were more confused after listening to Sierra then before.

"That girl is wack-o." One officer said to another officer.

"You said it." He responded.

"So, what did you find?" Sierra asked, climbing into the Crown Victoria.

Rose looked at her smiling. "I think we might be on to something." He informed her. "Your instincts might be paying off."

Then, as they drove off, Rose explained his theory to Sierra and showed her what he had found. As soon as they were turning off the block, 3 news vans were turning onto the block approaching from the opposite direction. Soon, everyone in Galveston County would know what was going on. Rose and Sierra were running out of time.

………………..

Back in Texas City, sitting inside of the On Point Barber Shop, business was being conducted as usual. All four chairs had someone in it getting their hair cut and the couches and chairs lining the walls were filled up with men waiting on their turn. Almost everyone that lived on the

Southside got their hair cut at On Point, but very few of them actually knew what On Point really was. It was nothing more than a front business for the leader of the Southlane Villains himself. Infamous.

There was a 'Do Not Enter' sign on the door in that back that led to the office. No one had ever dared to disobey that sign, and if they ever did, they would suffer serious consequences. Behind that door, Infamous sat at his large oak desk watching a 72' flat screen television with his right-hand man. They were watching an episode of their favorite show. 'The Next Great Singing Sensation'. It was a televised contest about R&B hopefuls who were competing to win a 1-million-dollar record deal. They didn't watch it for the winner though. They only watched it to laugh at the losers that made a spectacle of themselves on national TV.

Infamous was a large imposing figure, with dark skin and strong features, and he instilled in those around him with merely his presence. He stood about 6'3 and he weighed close to 350lbs. Most of his weight was fat, but it wasn't a sloppy type of fat. He was solid. His fat was built around muscle and he was surprisingly healthy. He exercised regularly and although he did eat anything he wished, he tried to keep a healthy mix included within his diet. Infamous liked to call his weight a product of good living. He mainly wore all red designer suits, but he changed the colors periodically. Every time you saw Infamous, he was puffing on a Cuban Cigars. Both of his hands were covered with gold rings, and he wore a diamond encrusted, gold Rolex watch, that had cost him $75,000 dollars.

Infamous laughed hard, in his signature deep guttural tone, and slapped his fat meaty hand down hard on his desk.

"You see that shit?" He asked chuckling, referring to a white kid with orange spiked hair that couldn't sing worth a lick. "Now why would his friends let him get on there and embarrass himself like that? "

"Yeah, I see him boss." His right-hand man informed him, standing like a soldier off to the side of Infamous desk with his hands clasped in front of his waist.

"He should be ashamed of himself." Infamous cried out. "Hahahahaha! He should…"

Infamous' laugh was cut short. "What the fuck?" He asked, leaning forward in his seat.

The scene on the TV had changed. A reporter from for the channel 10 news had come on, and they were standing in front of a home that was blocked off by police tape.

"We interrupt this broadcast to bring you a special news bulletin." She began. "Police Chief Robert Burby of the Texas City Police Department was murdered in his Alvin home earlier today along with his 10-year-old son, Robert Burby Jr. I'm Mindy Ray and I am live on the scene now. Behind me is the Police Chief's home. There were no witnesses to the crime, and as of now, there are no suspects. We did receive word from the police that they are looking for someone they are calling a person of interest, but they have yet to release any information about this individual to the general public. The Alvin Police Department is..."

Infamous stood up in his seat and his belly almost knocked his desk over.

"That mothafucka pulled it off!" He exclaimed, grinning from ear to ear. "I told you that Squeak was a reliable mothafucka. Damn. He got the son, too."

Infamous puffed his cigar.

"You thought you couldn't be touched, didn't you, Chief? You thought that fucking badge was going to save you? Motherfucker, I'm God. Big 'G'. You thought I was gonna let that shit slide? Well look at you now, Burby. Look at you now. We Villains, 'round here. Anybody can get it."

Infamous walked over to the wall and removed a painting of Marcus Garvey that he had hanging up. Once it was removed, it revealed the door to a safe that he had built into the wall.

"Shit," He said. "I might have to give Squeak a bonus this time. I have to admit. I wasn't sure if he was going to come through. I mean, I knew he was a bad man, but this was a tall order."

Infamous held the cigar in his mouth with his teeth and turned the dial to the set numbers and pulled the safe open. Inside was stacks and stacks of 100-dollar bills. On top of the money was a black 9mm hand pistol.

"Bring me that briefcase." He instructed his right-hand man.

Obediently, he brought it over to the boss and held it open while Infamous filled it up with $300,000 in cash.

After he was finished loading it up, he said, "I need you to deliver this to Squeak for me. You know where he lives."

His right-hand man simply nodded his head and headed towards the door. Right before he opened it, Infamous stopped him.

"Jesse." He called.

"Yeah boss?" Jesse answered.

"Be careful." Infamous told him. "By now, Sticks knows the truce is off and the police are going to seeking revenge for Burby. It's about to get hot out there. Texas City about to be on fire."

Jesse lifted his shirt revealing his pistol that he kept tucked away in his waistband.

"What did Shaka Zulu tell the British when they tried to convert him to Christianity by warning him of hell and the lake of fire?" Jesse quizzed him.

Infamous smiled. "What did he tell him, Villain?"

Jesse turned to walk out, but he looked back over his shoulder to answer his own question.

"Shaka Zulu told him, we don't need some white man named Jesus to save us from hell fire. We're the Zulu Nation. Around here, we eat fire."

Jesse worked for Infamous, but Jesse was also his best friend. They had rose to their present status together. In Infamous point of view, nothing made a bond stronger then committing violent acts together, and he and Jesse had been bringing pain to Texas City since elementary school.

He watched as Jesse left to go deliver the payment for the 3 jobs Squeak had completed. Infamous was feeling good because he knew that the Hooligans had no choice but to retaliate, and a blood bath is just what he wanted. He had swallowed his pride and made a truce, only to have his good intentions spit on by Sticks himself. Infamous swore that Sticks and everyone affiliated with him would pay the ultimate price for what he considered the ultimate act of betrayal.

Jesse left out of the barber shop through the back door and hopped into his candy red Cadillac Escalade. Tossing the briefcase onto the passenger side seat, he started the ignition and pulled out. Merging into traffic, he only drove one block before he was halted by a red light. Utilizing that time to adjust the dial on his radio, he looked down and began flipping through the stations. It startled him when he heard a tapping on his windshield. Instinctively, he reached for his pistol. He stopped when he saw who it was. It was just a homeless man washing his windshield for some spare change.

The man had long dirty dreadlocks and a tattered and torn white t-shirt on. Jesse felt sorry for him. As the man sprayed water on the glass and wiped it off with a towel, Jesse reached into his pocket and pulled out a $20 bill. Then, he rolled down his window and handed it to him.

"Thank you, mon." The man said in an extremely raspy voice and a broken Jamaican accent. "May the Gods of your ancestors bless you now."

Then, he pulled a small .25 caliber pistol out of his pocket and emptied the entire clip directly into Jesse's cranium. A woman driving a Honda Civic behind the Escalade screamed. Shock wasn't worried. He casually opened the driver's side door, reached over Jesse's dead body, grabbed the briefcase that was lying in the seat, and ran off. He left in his wake one dead man, one screaming lady, and several upset motorists honking their horns because the light was green, but traffic wasn't moving.

....

At the exact same time that Jesse was being murdered, Squeak was pulling back up to his house. The entire ride there, he had been trying to shake the memory of killing that little boy, but he couldn't. As heartless as he was, killing children wasn't his thing. Squeak entered the house on Anderson St. and heard the shower running.

"Shonda, it's me." He called out, letting her know that he was back from the job.

"Did everything go alright?" She asked.

Squeak thought back to the small boy he had just killed.

"Yeah." He lied. "Like clockwork."

"Good." Shonda yelled.

Squeak made his way to his bedroom and found the plate full of powder that he had left. Shonda had barely even touched it. In an attempt to silence the boys voice in his head, Squeak buried his nose into the pile of powder and sniffed as hard as he could. The rush caused his body to lurch backward.

"Cough! Cough! Cough!"

He began to cough as the excessive amount of cocaine bomb rushed his system.

"Auugghh!" He exclaimed, as he dropped down to one knee frantically rubbing his nose because of the intense burning sensation that had come.

Squeak felt his eyes begin to water and his entire face began to get numb. Rubbing his face, he still could hear the little boy in his head pleading with his fathers' dead body to come back to life.

"Daddy. Daddy. Get up."

Squeak could hear the child's voice as clearly as if he was right there in the room with him.

"Fuck." Squeak exclaimed. "What the fuck was his son doing there? Burby was supposed to live alone."

Pow!

Squeak heard the shot echo in his mind, and he saw the boy's skull open up. But... but... but he didn't have a choice, did he? What was he supposed to do? Was he supposed to let the kid live? No. He couldn't do that. The boy would've described him to the police. And then what? Then, him and Shonda would be hunted down like wild dogs.

Squeak opened his eyes, found the cocaine, and buried his nose in it again for another hit.

"Auugghh!" He exclaimed, shaking his head as he tried to sniff away the voices.

Cough! Cough! Cough!

"No." He proclaimed out loud. "It ain't your fault, Squeak. It's Burby fault. It was his lifestyle that got his son killed. He's the one to blame, not you. Fuck that shit. You had a job to do. That's it, that's all. A job. If Burby ass wasn't a crooked fucking cop, no of that would've happened."

Squeak looked down at the cocaine again.

"Yeah." He said, reassuring himself. "It's Burby's fault. He's the one who killed his son. Not me. Him."

Squeak was about to bury his face in the powder again when his bedroom door burst open. Shonda was standing there completely naked and dripping wet. Her hair was matted down to the sides of her face and her breasts were glistening.

"What the fuck are you in here doing?" She asked, clearly concerned.

She had heard him screaming and coughing uncontrollably and came in to investigate. Squeak could see her lips moving, but he had no idea what she was saying. His head was spinning faster and faster and his vision had become slightly blurred. As he blinked several times trying to bring his sister into focus, his brain began to register just how beautiful she actually was. The nicely trimmed hairs on her vagina had small droplets of water on them causing them to appear to be sparkling. Her dark skin was smooth and even, and her breasts were round and firm. Squeak could feel the lust demon that he had been fighting against for years getting stronger and stronger, but this time, his logical mind wasn't even attempting to fight back. The emotional overload, the cocaine he had inhaled, and Shonda's goddess like features were beating his moral resolve into submission.

Shonda made her way over to him to help him get off the floor, but the sudden rush of blood to his lower region had Squeak thinking about something totally different. As Shonda stood over Squeak, pushing the cocaine out of his reach, the lust overrode his logical mind. Reaching around Shonda and clutching her firmly on her butt cheeks, Squeak pulled her close and buried his face into her sweet smelling, freshly washed vagina.

At first Shonda flinched. The movement caught her off guard. It was not was she was expecting.

"What are you doing?" She asked, grabbing her brother by the sides of his head.

The sensation that his tongue gave her clitoris quickly answered her question. Shonda's knees buckled slightly as a tingle of pleasure shot through her entire body. Squeak caught her in his strong arms and prevented her from falling. Shonda gapped her legs and allowed Squeak to feast on the entirety of her love box. It had been years since either one of them had had sex, so Shonda was instantly sloppy wet.

Squeak pulled his head away from his forbidden meal. "What am I doing?" he thought, trying to deny the desire burning deep within him.

"No." Shonda protested with a breathy voice. "Don't stop. Please don't stop."

Forcing him to indulge in the obvious object of his lust, she begged him not to stop. Shonda maneuvered his head back and forth, left and right, and all around in circles. Squeak stuck his tongue out and allowed it to go wherever Shonda guided.

"Please don't stop, baby." She cooed. "It feels sooo good."

Squeaks head was spinning, and his dick was trying to burst out of his pants. Then, he skillfully took off his shirt in one swift motion and looked up at his big sister. Shonda grabbed her breast and bit down hard on her bottom lip. Squeak looked her deep in her eyes and licked his lips. The juices that covered his mouth tasted better than strawberries.

Squeak stood to his feet and locked gazes with Shonda. Both of them were breathing heavy. Squeak's mind was saying one thing, but his body was screaming something else.

Cautiously reaching out and placing his hands onto Shonda's breasts, he whispered, "This is so wrong. What are we doing? This is wrong."

Shonda reached out and placed a hand on his bulge. "But it feels so right." She said.

As Squeak gently fondled with her breast, Shonda unbuckled his pants and exposed his rock-hard tool. Squeak didn't know what to do.

He leaned in slowly mumbling, "But... but... but."

Shonda stuck her tongue out and licked the outside of his lips.

"No buts." She said softly, kissing him softly on the mouth.

"No regrets." She added, kissing him again.

"Only pleasure." She said through semi-clenched teeth like it was taking every ounce of will power she had not to take that dick from him right then and there.

Allowing his hands to slither up her frame, Squeak placed his palms on either side of Shonda's face. Pulling her close enough to where they could feel each other's breath, but just far enough away so that their lips wouldn't touch, Squeak swallowed hard. Then, he stepped closer and caused the tip of his dick to make contact with the hairs of Shonda's pussy.

"No regrets." He said slowly, emphasizing every syllable.

Then, as one, they closed the miniscule gap between their mouths and kissed passionately. Their tongues seemed to dance to a song that only they knew. A song that only they could hear. Shonda closed her eyes and let Squeak have total control over her. Squeak closed his eyes and allowed himself to be guided by his desires. He had not had sex with his sister since he was 18, and since then, he had not had sex with anyone else.

Becoming energized by the thought of once again penetrating the only female he had ever willingly experienced, Squeak grabbed her by her shoulders and shoved her down on the bed. The plate with the cocaine on it wasted all over the covers but neither one of them cared. Squeak pulled off his pants, boxers, socks, and shoes, while Shonda squirmed in anticipation.

"Are you gonna fuck me, daddy?" She asked aggressively. "Ooowww. Please fuck me good! I want you to hurt me, daddy! Beat this pussy up!"

Shonda had been waiting on this day for years. Squeak had been denying her for far too long. She couldn't believe that it was finally happening. He did love her. She knew that he did. They were meant to be together. To hell with what the rest of the world thought. Squeak was her world and she was his. They didn't need anyone to validate their affection for each other.

Squeak was turned on by Shonda's dirty talking. His body was on fire. He felt like an animal. Squeak grabbed some of the loose cocaine with his hand and inhaled the drug directly from the palm of his hand. He felt like he was powering up.

"You want me to hurt that pussy?" Squeak asked, as he dusted off his hands. Then he grabbed her by her thighs and drug her to the edge of the bed.

Shonda was caught off guard by the power behind the tug, but it turned her on none the less. Grabbing his thick piece of man meat, Squeak placed his dick head at the opening of Shonda's pussy and rammed every inch that he had inside of her as hard as he could.

"Auugghh!" Shonda hollered.

"Don't yell now, bitch." Squeak told her, as he pressed her legs all the way back to the bed and began to thrust in and out of her tight hole as fast and as hard as he possibly could.

Squeak had a nice sized penis and Shonda had not been penetrated since she was 19, so the pain she was experiencing was real. All she could do to cope was grit her teeth and grip the sheets. Squeak had forgotten how good his sister's pussy was. She was so wet that he could hear his testicles slapping against her skin and making a splish-splash noise.

"Ooohhh yeah." He moaned, as the grip of her vagina sealed tighter and tighter around the shaft of his dick.

Squeak noticed that Shonda was doing her best not to yell. He liked the challenge.

"So, you not gone yell, bitch?" he asked, not slowing down at all.

"You... ain't... doin'... shit... nigga!" She stammered out defiantly.

"Oh yeah?" He responded, as he stopped stroking long enough to climb on top of her.

Having more leverage from his new position, Squeak used the weight of his body to thrust inside of her with more force. It didn't take long before Shonda was yelling and moaning at the top of her lungs.

"Ok, daddy. Ok, daddy." She screamed. "You the man! You the man!"

"Oh? I'm the man now?" Squeak asked. "I'm the man now? Well tell me how good this dick is, then."

As he pounded away, Shonda declared, "This dick is the best! This dick is the best!"

That's all it took. Squeak felt an eruption swelling in the pit of his testicles.

"I'm about to nut." He moaned, as his strokes stopped coming rhythmically and became more erratic.

Shonda quickly pushed him off of her and hurried to his waist. Placing her mouth around his throbbing dick, she began to suck him fast and hard. Squeak grabbed her hair. When the cum started bursting forth from his penis, Shonda was there to catch every drop.

"Uuuggghhh." Squeak groaned as his body shook back and forth.

He felt every muscle in his body tense up. Shonda hungrily gobbled up every bit of nut that came from her brother's dick. Only when she was sure he was finished ejaculating; did she release his member from her mouth. He had unloaded a lot into her waiting oral cavity. Squeak watched as Shonda climbed out of the bed and headed towards the bathroom. By the time she made it back to the room, he was laying naked in the bed, sound asleep. Squeak had passed out.

"Yeah." Shonda said, rubbing herself. "I got that mothafuckin' bomb ass

pussy."

Chapter Five

Detective Rose pulled into the almost deserted parking lot of the Moore Memorial Public Library. The library was open for business, but only the diehard bookworms were inside. Ever since the internet had taken off, the public libraries around the country had seen a steady decline in patrons. The Texas City public library was no different. The staff there had to constantly come up with programs and events in order to give people reasons to come through the doors.

Moore Memorial Public Library had been around for as long as Rose had lived in Texas City. He was not one of the individuals who frequented the place, but Sierra was. Sierra was an avid reader. She liked all different sorts of books from all different genres. Her all-time favorite author was an African American author named Matthew Daniels. Matthew Daniels used several different names when he wrote. He had books under his legal name, Matthew Daniels, but he also wrote under the pseudonyms Chosen Phew and The Real Bookworm.

She also followed Matthew Daniels on Facebook. He ran an online book club under the group name, TheRealBookWorm, and he would always make videos talking about the different books he was either reading or writing. Matthew Daniels had several books out, but her favorite was called Suicide Note. Suicide Note was set in a town called Dickinson, Tx, which ironically, was a part of Galveston County. It was actually only 15 minutes away from Texas City. Sierra thought it was pretty awesome that a man born and raised in her hometown of Texas City had made it famous writing books and he wrote books centered around the area that she herself was from.

Part of the aura around Matthew Daniels and his books that helped him to blow up, was the fact that many people in the area, including law enforcement and politicians, swore up and down that his books were based on actual events. They claimed the crimes were real and the people were real. Everyone figured that he was just so intelligent, that he changed things around just enough to avoid any prosecution from the courts or retaliation from anyone who he may have been writing about. He had become a local legend.

During the entire ride from Alvin, Rose had been explaining his theory about the connection between The Hooligans and Chief Burby, but Sierra still seemed confused.

"I understand what you're saying." She told him. "What I don't understand is what we're doing at the Library. Shouldn't we be going to arrest Infamous?"

Rose cut off the ignition. Her words had reminded him that she was still new to this. He searched for a way to make her comprehend his approach.

"Ok." He said. "Let's follow your train of thought. What should we go arrest him for? What do you think we should charge him with?"

Sierra looked at him with a disbelieving look.

"The man is starting a war!" She exclaimed, tossing her hands into the air as if the answer was obvious. "You said it yourself. He's the one who ordered the hit on Abdul, he's the one behind those two homicides over in The Chelseas, and now, one of his soldiers has murdered the Chief of Police. What do you mean, what should we charge him with? We charge his ass with murder. That's what."

Rose remained calm and let Sierra get it all out.

"That's correct." He responded. "I did say that, but what evidence do we have to actually warrant an arrest and solidify a conviction?"

Rose looked around.

"Do we have the suspect in custody?"

Sierra rolled her eyes. "Well, no, but..."

Rose raised his index finger and cut her off. "Do we have any witnesses claiming that it was one of Infamous' gangbanger friends who committed the murders?"

Sierra folded her arms and tilted her head. "No, but..."

"Do we have the murder weapon, fingerprints, signed confessions, DNA, surveillance video? Do we have any physical evidence whatsoever?"

The string of questions hit Sierra like a ton of bricks. She dropped back in her seat and thought about it.

Whoever their killer was, he was an obvious professional. As of yet, he had left no witnesses or evidence of any kind. They were no closer to knowing who he was now than they were when they didn't even know he existed. All they had was a theory. In the court of law that would not stand up. Especially with a man as well connected and funded as Infamous. It was all conjecture. She doubted they could even get a Judge to grant them a warrant to search his home, let alone convince a Grand Jury to indict him.

Seeing that she was beginning to understand, Rose opened the car door.

"Remember," he told her. "It's not about what you know or what you think you know. It's about what you can back up with the evidence and facts. I've seen many a criminal bet a case that they were clearly guilty of because a cop ran into his investigation halfcocked."

Sierra climbed out of the car and followed him up the paved walkway. As the two of them passed by the small circular water fountain that graced the libraries landscape, Rose noticed an opportunity to impart some wisdom to the rookie. Wisdom he wished was imparted unto him when he was her age.

"Regardless of how bad the situation looks," he said, knowing that Sierra was listening, "you can never lose sight of the ultimate goal. As a detective, the goal is to figure out what's going on, build a solid case with facts and evidence, and keep yourself safe at the same time. I've seen a lot of officers lose themselves along the way. A lot. Have you ever heard of Officer Thorn?"

Sierra thought about it and then shook her head, no.

"Exactly." Rose said. "It's as if he never existed. He started out with good intentions like most of us. You know, trying to do the right thing. Trying to clean up the streets, as we say. But over time, he switched. Minor indiscretions became major indiscretions. He forgot all about the rule of law, evidence, and probable cause. He started acting like a person was guilty just because he said they were guilty. When he couldn't catch them with drugs, he would just plant drugs on them. When he couldn't plant drugs on them, he would assault them and claim they attacked him first, just to charge them with a crime. Eventually, it all caught up with him."

Intrigued, Sierra asked. "What happened to him?"

"Well, he never answered for all of his crimes he committed while he was an officer, but he eventually was arrested for assaulting his wife. When he got to prison, what do you think happened to him? What do you think all of those people he had wrongfully incarcerated did when they found out who he was?"

Sierra shuddered. Every cop knows what happens to a cop in prison. Especially the crooked ones.

Making it to the glass doors, they walked inside.

"I'm saying all of that to say this. No matter what, you never break the rules. It's a slippery slope. Once you compromise yourself just one time, it becomes easier and easier. It eventually becomes your style of police work, and it always drags you down. Always. As a homicide detective, you never go after a person for murder unless you can legally prove their guilt. To do that, you have to first establish a motive. You have to establish the why. Like, why did this person commit this crime. Without a motive, you have nothing. See, as a detective, you have to find out 'why' before you can find out anything else."

Sierra and Rose strolled into the lobby area of the library and Rose headed towards the bank of computers.

"So, how do we find the motive?" Sierra asked.

Rose stopped and surveyed the area.

"By piecing together clues, and a whole lot of luck." He told her.

The Moore Memorial Public Library was always a quiet place. They had only seen maybe 5 people scanning the shelves as they made their way towards the back. The computer area consisted of 5 rows of tables with 5 computers on each row. Of the 25 total computers, only 3 were being utilized and all 3 of those were on the front row. Deciding on the last computer on the last row, Rose and Sierra maneuvered down the aisles and took a seat. Sierra pulled up a chair from the neighboring computer so she could see the one that Rose was working on.

Rose smiled and nodded his head toward the front row. "You have an audience." He said coolly.

Sierra followed the direction of his eyes and saw the 3 other library patrons staring at her. When she made eye contact with them, they all quickly looked away.

Rose chuckled.

"What's so funny?" She asked, feeling a little uncomfortable.

"Nothing." He answered, trying to calm her down. "It's just been so long since I walked around in a police uniform that I had forgotten how much attention police garb could attract."

Sierra looked down at her uniform. In all of the excitement of the day, she had completely forgotten that she was still in uniform.

"Well," she stated, "when I become a detective like you, I won't have to worry about that anymore."

Wiggling the mouse, Rose caused the computers screen saver to go away and the libraries home page to come up.

"So, what are we looking for?" She asked, as Rose typed, clicked, and searched.

"Back at the Chief's house," Rose began, "you got me to thinking. How does Burby fit into all of this Villain against Hooligan mess? At first, I couldn't put my finger on it, but after I found that address book with Abdul's name in it, I was able to somewhat piece it together. Think about it. If Abdul was a Hooligan, and Burby had his name and number in his address book, it's safe to say that his connection to all of this is that he had some form of ties to the Hooligans, right?"

Sierra thought about it. "Well, yeah." She said finally. "Don't you think so too?"

Rose continued to type. "I did," he answered, "but one thing I know is that in this line of work, you never want to make assumptions. You want to back up everything with evidence. When I gave the matter more thought, I recalled an incident that occurred two years ago. Back then, one would have assumed that Burby's was somehow connected to the Villains instead of the Hooligans if such a connection was even present."

Sierra scratched her head. "And what incident was that?" She asked.

Rose punched a few more keys on the keyboard and then leaned back in his seat. "See for yourself." He instructed her.

Sierra directed her attention to the computer screen. Rose had pulled up an old newspaper article. Examining the article, she read the headline out loud.

"Drug Kingpin's Son Found Tortured and Murdered."

Sierra looked at Rose. She remembered hearing about that. It happened before she joined the force, so she didn't know too much about it. Rose motioned with his head encouraging her to keep reading. Sierra turned her attention back to the story.

Two years ago, on April 21, a 13-year-old boy named Korey Isaac was found murdered. The boy was the son of the notorious Gang Lord, Demetrius Isaac, a.k.a.

Infamous. As she read the article, she found out that the killer had beaten the boy severely before finally shooting him in the head. The police had no motive, no clues, and no suspects. Police Chief Robert Burby swore to find the person responsible and bring them to justice at all cost.

After reading the article in its entirety, Sierra came to an icon that read "click here for follow-up story". Reaching across the keypad, she placed the cursor on the icon and clicked the mouse. The first article was instantly replaced with a different one.

The new headline read, "*Police Chief Robert Burby, and the Texas City Police Department, makes arrest in the homicide case*."

Three days after the boy's body lifeless body was found discarded like a piece of trash, the TCPD arrested a local drug addict and charged him with the murder. Chief Burby speculated that the murder suspect, a man named Luis Wilkinson, had murdered the boy in retaliation for some drug deal gone bad. Luis was found in possession of the murder weapon, and an eyewitness had come forward and said that they had seen some of Infamous' men beating Luis the morning of the murder. The eyewitness claimed that the murder was retaliation for the beating.

Sierra clicked on the icon to pull up another follow-up story. The next headline really shocked her.

"*Gunman walks into police station and kills Luis Wilkinson*".

Before she was able to read the article, Rose spoke up.

"Now that's the one that intrigues me." He stated. "One of Infamous' men casually strolled into the Texas City Police Department Headquarters, shot and killed Luis Wilkinson, and then casually strolled right back out."

Sierra couldn't believe it. She had never heard that part of the story.

"And get this," Rose added. "The gunman only encountered one officer when this took place, and that officer did absolutely nothing to stop him. Care to guess who that officer was?"

Sierra's eyes got huge. "Don't tell me." She said. "Police Chief Burby!"

Rose nodded his head.

"I don't believe it." Sierra said, leaning back in her chair.

She placed her hand on her forehead. Immediately her analytical brain started processing the new information. This case had more twists and turns in it than a video game racetrack. Every time things started to somewhat make sense; another piece of information came into play that totally caused her to rethink her theory.

"Maybe," she said, coming to a different conclusion, "Burby wasn't murdered because of his affiliation to the Hooligans. He could've been murdered for his affiliation with the Villains and he had violated their trust somehow. I mean, why would he allow someone to execute Wilkinson if he was not working for Infamous?"

Rose sat back and watched as Sierra tried to figure it all out. He was seasoned enough to know that they didn't have enough information to come to any solid conclusions, but her going over the facts was part of the process. Rose figured that the next piece to the puzzle would be found in understanding the numerical code underneath Abdul's name in the Chief's address book. Reaching in his pocket to pull out the little black book, he felt the little notebook inside of his pocket also. He had completely forgotten about that. Retrieving them both, he sat the address book down on the table next to the keyboard and he flipped open the notebook. At the top of the first page was 4 numbers.

'6102'.

On each line below that, there were more seemingly random numbers. On the first line there was a 6-digit number, 615110. On the next line there was the number 612120. On each line there was a 6-digit number.

Looking at the notepad in Rose's hand, Sierra asked, "What's that?"

Rose shook his head trying to make out what the numbers could represent. "I'm not sure, but whatever it is, my instincts tell me it's important."

Rose and Sierra both stared at the list of numbers and racked their brains to figure it out.

....

Meanwhile, just outside the Moore Memorial Public Library, a candy blue H3 was driving down the street. The Hummers only occupant was talking on his cellphone using its Bluetooth. He was also smoking on an apple flavored mini-blunt filled up with hydro weed.

Sticks inhaled the weed smoke and held it within his lungs.

"Is it done?" He asked casually.

Shock replied, "Yes sir. That problem is no longer a problem."

Sticks smiled as he exhaled slowly through his nostrils. "Good, because I have another job for you. Are you ready for another one?"

There was a short pause. Shock rubbed the scar on his throat. Reality was, he was always ready to do a job.

"I'm listening." Shock told him, breaking the silence.

Sticks knew that he could count on Shock. In all of the years he had known him, he had never once turned down a job and he had never once failed to eliminate the target. Sticks could send Shock after men, women, children, disabled people, whatever. It didn't matter. He would always deliver. The only thing that mattered to Shock was the price on the individuals head. Admittedly, Sticks was concerned about working with a man like that. True, Shock was loyal, but he was also extremely volatile. He enjoyed killing a little too much. A man like that could be dangerous. At the end of the day, you could never fully control a man like that.

"Someone in our organization has tipped off Infamous." Sticks said. "That's the only explanation for why he would be coming after us like he is. Someone told him what we did. I can't prove it yet, but I'm 100% sure that they did. I need you to figure out who the rat is and exterminate him. It's time to clean house."

Shock considered the request. He had been asked to kill a Hooligan before, but he had never been asked to conduct a quasi-investigation of his own crew and weed out the rats. Not that it really mattered though, he didn't mind conducting an investigation. In fact, now that Sticks had presented the idea, he was somewhat intrigued. This would give him the opportunity to actually play with his victim before killing them. This was a license to torture before the kill. So what if it was a Hooligan. If they were feeding information to the other side, they deserved to be dealt with.

"Do you have any idea who it might be?" Shock asked, in his always raspy voice. "Where do you suggest I begin?"

Sticks knew that there were only three people on the planet, other than himself and Shock, that were supposed to know about what had happened. Sticks also knew that one of those three people were dead. That only left two possible candidates. Sticks figured Shock should begin there.

"Check out Trot and Archie." Sticks instructed him. "It has to be one of them. Or, both of them."

Shock wrote the two names down on a piece of paper in his typical ritualistic fashion. He could already feel his spirits slowly beginning to rise as thoughts of torture and homicide began to creep into his mind.

"I got you covered, Hooligan." Shock told him. "Consider it done."

Hanging up the phone, Shock knew that he would be able to visualize himself killing one of them pretty easily. He knew both of them well. He wasn't exactly looking forward to his new job, but Archie did argue with him one time when they were younger, and Sticks wouldn't let him fight him. So, he figured maybe he could view this as his opportunity to finally settle that old instance of disrespect.

When Shock had received the call from Sticks, he was in the middle of counting the money he discovered inside of the briefcase that he taken from Jesse. He expected to find something of value within it, but nothing could've prepared him for the stacks and stacks of 100-dollar bills that he did find. It was like Christmas. He got to kill Jesse, he found a briefcase full of cash, he was still going to get paid for killing Jesse, and now he had two more names on his list.

"I really came up this time." Shock told himself.

He had counted up to $65,000 when the phone call from Sticks came in, and he wasn't even halfway finished.

The thing he liked the most was that it was all extra. Sticks still owed him $50,000 for the actual hit.

As Shock began stuffing the cash into his safe, he decided to finish counting the rest of it later. To think, Shock had only had two jobs his entire life. His first job was that of a drug dealer, and his second was that of a hitman for hire.

Looking at all of the money inside of his safe, he said, "And people wonder why I do what I do."

Then he laughed long and hard.

A few more jobs and he would be able to retire. He knew that Sticks wouldn't want to let him go because he knew too much, so he had plans on just disappearing one day. One day he would be there, and then the next day he would be gone. Like a ghost. He would fade into the night and never look back. Shock knew that he had spilled too much blood onto the streets of Texas City, and he knew that one day he would grow tired of killing. Common sense told him that he would never find peace in the same location that created and nurtured his demons. He knew that if he would ever find solace in this life, it would be far away from the polluted air and crime ridden streets of his hometown.

Still energized off of his fresh kill, Shock was eager to complete his new job. As he changed out of his homeless man clothes, and tossed off his dreadlocks wig, he peeked out of his bedroom window. The sun was beginning setting and evening was creeping across the landscape. Oh, how he loved the cover of darkness. Shock tossed his dreadlock wig to the side and replaced it with an afro wig.

"Black power, motherfucker." He mumbled with a devilish grin as he lightly patted the fake hair.

Shock was really bald, but no one knew it. He shaved his head every night when he took a shower. He wasn't naturally bald, he did it for a reason. He knew that it was easy to disguise himself as a person with hair, and then remove the hair and fool any witnesses. Changing into a black t-shirt and a pair of black jeans, he walked over to his closet and opened it. There were absolutely no clothes in his closet. There were only weapons.

Shock loved guns. He had assault rifles, A.K. 47's, S.K.S.'s. hand pistols, and revolvers. On the top shelf he even had an assortment of army knives, pocketknives, brass knuckles, two tasers, and a can of mace.

"Hmmm." Shock hummed, as he tried to decide which weapon to use.

He smiled big and rubbed his hands together like a kid in a candy store. He had been itching for the opportunity to use his A.K. 47, but he didn't want to be guilty of overkill. No. He thought of killing as an art form. His weapon was like painter's paintbrush. He needed just the right weapon for the job. Nothing more, nothing less. Not knowing exactly what to expect when he confronted Trot and Archie, Shock decided to just reload his .25. As a last-minute addition, he grabbed his 6-inch army knife and headed out the door.

Outside his apartment complex he saw the usual sights. Drug addicts and their children all running around and congregating. No one gave him a second look. Shock knew where Archie lived, so he chose to go and question him first. Archie was a short but stocky red skinned dude that had been working for Sticks for years. All he would do is pick up dope from one location and drop it back off somewhere else. Just doing that simple act, being a drug runner, provided him with enough money to afford a nice brick house over on the Eastside. He lived there with his babies' mother, Veronica.

Shock climbed inside of his maroon colored Pontiac Sunbird and headed in the direction of Martin Luther King Jr St. Turning on his c.d. player, he scrolled through the tracks on the disc until he reached the one he was searching for. It was a song by Scarface called Burn. It featured the Houston based artist Z-Ro. He loved to listen to this particular song when he was headed out to complete a mission. There was something about the lyrics that got him in the right state of mind to handle his business.

Shock figured either Archie or Trot could easily be the rat. In his mind, both of them were just as good a choice as the other. He wasn't sure how he would find out, but he enjoyed the idea of extracting the information. Besides, if all else failed, he could always just kill them both. When the thought of killing them both crossed his mind, he smiled. Maybe he would just do that anyway.

By the time Shock was close to Martin Luther King Jr St, the sun had already completely descended below the horizon, and night had officially rolled in. Preparing himself for the fun up ahead, he grabbed his .25 out of his waistband and sat it down on his lap. Then, he noticed a blue dodge Durango pulling off of MLK St. Leaning forward in his seat, he was able to see a red-skinned driver with braids in his hair.

"Archie." He mumbled to himself. "Just where do you think you're going?"

Being careful to stay a few cars back, Shock began trailing him. Archie turned onto Texas Ave. bobbing his head up and down to the song on the radio. As he made his way to Loretta's house, he was completely oblivious to the man in the Pontiac 3 cars behind him. Not having far to go, Archie reached his destination in 15 minutes.

Pulling up in front of a small brown home on 14th St, he got out of his car, walked up to the front door, and then knocked. Knowing that Archie didn't know his car, Shock slowed down and drove by. He was silently praying that he could get a glimpse of the person that lived at the residence. As if his prayers were answered, as soon as he was directly in front of the house, he saw a brown skinned woman emerge and give Archie a hug.

Shock's blood instantly began to boil. He did not recognize the house, but he definitely recognized the woman who was embracing Archie. Her name was Loretta Gilmore. Gilmore, however, was her maiden name. The name she returned to after her divorce was final. Shock had first met her by her married name. Shock knew her as

Loretta Isaac. The same Loretta Isaac that was once married to Demetrius Isaac, a.k.a. Infamous.

"So," Shock said, glaring at the pair menacingly. "I've caught you red handed, Hooligan. Hugged up with the ex-wife of the enemy. Are you fucking his ex-wife? She gives you sex and you give her information? Is that how it goes? Tender dick nigga falling victim to pillow talk."

Shock watched them until they disappeared inside the house together.

"You disloyal piece of shit!" Shock spat out.

Seeing Archie with Infamous' ex-wife was all the evidence he needed. Lucky for Trot, he had gone to check Archie temperature first, or Trot might've lost his life simply as a technicality. Enraged, Shock hit the gas and sped off.

Archie was inside the house for about 30 minutes before emerging once again. Giving him another hug before he left, Loretta whispered in his ear, "Thank you."

Smiling, he responded by saying, "Any time."

Then, he walked toward his Durango looking up and down the block. Not seeing any cars, he hopped in and drove off. Every time he went to go see Loretta; he was afraid that someone might see him. He didn't even want to imagine what would happen to him if the wrong person found out about his little visits. Archie was on edge the entire way back to his home. He kept expecting someone to come out of nowhere and expose what he had been doing. Archie didn't relax until he was pulling into his driveway. Breathing a little easier, he climbed out of his truck and walked inside of his home.

"Veronica!" He called out, stepping into the living room. "I'm back."

He heard their 9-month-old son crying, but Veronica didn't respond. Archie figured she was in the backroom consoling their child. Making his way to the bedroom, he opened the door. The lights were off.

Stepping in and feeling around for the light switch, he asked, "Why is lil man cryin', baby?"

Then, finding the switch, he turned on the lights.

"Auugghh…" was all he managed to get out before Shock's fist connected with the bridge of his nose.

Archie stumbled back into the wall. Shock took two-steps forward and continued to strike Archie in the face. Archie tried to curl up, but Shock was swinging with too much force. His punches were penetrating Archie's defenses.

Veronica hollered, "Please stop!"

Shock swung one more hard left hook and knocked Archie down.

"Fuck." Archie screamed, as he placed his hands over his bleeding nose.

Shock backed away from him and pulled out his pistol.

"Shut-up. Both of you." He ordered.

Archie knew why Shock was there.

"Shock," he pleaded. "Let me explain."

Shock kicked him in the face. "I said shut-up." He told him. "Roll over and lay face down."

Archie knew that Shock was a stone-cold killer, so he obeyed. Placing a knee into Archie's back, Shock pulled out his knife.

"I don't talk to traitors." He said coldly.

Then, he raised the blade high over his head and brought it down hard into the back of Archie's neck. The sound of metal tearing through flesh and bone was sickening. Veronica started screaming again when the intruder stabbed Archie. Not wanting to shoot his .25, he jerked the knife out of Archie's neck. Blood squirted out of the wound and stained the floor. Then, Shock ran over to Veronica and buried the blade deep within her left breast. He dug in with so much force that the blade ruptured her heart. Shock was well learned in the anatomy of the human body. He knew a thousand different ways to kill.

Feeling the life leaving her body, Veronica looked one last time at her now silent baby boy. He was watching his parents get murdered right before his eyes. As she coughed up blood and breathed her last breath, she asked God to wipe this day out of her child's memory. Even in her final moments, her motherly instincts caused her to care more about her child than herself.

Shock withdrew the knife from her chest and watched as her body slumped over on the bed. She twitched a few more times and then she was eternally still.

Shock turned his attention to the child he had just orphaned. He looked at the two dead bodies and at all of the blood covering the room and covering him. For a brief moment, a fleeting memory of his own childhood tried to resurface. In his minds eye, Shock could vaguely see himself as a small child. There was blood and chaos everywhere. He could hear faint voices screaming, but he could not see any of the faces of those that were making the noise. Shock rubbed on the scar on his neck. Something about the memory made his scar tingle. Then, as quickly as the memory came, it faded back into the eternal darkness of his subconscious mind.

"You don't want to grow up and be like me." He said to the little boy, thinking about how he had just orphaned him. "This will haunt you for your entire life."

Shock walked over to the crib and peered down at the boy. With his free hand, he gripped the top of the child's head. Assuming the man was playing, lil man grabbed his wrist and giggled.

"Oh so innocent." Shock mumbled, staring into his eyes. "This world will snatch that from you."

Then, Shock allowed his blade to forever end the child's laughter. Deep down, Shock knew he had done the right thing. He had brought peace to the child like he often wished his own parents would've done for him instead of giving him away.

Chapter 6

Reluctantly, Tameka said, "Alright partner. I trust you. Let's do this."

Rose smiled. Not because Tameka had decided to go, but because he could almost taste the recognition; and to him, it tasted good. Rose put the cruiser back in drive and continued in the direction of 3rd Ave. As they approached the block that the house was on, Tameka's palms had begun to sweat. Nervously, she wiped them off on her pants. Out the corner of his eye, Rose witnessed her gesture and shook his head. He regretted the department's decision to give him what he considered to be such a scary partner. Rose figured that he would have to mold her into someone worthy to be called an officer of the law.

Trying to ease her nerves, he said, "We'll be alright, Tameka."

When Rose turned on to 3rd Ave., his own heart started to beat a little faster. Someone had used rocks to knock out all of the streetlights, so the entire block was eerily dark. There were several people walking up and down the street. Rose figured they were drug addicts. The Southside was full of them. They would wander up and down the streets all night looking for men to prostitute with and crack to smoke.

Pulling his cruiser over 4 houses down from the house they were looking for, he tried to plan his next move. Tameka watched as all of the drug addicts stopped what they were doing to watch the cop car that had just appeared on the block. From their position, they could see the house that the suspect was reportedly hiding out in.

"Do you think he's in there?" She asked.

Rose trusted his informant. This wouldn't be the first time that he had given him accurate information.

"I'm positive." Rose answered.

Not taking their eyes off of the cruiser, two of the prostitute crack addicts, Aisha and Marie, slowly walked up to the porch of the house they were watching.

Adjusting himself in his seat, Rose said, "Here we go."

Tameka looked around. "What?" She asked, confused as to what her partner was referring to.

Rose smiled and tightened his grip on the steering wheel. "You'll see." He told her. "Just wait for it."

Alerted to the presence of the police by the two addicts, the suspect inside of the house grabbed his pistol and jumped in his car. There was no way in hell he was about to go down that easy. Cranking up his car and rolling down the passenger side window, he kissed his gun and floored the gas pedal. Pulling out onto the street, he turned his car and drove in the direction of the cruiser. Speeding pass Rose and Tameka, the suspect let off two rounds into the side of the cruiser as he drove by. Tameka hollered as the sound of the shells struck the back door and the trunk.

Rose ducked down.

"Son of a bitch." He growled, as the realization of what just happened set in.

Using a trick that he learned in the academy, Rose turned the wheel hard and peeled out. Looking like a stunt driver from the movies, Rose expertly executed a U-turn from a stable starting point.

"Hold on!" He yelled, as he smashed the gas and got in hot pursuit of the suspect.

Tameka placed both of her hands on the dashboard and held on for dear life.

"Why didn't we call for backup?" She thought, as she noticed the situation escalating quickly.

Knock! Knock! Knock!

Rose sat straight up in his bed, knocking his blanket off of himself. The sound of someone knocking on his front door had awakened him from his sleep. Wiping the sweat off of his face, he glanced over at his still sleeping wife. Rose was half upset that someone was knocking on his door and half relieved. He was upset because the digital clock next to his bed read 1:15am. He was relieved because the interruption woke him from his dream. Rose knew all too well how that situation from his past was going to end, and it wasn't something that he enjoyed reliving.

Knock! Knock! Knock!

Not wanting to wake his wife, Rose quietly slid out of the bed, put his robe on, and headed towards the front door. It had been four full days since Abdul was murdered at the Economy Lodge Hotel and he still didn't have any solid leads on who was responsible. The body count was steady rising, and the media was having a field day. Plus, social media was going wild with talk of how inadequate the TCPD were at controlling the local gangbangers. To make matters even worse, the Hooligans had started to retaliate. So, instead of trying to prevent a war, his new objective was to stop a war. Rose knew that the only way to do that would be to find out what started the war, find out who his killers were, and use them to build a case against Infamous and Sticks. As long as the two of them were on the streets, Texas City was going to be dangerous. Of course, that was proving to be easier said than done.

"Who is it?" Rose asked, when he made it to the door.

"It's me, Sierra." The visitor called back.

"What is she doing at my house at one o'clock in the morning?" He thought, as he unlocked the door and opened it.

Sierra was standing there in a form fitting pair of blue jeans and a spaghetti string pink shirt that allowed Rose to see the top half of her cleavage. He could also see imprints of her nipples indicating that she was not wearing a bra. He mentally chastised himself for looking down at her breasts, but his subconscious mind had caused him to do it before his rational mind could warn him against it.

Smiling from ear to ear, she proclaimed, "I finally figured it out. It was so simple it was hard."

Rose was caught off guard by her enthusiasm. "Figured what out?" He asked, not having the slightest idea what Sierra was talking about.

Sierra reached into her back pocket and pulled out a folded-up piece of paper. "Have you ever heard of the Essenes?" She asked.

Rose folded his arms and gave her a look that said, "Now you know damn well I haven't heard of any Essenes."

Accurately interpreting his expression, she continued, "Well, don't feel bad. Most people haven't. See, the Essenes were a group of extremely religious sect of Jews who lived in highly organized groups from about 200 BCE until about 200 CE. They were an organization completely devoted to preserving what they claimed to be the true teachings of the Israelite people. Back in those days, the Romans were persecuting the Jews harshly. A series of revolts, that began with Judah Maccabees, caused the Romans to become increasingly more violent with the Jewish people in Judea. Plus, all of their religious material was being burned in massive piles in an attempt to erase all memory of the overzealous Jewish people. So, in response, a sect of Jews known as the Essenes, relocated to a series of caves that surrounded the Dead Sea, and they began hiding all of their cultural literature. They stashed copies of the Torah, the Tanakh, and several other writings that were considered sacred to the Jewish people. They also began devising ways to encrypt their writings, so that if discovered, the Romans would not know that they were looking at Israelite documents.

"Wait a minute." Rose cut her off. "The Dead Sea? As in Dead Sea Scrolls, Dead Sea?"

Sierra smirked. "Yep. One in the same. The Dead Sea Scrolls were actually hidden in those caves by the Essenes. If it were not for the Essenes, the world would not have those documents today. The Dead Sea Scrolls is not the only thing that they passed down to us, though. They also bequeathed unto us a special code. It is simple, but effective."

"A code?" Rose repeated.

"Exactly. It is known as Dyscletia."

For some reason, that word sounded oddly familiar to Rose. Sierra noticed the hint of recognition in his eyes.

Offering the explanation, she said, "It's where we get our word Dyslexia from."

Rose stopped her. "You mean that disease that causes someone trying to read to see the words backward?"

Sierra nodded her head and smiled. "Exactly." She told him. "Over the years, their codes gradually became more complex, but the very first form of their style of writing was simple. It was a quick and easy way to encrypt their sacred documents so that they would not be destroyed by the Romans."

Sierra paused for dramatic effect. Then she handed the folded-up piece of paper she was holding to Rose. Unfolding the paper, he discovered Sierra's copy of the numbers that they had found in Burby's notepad.

"All they did," she began, "was write backwards."

Rose held the paper in his hand and stared at it. Sierra's revelation was ringing in his ears. He felt so stupid. So blind. The numbers on the page began to instantly take on new meaning. The 6102 at the top of the page became 2016. The 615110 became 011516. His new understanding made the numbers easily understood. They were dates. Dates for the year 2016. That's why they all began with '61'. 615110 was 01-15-16. January 15, 2016. Sierra grinned as Rose started to see what she saw. Using this new method of reading the numbers, Rose realized that the last number written down was on the page headlined 7102, or 2017. More intriguing than that, the date it represented was May 10, 2017. Rose looked at Sierra wide eyed.

"That's the date…" he began, but Sierra cut him off.

"That's when Burby was murdered." She said, finishing his sentence.

Rose looked back down at the paper. This just might be the break in the case that he needed. If only he could figure out what the dates represented.

"How do you know about all of that stuff you just told me?" He asked, clearly amazed.

"I told you." She answered. "My father is a pastor. I know a lot about Jewish history. Plus, I read a lot. One of my favorite authors, Matthew Daniels, has an online Facebook group called TheRealBookWorm. He makes a lot of videos about books that he is reading. I was just at home watching his videos and I came across one about the Essenes."

Rose was so excited that he didn't know what to do, so he just leaned forward and gave Sierra a hug. The show of affection caught her off guard. Not sure how she should respond, she simply hugged him back. The mood turned from joy to apprehensive awkwardness when the two of them heard someone clearing their throat behind them. Releasing Sierra and turning around, Rose made eye contact with his wife. She was standing in the hallway, arms folded across her chest, and her she was tapping her foot against the floor.

"Ummm." Rebecca, Rose' wife said. "What the hell is all of this?"

Rose knew that Rebecca was mad. It was 1:00am and he was standing in the doorway hugging another woman.

"Baby," he said, trying to pretend like it wasn't a big deal, "she just came over to give me some new information about the case I've been working on."

Rebecca rolled her eyes. "At one o'clock in the morning?!?" She said, in disbelief. "Look, Bitch! For the past few days you've been spending an awful lot of time with my husband, and I don't like it."

"Bitch?!" Sierra repeated.

"Whoa! Whoa! Whoa!" Rose said, throwing his hands up trying to calm the women down. "It ain't even like that, baby. This is really about the case."

Rebecca walked up to Rose. "Oh naw. I don't doubt that it's about the case." She began. "But I'm a woman. So, I know how a woman is."

Then turning her attention to Sierra, she said, "I'm not going to do anything to jeopardize my husband's job, but I just want you to know that I can see right through all of that innocent co-worker role you trying to play."

Rebecca pointed a finger at Sierra. "I don't play behind mine. Trust that."

Then, she turned around to walk off.

Rose knew that Rebecca had actually let Sierra off easy, so he didn't say anything. Rebecca was a fighter. She grew up fighting her entire life. She had no problem going there. Sierra just stood there silently and watched as Rebecca walked back inside of their room and slammed the door.

"I'm sorry." Rose apologized to Sierra.

She shook her head. "No. Don't apologize." She said. "Really, I'm in the wrong. Not your wife. I knew that this was an unprofessional hour... I was just so excited when I realized what those numbers meant, that I wanted to tell you right away."

"But still," Rose responded, "Rebecca shouldn't have called you out of your name like that."

Rose was doing his best to repair some of the damage that his wife had done. In his mind, he felt that he was partly responsible for how his wife reacted. He had to admit to himself that he was very attracted to Sierra. Maybe that was the vibe that Rebecca had picked up on.

Not wanting to cause any further problems, Sierra decided to leave. "Well," she said, backing away from the door. "I'd better go. Besides, you need some time to go make up with your wife."

Rose just stood there silently as Sierra made her way to her car.

"Oh yeah," she said, turning around right before she made it to her vehicle. "I know what that 9-digit number stands for inside of that address book."

Rose couldn't believe it. This girl had to be some type of genius.

"I'll explain how I figured it out later." She assured him. "The number in the book is 1864-77-723. It stands for 327 77th St. That's the address to Amir's Safe Deposit. The last four numbers, 4681, is no doubt the number to a safe deposit box. I'm willing to bet that that particular box belonged to Burby."

Rose instantly began to speculate. If Sierra was right, the contents of that safe deposit box just might be the key he needed to bust the case wide open. His police instincts started to override his good judgement. He knew that his wife wouldn't be pleased with him leaving at one o'clock in the morning with Sierra, but he wanted badly to know what was in that box.

Sierra climbed inside of her car and started it up. Just as she was about to pull off, Rose was opening her passenger side door.

"Is Amir's open 24 hours?" He asked.

"I think so." Sierra answered.

"We need to go back to the Chief's house in Alvin, then." He said. "Wait right here."

Sierra watched as Rose ran back into his house. Smiling to herself, she said, "I knew you wouldn't be able to resist."

Ten minutes later, Rose came back out of his house wearing a brown suit. Climbing into her green Neon, he said, "With any luck, the key to the deposit box will still be inside of the Chief's house somewhere."

Sierra put the car into drive and headed in the direction of Alvin. Speeding slightly, they made it to the Chief's house in 20 minutes.

"Good." Rose stated, when he saw the yellow police tape around the Chief's house.

The police tape meant that the crime scene was still virtually untouched since the morning of the murder. That drastically improved their chances of finding the key that went to the safe deposit box.

"What now?" Sierra asked, as she killed the engine.

"Now," Rose answered, surveying the block, "we have to tip toe on that gray line that separates legal and illegal. If you want to wait out here, that's ok."

Sierra looked hurt. "What?" She questioned. "We in this thing together. If you're going in, I'm going in." She assured him.

Rose appreciated the loyalty. Besides, he knew that two people searching for one key in a dark house was better than one person.

"Fine." He said, knowing that time was of the essence. "Just remember this. Safe deposit box keys are long, sliver, and the top part of them is a large circle with a number engraved into it. I wouldn't be surprised if the number is the exact same as the number of the actual box."

Sierra nodded her head to let him know that she understood.

"Ok." He said. "Let's go. In and out."

The pair exited the Neon and approached the house crouched down. They knew that all of the neighbors were probably sound asleep, but still, why take chances. Crawling underneath the police tape that stretched from one of the trees in the front yard all the way to the mailbox and around to the back of the house, Sierra followed Rose up to the front door. Rose knew that what he was doing went against everything his badge stood for, but he excused his actions by telling himself that he was trying to stop a gang war.

To his surprise, the door was unlocked. When they entered the home, it was a lot darker than either of them had expected. Still, they couldn't risk turning on the lights. Just when Rose was about to venture out into the darkness, he felt Sierra grab his hand and place something in it. Then she shut the door behind them. Bringing the object up to his face, he noticed that it was a pen.

"What is this?" He whispered.

Instead of getting an answer, he heard a 'click', and a thin beam of light cut through the darkness and cast a soft glow on the couch over on the far wall.

"It's a pen light." Sierra whispered, as she made her way around him and used the small light to guide her path.

Rose pressed the button on the side of the pen that he held, and a light cut on. It wasn't much, but it was definitely better than nothing.

As Rose watched Sierra's light disappear around a corner, he said to himself, "That girl has thought of everything."

Following her lead, Rose made his way to the back and began his search in the master bedroom. He had no idea where the key might be, so he just decided to look everywhere. Using the light to find the dresser, Rose opened each drawer and sifted through the contents. After only 4 drawers he became discouraged.

"Think." He urged himself. "If I were Burby, where would I hide a safe deposit box key?"

Rose turned in circles trying to light up, one at a time, each section of the room. He paused when he made it back to the dresser. Sitting on top of it, in plain sight, was a hand carved jewelry box. Rose thought for a moment. Burby lived alone with his son. What would he need with a jewelry box? Feeling energized, he lifted open the top. Shining the light inside, he found that the jewelry box was empty.

"So much for that." He whispered.

Then, having an idea, he reached inside of it and rubbed his fingers against the velvet cloth. Gripping the cushion that was meant for placing the jewelry on, he gave it a tug. To his surprise, the cushion came out with ease. Peering back inside of the jewelry box, he grinned. Right there, hidden underneath the cushion of the box was a long, silver key. Engraved in the head of it were the numbers 4681.

"Jackpot." He said, placing the key inside of his pocket.

Finding what they had come for, Rose knew that it was time to go.

"Sierra." He whispered, as he tip-toed out of the room.

Flashing his light left and right down the hallway, he called to her again.

"Sierra. I have the key."

Rose started making his way back towards the living room. That's when he noticed Sierra's light moving around up front. Speeding up a bit, Rose hurried into the living room. Sierra heard a loud 'thud', and then Rose groaned in pain. Shining her light in the direction of the noise, she saw Rose holding his knee and grimacing.

"What happened?" She asked.

Rose pointed his light at the object that he had clumsily ran into. "I bumped my knee against Burby's computer desk." He reported.

"Are you alright?" She asked, genuinely concerned.

Rose knee was throbbing, but he did his best to shake the pain off. "Never mind that." He told her, limping towards the door. "I found the key. Let's get out of here."

"That was quick." Sierra said, following Rose to the front door.

Rose made it to the door and peaked his head out. Looking around to make sure that no one was watching, he opened the door completely and sprinted towards the

Neon. Sierra was right on his heels. After they had made it back to the car, they climbed in and Sierra wasted no time driving away. Rose looked and saw that Sierra forgot to close the front door, but he figured the police would suspect that juveniles had entered the home. At that particular moment, he didn't even care if the Alvin police could figure out that it was him that went into the residence. All he really cared about was finding out what was inside of that deposit box. Digging around in his pocket, he withdrew the silver key and held it up in front of him.

Sierra momentarily took her eyes off the road to look at it. "Is that it?" She asked.

Rose returned the key to his pocket. "Yep." He answered. "Now let's go find out what's inside of that box."

Sierra had just as much anticipation built up inside of her as Rose did. She could remember watching police movies on TV when she was small. The excitement of following clues and cracking codes had made the life of a police officer seem so grand. Actually, it was the non-stop thrill rides of the big screen that made her want to be a police officer when she grew up. She often fantasized about high speed chases, shoot-outs, and solving previously unsolved crimes. She couldn't believe that within her first year on the force, she was actually a part of a real live investigation. She knew that it would be awhile before she was able to make detective, so she figured it would be a minute before she had the chance to be involved in the things she remembered from TV.

Assisting Rose in his most recent case was a dream come true. Rose was a legend on the force. His exploits were widely known. Some of the tales may not have even been true, but the aura surrounding him made him see larger than life. Cutting her eyes at Rose, she thought about how sexy he was as well. Physically, he was just an average man, but his occupation made him very attractive. She had been dropping subtle hints since she met him, but he never seemed to pick up on them. His wife sure did though. Sierra couldn't help but to wonder if Rose had noticed and just chose not to respond to it. She couldn't imagine why, though. It wasn't like she was trying to break up his happy home or anything like that. All she wanted to do was borrow him a few times and then give him back.

Sierra was only 22 and she was looking to have a good time. She didn't need a husband. The entire way from Alvin to Texas City, Sierra entertained herself with thoughts of her and Rose partaking in various sex acts with absolutely no strings attached.

Rose looked at Sierra and saw a smile on her face. "What are you smiling about?" He asked her casually.

Sierra raised one eyebrow and gazed at him seductively. "Oh, you'll know soon enough." She assured him.

Rose said nothing else. He thought that he detected a hint of desire in her voice, but he figured he must have been projecting his own feelings onto her. Rose had been picturing himself with Sierra ever since she showed up on his doorstep with the top half of her breast exposed. His mind told him that his fantasies were wrong because he was a married man. His penis, however, was telling him that his fantasies were not enough. If it could talk, it would probably say, "What Rebecca doesn't know won't hurt her".

Rose looked at Sierra and then quickly looked away. Sierra thought, "I'll get him. It's just a matter of time."

For the rest of the ride they were both silent. Rose was relieved when they pulled into the parking lot of Amir's Safe Deposit. The tension was so thick inside of the car that he could almost feel it. Stepping out of the car. Rose looked at the shop. Amir's was one shop amongst 3 others that all used the same building and shared the same parking lot.

From left to right, there was a corner store, a donut shop, a check cashing place, and finally at the end, Amir's Safe Deposit. The owner, an Iranian man named Amir, knew that people might need to get to the contents of their boxes at all hours of the night, so he stayed open 24 hours a day, seven days a week.

The building was a simple structure from the outside. No windows and a solid wood door. Along the top of the store, painted in orange box letters was the name of the store. There was a small sign posted on the door that read, "Open 24 Hours".

Approaching the door, Sierra asked, "Have you ever been inside of there?"

Rose looked at the large wood door. "Nope." He replied. "Have you?"

Sierra shook her head.

"Well," Rose said, turning the knob and pushing the door open, "we both have now."

Immediately inside of the front door, there was a hallway that extended from left to right about 10 feet in each direction. There was a wall directly in front of them that was painted a solid beige color, and the carpet covering the floor was a matching beige. Along the top of the wall, spaced about 4 feet apart from each other, were 3 hanging lamps that provided a dim but sufficient amount of light.

Rose and Sierra stepped inside the building and looked around. To their left, at the end of the hallway, was a small wooden table with two wooden chairs seated next to it. The pile of magazines resting on top of the table let Rose know that the area most likely served as a waiting area. Looking to the right, Rose noticed a small rectangle window built into the beige wall.

Leading the way to the window, Rose commented, "I guess that's where we're supposed to go."

Without responding, Sierra followed Rose over to the window. Reaching it, Rose noticed that the window wasn't made out of regular glass. Tapping on it lightly with his finger, his suspicions were confirmed. The glass was bulletproof. It reminded Rose of the Ace Check Cashing place that stood next door. The only access one had to the individual behind the glass was a 5x8 inch hole cut into the bottom of it. There was no one inside of the little room behind the glass. The only thing that Rose could see was another door.

Sierra peered over his shoulder. "Where do you suppose everyone is at?"

Rose leaned in close to the glass and strained to see what all was behind it. "I'm not sure." He admitted. "Helllooo!" He called out, placing his mouth up to the 5x8 inch hole. "Hello. Is anybody in there?"

Rose waited on a response. Not getting one, he called out into the hole again.

"Hellooo."

This time, a rustling noise could be heard approaching from behind the door. Rose and Sierra exchanged glances. Opening the door and entering the little room, Amir stepped up to the glass smiling. Amir was an extremely tall Iranian with a thick mustache and beard. On top of his head he wore a red and white turban. Sierra couldn't help but to think that Amir resembled Osama Bin Laden. Since 9/11, all people from the middle east looked like Osama Bin Laden. She mentally checked herself for being so stereotypical. If anyone could understand the pain of being stereotyped, Sierra could.

For one, she was African American. For two, she was a female police officer. Lastly, she was a pastor's daughter. For that reason alone, everyone assumed that she was an extreme freak.

Sierra thought it over. "Well," she reasoned within herself, "maybe that last one is true."

"Hello. Hello." Amir greeted them. "My humblest apologizes for keeping you waiting."

His accent was extremely thick, but his English was good. "Do you have your key?" Amir asked.

Rose was silently praying that Amir wouldn't ask for any form of identification. He knew, however, that he probably would. If that happened, he didn't know what he would do.

Opting to not talk and just pretend like he was supposed to be there, Rose withdrew the key from his pocket and passed it through the hole to Amir. Amir accepted the key and held it up to his face to examine it. Rose and Sierra were both holding their breath.

Obviously satisfied, Amir simply handed the key back to Rose and said, "Take all of the time that you need."

Then, with no further words, he turned around and exited the room the exact same way that he had entered it.

Sierra looked around. "O....k." she said. "Now what?"

Rose scratched his head. He had no idea. Just when he was about to call to Amir again, he was caught off guard by the sound of gears cranking up. Snapping his head to the left, he was shocked to see a section of the wall slowly rising. Apparently, the door to the back was simply disguised as a part of the wall. Making his way over to the opening, he was impressed. No one would be breaking into Amir's and stealing anything.

The section of wall that had risen was every bit of two feet thick and from the sound of it, solid iron. Rose wondered what could be of so much value that Burby would go through such extreme lengths to keep it protected. Looking over Rose's shoulder, Sierra realized that this new hallway was darker than the first one. Stranger still, it was completely empty except for a computer screen and a keypad built into the left-hand wall about 10 feet in.

Rose walked up to the computer screen. There was a single sentence written across it.

'What is your box number?'

Rose looked at Sierra.

"4681." She recited.

"I know that." Rose stated. "But do you think this is a little too easy?"

Sierra rolled her eyes. "Don't tell me." She said. "You thrive off of a challenge."

Sierra typed in the 4-digit box number and pressed 'enter'. In a second, another sentence appeared. Reading it, Sierra folded her arms and glared at Rose.

"Looks like you got your wish."

Rose read the sentence and rubbed the back of his neck. He didn't know what they should do next. There, on the screen, were the words, 'Enter your password.' Along with that was a box in which they were expected to type in a 5-character password.

"Damn." Rose muttered, as he realized why Amir didn't bother to ask for any identification. He knew that you needed a password to access the actual safe deposit box.

"Don't damn, now." Sierra mocked him. "This is exactly what you were looking for. A challenge."

Rose cut his eyes at her. Sierra backed up and threw her hands up as if to submit.

"Heeey." She said. "Don't look at me. I figured out the code to the numbers, so now it's your turn, Detective." She waved a hand at the screen. "Go ahead. Impress me."

Rose turned back to the computer screen. There was no way he was going to be outdone by a rookie. He knew that if he applied himself to the task at hand, he would be able to guess at Burby's code. Rose thought for a minute.

"Maybe his sons name." He wondered.

"No." He told himself. "Robert has six letters in it."

Sierra watched as Rose dug around in his pocket for the piece of paper with her copy of the numerical codes on it. She knew that Rose could figure it out. Especially since she issued a challenge to his skills as a detective. Rose stared down at the paper in his hands. There had to be something that they were missing. Maybe the password was a number. Rose scanned the page. He scanned it a second time. No 5-digit numbers anywhere.

Rose studied the page for 5 full minutes. When nothing jumped out at him, he became frustrated. Maybe Sierra didn't copy everything down exactly how it was in the address book and the notepad. Returning the paper to his pocket, he pulled out the notepad and the address book.

"What if the password were under a different name?" He wondered.

Acting on a hunch, he flipped through the address book looking for any 5 letter words of 5-digit numbers. He didn't have to look far into the book before his heart stopped.

"Could it really be that simple?" He mumbled.

Sierra heard Rose murmur to himself and figure he was on to something. Following his gaze to the page in the address book, big as day, was the name 'Abdul'. Not only that, it was the name used to signify the address and number to the safe deposit box. Plus, the name had 4 stars next to it, making it stand out amongst all of the other entries.

"Do you think…" Sierra let her question trail off.

"Well," Rose answered, knowing what she was thinking, "there's only one way to find out."

Rose knew that this was probably the password, but he was still a bit reserved. What if he was wrong? Then again, what if he was right? Throwing caution to the wind, Rose slowly typed in 'A-B-D-U-L'. Hanging his index finger over the enter key, he thought it over one last time. Nothing else made any sense. Just as Rose was about to press down, something Sierra had told him earlier that night was ringing in his ears.

She had said, "All they did was write backwards."

Sierra wondered why Rose had hesitated. "What's wrong?" She asked.

"That's not the password." Rose told her.

She looked shocked. "How do you know that?" She questioned.

Rose didn't respond. He simply deleted the name Abdul, and then typed in 'L-U-D-B-A'. Then, with no hesitation, he pressed the enter key. They both watched nervously as the screen momentarily went blank. When it blinked back to life, it read, 'When you are finished, place box back in slot and press the enter key.'

They couldn't help but to smile when they heard more gears cranking up and saw a small door about a foot long and a foot high open in the wall behind them. It seemed like everything within Amir's was hidden behind false walls. Rose and Sierra watched with anticipation as they waited to see what was going to emerge from the newly opened door. It wasn't long before they saw a small metal box appear.

Rose reached inside the opening and retrieved the box. Sierra wondered what could be inside of it. Holding the box precariously in one hand, Rose fished the key out of his pocket and handed it to Sierra. She took it like she was accepting a rare diamond.

"Go ahead." Rose urged her, holding the box in front of him. "Open it up."

Sierra obeyed.

The lock was on top of the box, so she inserted the key into the keyhole and turned it to the right. They heard a low 'click' sound and the top popped open slightly. Knowing that this box could hold the key they needed to solve the case, Rose held his breath. When Sierra lifted the top all the way up, they both peered in.

Inside, there was a stack of papers and a C.D. Sierra picked up the C.D. and noticed that it was a computer disk C.D. Returning it to the box, Sierra pulled out the stacks of papers. They were bank statements. According to the statements, Police Chief Robert Burby had close to $500,000 stashed away in an offshore bank account. Examining the bank statements, Rose and Sierra noticed that Burby was making large deposits into the bank account monthly. No less than $5,000 and some as high as $25,000.

"What the hell is that?" Rose asked out loud.

"Looks like the Chief didn't need his job as police chief." Sierra commented.

Then, noticing something, she said, "Wait a minute."

Sierra reached into Rose's pocket and pulled out the notebook. Comparing the dates in the notebook to the dates of deposits on the bank statements, the correlation between the two was obvious. Every day after one of the dates in the notebook, there was a deposit. Rose and Sierra looked at each other.

Then, at the same time, they both said, "The Chief was on somebody's payroll!"

Chapter Seven

Shock opened the front door to his apartment slightly and peered out. It was still early in the morning and the sun had not yet risen. On average, his apartment complex was always buzzing with activity, but this morning seemed oddly different. The entire area was pretty much void of movement. He knew that the abnormal quietness would be infinitely beneficial to his mission.

Shock then ducked back into his apartment. Like a lion on the prowl in the jungle, he stood perfectly still, and waited. Using a trick, he had learned from studying Hinduism, he closed both of his eyes and slowly regulated his breathing. Mentally increasing the decibel reception of his ears, Shock tuned in to the world outside of his door. Relaxing himself to a point of meditation, he listened as the silence itself seemed to grow louder and louder.

Shock stood perfectly still. There was no way of knowing how long it would take, so he was prepared to wait for hours.

'Creek'.

Shock's eyes moved behind his eyelids.

'Creek'.

The wooden walkway that lined the upstairs units of the Rancho Santa-Maria had given away his prey.

'Creek'.

"Yes." He thought. "Those are the footsteps of the unknowing."

The scent of perfume went before the prey and found the waiting nostrils of the hunter. Slowly, as if the prey were capable of hearing like he was, Shock withdrew his 6-inch blade. Licking his lips, Shock waited for the prey to get closer. The woman outside of Shock's apartment lived 5 doors down from him. The plastic bag lying on the ground in front of his door had drawn her attention. From a distance, it appeared to be drugs.

She smoked crack cocaine but was still decent looking. She had dark skin and short black hair. Her breasts were about a size 34DD and her thighs were extremely thick. The biker shorts she was wearing hugged her hips beautifully. She stopped when she noticed that Shock's door was cracked.

She waited.

From where she was now standing, she could see a few chunks of white dope inside the plastic bag. Not wanting to be accused of stealing, she debated on whether she should try to take it or not. Looking around, she made a mental note of her surroundings. No one was watching. She rubbed her mouth. Giving in to her addiction, she decided to go for it. She hurried to Shock's door and knelt down.

As soon as she had wrapped her hand around the bag of dope, Shock swung his door open, placed one hand across her mouth, used his other hand to put his knife to her throat, and then he drug her into his lair.

"If you scream, I'll kill you." He warned her in his raspy voice.

Completely paranoid, she decided to just obey him. Once he had her entire body inside, Shock kicked the door closed with his foot. Darkness enveloped them both. Confident now that they were inside, Shock took his hand off of her mouth.

"What... what... what do you want from me?" Regina asked.

Shock grabbed her by her t-shirt and led her into his bedroom. Shoving her down on the floor next to his mattress, he replied, "I want relief."

Regina didn't know what he meant, but she could imagine.

"If you don't want to die," Shock told her, "do exactly what I tell you, when I tell you."

He pointed his knife at her.

"Get undressed."

The fear had Regina shaking like a leaf. She had never been raped before. Thinking that death was far worse than non-consensual sex, Regina nervously took off her shirt and bra. Shock watched as her breasts jiggled. They seemed to be happy to be free from the confines of her clothing. Shock noticed that she had large dark colored nipples also. The sight of them was the beginning of his arousal.

Tossing her bra to the side, Regina peeled off her biker shorts. They didn't come off easily. Her ass and thighs were practically stretching them to the limit. When she was finally able to get them off, Shock saw that Regina wasn't wearing any panties. That revelation caused him to stiffen up even more.

Shock rubbed his manhood through his pants as he gazed at her freshly shaved vagina. He quickly pulled his shirt over his head and came out of his pants. His now rock-hard member was pointed straight out in front of him. Tapping on his penis with the blade of his knife, he instructed Regina, "Now, come and suck it."

Regina knew that her best chance of survival was to comply and leave her attacker fully satisfied. Swallowing the lump in her throat, she tried to fool herself into thinking this was something that she wanted. She got on all fours and crawled like a cat up to Shock's legs, making sure to put a dip in her back so that her ass would poke out. Slowly raising herself up, she felt Shock's dick come into contact with the back of her head.

Lifting up until it rolled off of her head and slid down the side of her face, Regina was now kneeling in front of him. Without using her hands, she skillfully took him into her mouth.

"Ahhh." Shock moaned, as the suction shot sensations through his entire body.

With one hand, Regina grabbed the shaft of his dick and combined oral sex with masturbation in a way so unique that Shock tossed his blade onto the bed and grabbed two fistfuls of her short hair. Regina showcased her coordination by using her free hand to gently massage Shock's testicles.

"Umm-huh." She moaned, as the taste of his dick started to grow on her.

When she realized that he had thrown away the knife, she felt more confident in the fact that she would live. Pausing to breathe, she cooed, "Oouuww. This dick so big, I can't even fit it all in my mouth."

Then she opened up wide and stuffed his entire tool down her throat without touching the shaft of it with her lips. By the time her nose became buried in his pubic hairs, the tip of his dick was pressing up against the back of her throat. Shock watched with joy as her eyes started to water. Regina closed her mouth around his member and began bobbing again. Only this time, she buried her nose in his pubic hair with each forward motion. Shock heard her gagging, but she wasn't missing a beat. Tears slowly rolled down her cheeks, but she kept moaning with pleasure.

"Ummm. Ummm. Ummm." Was all Shock heard.

The constant friction against the tip of his penis was proving to be too much. Not wanting to cum yet, Shock grabbed Regina by her hair and yanked his dick out of her mouth. She licked her lips aggressively and pulled against his grip, trying desperately to continue sucking him.

Shock loved her enthusiasm, but he wanted to penetrate her. Bending her over and forcing her into a doggy style position, Shock guided his dick into her already wet hole and buried himself deep within her walls. The warmth caused him to lean over on top of her and hug her from behind. As Shock began stroking, he was playing with her breast.

"Yeah, baby." Regina moaned. "Stretch them pussy walls."

As Shock went in and out of her over and over, he felt her body quiver. Regina gritted her teeth and sucked in air through them. Her dark chocolate frame convulsed and rocked. Shock grabbed her around her waist and continued to pound. He could hear her mumbling under her breath, but he couldn't make out the words. Suddenly, as his testicles slapped up against her pearl tongue, Regina threw her head back and moaned loudly.

"Ooohhh!" She yelled. "Don't stop! Don't stop! Don't stop!"

Her words encouraged him. Shock began to stroke faster and harder.

"Don't stop! Don't stop!" Regina continued to plead.

Then, her entire body tensed up.

"Oh… my… fucking… GOD!" She screamed. "Yeeesss!!!"

Shock felt the inside of her pussy become more slippery. Looking down to watch himself fuck her, he noticed that the entire length of his penis was covered in white cum.

Regina had orgasmed.

The snow-white pleasure juice had come out of her in so much excess that Shock could feel it running down his nuts and dripping down his inner thighs.

"Yeah girl." He told her. "You glad I took this pussy, ain't you?"

Shock slapped her on her right butt cheek. "Yo' body done told on you."

Regina's ejaculation had increased the heat produced by her hole. Shock once again felt himself about to blow. This time, there would be no holding back. Shock reached down and gripped Regina by her hair. Pulling her head back so far that Regina thought her head was going to snap, Shock pumped his last few pumps. Burying his member as deep inside of her as his 8 inches would allow, he grunted as his tool unloaded.

Shock made sure that every drop of his cum came to rest within her. Once he pulled out of her, Regina collapsed on the floor exhausted. Shock had given her a better orgasm then her boyfriend. Shock stood up and looked down at her.

"I'm finished with you." He whispered.

Regina payed no attention as Shock reached over onto the bed and quietly picked his knife back up. She squirmed a little and licked her lips. She was still experiencing aftershocks.

Picking up his pants, Shock said, "I have something for you."

Regina rolled over and smiled. Her smile soon faded when she laid her eyes on the knife. "But... but..." she stammered out. "Didn't I satisfy you, baby?"

Shock looked at her nude body. "Oh yeah." He told her. "You were better than what I expected."

Regina watched as Shock reached into his pants pocket and pulled out a 100-dollar bill.

He tossed her the money. "Keep the change."

Regina smiled and climbed to her feet.

"You a freak." Regina began putting her clothes back on. "I ain't never had one of my customers want to role play with me before. I like it though. I wish my boyfriend would do that sometime."

Shock just watched her get dressed. He had nothing more to say to her. Walking her to the door, still completely naked, Shock showed her the way out.

"Thank you for the extras baby." Regina walked out of the room and headed back to her own apartment.

She was so excited about the $50 extra she received, that the green Dodge Neon she saw passing by didn't even warrant a second look.

....

Sierra glanced at Rose. "How do you figure that?" She asked, as they made their way back to her apartment so they could use her personal computer to see what Chief Burby had saved on that C.D.

"Think about it." Rose began, happy to have the opportunity to explain something to her for a change. "We know from the bank statements we just found, that Burby was getting paid off by either the Hooligans or the Villains. At first glance it would appear that he was working for the Villains. Why? Well, back in 2015 he allowed an armed man to walk into the police station, murder the man suspected of killing Infamous' son, and then walk back out. That alone is reason enough to suspect an alliance to the Villains. Plus," Rose continued, "we know for a fact that Burby's killer was a Villain."

Sierra cut him off. "Wait a minute. How do we know that?"

"If you remember," Rose answered, "the very first murder committed was a Villain hit on the second in command of the Hooligans. It was carried out in a very unique way. One bullet into each shoulder and the kill shot placed into the victim's forehead. That's the exact same way the two young men in The Chelseas were killed."

Realizing where Rose was going, Sierra added, "And Burby was killed the same way, too. Well... Burby was shot in the legs also, but he definitely was shot in the shoulders and in the head."

"Right." Rose agreed. "So, that particular style of killing is unique to the Southlane Villain hitman, while the assassin for the Dramaside Hooligans appears to take more of a 'by any means necessary' kind of approach."

Sierra understood the logic, but she was still confused about something. "I thought the Hooligans wore blue and the Villains wore red."

Nodding his head, Rose told her, "They do."

Sierra scratched her head. "So why did we see Burby's killer wearing all blue if he was a Villain?"

Rose had been waiting for that question to come up. He smiled. "We know from the notebook we found that Burby was expecting another payoff the day he was murdered. So, the only logical explanation for his killer posing as a Hooligan, was..."

Rose left the statement unfinished. He wanted Sierra to figure it out. She didn't have to ponder long before it dawned on her.

"Burby must've been expecting his payoff to be delivered by a Hooligan." She said.

Rose just grinned. She was good at detective work.

••

"So," she added, "Burby was working for both Infamous and Sticks, Infamous found out, felt betrayed, and had him killed?"

"That's a totally plausible theory." Rose told her, "but let's not jump the gun. We'll just take it one step at a time. As for now, we only know that Burby was being paid off by the Dramaside Hooligans, and the Southlane Villains had him killed."

Rose lifted the C.D. from off of his lap. "Hopefully, this will give us a little more insight into what actually happened."

∙∙

"I know one thing." Sierra said. "We won't have to wait much longer to find out."

Rose looked at her. "Why is that?"

"Because we're here." She answered, pulling up to an all white house with old Christmas lights hanging up.

"Ummm." Rose said, wondering about the lights.

Sierra giggled. "No excuse." She admitted. "Just laziness."

Rose could do nothing but respect the honesty. Saying nothing more, they exited the vehicle and Sierra led the way inside of her home. Walking inside and turning on the living room light, she opened her arms wide.

"Welcome to my humble abode."

Rose quickly took in the décor. Sierra had two black leather couches pushed against the wall to his right and to his left. There was a small glass table with black metal legs in the center of the room. On it was a book titled, 'The Secret Codes of the Essenes'.

Following Rose's gaze to the book, she said, "Some daughters get money as a birthday present, but I get religious based literature."

Thinking about how important the information in that book was to his case, he said, "Remind me to thank your father if I ever meet him."

Next to the book was a Bible opened to the book of Proverbs. Rose had no idea how he went straight to this particular verse on the page, but Proverbs 5:18, 19 seemed to jump out at him.

It read, *'Let thy fountain be blessed: and rejoice with the wife of thy youth. Let her be as the loving hind and pleasant roe; let her breasts satisfy thee at all times; and be thou ravished always with her love.'*

The passage made him think about Rebecca. He would have to do something to make things back right with her. She was upset when he left with Sierra and he didn't blame her. Rebecca knew how he got when he was dealing with a tough case though. He couldn't focus on anything else until it was solved.

Sierra was already seated at her computer desk starting up her HP.

"Rose." She called. "Bring me the C.D."

Shaking the thought of his wife off, he walked over to Sierra and handed her the C.D. She took it without looking up. When the menu screen popped up, she fed the disk into the hard drive. The computer whirred as the C.D. began to spin and the mini lasers started to read the information on it. It wasn't long before two new icons 'bleeped' onto the screen. Rose placed one hand on the desk and one hand on the back of Sierra's chair so he could lean in for a closer look. The icons resembled those black and white boards that people used on a movie set to begin a new scene.

"What is that?" He asked.

Sierra clicked on one of the icons. "It means that Burby has video clips of something saved onto this disk."

Rose watched as Sierra maneuvered through a few more screens before an actual image came up. A small box appeared on the screen. Along the top of it was several buttons. There was a play, stop, fast forward, rewind, and pause.

"That's the police station." Rose declared, recognizing the image. "What is Burby doing with video of the inside of the police station?" He wondered out loud.

Sierra clicked the play button. They watched as Burby sat at the front desk inside of the station. The clip was footage from one of the security cameras inside of headquarters. The date that flashed across the bottom left-hand corner of the screen revealed to Rose what they were about to see. The date read '4-25-2015'.

"That's the same day Wilkinson was murdered while in police custody." Rose informed her.

Sierra's eyes got wide as she realized what she was about to witness. As Burby sat at the front desk, a man in a trench coat walked in. He walked right passed the desk towards the back without even acknowledging Burby. Judging by the time at the bottom right hand corner of the screen, he was only in the back for 30 seconds.

"A professional." Rose thought. "A professional with enough guts to kill inside the police station."

Emerging from the back, the man walked with a slow stride back towards the front door.

"Wait a second." Rose said, grabbing the mouse.

For a brief instant, the killers face was visible to the camera. Rose pressed rewind and then paused it on the frame he was looking for. Staring hard, Rose tried to get a good look at the killer. The longer he looked, the more he felt as if he recognized the individual. Sierra watched as Rose slowly began to zone out while looking at the screen.

"No... way." Rose muttered.

Being transported to another place, Rose backed away from the screen. The slight fear on his face worried Sierra. She couldn't recall a time that she had ever seen fear on Rose face.

"Rose." She called. "Rose. Are you alright?"

She was calling his name, but Rose couldn't hear her. He was in another place. Sierra watched him quizzically as Rose slowly removed his jacket, but kept his eyes glued to the screen. Dropping his jacket on the floor, Rose removed his shoulder holster and began unbuttoning his shirt. Sierra watched as he pulled his shirt down over his left shoulder. Surprisingly, Rose had a gunshot wound on his shoulder. He began to rub it gently, staring off into space. Once again, against his own freewill and better judgement, his mind began wondering back to that night he'd rather forget. Normally, he would try to fight the memory off, but this time was different. This time, he allowed the memory to come.

"Hold on!" Rose yelled, as he smashed the gas and got in hot pursuit of the suspect.

Tameka placed both of her hands on the dashboard and held on for dear life. "Why didn't we call for backup?" She thought.

Rose was not about to lose this guy. He had already killed two people a few days before, and he had just shot at him a few minutes ago. After only two blocks into the chase, Tameka grasped at the C.B. radio inside of the cruiser.

"What are you doing?" Rose shouted.

"I'm calling for backup!" Tameka shouted back. "What do you think I'm doing?"

Rose took one hand off the wheel long enough to snatch the radio out of Tameka's hands. "Oh no you're not!" He yelled. "This is my collar!"

Tameka couldn't believe how bullheaded Rose was acting. They were in a high-speed chase with a suspected murderer, shots had already been fired, and he still didn't see the need for assistance. This was definitely not the man she had fallen in love with back in high school. That Derrick Rose would never endanger her and their unborn child, unnecessarily. This new Derrick Rose would do just about anything for a detective job. She didn't like this new Rose.

The suspect hung up his cellphone and swerved into the parking lot of the Ashton Park Apartments. Rose swerved in right behind him. Without pulling into a parking space, the suspect simply turned his car sideways in the middle of the lot and made his passenger side door face Rose and Tameka.

"We got him now." Rose declared triumphantly.

The suspect opened his door and climbed out. Squatting down with his back against his car, he gripped his pistol tight and prepared to shoot. Rose and Tameka parked their cruiser facing the suspect. Using their doors as shields, they jumped out, guns drawn.

"Throw out your weapon and come out with your hands up!" Rose commanded.

The suspect laughed. "Yeah right." He thought. He was waiting on his signal.

"Did you hear me?" Rose screamed. "I said throw out your weapon and come o......"

His sentence was cut short by the sound of gun fire. Someone was shooting at them from behind. Suddenly afraid, Rose turned around to return fire. He was shocked to see a dark-skinned black girl who couldn't be no more than 16 years old, holding a chrome revolver and shooting at him. When the suspect heard the gun shots begin, he sprinted around his car and began releasing shells in the direction of Rose and Tameka. Before Rose could get off a shot in the direction of the girl, a bullet from the suspects gun pierced the door of his cruiser and buried itself in his back.

"Auugghh!" He cried out in pain as the heat from the bullet sent shockwaves through his body.

Rose dropped his gun and fell over. Looking in the direction of Tameka, he saw her slumped over in the seat. A hole in the side of her head told him that she had been hit. Rose wondered how he could be so stupid as to allow himself and his high school sweetheart to get ambushed. The bullets coming from both directions made him sure that he was about to die. He knew that he had only one chance. He grabbed his gun and rolled over onto his back. When he did, he found himself looking deep into the eyes of the suspect. The suspect let off one more shot that struck him in his left shoulder. Rose cried out in anguish and dropped his gun again. As he laid there helplessly, he heard the female calling for his death.

"Kill that pig!" She yelled. "Kill that pig like you killed those two Hooligans in front of the store!"

The suspect grinned. "Southlane Villains!" He yelled. "Big Squeak!"

Then he pointed his pistol directly at Rose's forehead and pulled the trigger.

Click.

Rose heart skipped a beat. Squeak pulled the trigger again.

Click.

"He's out of bullets." Rose thought.

Squeak looked at the pistol. "Fuck." He growled, slapping the gun with his free hand.

Trying one more time, he pointed the pistol at Rose.

Click. Click. Click.

"Damn. You one lucky motherfucker. If I ever see you again." Squeak told him, "I'll kill you."

Then, turning to the girl, he said, "Come on Shonda, we gotta get out of here."

Rose laid there while the two teenagers ran to the car he was chasing, hopped in, and peeled out. Summoning enough strength to pull himself up into the cruiser, he saw Tameka again. By the time he got on the radio to call for backup, he was in tears. His girlfriend and his child were both dead. Sad part about it, he couldn't blame anybody but himself. It was his own reckless attitude that ended their lives.

Sierra sat there bewildered while Rose rubbed the wound on his shoulder. "Squeak." He whispered. "You killed my Tameka."

Rose collapsed down to all fours and started sobbing uncontrollably. Sierra jumped up and rushed to his side. "Rose. Rose. What's wrong?"

Rose looked up at her with tears streaming down his face.

"That's Squeak." He said in between sobs. "The same Squeak that murdered Tameka."

Rose hollered and tore his shirt from off of his torso. Sierra had never heard the name Tameka before, but she guessed that she was his old partner. Doing her best to comfort him, she grabbed Rose head and embraced him into her bosom. His tears made her breast somewhat slick. Whenever he remembered the entire episode, he became emotionally vulnerable. The memory had a way of breaking him all the way down. Rose tried fought hard, both day and night, trying to suppress what happened so long ago. He presented an image of strength and confidence to the world, but the truth was, he was a broken man.

He was broken on the inside, and his bravado was the proverbial band aid on a bullet wound. He knew that he did not pull the trigger, but he was definitely responsible for Tameka's murder. He was also responsible for the murder of their unborn child. He may not have pulled the trigger, but he might as well have pulled it. He refused to call for backup even after Tameka begged him over and over again. And for what? A title? A cool arrest story? For bragging rights?

As he heaved and cried, Sierra rubbed his head. "Shhh." She hushed him tenderly. "It's ok. You're ok."

Rose rocked back and forth in her arms and allowed her to console him. Hearing her say that everything was going to be ok had a calming effect on him. His wife, Rebecca, would always hold him in a similar fashion whenever he lost control. Although he was mourning over a love he had before he met her, Rebecca understood that the event was devastating. She knew that it was the duty of a wife to heal all wounds. Strangely, Sierra now found herself trying to put him back together again.

Sierra held Rose tight. She was finally beginning to understand his past in a more meaningful way. There were still a lot of blanks needing to be filled in, but Rose was definitely a human. He was a man with a lot of pain. Before that very moment, Sierra assumed that all of her respect for Rose came from how strong he was, but now that she was witnessing him cry, oddly enough, she didn't lose any admiration for the man. In fact, she revered him more.

The two of them held each other close until Sierra's shirt began to slide down to just below her left breast. She wasn't wearing a bra, so when her shirt fell, Rose found himself with his mouth seductively close to a mildly moist nipple. Between his tears he saw that she was exposed. He often wondered what she looked like under her clothes, and now he now he had an answer.

Her breast appeared smooth and soft. There were no bumps or scars on the portion before his face, and because of her youth, it was still perky and firm. Without considering the consequences of his actions, Rose adjusted his head slightly and kissed the side of her breast. He didn't know what he was doing, and he didn't care. The entire situation placed him into an emotional frenzy. He wasn't thinking, he was only acting.

Rose waited a few moments after the initial peck, and gauged Sierra's reaction. When she did not react, he took it as a sign to go further. Pushing the envelope, Rose gently placed his mouth around her nipple and sucked lightly. He let his tongue toss it to and fro inside of his mouth.

Sierra was caught off guard by the action, but she didn't resist. Instead, she moaned and began massaging the back of his head. Beginning to breathe harder, Rose pulled her shirt down below both breast and gripped them firmly. The light brown nipple on her high yellow skin was a very sexy contrast of colors. Going back and forth from left to right, Rose did his best to give each of her titties an equal amount of attention.

Sierra couldn't believe what was happening. Her fantasy was coming true. She knew that she would get him eventually. Rose was the gentle lover that she expected him to be. His touch was relaxing and welcome. Releasing her twin mountain peaks long enough to remove Sierra's shirt, he took in her frame as her body became exposed. She looked so beautiful to him. Not knowing exactly how Sierra felt, he wanted to make sure that she wanted it as much as he did.

Licking his lips, he asked, "Can we make…"

Sierra placed a single finger up to his mouth. Then, without breaking eye contact, she took him by the hands and stood up. Walking backwards, she slowly led him to her bedroom. When they passed by the glass table in the center of the room, Rose looked at the Bible still opened to Proverbs. He paused and looked at Proverbs 5:18, 19.

Sierra tugged his hands gently. Directing his attention back to the young, beautiful, willing woman in front of him, Rose was glad that he wasn't a very religious man. He followed her into her chambers and cast all thoughts of the wife of his youth from his mind. Tonight, he would indulge in the strange woman, and tomorrow, he would not be ashamed.

Once they crossed the threshold of her room, Rose picked Sierra up in his arms and carried her over to the bed. After laying her down on her back, he climbed on top of her. Starting at her neck, he licked and kissed down the length of her body. At the same time as he was descending with his mouth, he was pulling her pants off with his hands.

Sierra wiggled with anticipation. Spending a little extra time on her belly button, Rose heightened the pleasure with his tease tactic. He pulled her pants all the way off and kissed around on her inner thighs. Sierra's constant twitching let him know that he was doing something right. After a while, Sierra couldn't take it anymore. She grabbed the back of his head and forced his tongue to enter into her.

"Yes." She squealed, as Rose caused his slippery tongue to dance within her walls.

As much as Rose hated to admit it, she actually tasted better than his wife. Rose slid his hands underneath her butt cheeks and lifted her off of the bed a little. Sierra spread her legs wide.

"Mmmm." She cooed. "I love what you're doing down there, Rose. Keep going. Please, keep going."

Rose obeyed.

He pressed his tongue flat up against her love box so that he could hit as many nerves as possible. Then, he bobbed his head up and down, licking from Sierra's pearl tongue to her hole. The sensation caused her to squirm. Rose licked faster. Sierra began rotating her hips to help him hit all of the critical spots.

"Shit, daddy." She said, with her eyes closed. "Work that tongue! Mmmm. Work that mothafuckin' tongue, daddy."

Rose knew that he could give excellent oral sex and he was glad that Sierra now knew also. He stopped licking up and down and focused solely on her clitoris. Then, he used one of his hands to stick two fingers inside of Sierra's wetness.

"Uuuhh." She exclaimed, at the unexpected entry.

Rose was surprised that she was as tight as she was. Using his fingers to stroke her, and his mouth to stimulate her clit, Rose made her moan out in ecstasy. Soon, the taste to her became slightly salty. Withdrawing his fingers and his mouth, he noticed a small stream of white cream issuing forth from her. Turned on by making her cum, Rose buried his face in her pleasure box once again and licked up her orgasm from inside of her.

"Damn boy." She exclaimed, when she felt what he was doing. "You a freak for real."

Rose swirled around inside of her until he had felt satisfied with his cleaning process. When he finished, he stood to his feet, wiped his mouth off, and licked his hand clean. As he took off his pants, Sierra reached in her nightstand and grabbed a condom. Giving it to him, Rose slid it on quickly.

"Come on, daddy." Sierra invited. "Come get this pussy. You earned it."

Rose climbed back on top of her and penetrated.

"Uuuhh." He groaned, when he felt how warm and tight it was. Like a virgin. Rose looked Sierra in her eyes and slow stroked her until long after the sun came up.

Chapter Eight

Rose sat on the edge of the bed, still naked, with his head in his hands. Sierra laid naked behind him.

"What's wrong, baby?" She asked in a pouty voice. "Wasn't I good enough for you?"

Rose looked up, "Of course you were, Sierra." He assured her, using the back of his hand to brush away the hair that was hanging in her face. "I was just thinking about something."

Sierra rolled over onto her side and propped her head up on her hand. Rose almost became aroused again off the sight of her breast bouncing around so freely.

Sierra smiled. "Oh yeah. What were you thinking about?"

Rose turned back around and faced the dresser on the far wall. He couldn't possibly tell her what he was really thinking. It might hurt her feelings. Rose thought that Sierra was a very attractive young woman, and he could tell that she was very intelligent, but despite the impression his actions might have given off, he was still deeply in love with Rebecca, his wife. When Rose was younger, he often wondered how a cheating man could profess, with a straight face, that they loved their wives. He now knew because of personal experience.

Rose had been with Rebecca for 5 years now and he only cheated on her with 3 different women. The adultery was always the same though. There was nothing wrong with the other woman, his heart just belonged to Rebecca. His escapades with Sierra was nothing more than an indulgence in carnal pleasure to him. Rose hoped that she understood that, but he wasn't sure if she did. He faced her again. Sierra was extremely beautiful, but Rose was not prepared to sacrifice his marriage because of her good looks. Not wanting to get on bad terms with her, and really not wanting to jeopardize his marriage, Rose decided to just pray that Sierra would expect nothing more than the night of passion that he gave her.

Lying about what he was thinking, Rose replied, "I was just racking my brain about this case we've been working on."

Rose stood to his feet and began to gather his clothes.

"Really," he said, getting dressed to avoid further conversation. "I think it's time we checked out that other video clip on Burby's C.D."

Sierra sat up as Rose was putting his pants on. Slightly relieved, she released the breath that she had been holding. For a second, she thought that Rose was going to say that he had actual feelings for her. True, she found Rose attractive, but she didn't want to be in a relationship with him. She was just turned on by the atmosphere in which they were having sex. The danger, mixed with mystery, and mingled with the physical rendezvous that should have been off limits was more than enough to get her juices flowing.

Sierra knew that she had some exceptional love making tactics, but she silently prayed that Rose wasn't getting hooked. If he was, she knew that she would have to eventually let him down easy.

Appreciating the fact that Rose mentioned their case, she said, "Yeah. We need to finish checking out that C.D."

Neither one of them said anything else until they were completely dressed and back in position in front of the computer. They found it just as they had left it. The image was still paused on the frame with the hitman, now identified as Squeak, facing the camera.

"Why do you think Ellis saved that on a computer disk?" Sierra asked, getting comfortable in her swivel chair.

Rose thought about it for a moment. "Well, my guess would be that he kept it for collateral. After the shooting inside of the station, that particular surveillance tape came up missing. I suppose Burby initially took it to weaken any criminal case that might get brought up against him. The original is no doubt destroyed, but Burby probably wanted to keep something that he could use against the Villains if he ever needed to."

Sierra nodded.

It made sense to her, so she didn't ask about it anymore. Instead, she reached for the mouse and clicked various icons and buttons until the second video clip appeared. The first image to appear was fuzzy. Both Rose and Sierra tried to figure out what it was. It seemed like a large white object, but that was all. Sierra placed the cursor over the 'play' option and clicked the mouse. The white object moved, and Rose was able to recognize the image. It was Police Chief Burby standing in front of the camera wearing a white shirt.

Sierra and Rose watched without blinking.

"Why would a video tape of Burby be locked away in baby fort knots, a.k.a. Amirs Safe Deposit?" They both wondered.

Burby sat down in front of the camera. He was inside of a room that they did not recognize, and behind him there was a door. Burby appeared to be facing the camera, but his eyes were directed just below it.

Click, click, click.

"What's that noise?" Rose asked.

Sierra placed her ear next to her computer's speaker. Listening hard, she said, "I... think... he's typing."

Rose stood up straight. "Typing? What is he typing on?"

They both continued to watch the screen trying to figure out what was going on. About 45 seconds into the video clip, someone started knocking on the door behind Burby. Just then, Rose recalled the bruise on his knee. He had bumped into a computer desk back inside of Burby's house. Suddenly, he recognized the room as the Chief's living room.

"Burby is sitting in front of his computer at home." He declared.

Sierra watched Burby walk over to his front door. As soon as he opened it, 3 men burst into the room.

The tall, skinny visitor spoke first. "I need to talk to you."

Burby looked at the 3 men strangely and then peaked out of his door.

"Who is that?" Sierra asked.

Rose stared at the screen in disbelief. The tall skinny man was none other than Sticks himself, and one of the men with him was his first murder victim, Abdul. He had no idea who the man with the afro was.

"That's Sticks and Abdul." Rose informed her.

Without looking up, Sierra asked, "Abdul?! You mean the man that got murdered at The Economy Lodge Hotel?"

"Yep. The very same. They must be there to make a payment."

While most of the conversation was out of the view of the camera, what they were saying was easily heard.

"What are you doing here?" Burby asked, after he made sure that all of the blinds were closed. "You weren't scheduled to come here today. What if I had company?"

Rose could tell that Burby was agitated by their visit. This was obviously not a drop off.

"Look." Sticks told him calmly. "I'll gladly pay you extra for the inconvenience, but I have a situation that couldn't wait."

Burby appeared in the camera shot with his arms folded. "This better be good."

Sticks stepped into the camera shot and stood in front of Ellis. "I'm going to get straight to the point. You know that I have a truce agreement with Infamous, right?"

Burby nodded.

"Well," Sticks continued, "I have accidentally breached our agreement and I need your assistance in cleaning it up."

Burby looked confused.

"Accidentally breached your agreement. Help you clean it up?" He repeated. "What are you talking about?"

Sticks placed his hands onto Burby's shoulders. "You know as well as I do that if Infamous finds out that I betrayed his trust, the streets of Texas City will be caught up in another war. You don't want that, do you?"

Burby thought about it.

"Of course, I don't want another war to erupt." He told him. "But you still haven't even told me what the situation is or how I could possibly be of any assistance.

What is all of this about? Stop being vague and enigmatic. Spit it out."

Sticks took his hands off of Burby's shoulders and rubbed his head. He inhaled deeply and exhaled slowly. Then, looking Burby directly in the eyes, he said, "One of my men just killed Infamous' son."

Burby backed up. "What?!?" He asked in disbelief.

"What?!?" Rose asked, at the same time that Burby was asking the question.

"No... way!" Sierra stated.

Rose felt the entire room spin. He could not believe what he had just heard. Sticks was the one responsible for the death of Korey Isaac. Rose mind began to piece all of the events of the past few days together. He stood there in amazement as the case suddenly began to make sense. Somehow, Infamous must've found out that Sticks was responsible for his 13-year-old son's death and that Burby had helped cover it up.

That was why Infamous went on his killing spree. That was the reason for the war that was now being fought on the streets of Texas City. It even explained the Bible verse that Squeak had left spray painted on the wall of the house in The Chelsea's. Infamous was sending a message that the murders were in response to the murder of his son. This war was about vengeance! Rose knew that vengeance was one of the most powerful emotions in a human being's arsenal. Its drive rivaled the drive produced by love. In fact, vengeance is most often love mingled with hate. Love for the one you are avenging and hate for the one you feel hurt the one you love.

After Sticks revelation, Burby casually stopped recording in such a way that didn't alert Sticks to what he was doing. He obviously didn't want to incriminate himself with the footage, and he didn't want Sticks to know that he had all of the conversation up until that point on tape. Sierra turned to Rose when the clip stopped.

"Who would've thought?" She said, not really comprehending the magnitude of the situation.

Rose silently walked over to her couch and sat down. Sierra joined him.

Mostly talking to himself, Rose said, "That poor man."

Sierra looked at him. "What man?"

Rose shook his head. "Think about it. If Sticks was responsible for the death of Korey, then that means that Luis Wilkinson was actually innocent."

As Sierra thought back to the man who got killed in police custody, her stomach turned.

"That son of a bitch!" Rose said. "He actually framed an innocent man for the murder of a 13-year-old boy."

"Not only that," Sierra added, "he also sat idly by while that boy's father sent his hitman to slaughter him in cold-blood."

Rose was disgusted. At one point he actually looked up to Police Chief Burby. Now that he knew what type of person he really was, he couldn't even make himself feel sorry for the man. Ironically, his own underhanded act had come back to haunt not only him, but also his own son.

"Burby must've known that the case against Wilkinson wouldn't hold up in court." Sierra noted.

For a moment, they both sat there in silence. They now knew the 'why' behind their war. They also had a 'who', but they still needed to actually find the 'who'. Rose was excited to have a name.

Squeak.

That was probably the biggest break they had in the entire investigation. Plus, Rose felt as if he was going to finally be able to get a little justice for his first love and his unborn child. For years, the names Squeak, and Shonda haunted him. He often thought that the pair left the state and he would never be able to get his revenge. Now, he found out that at least one of them was still in town, and that one was still up to his old tricks. Killing in the name of the Southlane Villains. Rose knew that if he could find Squeak, he would have a chance at ending this war.

"So, what do we do next?" asked Sierra, waiting for Rose to figure out their next move.

Rose stared straight ahead and placed his hand on his firearm through his jacket. "Next," he said, picturing the assassin in his mind's eye. "We find Squeak."

....

Shonda laughed out loud inside of the movie theater.

"Did you see that shit, Squeak?"

Squeak only lightly chuckled. For the fourth time, the white couple sitting in front of them turned around and glared.

"Could you please keep it down?" The white woman asked, with agitation in her voice.

Shonda looked around. "Who the fuck you think you talkin' to, bitch?" She snapped, swerving her head from side to side.

The woman looked shocked. "Bitch?" She placed her hand against her chest as if she couldn't believe how Shonda had responded.

"Ummm. I ain't stutter. I called you a bitch. Bitch!

Squeak smiled. He knew that it was only a matter of time before Shonda went off. The lady in front of them had been complaining about the noise she was making the entire movie. Actually, Squeak was surprised that it took her as long as it did to check the woman. Usually, it only took one comment.

"There's no need for name calling." The woman said. Then she turned back around in her seat.

Squeak burst out laughing.

"Oh." Shonda said, smirking. "You only giggle at the movie, but you laugh out loud when I check that hoe."

Squeak shrugged his shoulders. What could he say? He loved being black. At times it seemed that African Americans always got the short end of the stick when it came to survival in the US. They were on top when it came to physical combat though. Hands down. Squeak figured it came from them being warriors back in Africa. That instinct must be bred into them.

That's what caused the white lady to back down. She had no way of knowing if Shonda could fight or not, but just because of her skin color, she assumed that she could. Squeak knew all too well that she guessed right. Had the lady challenged Shonda in any way, she would have gotten beat bloody right there in The Mall of The Mainland movie theatre. Shonda could fight like a man. Growing up in the streets, she had no choice but to learn how to fight. If they wouldn't fight over even the smallest disagreement, their father would whoop them mercilessly. He called it beating the weakness out of them.

They quickly learned that it was easier to fight people their own age in the streets then to face their father at home. Shonda knew that Squeak enjoyed seeing her get gangster, so she kept up the shit talk for a while.

"Yeah." She said, leaning back in her seat and crossing her legs. "I thought I was gone have to beat a bitch up. Lucky fa' that hoe, she got her mind right. Hmmm. Gone tell me to be quiet. Like she my mothafuckin' mama or somethin'."

Shonda pointed her finger and almost touched the back of the lady's head. "I swear fool. If this bitch says one mo' mothafuckin' thang to me, I'm gone whoop this hoe. I put that on mama grave."

Apparently feeling obligated to say something on behalf of his wife, the man that was with her turned around in his seat. Before he could say a word, Squeak stood to his feet and shook his head.

"It ain't worth it, bro." He informed the man, raising up his shirt to reveal the handle of an all-black pistol.

Squeak wasn't going to shoot him in a crowded movie theatre, but he would, however, shoot him in the parking lot. Seeing the gun, the man quickly changed his expression.

"Awww naw man." The dude pleaded. "It's nothing like that. I was just gonna apologize for my wife's behavior."

His wife glared at him. "My behavior?"

"Yes. Your behavior. Bothering those nice people while they try to enjoy the movie. I can't believe you."

The woman was shocked. "But… but… but."

"No buts," the man said, "let's go."

The woman looked bewildered as her husband grabbed her by the hand and practically drug her out of the theatre. Once they were gone, it was Shonda's turn to laugh out loud.

"You better not have let that white boy get in my business." She told him.

"Come on now, sis." Squeak said, placing his arm around Shonda. "You know how we do. You take the female and I'll take the male."

"You damn skippy." Shonda declared.

Shonda laughed and talked for the rest of the movie. Not surprisingly, no one else complained. When the film was over, Squeak and Shonda exited the theatre and started walking around the mall. With the money that Squeak had gotten paid from those 3 jobs, he decided that him and Shonda deserved some down time. It was only 1:15pm, so the mall wasn't all that packed. That was good because neither Squeak nor his sister liked big crowds. They always did their best to stay below the radar.

Shonda led Squeak to a shop called 'Behind Closed Doors'. It was a lingerie store that carried all of the latest name brand bedtime clothes.

"I'm going to get something for you, daddy." Shonda declared, twisting her hips as she entered the store.

Squeak followed behind her shaking his head. Ever since that night he gave in and had sex with her, Shonda had been acting like they were a couple. He tried to explain to her that that night was a mistake, but she wouldn't listen. In her world, his true feelings had finally come out. Squeak had to admit that the freak session was better than he had expected. Maybe it was because of all the time that had passed since the last time either of them had given in to the desires of their flesh.

Not that the attraction wasn't there, in fact, the physical attraction been there since they were young. Squeak's mind just told him that it was wrong, so he kept himself in check. Since that night that they once again experienced each other, Squeaks attraction to his sister had grown. At times it felt as if she could tell, because she was doing everything in her power to capitalize off of it. This trip to the lingerie shop was no doubt one of her schemes to break him down.

Squeaks brain didn't want to follow her inside the store, but his body did. When Squeak found himself watching as Shonda pulled skimpy outfits from the shelves, it was obvious that his body had overruled the warnings of his mind.

"What about this one?" Shonda held one of the items up to her body.

It was a red and black maids' outfit. The skirt was extremely short with ruffles along the bottom and it even came with one accessory. Attached to the top piece by a string was a small feather duster.

"We could do some thangs with this one, huh?"

Squeak swallowed the lump in his throat. Shonda's ass was so fat that Squeak knew the bottom of her butt cheeks would hang below the bottom of the skirt. Noticing how Squeak was staring at the outfit, Shonda knew that she would have to buy it. With joy in her eyes, Shonda grabbed Squeak by his hand and headed towards the dressing room.

"Come on, daddy." She said. "I wanna go try it on."

Ever since her brother made love to her, Shonda was on cloud nine. She loved him with all of her heart and soul. It angered her that society labeled her feelings as incest and considered them wrong. Who was society anyway? Society wasn't there to help when her own father raped her. Society wasn't there when that same father beat her until she bled. Where was society when her mother died? Or why didn't society keep her family from being split up? Society was nowhere to be found. The only help she ever received came from Squeak. He loved her and she knew it. She had no intentions of being with a man that might turn out like her father. Hell no! She trusted Squeak and only Squeak. Everyone else would never have access to her heart.

Shonda knew that somewhere along the way someone must have gotten to her brother and polluted his thinking. She resolved to be patient with him. In time, he would come around.

"After all," she thought. "he loves me just as much as I love him. He's just too ashamed to admit it."

Shonda disappeared into the dressing room with the maids' outfit. Squeak took a seat on one of the chairs that sat just outside of the dressing room area. He took a look around the store. One of them in particular was able to grab hold of his attention and keep it captive. It wasn't her beauty that caught his eye. It was more to the effect that she seemed somewhat out of place. Squeak reasoned that she was a good 300 plus pounds, easy.

The lady wasn't one of those big and nasty type of fat women though. From her appearance, Squeak got the impression that she took good care of herself. The fat lady was a Hispanic woman with hair that hung all the way down to the top of her butt. Squeak guessed that she was between 25 and 35 years old. She stood only 5'8, so she was pretty round. Her breasts were huge though. You could tell that she cared about how she looked because she was wearing a gold and black Baby Phat outfit that somewhat hid her size. She also had on a pair of D & G sunglasses that were resting on the top of her head.

Thinking it over, Squeak concluded that just because she was overweight didn't mean she couldn't dress up in lingerie. Big girls liked to feel sexy too. Squeak watched her as she searched the racks for an outfit that she liked. Pulling a light green silk nightgown from the rack, she held it up to her body and examined herself inside one of the many mirrors that were set-up throughout the store. Oddly, Squeak thought that she might actually look nice with the nightgown on.

The lady glanced over in the direction of the dressing rooms and caught Squeak staring at her. She instantly began grinning. The thought of a fine black man watching her as she shopped for lingerie turned her on. It had been so long since her own husband acted aroused by her, that any attention from anyone was welcome. She smiled and waved at him. Squeak was caught off guard by the gesture. He looked to his left, then to his right, and finally back towards the lady. She was pointing at him to let him know that she was waving at him.

Not knowing exactly how to respond, Squeak waved back. He instantly regretted his decision when the woman started walking in his direction.

"Shit." Squeak thought.

He wasn't trying to invite the woman over for a conversation. Especially not with Shonda only 10 feet away from him. She was one of the reasons he never had a girlfriend. Every time he would try to get close to a woman, Shonda would run them off. The lady was halfway to Squeak when Shonda emerged from the dressing room.

"Sooo." She sung, standing next to him and spreading her arms out wide. "What do you think?"

When the lady saw Shonda, she stopped, dropped her head, and made a casual detour to the left. Relieved, Squeak looked over at his big sister. He couldn't help but to stare wide-eyed with his mouth hung open. Shonda spun around in a circle. Squeak was right. Her butt cheeks hung well below the bottom of the skirt.

"Damn, sis. That shit looks live."

Shonda jumped up and down giggling. "I knew you'd like it."

Then, she leaned over and grabbed Squeak around his neck. Her breasts felt soft and warm against the side of his face. Squeak began to wonder why he couldn't just be with his sister. True, they say that it isn't right, but neither is killing people and he does that often.

Shonda released him. "Great." She proclaimed. "I'm going to get it."

Then she dusted off his crouch with her feather duster saying, "Maybe later we can put it to some good use."

With that, Shonda ducked back into the dressing room. The jiggling of her ass caused Squeaks dick to become rock hard. He rubbed it through his pants because it was throbbing so hard that it hurt. Scanning the store, Squeak made a carnal decision.

"Well." He thought. "We did it the other day, so fuck it."

Squeak stood to his feet and eased towards the dressing room door.

"Shonda." He called out, making sure that she was actually the one inside.

"Yeah." She answered.

Squeak looked around one more time to be sure that no one was looking, then he opened the door and entered the dressing room. Shonda was startled at first. She was still wearing the maid outfit top, but she had pulled the skirt off. From the waist down, she was only wearing a pair of red lace panties.

"What's up?" Shonda asked.

Squeak didn't answer. Instead, he turned around, locked the door, and then grabbed Shonda's arms.

"Ooohhh shit." She said, realizing what he was doing.

He spun her around and pushed her back, forcing her to bend over in front of him. Shonda loved that rough shit. She didn't protest at all. She simply placed the palms of her hands against the bench inside the dressing room and spread her legs. Squeak knew that they didn't have long, so he didn't attempt to get undressed. Removing his gun from his waistband, he set it down on the bench next to Shonda's hands. Then, her unbuckled his pants and pulled out his pulsating member. Sliding her panties to the side, he penetrated her. As always, that first thrust was like heaven. So wet, warm, and tight.

Getting into character, Squeak said, "I pay yo' mothafuckin' ass to clean up around here. But every time I come home; it looks like a tornado hit. So, I ain't gone tell you no more. I'm just gone start beatin' this pussy up."

After he said that, he began pounding away. Shonda's ass jiggled with every stroke.

"I'm so sorry." Shonda apologized. "I'm gone do better tomorrow. I promise."

She closed her eyes and gritted her teeth as the thickness of her brothers' tool stretched her walls to their limits.

"You... ain't... sorry." Squeak declared, pumping harder and harder with each word.

Her entire body began to rock back and forth with the force of his strokes. Shonda couldn't believe it. That maid outfit had a stronger effect on him then she thought it would. Squeak was actually giving it to her in the dressing room of a lingerie store. Unbeknownst to Squeak and Shonda, the overweight Hispanic woman was standing just outside of their dressing room listening to them having sex. In her mind, she was fantasizing about herself with the black man. The sound of the man going in and out of the woman was making her wet. She rubbed her thighs together in an attempt to cool down the burning sensation that was now beginning below her waist.

"Yes, daddy. Yes, daddy." She heard the woman moan. "It must be good." The Hispanic woman thought, biting her lip. "I want some of that." She decided.

Squeak didn't know if it was the possibility of being caught, the exceptional feeling of Shonda's walls, or a combination of the two, but whatever it was it didn't allow Squeak to last long. Before he knew it, the familiar feeling of a climax was creeping through his member. Shonda could tell from the change in his stroke that he was close to cumming, so she braced herself on the bench and started throwing her ass back to make Squeak erupt quicker.

Her actions did the trick. "Uuuggghhh!" Squeak groaned, as he grabbed her by her waist and pushed his penis as deep inside of her as it could go.

They both moaned and made twisted expressions as Squeak deposited his load within her. The Hispanic woman that was spying on them had quickly brought herself to a climax as well, with her left hand, as she imagined herself in the position of Shonda. Withdrawing her hand from her pants, she backed away from the door and zipped her pants back up. Looking at her hand, she noticed that she had gotten some of her juices on her wedding ring.

Still turned on, she licked her fingers clean. Pulling a piece of paper from her purse, she jotted down her name and number. When she saw Squeak emerge from the room without Shonda, she extended her arm to hand him the paper.

Squeak was shocked to see the Hispanic woman standing outside of the room. He wondered how long she'd been there.

"Here." The woman said, offering him the paper.

Squeak looked over his shoulder to make sure that Shonda was still inside of the dressing room. "What's this?" He whispered, accepting the paper.

The woman looked at him as if she was willing to gobble him up right then and there. "I'm feelin' you." She told him.

Then she turned and walked away before Shonda caught them talking.

"Damn." Squeak thought, unfolding the paper. "All I did was look at the bitch. She must be desperate."

When Squeak opened the paper, he found the woman's name and her cell phone number. It read, 'Adriana Martin.' (409) 771-2438'. Adriana had dotted the "I" with a heart. Squeak hurried up and stuffed the paper in his pocket when he heard the door to the dressing room open.

"Thank you, daddy." She said, giving Squeak a kiss on the cheek. "Come on. Let's pay for this and go shop at another store."

"Ok." Squeak agreed.

By the time they had paid for the outfit and exited the store, Squeaks cell phone was ringing.

"Wait a minute." He pulled his phone out of his pocket.

When he saw the name on the caller I.D. display, he held the phone up so that Shonda could see who was calling. She smacked her teeth.

"You know what that means." She said.

Of course he knew. It was time for him to do another job. Squeak answered the phone.

"What's up, boss?"

Infamous had spent the entire morning at Jesse's funeral. He still couldn't believe that Sticks had his best friend murdered. It was almost as painful as burying his own son. Infamous was a killer by nature but he still cared for those that were close to him. Tears of grief streamed down his face as he drove away from the funeral in his all black Maybach Benz.

"It's time to raise the stakes." Infamous said, with hatred in his voice. "That motherfucker wants to hurt me; well I'm going to hurt him right back."

Squeak listened as Infamous went on and one for a few minutes about how committed he was to completely crushing Sticks, and the Hooligans as a whole. Squeak knew that the boss just needed some time to vent. Jesse's funeral was today. He knew that the boss would be amped up for the next few days. In the days following Jesse's murder, he had ordered all of his soldiers to shoot on sight when they encountered a Hooligan. Likewise, Sticks had given the order for his soldiers to ride on the Villains. Texas City had seen more homicides and shootings in the past 3 days, then it had seen in the past two years combined. No exaggeration. Squeak knew that he would only be called when someone important and specific needed to be taken out. Obviously, that time had come.

After Infamous was finished swearing revenge, Squeak said, "All I need is a name, boss."

Infamous puffed on his cigar while he waited for the light to turn green.

Infamous held it in momentarily and the exhaled. "This one is a little different, Squeak."

"How so?"

"It's time for my ultimate payback for Sticks betrayal. It's time that bastard felt the pain that I felt. He needs to experience what I experienced. I need you to bring me one of his sons."

Squeak looked over at Shonda. He knew that this day was coming. Infamous entire plan revolved around killing one of Sticks sons like Korey was murdered. Squeak figured he could pull it off, but he was also realistic. Kidnapping the son of a gang lord was easier said than done. He sat on the phone for a moment and considered the danger. Squeak knew that he could very well be killed attempting this job. He couldn't refuse though. His loyalty to Infamous ran deep. The only person he was more dedicated to was Shonda, and that was because she was family. In Squeaks opinion, blood was thicker than water.

"Hello." Infamous called into the phone, concerned after the moment of silence. "Squeak. Are you there?"

"Yeah, boss. I'm here."

"So, what do you think? Can you bring me one of his children?"

This time, without hesitating, Squeak told him, "Consider it done, boss"

Infamous smiled. "That's what I like to hear."

Then, they hung up.

Seeing Squeak get off of the phone, Shonda was curious as to what job Infamous had for Squeak.

"So." She said, with an inquisitive look. "What did he say?"

Squeak hung his head. "I have to bring him one of Sticks sons."

Squeak couldn't help but to think about how he felt after he murdered the Chief's son. He hoped that he could bring himself to do it again.

Chapter Nine

Traffic was beginning to pick up a bit, but that was normal. Every day in Texas City, at around 2:00pm, you would see more cars on the road. People were getting off of work, going to work, or just on their way to the grocery store. The number of vehicles on the road caused the green Dodge Neon making its way through the streets nothing more than another traveler. No one on the road would have ever guessed at the complexity of the situation the man and woman inside of it faced.

Sierra had the A.C. turned on medium to combat the heat outside. Most people thought that 12:00 noon was the hottest part of the day, but they were wrong. The hottest part of the day was between 1:30pm and 2:30pm. Why? Simply because at noon, the sun would be directly overhead. So, by the time 1:30pm hit, the asphalt, concrete, and overall ground below would be heated up by the rays of sunlight beaming down.

Rose reached out and adjusted the A.C. vent that faced the passenger seat. A cool gust of air blew across his face and neck. Closing his eyes, he tilted his head back to let the air hit his chin.

"So, when does your shift start?" He asked, with his head still leaned back.

Seeing Rose trying to cool off, Sierra cranked the A.C. up to high. Rose smiled as the air began to blow more forcefully.

"I don't have to be on the clock until 10:00pm." She answered. "I got the graveyard shift tonight. Why do you ask?"

"Well, since I'm a detective, I get to pretty much make my own hours. So, what I was going to do was this."

Rose turned to face her.

"We've both been working pretty hard lately. Ever since we started working this case. Soon, we'll be running on nothing more than fumes. Now, to a certain extent, we have to be diligent and remain focused, but at the same time, if we push ourselves too hard, we won't be able to think clearly enough to solve the case. So, this is what I want you to do. After you drop me off, go back home, rest, wash-up, and relax until your shift starts. Then, when you get to work at 10:00pm, I'll be there, and we can pick up where we left off."

Sierra cocked one of her eyebrows up and grinned.

"Don't tell me the 'Lone Ranger' is finally starting to see me as a partner."

At the mention of the word partner, Rose thought about Tameka.

"Naw." He said. "I do not do partners, but I'm not crazy neither. I'm man enough to admit that I wouldn't have made it this far in the case if it had not been for you, and I'm pretty sure that you will prove valuable in seeing this thing all the way through."

Sierra felt flattered. She knew that it was a very rare thing to hear Detective Rose admitting that he could not do something on his own. She knew that she must have really made a good impression on him. Maybe, by the end of this case, she could convince him that she would make an excellent partner. She decided that she would just wait on the opportunity to present itself and she would capitalize off of it.

Deep down, Rose felt that he was coming dangerously close to a partnership type of relationship with Sierra and it made him a little uneasy. Ever since Tameka got murdered because of his lack of good judgement, he promised himself that he would never have another partner. Rose did not want to give fate the chance to put him in a predicament like that again, but he knew that he probably wouldn't be able to solve this case without Sierra's help.

Rose thought back to the codes in the notebook and the bible verse spray painted on the wall. He would not have known what either one of them meant if it had not been for her.

The pair made the remainder of their trip in silence. Both still thinking about the case and both anticipating the coming opportunity when they could stop thinking about the case. It wasn't long before Sierra was pulling over in front of Rose's house.

Opening the car door and getting out, Rose said, "Don't forget. Relax a bit. We'll get back on the case tonight."

"Alright, Rose." She called after him, right before he closed the door.

Rose listened to Sierra pull off as he made his way up to his front door. When he was halfway there, he paused.

"Shit." He cursed under his breath, when he remembered what he had done.

"Sierra and I had sex!"

Rose knew that he was no doubt reeking of the smell of sex. It was a very distinct smell. If he knew his wife, and indeed he did, she would know what he had been up to if she had the chance to smell him. Thinking fast, Rose told himself that he would just do his best to make it to the shower. Once he had washed off, she could accuse, but she couldn't prove. Using his key to enter his home, he was relieved to not see his wife anywhere.

"Maybe Rebecca is still asleep."

Tiptoeing as fast as he could, he hurried to the bathroom. Rose quickly got undressed and turned on the shower water.

"I'm home free." He said to himself, testing the temperature of the water with his hand.

He withdrew his hand immediately. It was way too hot. Rose adjusted the hot and cold dials. As he did, he heard a loud 'BAM'.

Rebecca burst into the bathroom with anger plastered across her face.

"Just what the fuck do you call yourself doing?" she questioned.

Rose tried to play it off. "I'm about to take a shower. What does it look like I'm doing?"

Rebecca put her hands on her hips. "It looks like you're trying to cover something up."

"Cover something up?" Rose repeated. "You sound crazy."

He knew that Rebecca was anything but lame. His only hope was to clean the scent of Sierra's sex off of his penis before she caught wind out it. Rose turned and stepped one foot into the tub. Rebecca hurried up and grabbed his arm with both hands and pulled him back before he could get in the water. Rose had to break his fall by grabbing the countertop and the wall.

"What the hell is wrong with you?" He asked, trying to break free of his wife's grip.

"What's wrong with me?! You leave this house at 1:00am with some fast ass bitch that I knoooow is trying to fuck you, you stay gone for 13 mothafuckin' hours without calling so much as once, and then, when the bitch drop you off, you run straight to the shower. Come on, Derrick. I'm not stupid. You fucked that bitch. Didn't you?"

Rose and Rebecca were engaged in a tug of war. Rose was trying desperately to get in the water, and Rebecca was doing everything in her power to stop him.

"So what if I left the house with, Sierra." Rose said in response to what Rebecca had said. "We work together. We were following up on a lead. We weren't fucking. Me being gone for 13 hours and me trying to take a shower doesn't mean anything."

"The HELL it doesn't! It means you fuckin' that bitch! That's what it means."

Rebecca had an extremely tight grip. Rose didn't want to hurt her, but he didn't want to get caught either.

"Woman, look." He said, trying to sound serious. "I did not have sex with Sierra. We just work together. You need to stop being so insecure."

Rebecca looked hurt. "Oh, so I'm insecure now, Derrick? Ok then. If you're telling the truth, let me smell your dick. If I don't smell that bitch on your dick, I'll apologize, and I'll never accuse you of cheating again."

Rose knew that it was eventually going to come to that. There was no way he was about to let his wife's nose get anywhere near his groin. He had to get in the water, and fast.

"Smell my dick? You are crazy for real."

Rebecca was finished talking. She dropped to her knees and grabbed his hanging penis. As she leaned in to sniff, Rose knew he had to do something. Using the palm of his right hand, Rose pushed Rebecca's forehead. When he extended his arm, her head snapped back, and then her entire body fell over backwards. Rebecca grunted as she fell down, but Rose didn't bend over to help her. Instead, he used that time to jump in the water.

As he rubbed the soap directly on his penis and abdomen, he knew that his actions were incriminating, but allowing Rebecca to smell Sierra's juices on him would've been far worse.

Rebecca looked up from the floor at Rose. "You slick, mothafucka'." She said, climbing to her feet. "Alright. You did that. Just don't be mad when that bullshit come back on your ass."

She stormed out of the bathroom and slammed the door behind her.

"Come back on me?" Rose repeated. "Yeah right."

He pulled the shower curtain closed and began to bathe regular. He would just have to make it up to her later. That's all. Rebecca was fuming. She wasn't a dumb woman by far. She knew what was going on. That bitch Sierra was seducing her husband. She wasn't crazy though. Trying to stop him from going around her would cause problems with his job. Rose paid all of the bills and took care of her, so she wasn't about to mess up his paycheck, but she could get even. That's what she did the other two times he cheated. He thought he was so smart and smooth that he had gotten away with it, but she knew all along. She didn't confront him though. She just went out and had an affair of her own. Rebecca liked to get even.

Still highly upset, she started pumping herself up to go out and do Rose how he did her. Some man was going to score, simply because she was scorned.

Knock. Knock. Knock.

Her thoughts of revenge were interrupted by a knock on the door.

"Who the fuck is that?" She wondered, as she went to answer the door.

Without looking out the peephole, Rebecca just swung open the door and got the surprise of her life.

"Hey, Rebecca." Sierra said, holding a wallet out in front of her. "Rose dropped this in my car."

Rebecca stood there and stared at the smiling Sierra.

"You got some nerve."

Sierra looked confused. "Excuse me?"

Rebecca shook her head. "Don't worry about it."

Then, without warning, she punched Sierra as hard as she could in the face.

Sierra screamed as she stumbled off the front porch and hit the ground hard.

"She must know." Sierra thought, as pain shot through her face and back.

Rebecca stood over her with her fist balled up. "Get up and fight, bitch." Rebecca shouted.

"Oh." Sierra shot back, shaking off the first blow, and climbing to her feet. "You thought I wasn't?"

Sierra was a preacher's daughter, but she was far from a good girl. She had had her fair share of fights and her father even let her take a few boxing classes. The two women posted up in front of each other like boxers in a ring. Rebecca, fighting out of rage, rushed Sierra with a series of jabs. Sierra kept her cool and just backed up out of her reach. Then, after she timed Rebecca's punches, she side-stepped to the right and hit Rebecca with a solid right hook.

"Ungh." Rebecca grunted.

"Yeah, bitch." Sierra taunted. "You thought it was gone be easy, huh?"

Rebecca started swinging again. Sierra tried to block the blows, but Rebecca was too strong. Her punches penetrated Sierra's defenses and connected repeatedly with her face. Sierra started to swing back. Before long, the two of them were engaged in an all-out slugfest. Sierra was landing more punches, but Rebecca was making more of her punches count. Rose climbed out of the shower and wrapped a towel around his waist. He thought he could hear someone yelling. Walking out of the bathroom without even drying off, Rose heard something going on in the front.

The closer he got, the more it sounded like Rebecca cursing. When Rose made it to the front door, the sight he saw didn't seem real. There, in his front yard, being watched by all of his neighbors, was Rebecca and Sierra trying to kill each other.

"Oh no." He thought.

Forgetting that he was only wearing a towel, Rose ran towards them.

"Rebecca! What in God's name are you doing?"

The neighbors watched in amazement as Rose grabbed Rebecca and pulled her away from Sierra. They all knew that Rose was a cop, so they never in a million years expected to see so much drama unfolding at his house. It was more entertaining than television.

"Let me go!" Rebecca screamed, as Rose carried her back towards the front door.

Rose was so embarrassed. "Sierra, I'm sorry." He called out.

"Don't apologize to that bitch!" Rebecca screeched.

Sierra smiled. "Yeah, don't apologize to me. I should be apologizing to you for beatin' yo' wife ass like that."

That comment enraged Rebecca even more. She started struggling fiercely to break free. In all of the commotion, the towel Rose had around his waist came off. The female neighbors gasped as they all got an eye full of his package. Rebecca looked down to see what they were staring at. It upset her even more to know that her neighbors were now gazing at her husband's tool.

Grabbing Rose' dangling manhood, Rebecca shouted, "You hoes see this? This my dick. My… MOTHAFUCKIN'… DICK!"

She made sure that they understood each word. Rose had enough. He lifted Rebecca onto his shoulder and packed her back into the house. All of the spectators turned to Sierra. She just grinned, shrugged her shoulders, and got in her car. They all watched as she drove off and then the gossip and speculation began. Sierra couldn't believe she had to fight Rose's wife. She looked at her reflection and saw that Rebecca had bust her top lip.

"Just for that," she said, touching the bruise with her fingertip. "I'm gone fuck yo' man again."

Rebecca shook herself loose from Rose grip. "Put… me… down." She demanded.

Rose was mad as hell.

"Why did you do that shit?"

"Fuck you!"

Rebecca stormed out of the living room and Rose followed her, still completely naked.

"I'm not finished talking to you." He told her.

Rebecca snatched one of her favorite outfits out of the closet. "Too bad, Derrick. I was finished talking to you when you pushed me down in the bathroom.

Rose watched as Rebecca got dressed.

"Where do you think you're going?"

Rebecca ignored him. She simply put on a pair of black capri jeans and a black shirt that was designed with only one strap. Rose continued to ask questions and she continued to ignore him. He followed her all the way to the front door, but he wasn't going to go back outside with no clothes on. They already put on a big enough show. Rebecca opened up the door and walked out.

Stopping to pick up the wallet that Sierra dropped when she punched her, Rebecca said, "Your little hoochie brought this back to you."

She threw it over her shoulder and walked off the porch. Rose looked at his wallet. He was wondering why Sierra came back to his house. Rose stood in the doorway and watched while Rebecca got into her purple Nissan Maxima and drove away.

....

Meanwhile, on the other side of town, two brothers were leaving a Shell service station and heading up to the mall.

"Are you sure they came out yesterday?" Suko asked, as he merged in with the traffic."

"How many times I gotta tell you?" Tao asked. "Everybody on Facebook has been posting about it. The new Jordan's just came out yesterday."

Suko picked the weed blunt up out of the ashtray, puffed on it, and held the smoke inside of his lungs. "We gone be one of the first ones on the block with them hoes."

....

Shock pulled out of the Shell station parking lot and turned in the direction of the gray Cadillac. Sticks hadn't sent him on a mission since he took care of Archie and he was itching to get into something. He knew that there was a war going on between the Hooligans and the Villains, so he figured that any Villain would do. Shock didn't know what he might have to get into, so he had his A.K. in the trunk, his knife on his hip, and his Glock 9 on his lap.

Shock considered himself a predatory chameleon. He was wearing a black and red du-rag with a black and red hat. The hat had the letter 'V' stitched into it. He also had on a red t-shirt, black jeans, and some red and black tennis shoes. He was a Hooligan, so he normally wore blue, but to complete a job he would wear anything. Shock was hunting Villains, so he camouflaged himself like one.

"I'm the wolf in sheep's clothing." Shock thought devilishly.

He had spent the last 45 minutes prowling around on the Southside when he noticed two light skinned men wearing all red enter into the Shell station. Shock had been in Texas City long enough to know that if he saw two dudes flamed up on the Southside, they were Villains. He had made the decision then and there to murder them both. Shock didn't know where they were headed, and he didn't care. If they slipped up and led him to a secluded spot, he would put his Glock to work. On the other hand, if they took him to an area infested with Villains, he would utilize the A.K. that he had in the trunk.

Shock ended up following the pair all the way to The Mall of The Mainland.

"Hhhmmm." Shock thought. "This just might be interesting."

Shock climbed out of his Pontiac Sunbird and followed the brothers across the parking lot and towards the entrance to the mall. As he approached the glass doors, he noticed a man and a woman exiting the mall. His prey stopped to talk to them. Shock stopped, bent down, and pretended to be tying his shoe. His prey shook hands with the man and Shock noticed them exchange the Villain handshake.

"Oh." Shock whispered. "So, you're a Villain too?"

Noticing that the woman was carrying a bag from the lingerie shop 'Behind Closed Doors', he said, "I bet I know what ya'll are about to go do."

Shock turned around and headed back out to the parking lot. He zig-zagged aimlessly long enough to see what kind of car the couple got into. It was a black Chevy

Cavalier. He made a mental note of the car and the license plate number. FWM-9116.

"I'll catch you later." Shock mumbled under his breath.

Then, he rushed inside of the mall trying to catch up to his prey.

"Come on." Tao urged. "Foot Locker is this way."

Suko and Tao made their way to Foot Locker and took a moment to scan their inventory. Shock stopped in front of one of the stores that were close by and sat down on the bench in the middle of the floor.

"The predator must possess patience." He said, as he kicked back and peeped the scene.

From a distance, he noticed a brown skinned lady exiting Dillards. She was jazzy too. She had on a pair of black capri jeans and a black shirt with only one strap on it. She wasn't just extremely thick, but she wasn't skinny neither. Shock noticed that when she walked, she was twisting her hips hard. If she was trying to get his attention, she defiantly succeeded. When they made eye contact with each other, the woman smiled and headed in his direction. Shock rose to his feet when she got close.

"How you doin' ma?" He asked.

"Oh, I'm fine." She responded.

Shock smiled. "I didn't ask how you look. Anybody with two eyes can see that you're fine. I asked how you were doing?"

The lady giggled. Shock knew that he had her. As the saying goes, if she grin, she in.

"I meant that I was doing fine, but thanks for the compliment." She smiled from ear to ear. "How about you?"

"I'm doing a whole lot better now that I've met you." He answered.

Shock grabbed her left hand. "My name is LaQuincy, but everyone calls me, Shock."

He kissed the back of her hand. "What is your name, beautiful?"

When he kissed her hand, she was glad that she had enough forethought to remove her wedding ring and leave it in her car. "My name is Rebecca."

As the two of them made small talk, Rebecca was sizing Shock up. He looked like a thug. The complete opposite of her husband. In fact, he looked like the type of man that her husband would arrest. That turned her on immensely. His voice was also attractive. It was really raspy and unique. He sounded dangerous.

By the time they exchanged cellphone numbers, Rebecca already made up her mind to have sex with her new friend. She wondered if he had any idea how lucky he was to be the first cute guy to approach her on a day like today. While they were conversating, Shock saw his prey leaving the Foot Locker with bags in their hands.

"Ummm." He said. "I really do hate to rush off like this, but I have to take care of a little business."

Rebecca waved it off. "Don't worry about it, Shock. As long as you remember to use that number, we're good."

Shock looked up and down at her body.

"Believe me." He said, rubbing his hands together. "I'd be a damn fool if I didn't use this number."

Rebecca liked the compliment. Shock gave Rebecca a hug, told her goodbye for now, and once again became the shadow of Suko and Tao. The mall was beginning to get more crowded, so Shock thought that he would have to wait until later to get them. He enjoyed the knowledge that none of the other patrons of The Mall of The Mainland knew that he was a hunter on the prowl. To Shock, the crowds were the tall grass, the brush, and the trees. All working together to provide cover for the lone lion.

He licked his lips as he stalked his unknowing prey. Their ignorance was almost sufficient enough to arouse him. As he tailed his two gazelles, he noticed them breaking off from the rest of the herd. Attempting to guess where they were going, he realized that they were heading in the direction of the bathroom. Shock prayed to every god that he had ever heard of that the pair would be foolish enough to enter the isolated restroom area.

They passed by the jewelry shop. The white woman standing inside of the booth tried to get his attention.

Shock waved her off.

They crossed through the food court.

"Yes." Shock thought, as they entered the long hallway that led to the bathroom.

Shock looked at his surroundings. There were two females coming from the lady's restroom. Shock did his best not to look at them. As they neared the end of the hallway, Shock petitioned the same gods that assisted him in herding his prey down this hallway. He asked that the bathroom be empty.

Suko and Tao made it to the bathroom.

"Hurry up, Suko." Tao said. "We gotta get back to the trap."

Suko handed him the Foot Locker bag. "Aiight my nigga." He told him. "I just gotta piss."

Tao accepted the bags from his brother and took a seat on the bench outside of the bathroom door. After he set the bags down, he looked up and saw a man flamed up in all red.

"What it do, Villain?" Shock asked in his raspy voice, before entering the bathroom behind Suko.

Tao looked at the man strange. He didn't recognize him, but the man addressed him as a Villain. The man was dressed as a Villain also. Tao shrugged his shoulders. There were plenty of Villains that he didn't know. Infamous had an army of soldiers.

Shock entered the bathroom and saw Suko standing at the urinal.

Suko looked over his shoulder. Seeing a man in red, he said, "What it do, Villain?"

Shock scanned the area. "Shit," he responded. "Riding it out like a, G."

"Already." Suko told him.

Shock thanked the gods for once again lending him a helping hand. The place was empty. Not knowing how much time he had, Shock pulled out his knife and snuck up behind Suko. With his left hand, he grabbed his mouth to muffle his cries, and with his right hand he slit his throat from ear to ear. It all happened so fast, that Suko was still holding his penis when Shock released him. Blood squirted out of his neck and colored the wall in front of him. Shock backed away from the body as Suko crumbled and fell to the floor.

Shock stood over him and looked him directly in his eyes. The last thing Suko would hear, was a raspy voice saying, "Dramaside, bitch."

Shock tucked his knife away and walked out of the restroom. Tao spoke this time.

"What it do, Villain?" He asked.

Shock didn't even look at him. He just kept on walking. Tao looked him up and down. When he gazed at his hand, he thought he saw drops of blood.

"What the fuck...?" He asked under his breath.

Watching the man walk off, Tao could sense that something was wrong. He rushed into the bathroom.

"SUKO!" He shouted, when he saw his brother stretched out on the floor. "SOMEBODY GET SOME HELP DOWN HERE!"

It was too late though. Suko was gone, and so was the man responsible for Suko's death.

Chapter Ten

"Alright girl." Sierra said into the phone. "I have to go to work in a little bit, so I'm about to go."

"Ok." The woman on the other line answered. "And say, sis-in-law," she added. "Next time you get into it with that bitch, call me."

Sierra laughed and waved her hand around in the bath water that she was relaxing in. "Ain't nobody worried about Rebecca." She told her. "I got that hoe. Trust that."

"Well, you know I'm here if you need me, but I guess I'll let you get on to work. Your brother will be home in a minute anyway and I haven't even started to cook yet."

"Alright then. Don't forget to tell my big head brother that I love him."

Sierra said goodbye and hung up the cellphone. Reaching out of the tub, she sat the phone down on the toilet seat. Then, with her now free hand, she picked up the weed blunt she had burning in the astray next to where she just placed the phone. Sierra inhaled deeply. She loved nothing more than to relax in a nice warm bath and get high all by herself.

As the marijuana entered her lungs, Sierra tried to think back to when she first started smoking weed. If her memory was correct, she was about 13 years old. Her first love, a boy named Cameron, had given her her first hit. He was 16 years old and he ran with the Hooligans. At the time, she was rebelling against everything that her father stood for. She was hanging with the so-called gangster girls, dating a thug, and when the opportunity to get high presented itself, she took it.

It was like nothing she ever experienced before. Almost instantly she was hooked. To her, it seemed like she was an entirely different person on weed. It helped her to relax no matter what was going on around her. Even after she began to calm down, the weed smoking was something from her past that she held on to. Since she first started smoking, she could only remember one time when she went without getting high for more than one week, and that was when she was trying to get her job with the police force. As soon as her probationary period was over, she locked herself up in her house and spent an entire day getting reacquainted with the weed.

Sierra hit the blunt one last time before climbing out of the water.

"Here we go again." She said, as she grabbed a towel and dried off.

Rose was correct. She didn't realize how much she needed that down time. After taking some time to herself, she felt refreshed and ready to get back to working the case. She had gotten a chance to talk to her sister-in-law, smoke a little weed, and take a nice relaxing bath. Her sister-in-law had been at the mall earlier and said that someone had gotten killed in the bathroom area.

She wasn't surprised by the news. Every day that the war went on, the violence got worse and the gangsters became more brazen. The only strange part about it was that she told her a Villain had murdered another Villain. After giving it some thought, Sierra concluded that it was most likely similar to the Villain dressing up like a Hooligan to get to the Police Chief. It seemed like disguising yourself as a rival gang member was becoming common place. That complicated things. You couldn't tell who you were looking at by their clothing anymore.

"Perhaps Rose will have some insight into how we should proceed." She thought.

Sierra laid her uniform out before she got in the tub, so it didn't take long for her to get dressed. After getting in uniform, rinsing the smell of marijuana out of her mouth, and spraying herself with perfume, Sierra grabbed her keys and headed towards the door. Just when she was about to walk out the front door, her house phone rang. Trying to hurry up so she wouldn't be late for work, Sierra rushed over to the phone.

"Hello." She answered.

"Are you alone?" The voice on the other end asked.

Recognizing the voice, Sierra spoke softly into the phone even though there was no one else there with her.

"Yes. I'm alone."

"Good. So, have you located the money?"

Sierra had not forgotten about the mission. "I have some good news and I have some bad news." She reported.

There was a momentary pause. Then, the voice broke the silence.

"Proceed."

"I found out which overseas bank that Burby was using. I also have the account number to his account. The only problem is that the balance from the most recent bank statement says that Burby only has about $500,000."

"$500,000?!" The voice repeated confused. "There must be some mistake. There is no way that's all he had. There must be more."

Sierra thought about it. "Well, maybe he hid it some place."

"There's not too many places that someone can hide $20 million in cash."

"Just give me a little more time. If the money is out there, Rose can find it. I've seen him in action. He's a pretty good detective."

The voice chuckled. "He's not good enough to see through you."

"Well, he's good, but I'm great. Besides, I already put this pussy on him. He looks at me with his dick now and not his eyes."

Both Sierra and the voice laughed.

"Just keep me posted." The voice said.

"Just hang tight. I'll find it. I promise."

With that, they hung up, and Sierra headed out the front door. After a short drive, she was pulling up to the police station. As soon as she entered the parking lot, she saw Rose standing next to his car. It was dark outside, but he was illuminated by one of the many lights that cascaded the entire lot. Some of the veteran officers had told her why there were so many lights. Apparently, about 15 years before she joined the force, criminals with grudges against certain officers would lay in wait in the parking lot and gun them down as the officer approached his or her cruiser.

Sometimes they caught the suspect and sometimes they didn't. They figured their best defense was to take away the shooters hiding spots. At least now the officers would be able to see their attackers coming and return fire. Sierra parked next to Rose and exited her vehicle. Rose flicked the cigarette he was smoking.

"Sierra, I just want to apologize again for..."

Sierra cut him off. "Please, Rose. It's not that big of a deal. If you really want to make it up to me, just don't bring it up anymore."

Rose sighed. He didn't know what to say, so he guessed it was good that she didn't want to talk about it. Rose made up his mind then and there to let it go.

"Ok." He said.

Sierra caught him off guard and kissed him on the lips.

"Good." She said. "Now wait right here while I go clock in, daddy."

Sierra walked off before Rose could respond. He was left grinning. If he was a white man, he would have been blushing. Rose took out another cigarette and puffed on it while he waited for Sierra to come back out of the station. He was trying to get his mind back on his job, but it was hard. Rebecca had not come back home yet, and to make matters worse, she wasn't answering her cellphone.

Rose knew that he had messed up bad this time. There was no telling how long Rebecca would hold it against him. All because he couldn't keep his dick in his pants, and strangely, even though Sierra was at the root of all of his current woes, seeing her somehow eased his mind. Rose shook his head from side to side.

"You trippin' man." He told himself. "She was not that good."

It wasn't long before Sierra was coming back out of the building. Rose took one look at her and thought back to the sexual rendezvous that they had.

Reconsidering his initial position, he said, "Maybe she was that good."

Sierra walked up smiling and eager to get started. "So, Where to next?"

Rose made his way around to the driver side door and opened it.

"We can talk on the way." He told her, getting into his vehicle.

Sierra climbed in on the passenger side and Rose drove off. When he turned on to the street, Sierra buckled her seatbelt and said, "I'm listening."

Rose liked her enthusiasm. He could tell that Sierra was really into the whole process of detective work. At times she appeared a little too eager. Rose chalked it up to her aspirations of becoming a detective.

Turning his left blinker on, Rose said, "I got to thinking. We have a description of one of our killers and we also have his street name. Usually, that's enough to find out who the guy really is. So, before you made it to work, I ran the alias, 'Squeak', through our computers database. Unfortunately, the only hit I got was a Squeak name Anthony Tune."

Sierra scratched her head. "Why is that unfortunate?"

Rose shot her a glance. "I know for sure that our Squeak is in his mid to late 20's. The Squeak I have in our computer is 47 years old."

"Oh." Sierra responded, hanging her head in disappointment.

Rose saw her new demeanor and placed his hand on her shoulder.

"It's not a complete dead end."

"What do you mean?"

"This particular Squeak has a rap sheet a mile long. What I'm hoping is that either he's our Squeaks' father, or one of the older gang members in the Villains. A lot of the time these guys get their nicknames from people they look up too and respect. Knowing firsthand how violent our hitman Squeak is and reading how violent this Anthony Tune guy use to be, I figure that there just might be a connection."

"So, you want to go question him?"

"Yep. That's where we are headed to right now."

Sierra looked at the time on the radio display. "But it's 10:15pm."

Rose shrugged his shoulders. "He'll be alright."

Sierra sat back and thought for the rest of the drive. All of this hunting down the killer was cool, but she needed to be trying to find that money. She thought for sure that the location of the money would be found back at Amirs Safe Deposit. Police Chief Burby was becoming a nuisance even in death. Sierra racked her brain trying to figure out who could possibly know about the money. For the life of her, she could only come up with one person. The Chiefs' wife, Bianca Burby.

Common sense told her that if the wife knew anything about the cash, but couldn't find it, she would tell all in the hopes of getting some of the money for herself.

Sierra knew that Bianca and Burby were separated but still legally married at the time of his death. She just needed to figure out a way to convince Rose that she was worth investigating. To Rose, the Chief had no more significance. Rose was focused on Squeak. Sierra knew that she could probably come up with some lie to change his mind. Hell, she'd better if she ever hoped to get rich.

Rose looked out of the window as he turned onto the street that Anthony Tune lived on. From his days as a regular cop he knew that Tune lived in a very rough part of town. In fact, it was on this very street that he had arrested his first drug dealer. The obvious addicts that lined the streets let him know that not much changed about the area. Only this time, the people didn't know that he was a police officer right off the back.

"It's dark on this block." Sierra noted.

Rose looked at the busted-out streetlights. He had seen busted out streetlights before. The sight made him swallow hard.

"Stay with me." He urged himself softly. "You gotta stay focused, Derrick."

The scene was eerily similar to the night Tameka was killed. It took every ounce of will power that Rose had to keep himself from falling into a trance and remembering the pain of that night. In his head, Rose started talking to himself about the task at hand. It was a mental exercise a therapist taught him years ago. He would begin mentally talking to himself about whatever task he was currently engaged in and that would assist his mind in resisting the regression. He stared straight ahead as he tried desperately to remain in the present.

Sierra looked over at him. "There he goes again." She thought.

It seemed like every 20 minutes he was zoning out. Sierra started expecting that out of him. She assumed he just been through so much, his past sometimes haunted him. Sierra often wondered what demons he faced, but then again, she wasn't 100% sure that she wanted to know.

Finally gathering himself, Rose turned into the driveway of the residence that he had on file for Tune. It was in the area of Texas City known as 3rd Ave Village. He quickly scanned his surroundings. The house was a yellow, shot-gun style house. The porch was small with 3 cracked cement steps leading up to it. Rose could tell that the grass hadn't been cut in a while but there were just a few scattered patches of it, so it really didn't matter. Most of the grass that had been lost appeared to have been the victim of foot traffic. There were several trails walked into the yard. The paint on the walls was peeling off and the roof had several patches on it.

Rose pulled up behind a gray truck, so he felt reassured that Tune was at home.

"Let's go." Rose said, getting out of the car.

Sierra got out and followed him up to the front door. She stood there while Rose knocked. Sierra didn't know why, but she felt uneasy about the whole thing.

With the way Rose said this guy's attitude was, she doubted he'd be cordial to two police officers showing up at his house at 10:00 at night. To make matters worse, they came unannounced to question him about a killer that just so happens to have the same street name as him. The more Sierra thought about it, the more she was ready to go.

Not getting an answer, Rose knocked on the door again, harder this time. Sierra fidgeted with her hands nervously.

"Maybe we should just go?" Sierra offered.

"He's here." Rose told her. "He's probably just asleep."

Rose knocked a third time, harder still. "Squeak!" He yelled out, thinking that he might get a response if he could make Tune believe it was one of his friends at the door. "Squeak, it's me. I really need you man. Come to the door."

Sierra thought for sure things were going to turn out bad now. Rose was trying to pretend he was a friend.

Knowing that Sierra didn't understand his approach, Rose whispered to her, "When you don't have a warrant, you get them to open the door the best way that you can."

Sierra forced a smile. She was finding out firsthand that a detective had to be just as slick as the people they were trying to find. Rose was about to knock again when his tactic paid off.

A voice from within the house called out. "I'm coming damn it. Quit banging on my door."

Rose looked at Sierra and winked. Every chance he got to show the rookie how real detective work went, he reveled in it. Sierra gave him a slight head nod to let him know that she was aware that his little technique worked. She was still apprehensive though, as the man on the inside unlocked the locks. When he swung the door open, a cloud of white smoke rushed out of the house and hit Rose and Sierra in the face, on its journey to blend in with the cool night air.

Rose encountered the smoke and gagged.

Sierra encountered the smoke and inhaled. "Good ol' weed." She thought.

Behind the cloud of smoke was Anthony Tune. Tune was a 5 '8 dark skinned black man with tattoos covering his entire body. His many stints in the Texas penitentiary had left him scarred, tattooed, and muscular. He wasn't wearing anything except a pair of white boxers, white socks, and black house shoes. When his eyes focused in on Rose and Sierra, the blunt that was in his mouth fell to the floor.

"ONE TIME!" He yelled out, as he turned around and sprinted full speed down the long hallway toward the back of the building.

He was moving so fast that his house shoes came flying off of his feet.

"Wait!" Rose darted into the home and ran full speed after Tune through the house.

"ONE TIME! ONE TIME! ONE TIME!" Tune kept screaming as he ran.

Not knowing what to do, Sierra just stood there. Tune made a beeline for the backdoor and shot off into the night.

"Come back here!" Rose called after him.

The hallway led directly to the back, so Sierra saw when they exited the building. Realizing that Rose might need her assistance, Sierra pulled out her sidearm and stepped into the house. She didn't make it far before she noticed a completely naked woman come tiptoeing out of one of the side rooms with a brown duffle bag in her hands.

Sierra raised her pistol. "Freeze!"

The naked lady looked at her, dropped the bag, and raised her hands up. "Don't shoot. It's not mine."

As Rose chased Tune down the alley, he thought, "What the hell is wrong with this guy?"

Hoping to get Tune to stop running, Rose shouted after him, "I'm not here to arrest you, Tune." I just want to talk."

Tune didn't slow down one bit. "Fuck you, pig."

Tune turned and jumped over a chain-link fence.

"Why do they always start zig-zagging?" Rose asked himself as he cleared the fence, still in hot pursuit.

Sierra made the woman put her clothes on and sit back down on the bed. With her gun still aimed at the woman, Sierra used her free hand to unzip the duffle bag. "Ooohhh. So ya'll selling marijuana up in here, huh? That's why he ran?"

Sifting through the bag, she counted off, "One... two... three... What is this? About 5 pounds?"

"Officer, look." The lady pled. "Ain't none of this mine. Anthony is just my boyfriend. I swear to you. None of this is mine. I don't even live here"

Sierra looked down at the weed. "He's just your boyfriend, huh? Well, what were you about to do with these drugs?"

"I'm sorry." The lady began to fake cry. She was trying hard to force out a few tears. "Anthony just always told me that if the police ever showed up while I was here, that he was going to run to distract them, and I was supposed to get rid of the stuff. It was stupid, I know, but I was just trying to..."

"Ok. Ok." Sierra said, cutting her off. "No need to cry about it. Just answer me one question. Do you want to go to jail today?"

The woman rocked back and forth on the edge of the bed. "No ma'am. I can't go to jail, Officer. I have children. Please don't lock me up."

"Alright then. Here's what we're going to do."

Tune was starting to get tired. He figured he ran long enough for April to get away with all of the weed. If he hadn't, too bad. Rose watched as Tune stopped abruptly and then laid face down on the ground and put his hands behind his back.

"Ok." Tune yelled. "I give up. Don't shoot."

Rose closed the gap between himself and Tune. He was breathing heavily as he knelt down and placed his handcuffs on him. The man's actions upset Rose. He chased the dude for about two and a half blocks, only to have him surrender. Rose concluded then and there that Anthony Tune was indeed just as crazy as his police record implied.

Helping the now handcuffed Tune to his feet, Rose asked, "Why in the hell did you run, man?"

Tune took a couple of deep breaths. "I got warrants."

Rose thought back to when he looked Tune up in the computer. "No, you don't."

Tune looked back over his shoulder as Rose walked him back to his house. "I don't? Damn, my bad, homie. I thought I did."

Rose shook his head. They both did all of that running for nothing. Rose wanted to do his questioning back inside of the house, so he led Tune back in silence.

After they made it within a block of the house, Tune broke the silence by asking, "If I don't have any warrants, what did you come knocking on my door for?"

"All I wanted to do was ask you a few questions."

"Shiiit. I don't answer questions from cops. I ain't neva been no snitch."

Rose sighed loudly. He expected this type of response. No one ever willingly talked to the police. Especially a detective. He was pretty good at getting people to talk though. It was something like an art form. All he needed to do was offer them some type of incentive and seeing how Rose smelled marijuana back at the house, and how Tune had evaded arrest, he thought that he could easily find a way to get him to talk.

When Rose and Tune made it to his backyard, they saw Sierra standing in the back door holding a brown duffle bag.

Tune's heart sank. "April ran off and left the weed." He thought.

Sierra held the bag up and swung it from side to side. "Look what I found, partner."

Tune thought about going back to the penitentiary. "Fuck that shit. That bag ain't mine."

Rose cocked one of his eyebrows up and grinned. His instincts told him that he had just ran across a much better bargaining chip then the threat of an evading arrest charge.

Sierra laughed to herself. "That's funny. Your girlfriend said the exact same thing."

Once they were all back inside of the house, Rose sat Tune down on the couch in the living room.

"So." Rose said to Sierra. "What's that?"

Instead of answering, she opened the duffle bag and dumped out the contents onto the floor in front of Tune. Tune watched as two ziplocked pounds of weed tumbled to the floor. He looked at it strange. "Maybe April couldn't get away with all of it." He thought. "Well, at least she tried." Tune knew that getting caught with two pounds was better than getting caught with five pounds.

Rose looked at the marijuana and picked the bags up off the floor. "Hmmm. Looks like regular grass to me. There's no laws against saving grass in Ziplock bags."

Both Sierra and Tune looked at him as if he were crazy. It was obvious what was in the bags.

"Now." Rose said, pulling up a chair in front of Tune. "Back to the reason why I'm here. They call you Squeak, right?"

Tune turned away. "I told you, man. I don't talk to the police."

Rose slapped his forehead as if he just had a revelation. "Damn. I made a mistake. This isn't grass." He lifted one of the bags of weed up to his face and inhaled. "This is... this is... Naw, it can't be. I know a man that has already been to the penitentiary four times is not in possession of illegal marijuana. It can't be. This has got to be regular grass. It can't be marijuana. It just can't be."

Sierra couldn't help but to smile when she realized what Rose was doing.

Rose looked Tune directly in his eyes. "They call you Squeak, right?"

Tune looked from Rose, to Sierra, to the bags of weed. He weighed his options. Going back to prison was not something that he wanted to do. Especially not over a weed case.

Tune hung his head and let out a long sigh. "Yeah, man. They call me Squeak. Why?"

Rose glanced at Sierra. Once again, he was able to get the results that he wanted. Sierra did good by finding that marijuana. He wondered how she knew where to look. He figured he'd ask her later.

"Well," Rose began, turning his attention back to Tune, "I have a problem. See, there's been this guy named Squeak going around doing all sorts of things these past few days. Bad things. I mean, really bad things."

Tune adjusted how he was sitting to get some of the pressure off of his wrists. The handcuffs Rose had placed on him kind of hurt. They were too tight.

"Come on, man." Tune pled. "I sell weed. That's all. Whoever said I was out there troubling your streets is lying. I don't get down like that no more."

Rose nodded his head. "Oh, I believe you. I know it wasn't you. I have a picture of the guy. Thing is, he goes by the name Squeak too. So, I got to wondering if maybe you knew him."

Tune frowned up. "Just because we got the same tag don't mean we're friends."

Rose tossed the bags of weed onto Tune's lap. "I want you to think really hard, Tune. The guy is about 25-30 years old, brown skinned, and maybe 6ft tall with a medium build. Maybe he's someone you brought up in the streets and he just adopted your alias. Or maybe he's your son. Who knows?"

When Rose mentioned Tune's son, his mind instantly went back to his junior. Anthony Tune Jr. He called him Squeak all through childhood too. It had been so long since he had any contact with him though. Every now and then the streets would bring him word on how his daughter and son were doing. Neither one of them wanted anything to do with him. He couldn't blame them either. The things he put them through coming up were horrific. Tune wasn't surprised that Squeak finally did something so bad that the police came knocking on his door.

Tune thought it over. Even though Squeak didn't fuck with him anymore, he couldn't help the police track him down. It just wouldn't be right. Tune once again laid eyes on the two pounds of weed in his lap. On the other hand, he couldn't see himself going back to jail either.

"Life comes with choices." He thought to himself.

Rose sat back and watched Tune's expression. He could tell that he knew who Squeak was. Rose hoped the threat of prison was enough. The longer Tune took to think, the better Rose felt. If he was adamant about not telling them what he knew, he would've professed it by now. Experience taught Rose that prolonged silence meant they were trying to find a way to justify breaking the code of the streets. When really all it boiled down to was self-preservation. Not many people would sacrifice themselves for another person.

Tune licked his lips. "The Squeak you're looking for... he's my son."

"Bingo!" Rose thought.

Tune nervously moved around on the couch. "But that doesn't mean I know where he is now." He added, trying to somewhat hold out.

Rose tried to read his expressions, but he couldn't. It wasn't uncommon for a person in the streets to lose complete touch with their parents. Something told him that Squeak's father could tell him more then what he said though.

"Look." Sierra said, stepping in. "We already know about this war that's going on, and we already know that your son is the hitman for Infamous." She went and stood directly in front of Tune and leaned over in his face. "So, believe you me, we'll find him. The only thing you have to ask yourself is will you already be keeping the cell warm for him when he gets there."

"I already told you." Tune replied. "I don't know where he is."

Sierra grabbed him by his arm and lifted him off the couch. "Fine. It makes no difference to me."

Tugging him towards the front door she called back to Rose. "Pick up that evidence partner."

Tune got frightened. "Wait a minute. What are you doing?"

Sierra rolled her eyes. "Sending you back to prison. What do you think?"

Tune stopped her before they made it to the front door. "Ok. Ok. I'll tell you what I know."

Sierra looked back at Rose with the same smug look that he had been giving her whenever he did something right. Rose, who was confused as to what she was doing until just then, liked what he saw.

"You didn't hear this from me." Tune began.

Sierra nodded her head.

"Like I told you. I have no idea where he is at these days, but I do know something about his boss, Infamous. He has his main headquarters in the back of the On Point Barber Shop. Not many people know about it, but I do. Now, don't get me wrong. I'm not saying that you can just barge up in there and start asking questions. That's a good way to get yourself killed. I'm sure though, that if you watch that barber shop long enough, you'll eventually see my son show up."

Sierra looked at Rose to see if that was good information or not. Rose dropped the bags of marijuana and unlocked the handcuffs. Then, he dangled them in front of Tune's face.

"One more thing." He said. "What's your sons real name?"

Tune looked at Rose and rubbed his wrists where the handcuffs had been. Then he said, "His name is the same as mine. Anthony Tune Jr."

As they headed out the door, Sierra let him know that they appreciated his cooperation. Tune followed them to the front door and watched as they got in their car and drove away. There were several people lurking around in the streets watching them drive away too. Tune knew that he would have a whole lot of explaining to do. The police had just raided his weed house, and nobody went to jail.

Tune thought, "The good thing is no one would ever guess the real reason why they had shown up."

Everyone knew that he no longer had contact with his son. Tune shut the door. Really, he lost contact with all of his children years ago. Thinking about his kids, his wife that passed away, and all of the mistakes he made, Tune walked into his room and picked up the picture he had sitting on the nightstand. Taking a deep breath, he reminisced about the family that he lost.

....

As Rose was driving back towards the station, he commended Sierra on her interrogation skills. "I like how you made him tell us where we could find his son."

Sierra smirked. "I learned from the best. I was just following your lead. Once I saw that he was willing to talk in exchange for his freedom, I exploited it."

Rose couldn't help but laugh. He realized that Sierra caught on quick.

Becoming serious, Sierra asked, "Hey Rose. Can I ask you a question?"

Rose glanced at her. "Shoot."

"Was it right to know that Tune had those drugs inside of his house and not arrest him because he answered our questions?"

Rose thought it over before he answered. He knew where she was coming from. In the academy they teach you to uphold the law at all cost. You even have to take an oath. It's hard for all rookies when they come into the knowledge that there is a lot of gray area in real police work.

Rose chose his words carefully. "Have you ever heard of the phrase, 'The lesser of two evils'?"

Sierra nodded.

"It's kind of like that. Except it's the greater of two evils. True, selling or possessing marijuana is wrong, but murder for hire is far worse. Our main goal in this investigation is to get these killers off the streets and bring a stop to this war. Now, if we have to let a two-bit weed pusher off the hook in order to do our job, then so be it. I mean, it's not right, but the end justifies the means."

Sierra sat back in her seat and let what Rose just told her sink in. After she analyzed the situation, she concluded that if the information they received could actually help them bring down Squeak and topple Infamous, it was worth immunity for Tune.

"I understand." She told him. "But, if the information he gave us doesn't turn up anything, I'm going back to bust his ass."

Rose laughed at how gung-ho Sierra was. He had no idea that she was just talking trash. Rose thought she was serious. Sierra, on the other hand, couldn't really see herself taking one of the weed men off the streets. People in Texas City needed to get high. Life is too stressful to be forced into facing it sober.

"Look." Rose said, as he made a right turn onto the street that the police station was on. "It's too late to go on a stakeout at On Point, so we are going to have to follow up on that lead tomorrow."

Rose pulled into the parking lot of the station. "In the meantime, you can make your usual rounds and we'll go watch that barbershop tomorrow."

Sierra didn't want to get out of the car. She knew that she still needed to go talk to the Chief's wife. Her only problem was that she didn't know how to bring it up without alerting Rose to her real intentions. Rose parked next to Sierra's cruiser. Turning off the ignition, Rose glanced at Sierra and could tell that she had something on her mind.

"What's wrong?"

Sierra's mind was racing for a way to bring it up, but she was drawing a blank.

"Fuck it." She thought. "I'll come up with something later."

"Nothing is wrong." She said, opening the door.

Rose felt as if she was lying, but if she didn't want to talk about it, so be it. "Well, ok then."

The both of them climbed out of the car and began walking towards the entrance to the building. When they made it to the glass doors, Sierra stopped.

"I'll meet you inside."

Then, she turned around and started walking back towards the parking lot. Rose watched her for a moment before disappearing into the station. When Sierra reached her cruiser and Rose's Crown Victoria, she looked back to make sure that she was alone. Not knowing if anyone was on their way outside or not, she hurried up and opened her driver's side door. Scanning the parking lot one last time, she dropped down to her hands and knees and peered underneath Rose's vehicle. Finding what she was looking for, she reached under his car and peeled off the 3 bags of weed that she had stashed under there.

"It's still here." She proclaimed, smiling. "I thought for sure that it would get knocked off on the ride back up here."

Sierra quickly transferred the 3 pounds of marijuana from underneath Rose's car to under the seat of her cruiser. She figured she could drop it off at her house while she was on patrol later on that night.

She closed the door. "I appreciate you, Tune. This should last me for months."

Then she laughed out loud as she made her way inside the station.

Chapter Eleven

It had been 2 full days since Squeak was approached by Adriana in the mall and he still had not been able to get her out of his mind. He didn't know why. Maybe it was the fact that she was listening to him have sex with Shonda. Or maybe it was just because he had not had a woman, period, besides Shonda and his mother his entire life. Either way, he really wanted to use the number that she gave him. Squeak held the phone in his hand and looked around the room. Shonda was gone on a reconnaissance mission of sorts. He sent her to stake out Sticks home so that they could figure out a way to snatch one of his little boys. Infamous knew that this new job was a pretty tall order, so Squeak had some time before he was expected to deliver. Kidnapping and murder were two totally different things.

Squeak tossed the phone up and caught it. The best time to get at her would be while Shonda was gone. Squeak weighed his options.

"Fuck it." He began dialing the number she gave him. "You only live once."

....

Adriana was driving down the street talking to her husband's sister. "I'm on my way over there right now, girl."

"Well hurry up." Her sister-in-law urged. "I can't smoke all of this by myself."

Beep-Beep.

Adriana's phone beeped.

"Hold on girl. I got somebody calling me on the other line."

Adriana clicked over.

"Hello." She answered.

"Ummm. May I speak to Adriana Martin please?"

Adriana frowned up. She didn't recognize the voice and they were asking for her by using her full name. Only bill collectors and scammers did that.

"Who is this?" She asked, slightly nervous.

Squeak quickly remembered that he didn't get to introduce himself the other day. "This is Ant. We met the other day in The Mall of The Mainland."

Adriana tried to recall who she gave her number too. Then, it hit her.

"Ooohhh. The guy from Behind Closed Doors?"

"Yeah." Squeak answered, glad that she remembered him. "The one from the dressing room."

Adriana's pussy instantly got hot at the mention of the dressing room. Memories of how he made the woman he was with moan and squeal in ecstasy still had the power to turn her on. It had been so long since she was made to cry out because of the pleasure delivered to her nether regions, that she was just about ready to burst.

"So, the mystery man's name is Ant?"

"That's what they call me."

Squeak was a little apprehensive about telling her his real name. The majority of his life was spent in the underworld. People that knew him by Squeak knew him as a ruthless, no nonsense individual. If Adriana heard about him around the way, he didn't want to run her off before they had the chance to really get to know each other.

Adriana's sister-in-law sat on the phone and kicked her feet up on her couch. "What the hell is taking so long?" She mumbled to herself.

Adriana left her on hold for what seemed like an eternity. Just when she was about to hang up, Adriana clicked back in.

"Biiitttccchhh!" She squealed like a schoolgirl. "Guess who that was."

Her sister-in-law rolled her eyes. "I don't care if that was the King of Zamunda. Don't leave me on hold like that no more."

Adriana ignored the attitude. "Remember that dude I told you about from the mall? Well, that was him. He wanna come over to your house with me and smoke with us."

Her sister-in-law thought about it. "Are you talking about that nigga who was fucking the shit out of his girlfriend in that dressing room?"

Adriana got turned on again. "Yes, girl. Yes!" She exclaimed. "I told you I was gone get him."

Her sister-in-law laughed. "Well, you know the rules. If I let you fuck around on my brother, you gotta share the dick."

Now it was Adriana's turn to laugh. "Come on now, girl. When have you ever known me to be stingy with a man? I don't love 'em, I just fuck 'em. I already got my soulmate. Terrance just been bullshitting lately."

………………..

Squeak was more nervous than he had been in a long time. To a certain extent, he was a little anti-social. The prospect of going out with some woman he just met and chilling with her and her sister-in-law scared him. For one, he had no idea that Adriana was married, and if she was married, what did she want with him? Squeak decided to just play it by ear. Shonda had the Cavalier, so he gave Adriana directions to his house. He only hoped that he could leave, hang out for a while, and come back before Shonda returned.

Squeak figured that Adriana must just want him for a friend if she's already married. On the other hand, people cheat on their significant others every day. As Squeak thought about what he should wear, he pondered whether he should try to have sex with her or not. It wasn't long before Squeak heard a horn blowing outside.

"Damn." He thought. "She must have already been in the neighborhood."

Squeak took a deep breath and walked out the front door. He was surprised to see Adriana parked in front of his house in an all-black Yukon. Either her or her husband had some change. That was obvious.

Squeak made his way over to the passenger side of the car and opened the door.

"Hey boo." Adriana sang out.

"Shiit. What it do, lil mama?" He replied, trying to shake off the butterflies that were fluttering around in his stomach.

Adriana had the A.C. up so high that the entire car was feeling like an ice box.

"What took you so long to call me?" She asked, after Squeak shut the door and she pulled off.

"To be honest, I normally don't just meet women like this and just go out with them."

Adriana thought about the female he was having sex with is the dressing room. "Oh yeah? That dark-skinned lady is your girlfriend, huh? You had to find time to get away?"

"Oh... uh... yeah." Squeak lied.

He knew that Shonda wasn't his girlfriend, but after he gave it a second thought, he didn't want to give her the real reason it took so long for him to call. He didn't want to appear scared.

"I can understand that." Adriana said. "I be trying to find time to get from under my old man, too."

Squeak looked at her unsure of how to respond. She picked up on his discomfort and scolded herself silently for mentioning his girlfriend and her husband. The last thing people wanted to think about when they were about to go outside of their relationship for passion, is the person that they are in a relationship with.

"But say though," she added, trying to fix the damage she might've caused. "For the rest of the day, let's not mention the people that we're with. You focus on me, and I'll focus on you."

With that, Adriana reached her right hand over to Squeaks lap and rubbed up and down his thigh. He knew then that she wasn't trying to just be his friend.

"O...k." He said, stuttering a little.

Adriana cut her eyes at him. To her, he seemed a little intimidated by her. "Oh yeah." She told herself. "Me and my sis-in-law gonna have some fun with you."

The two of them made small talk for the remainder of the ride. During the conversation, Adriana made sure to complain about how long it was since she was satisfied sexually. Squeak sat in the passenger seat absorbing every word. From the topics of conversation alone he was aroused the entire ride. The way that Adriana was dressed didn't make it any better either. She was wearing a pink t-shirt that hugged her breast erotically. The jeans she had on were pink also and her tennis shoes were white and pink. Squeak didn't know why, but Adriana made that pink look extravagant.

He only saw her twice, and both times she was dressed so nice that he didn't even care about her weight problem. Not that he had a problem with heavy women or anything, but the way she carried herself made her sexy. He was cutting for her attitude also. Adriana was Hispanic, but she spoke like a black girl. Squeak liked that because he was more accustomed to black women than any other race. He was more relaxed around her because of how she carried herself. Squeak looked out the window as they pulled up in front of an all-white house.

"This is our stop." Adriana informed him.

Squeak looked at the residence. "Your sister-in-law lives here?"

"Yep." She answered, climbing out of the S.U.V.

Squeak followed her lead and got out of the vehicle. He Looked at the old Christmas lights hanging up, and thought, "She must be lazy."

The two of them made it to the front door and Adriana knocked.

"Come in." A female voice yelled out.

Adriana opened the front door and entered the house. Squeak followed right behind her. Once inside, Squeak noticed a bright skinned female sitting on a black leather couch with her feet up on the cushions. She was wearing a pair of gray jogging pants and a white t-shirt. Squeak noticed that she had a Bible laying on a tabletop in the middle of the living room. He wondered if she was religious.

Adriana did the honors of introducing everyone.

"Ant." She said, speaking to Squeak. "This is my sis-in-law, Sierra. Sierra, this is my new friend, Ant."

Sierra sat up straight on the couch when she saw Squeak. Squinting at him, she asked, "Have we met?"

Squeak had no idea what she was talking about. He didn't know her.

"You look really familiar." Sierra added.

"Naw." Squeak told her. "You got me mistaken with someone else."

Sierra hit the blunt she was holding and then passed it to Adriana.

"You know what they say." Adriana offered. "Everybody has a twin."

Sierra exhaled slowly and tried to remember where she knew him from. "Ant... Ant." She thought. The name didn't ring a bell, but the face did. Everyone in the room just sat quietly for a moment. Adriana was worried that maybe the two of them use to fuck around.

"Maybe I'm tripping." Sierra finally said.

Happy that she left the issue alone, Adriana sat down on the other couch with Squeak seated right next to her.

"Ya'll wait right there." Sierra said, getting up and heading to the back.

While she was gone, Adriana rubbed Squeak's leg. "Relax boo." She urged him. "I don't bite."

Squeak laughed it off, but he was still trying to figure out where Sierra knew him from. For the life of him, he couldn't place her face. Deciding to forget about it, he took the blunt from Adriana and puffed on it. After he got some weed in his system, he felt more comfortable.

Referring to Adriana's hand on his lap, he said, "You might want to watch out before you start something that you can't finish."

Her eyes lit up. "Now you're talking, daddy." She said, letting her hand slide all the way up to Squeak's crotch. "Trust me. I can finish anything that I start."

When she encountered his member, her eyes got big. "Is that all you?" She cooed.

Squeak was about to respond when Sierra came out of the back with a Ziplock bag full of weed and a 50 box of cigars. Dropping it down on Squeak's lap, she said, "I provide the weed, Adriana breaks it up, and you can roll it up, Ant."

Adriana eyed the weed suspiciously. "Where did you get all of that from?"

Sierra waved a finger from left to right. "Now you're worried about a little too much. Just know that I have my ways."

Squeak picked the bag up and looked at it. "This is close to a pound." He thought.

Then, tossing the weed to Adriana, he said, "You heard the lady. Gone break that shit down."

Adriana rolled her eyes, but at the same time, she was turned on by Squeak emerging from his shell a little bit. Pulling the glass table close to her, Adriana pushed the Bible to the side and dumped out some of the weed onto the tabletop. As she picked apart the buds with her hands, Sierra sat back down and turned her attention to Squeak.

"So, Ant. Tell me a little about yourself.

"There's really not too much to tell." He replied.

"Sure there is." Sierra pressed. "You got any brothers or sisters?"

Squeak fidgeted in his seat. He was being made uncomfortable by all of the questions. He didn't like talking about his personal business. Yet and still, he didn't want them to think he had something to hide.

"Well, I have one big sister and I had one little brother."

Adriana looked up from what she was doing. "What do you mean, 'had'?"

Squeak shook his head. "It's a long story."

Sierra looked at her wrist as if she was wearing a watch. "We got nothing but time. Seeing how slow Adriana breaking down that weed, it's gone be about 3 hours before another blunt get put in the air."

"Bitch please." Adriana smacked her teeth.

Squeak leaned back in his seat. It had been so long since he thought about what his father did to his little brother. He tried to come up with reasons not to talk about it, but Adriana and Sierra were persistent. They begged and pleaded until Squeak finally conceded to tell them the story.

Making a disclaimer, he said, "It's not the kind of story you think."

As Squeak began to paint them the picture, using fake names, his own mind summoned the memories. Squeak could remember back when he was only 6 years old and Shonda was 7. Their parents had one other child then. A boy named Richard. Richard was only 5 years old at the time. Squeak could recall that this was after the sexual, physical, and mental abuse of Shonda and himself had begun. Their father was an alcoholic and he would come home drunk and raise hell over any little thing that he thought was wrong. The night that he lost his brother was one such night.

"Laina!" Tune called out, as he burst through the front door with a 40-ounce Olde English glued to the palm of his hand.

Squeak, Shonda, and Richard were all playing in the living room when he came in. Storming past the children without acknowledging them, Tune went on the hunt for his wife.

"LAINA!" He screamed again, with so much anger in his voice it was almost tangible.

Squeak, Shonda, and Richard all exchanged nervous glances. This wasn't the first time their father came home in this manner. Actually, it was normal for him to act this way. History told them what was about to happen. The alcohol was about to pick a fight with Laina, and she wasn't going to back down. That's one thing the kids never understood. Their mother was no match for their father, but she always stood up to him.

"Laina!" He called out again, entering their bedroom.

Laina was sitting on the edge of the bed watching TV.

"Laina, why in the hell didn't you answer me?"

Laina looked up as Tune crossed the room and she wasn't the least bit afraid. She knew what was coming next, and she didn't care.

"Anthony." She replied. "I am not in the mood for your shit tonight."

Tune's bloodshot eyes got huge. He raised up his free hand and slapped Laina off the bed.

"Woman!" He hollered, hovering over her. "Don't you EVER disrespect me like that."

Laina grabbed the side of her face. The blow stung like hell. She rolled over onto her back and said through clenched teeth, "You... bastard!"

Then, with all of her might, she kicked Tune directly in his crotch. He instantly dropped the 40-ounce and keeled over. Hearing him cry out in pain encouraged her to keep going. While Tune held his groin and rolled around on the floor, Laina jumped to her feet and picked up the 40-ounce.

"You... don't disrespect... ME!" She declared, as she swung the bottle and struck Tune in the side of his face.

"Aaauuuggghhh!!!" He cried out, as the bottle shot waves of pain throughout his entire head.

Laina looked at the bottle. She had expected it to break, but it didn't. Realizing it was still a good weapon, she drew back and swung it again. Tune did his best to block the blow with his arms. He'd rather get hit in the arms than the head again.

By now, the kids made it into the room, and they were watching the fight. Richard was jumping up and down.

"Get him, mommy! Get him, mommy!" He kept chanting.

He liked it when Laina would get the best of Tune. Really, they all did. Richard just didn't care if Tune knew it. Squeak and Shonda were afraid to go against their father. When Laina heard Richard, she looked up.

Not wanting them to witness the beating, she urged them to leave. "Ya'll go back in the living room and play. Mommy is alright."

The momentary distraction was all Tune needed. Catching Laina off guard, he grabbed her ankle and pulled her leg out from under her. She dropped her weapon as she fell, and Tune climbed on top of her.

"Yeah, bitch." He said, regaining the upper hand.

"Get the fuck off of me." Laina screeched, trying in vain to get from under him.

Tune grabbed her by her hair and punched her hard. "Shut-up." He spat out.

The punch almost knocked her out. She instantly became dizzy. Tune noticed he done some damage and laughed. Looking in horror, Richard was fed up with Tune beating Laina. He crept up behind him and picked up the bottle that Laina dropped. Then, doing what he saw his mother do, he gripped the bottle with both hands and swung.

Clunk!

It connected against the back of Tune's head. The bottle didn't hurt though. Richard was too young to make the lick count. Tune backhanded Richard to the ground.

"You little bastard." He called out, as Richard began to cry.

Tune reached out to grab him, but Richard scooted out of the way. Then, Richard leaped to his feet and ran full speed out of the room.

Laina became enraged and shrieked. "You hit my baby."

"Fuck yo' baby." Tune shot back.

Laina couldn't get free to hit him, so she did the next best thing. Gathering all of the loose saliva in her mouth, she spat the biggest loogie she could muster up, right in his face. Squeak and Shonda took in a deep breath. Tune continued to hold her by the hair with one hand and he slowly wiped off the spit with the other.

"No... the fuck... you didn't." he slurred.

Laina glared at him with hate in her eyes. "Yes... the fuck... I did."

Tune stood to his feet and drug Laina kicking and screaming by her hair over to the dresser.

"Bitch, I'll kill you for that shit."

Laina struggled to get free. "Let... me...go... Anthony!"

Tune heard her loud and clear, but he had no plans on complying. Instead, he reached into the dresser and pulled out a .38 snub nose revolver.

"You spit in my face?"

Then, he hit her in the head with the gun and knocked her down. When Laina realized he was holding his gun, she became frightened.

"Please Anthony." She begged. "Not in front of the kids."

Tune pointed the pistol at her and smiled. "Oh. Now Miss Bad Ass wants to beg?"

Tune laughed out loud. Squeak and Shonda were frozen in terror. They were so deep in shock by what they were witnessing that they almost didn't notice Richard running past them with a kitchen knife in his hand. To Squeak, everything from that point on seemed like it happened in slow motion. Laina had her arms outstretched trying to block a bullet. Tune stood over her laughing at her fear.

Richard rose the knife over his head and yelled, "Leave my mommy alone."

Before anyone could react, Richard had buried the blade deep into the thigh of Tune.

"Aaauuuggghhh!" He cried out.

Acting on instinct, Tune spun around and the gun that he was holding went off. A single bullet erupted from the barrel and stuck Richard. The force of the hot lead knocked him back.

"NOOOOOO!" Laina screamed, as the bullet tore through Richards neck and sent blood spraying from the open wound.

Tune released her and she scrambled to him as his body collapsed. "MY BAAAAABY!"

Seeing his son laying there, motionless, sobered Tune up quick. He dropped the gun.

"What have I done?" He asked himself, looking at his hands.

Laina yelled. "Call 9-1-1! Please, call 9-1-1!"

....

Squeak could remember the ambulance and the police coming. His father went to prison, and his brother went to the hospital. After 3 years, his father came back, and his brother, Richard, never did.

Sierra and Adriana sat silent. They had no idea that the story of how he lost his younger brother would be so dramatic. Amazingly, Squeak stayed stone faced throughout the entire narrative. A spectator would never have guessed that he was not only thinking about his brother, but also the 10-year-old boy that he had to shoot. The situation with Burby's son made him ask a difficult question.

Am I just like my father?

Breaking the awkward silence, Adriana apologized. "We're sorry we made you tell us that story and relive that event."

Her voice brought Squeak back from his daydream. "Sorry? No need to be sorry. It's cool. It happened a long time ago. I've had enough time to get over it."

Neither Adriana nor Sierra knew how to respond. Squeak read their expressions and did his best to lighten the mood.

"Man, that's good enough." He said to Adriana. "I can work with that."

Squeak pulled out a pocketknife and began to cut open the cigars so that he could roll up the weed. When Sierra's phone began to ring, no one was upset. In fact, everyone appreciated the distraction. Adriana and Squeak talked about other drugs that they tried while Sierra went to answer the phone. It was sitting next to her computers keyboard, so she sat down in her swivel chair before lifting the receiver.

"Hello." She answered.

"Hey, Sierra." Rose replied on the opposite end.

Sierra sighed under her breath and leaned back in the chair. "What's going on, Rose?"

It seemed like ever since Rose had started having problems with his wife, he was calling Sierra more often and it was becoming annoying.

"Ain't much going on. I'm just at the house enjoying my day off. What's up with you?"

Rose was parked at the Donut Shop that sat diagonal from On Point Barber Shop. "The situation is the same out here. Squeak still hasn't shown up."

Sierra frowned. "You don't think Tune sent us on a wild goose chase, do you?"

Rose lifted the binoculars back up to his eyes. "You know what? At first, I did, but not anymore."

"And why is that?" She inquired, getting her hopes up.

Rose lowered the binoculars. "Two reasons. Reason number one, almost everyone I've seen go into that Barber Shop has been wearing red, and the ones that weren't wearing red weren't wearing blue neither. That's in line with what Tune was telling us about it being the headquarters for Infamous."

Rose paused to take a drag of his cigarette. "And reason number two, I didn't realize it until earlier today, but right on this street is where Jesse was killed."

Sierra rocked back and forth in her seat. "Who?"

"Jesse." Rose reiterated. "The man that got shot in the head by a man witnesses described as having dreadlocks."

Sierra thought about it for a few seconds before it hit her. "Oh yeah. I remember that. But, refresh my memory. Why is Jesse important again?"

Rose thought that he explained who Jesse was a few days ago, but apparently not. "Jesse was Infamous right-hand man."

Suddenly, it all made sense. It was logical to assume that Tune told the truth. Jesse was most likely murdered after leaving the barber shop. While Sierra sat on the phone with Rose, Adriana and Squeak had fired up one of the blunts. Adriana knew that she didn't have all day to try to get laid because she had to go home soon. She was desperately hoping that Squeak would make the first move, but he didn't. She wondered if he was holding back because Sierra was there. Finally, after waiting as long as she could wait, Adriana decided to open up the door herself.

"Ant." She said. "Do you know why I gave you my number?"

Squeak looked at her and shrugged his shoulders.

Adriana leaned in close to him and said, "I wanna fuck with you."

Squeak couldn't help but to think about her husband. Surely, she didn't mean that she was prepared to leave him for a guy she just met. She didn't even know anything about him.

"What do you mean by that?"

Adriana got a little frustrated. She thought it was self-explanatory.

"I want to put you in this pussy." She thought.

Adriana tried to find a way to say what she meant without coming off as a hoe. "When I say I wanna fuck with you," she said, straddling him on the couch. "I mean I wanna... fuck... with you."

She emphasized the word 'fuck' by gyrating her hips on top of him. Squeak looked around her at Sierra, who was still on the phone. He got the message loud and clear this time, but he wondered what Sierra would say if she caught them getting so close on her living room couch.

Adriana turned around and followed his gaze to Sierra. "Awww. She ain't nobody. To be honest, she wants to...fuck... with you too."

Squeaks stomach instantly balled up into knots. He wondered what he stumbled up on. Wiping his now sweaty palms off on his pants, he didn't know what to say or what to think.

"You bullshittin'." He managed to stammer out.

"Bullshittin'?"

To Adriana, it sounded like a challenge.

"I don't bullshit, baby."

She seductively climbed off of his lap and began to unbuckle his pants. Squeak watched in awe as she pulled his flaccid penis out of his boxers and started lightly stroking it. His eyes shot from Adriana's hand to the back of Sierra's head. He wanted to tell her to stop, but at the same time, he wanted to beg her to continue. The blood was beginning to rush into his manhood, and it felt good.

"Damn, Ant. You gone hurt somebody with this thing. It's like a big black snake."

Shonda always told Squeak that he had a really big dick, but he didn't know for sure. After all, he never went out of his way to check out other men, so he didn't have anything to compare himself to. He figured if Adriana was telling him that he had a nice package too, it must be true.

Squeak puffed on the weed.

"Mmmm." Adriana moaned. "I gotta taste you."

With that, she lowered her head and wrapped her lips around Squeaks now rock-hard tool.

"Shit." Squeak moaned, as Adriana began to bob up and down.

Adriana was something like an expert at giving head. She was a big girl, so she had to be. Squeak could feel his toes curling up in his shoes as Adriana sucked and slurped on him.

"Yeeeaaahhh." He encouraged her, as he used his free hand to grab a fistful of her long black hair. "Damn, girl. You good at that shit."

He closed his eyes and leaned his head back. Adriana actually liked the taste of dick. She liked the taste of cum even more, so she always tried extra hard to get a man off. Squeak kicked back as Adriana licked around the tip of his penis. Then, he felt her lick the tip and the shaft simultaneously.

"Uuuhh." He moaned, as the unexpected sensation made his entire body tingle.

Squeak picked his head up to see how she was accomplishing such a feat, and what he saw brought him to the brink of climax. Sierra had hung up the phone and came over to assist Adriana in servicing him. The two women were both hungrily licking up and down his entire penis. Their tongues were encountering each other, and they didn't mind. Squeak thought he was dreaming.

Sierra backed away from their shared meal and she grabbed Adriana by her hair. Forcing her to deep throat every inch Squeak had, Sierra said, "If you gone suck his dick, suck it right, girl."

Then, she guided Adriana's mouth up and down.

"Mmm-huh. Mmm-huh." Was all Adriana could mumble with her mouth as full as it was.

"Do you like that, Ant?" Sierra asked him.

"Hell yeah." Squeak answered. "Hell, yeah I like it."

Sierra licked her lips. "Do you wanna fuck her, Ant?"

Squeak could only nod. His voice turned into nothing more than a series of barely audible moans and groans.

Sierra yanked Adriana's mouth off of Squeaks throbbing member. "Take them clothes off." She ordered her.

Adriana complied as Sierra took over the job of sucking him. Adriana loved her sister-in-law to death. It was hard for her to get a man because of her size, but if she took the men to Sierra's house, everything would fall into place. Adriana got completely naked and stood in front of Squeak. He was so far gone by the level of ecstasy that the two women had created, he hardly noticed her folds of flesh.

Sierra stopped pleasuring Squeak with her mouth and said, "Let's take this to the bedroom."

Then, she led Squeak into the back by holding onto his penis and walking.

"These females are some freaks for real." Squeak thought.

Making it into the room, Sierra handed Squeak over to Adriana and she quickly undressed him.

"Come on, baby." She urged, climbing on top of the bed and getting on all fours.

Squeak got on his knees behind her and wasted no time guiding his meat inside of her hole. Adriana took in a deep breath as Squeaks manhood not only filled her up, but also stretched her walls in a way that her husband never could.

"Hell... fuck... yeah." Adriana squealed, as Squeak began to pump in and out of her. "I can feel it in my stomach."

Gripping the sheets tightly, Adriana was doing her best to maintain. Squeak could hear her, but his mind was in a totally different place. The heat that emanated from her goodies had his penis experiencing sensations that were all new to him. Sierra had pulled her swivel chair into the room so she could watch the action. As Squeak pounded away at Adriana, he heard a series of soft moans coming from the opposite side of the room.

Turning his head to investigate, he saw Sierra with her pants and panties off, and her legs gapped wide open. Squeak stroked Adriana more fiercely as he watched Sierra masturbating to his and Adriana's show. The room was dark, but he could still easily see Sierra's fingers sliding in and out of her wet pussy. When Sierra made eye contact with Squeak, she curled her lips back like an animal and bit at the air.

Squeak couldn't help but to start fantasizing about being inside of the much better-looking, Sierra. The rhythm of his stroke even changed as he became mesmerized by the sight of Sierra playing with herself. He started penetrated Adriana as deep as he could. Adriana buried her face in the bed and cried out into the sheets.

"I can take it! I can take it! I can take it!"

Squeak paid her no mind as he continued to pile drive Sierra in his mind. Sierra withdrew her fingers from her dripping wet pussy and inserted them into her mouth. She saw how Squeak was man-handling Adriana and she couldn't wait until she would have her turn with him. Squeak watched Sierra taste her own juices and lost all control. Before he knew it, his body was tensing up preparing to ejaculate.

Adriana heard him groan and felt his body jerk and she knew what was coming next. She crawled from in front of him and quickly turned around. This is what she was waiting on. Adriana began jacking Squeak off while she held her mouth open in anticipation of his cum. When Squeak finally released, his nut shot from his penis directly to Adriana's tongue. She did her best not to miss a single drop. The climax left Squeak exhausted. He laid down on the bed and took a few deep breaths.

Sierra walked over to him and rubbed him on his chest. "Yeah, daddy." She said. "Catch your breath. I don't want you half-steppin' when you get up in this pussy next."

Squeak looked up at the two women and thought, "With all the wrong I've done in my life, I still died and went to heaven."

Chapter Twelve

Rose looked at the time displayed on his cars radio. It was already 2:00 in the afternoon, and he had been watching On Point all day.

"I need a break." He told himself.

There had been zero signs of Squeak. Rose knew that if he was just patient enough, his diligence would eventually pay off. Not wanting to vacate his post for too long, Rose decided to just swing by his house and see how his wife was doing. Lately, they had been doing a little better, but his infidelity still disrupted the overall joy within his happy home.

Rose wasn't an ignorant man. He knew that he damaged the trust in his relationship, and trust could only be repaired with time. Cranking up his car and pulling off, Rose told himself that it would be a good idea to stop by the floral shop on his way home and buy Rebecca some carnations. He would've bought some roses, but they were played out. He couldn't count how many women received roses from Derrick Rose over the years. It was high time that he stepped his game up.

Feeling proud of himself, he turned onto his street with his flowers in his arm and smiling like a kid in a candy store with $100 to spend. He just knew that the spontaneous romance would do a lot to heal the wounds that his actions caused. His smile quickly transformed into a frown though. Through his windshield, he could see Rebecca standing in the doorway of their house, in her bathrobe, waving goodbye to some man driving away in a maroon colored Pontiac Sunbird.

Rose's heart sunk when his imagination told him of all the things that could've just happened. As he rolled up to his house, Rebecca looked in his direction and fear registered on her face. She jogged to the street trying to flag him down, but Rose didn't stop. Her actions had incriminated her enough to make him think the worse. There was only one reason for her to respond like that when he pulled up.

"She's cheating on me." He thought.

The realization hit him like a ton of bricks. He dished it out, but he sure couldn't take it. He didn't even look at Rebecca as he drove away. He was disgusted with her. His attention was now on this mystery man. Rose wanted to find out who he was and just what the hell was he doing at his house with his wife.

Speeding up so that he could follow the man from a comfortable distance, Rose made a mental note of the car's license plate. He knew that if he could get an address to go along with the license plate, he would more than likely be able to find out who this man was that was dipping in and out of his home while he was at work. Rose hadn't followed the man for two good blocks before Rebecca started blowing up his phone.

He looked at the name on the caller I.D. display and laughed. What was there to talk about? She had gotten her revenge. Now, the ball was back in his court. Rose tossed the phone in the passenger seat and allowed it to ring non-stop.

"I need a cigarette." He said, fishing one out of his pocket.

Rose nerves had become bad. His hand shook as he lit the Newport. Rose silently prayed that it was enough to ease his mind. Being honest with himself, he accepted that his pride was hurt more than his heart.

"How can Rebecca allow another man to enter her?" He thought.

Yeah, he had fucked Sierra, but men and woman were different. A man's wife isn't supposed to give up the goods no matter what the man does. Rose shook his head.

"Fuck!" He yelled, punching the steering wheel with his fist. He had no idea what he would do when the man stopped. More than likely he would just try to figure out who he was and then go from there.

Shock had only driven for about four blocks before he noticed an unmarked police car tailing him. Whenever he drove, he never continued on one set path. He made several unnecessary turns just for an occasion like this one. Shock knew that if any car followed his same route exactly, they had to be following him. He didn't know how long the cop had been behind him, but at this point it didn't even matter. The important thing was that he made him. Obviously, they were on to him. Shock wondered why he didn't just pull him over and get it over with.

"Maybe they're just watching me," he thought.

"Ok." Shock said out loud. "You wanna play? Let's play."

Rose watched the man raise a phone to his ear and he figured he was calling Rebecca. The game of cat and mouse had begun.

....

Back in Amburn Oaks, Sticks was lounging around the house with his family watching TV when his phone rang. Passing the apple flavored mini-blunt to his wife, Silvia, he answered the phone.

"We have a problem." Shock reported as soon as Sticks had said hello.

Sticks sat in silence while Shock filled him in on the situation.

Sticks listened to the description of the car. "That's Detective Rose. How does he know about you?"

"I have no idea." Shock replied. "What do you want me to do?"

Sticks thought about it for a minute. Rose couldn't have anything, or else he wouldn't be playing this little game of follow the leader. He must just be acting on a tip and hoping that Shock will lead him somewhere that will be useful in his investigation.

"I'll tell you what." Sticks began. "Don't panic. Just drive around until he gets tired of following you. If he had any reason to pull you over, he would've done it by now. He's just fishing. Hoping that something turns up."

"I got it, boss." Shock replied.

Then, they hung up. Shock was praying that Sticks would give him the green light to murk the pig.

Looking in his rearview mirror at Rose, Shock mumbled, "You got lucky this time cop, but the next time the hunter will become the hunted. I promise you that."

The only reason Shock allowed Rose to stay behind him this long was because he wasn't sure if he should lure him into a trap or not. Seeing that he wouldn't be able to get him during this round, he made provisions to shake him. Shock slowed down at the next light he came to and waited for it to turn yellow. Then, he hit the gas and turned left. Knowing that Rose would get held up by the red light, he used the head start to get out of dodge.

Rose shot off a string of curse words as he realized he lost his wife's lover. Thinking fast, he grabbed his notepad and jotted down the Sunbirds license plate number.

"If that vehicle is registered to you." He said. "I'll still be able to find out who you are."

When the light turned green, Rose tossed the flowers out the window and drove off. Rebecca had a lot of explaining to do.

....

Meanwhile, Sierra was walking around her house signing to herself as she got dressed. Adriana and Squeak had left 10 minutes ago, and she was feeling so satisfied it was a shame. When she got a piece of Adriana's new friend, she made sure she let him know that he was welcome whenever. It didn't matter if he came with Adriana or not. Squeak assured her that he would be returning for some more of her hospitality as soon as possible. She made him promise that he would.

Once Sierra was finished dressing, she went and looked herself over in the mirror.

"I could pass for a detective." She said, admiring her attire.

Sierra was wearing an all-white button-down dress shirt with a pair of black slacks. Her badge didn't read detective, but she hoped that no one would look at it that closely. She just clipped it onto her hip like she saw Rose wearing his and felt satisfied that it would do the trick.

Sierra finally gave up on trying to convince Rose to go question Bianca Burby. He was so caught up in catching Squeak that he developed tunnel vision. Sierra chalked it up to the fact that Squeak shot him some years ago and murdered his partner. He obviously wanted revenge. Sierra's mind was on that $20 million that police Chief Burby had stashed away somewhere. When she was at work the day before, she got an address for Bianca and decided to go question the woman herself.

Sierra smoothed out her shirt in the mirror and turned around in a circle.

"You are too fine." She complimented herself. "Now, let's go get paid."

Sierra walked out of the house, climbed in her Dodge Neon, and drove off.

....

Silvia followed Sticks from the living room to the bedroom. "Baby, what's wrong?"

She noticed that his entire attitude changed after he got off the phone with Shock.

"What's wrong?" He repeated, searching the walk-in closet for something to wear. "Shit is about to hit the fan! That's what's wrong."

Ever since this war began, Silvia was constantly on edge. She always wondered how long it would take before the carnage found its way to her doorstep.

"Well, what do you mean by that, Kenneth?" She asked, becoming frustrated.

Sticks grabbed a blue Makaveli branded t-shirt and a pair of blue Makaveli branded jeans.

"Long story short." He said, changing clothes. "Detective Rose is on to Shock. If he's on to Shock, he knows that Shock works for me. If he knows that Shock works for me, he can implement me in so much shit, I'll never see the light of day again."

Silvia tried to take it all in. It seemed like her whole world was crumbling around her and there was nothing she could do about it. She had no job, no money of her own, and two small children. If something were to happen to Sticks, she would be out of there. None of his money was legal, so all of it would be taken from her and confiscated by the state.

She walked on the heels of Sticks as he headed towards the front door. "So, what are you going to do?" She asked, desperate for some words of comfort.

Sticks opened the door and hesitated in the doorway. "There's only one thing I can do." He said, looking his wife directly in the eyes. "I have to get rid of Rose."

Silvia hugged herself as she watched Sticks climb in his H3 and speed away.

"This is getting totally out of control." She thought.

………………..

Bianca Burby didn't live in Texas City, so Sierra knew that she had a little travel time ahead of her. Bianca stayed about 1 ½ hours away in a small town called Hitchcock. As she drove, Sierra had the radio blasting. She was jamming that Mary J. Blige song called, The Breakthrough. Sierra couldn't sing, but in the privacy of her vehicle, it didn't even matter. She was hitting a high note along with Mary J. when her cell phone started ringing.

Slightly upset by the interruption, she turned down the volume of track number 5 and reached for her phone. The caller I.D. read 'unknown caller'. Sierra quickly became serious. There was only one person that showed up like that when they called. She turned the volume completely down and took a deep breath before answering.

"Hello." She answered.

"I thought we were in this together." The voice replied.

Sierra could tell that they were upset.

"Why didn't you tell me that you were going after Shock?"

"Whoa. Hold on a second." Sierra said. "Who is Shock, and what do you mean, 'I'm going after him?'"

The voice paused.

"Where are you?" They finally asked.

"I'm on my way to question the Chief's wife. You know? Still trying to find out about that money."

"Well, look. We won't deviate from the original plan, but I have another job for you."

Sierra wondered what could be going on.

"Another job?" She asked.

"Just listen." The voice directed her. "As we speak, your partner is following around a man named Shock. Shock is the hitman for the Hooligans. Now, I have no idea how Derrick Rose made the connection, but somehow, he has. This is not good. It's bad for both of us. So, here's what we're going to do."

Sierra paid close attention as the voice instructed her on how to handle the new development. She had no idea that Shock was the other hitman that they were searching for. Even more mysterious was how Rose found out. She wondered why he neglected to inform her. What also surprised her was her contacts protectiveness over Shock, now that she knew who Shock was.

At first, Sierra was going to refuse the new objective, but the raise in pay had changed her mind. She was using her police influence to help find the money for a $2 million cut. Now, her piece of the pie was being boosted up to $5 million. She couldn't be mad about that. Sierra couldn't wait until she found the money that Burby stashed so she could quit her job with the police force and retire at an early age. The things she was willing to do for the love of money bothered her at times, but she figured it would all be worth it when she was a millionaire, chilling with her feet kicked up on some far away island.

....

In his attempts to lose Detective Rose, Shock found himself in a part of town that he very rarely went through. He was on the Southside. To make matters worse, he was just forced to flee from an enemy. Shock hated to run. He was silently praying that he could run across a Villain or two that he could take his anger out on. Circling around for a while, trying to find something to get into, Shock turned on to Anderson St. When he passed by a green and white house surrounded by a chain link fence, the car parked in the driveway caught his eye. Shock slowed down and grinned like a chess cat. He couldn't believe his luck.

"FWM-9116." He said, reading the license plate number out loud.

Shock recognized the black Cavalier from the Mall of The Mainland the other day. He remembered that a Villain and his girlfriend drove the car. Shock made it to the stop sign at the end of the block and weighed his options.

"Should I, or shouldn't I?"

He knew that he wanted to go in the house, but he wondered if he should wait until later on that night. Darkness could be an assassin's best friend.

....

Shonda paced through the house with the phone attached to her ear. She had been trying to get in touch with Squeak ever since she got back from staking out Sticks' house. Shonda felt like she had the perfect idea of how to snatch one of the boys, but when she returned, Squeak was no longer there. When she called his phone, it would just ring and ring until the voicemail picked up. She knew that her brother could take care of himself, but still she was worried about him. Worry came with love. He never intentionally ignored her calls before, so something had to be distracting him.

Shonda heard the voicemail come on for the sixth time.

"Damn!" She said, hanging up. "Where the hell are you at, Squeak?"

Shonda was just about to press the redial button when she heard someone knocking on the front door. She rushed to the front, thinking that Squeak had come back, but he didn't have his key.

Swinging the door open, she shouted, "Where the hell have you..."

She stopped mid-sentence when the man at the door, who was defiantly not Squeak, pointed the barrel of a pistol at her forehead.

"Ooohhh, so aggressive." Shock mocked, in his raspy voice. "I like that in a person I'm about to kill."

....

Sierra arrived at the address that she had for Bianca Burby. Looking around bewildered, she said, "This can't be right."

Sierra double-checked the address.

It was correct.

The residence was just nothing like what she expected. The house was very small and painted an off-white color. Sierra could tell, even from the curb, that the house was originally white, but years of neglect had left it dirty looking. The only car in the driveway was a purple Mazda 626 that Sierra assumed belonged to Bianca.

"Well," Sierra said, examining herself one last time in the rearview mirror. "Here goes nothing."

Stepping out of her vehicle, Sierra adjusted her badge so that it would sit right on her hip and she approached the front door. She thought she had it all figured out how she would approach the conversation, but now she wasn't feeling so confident anymore. Her initial plan was to mention the money and see what Bianca had to say about it, but now she wasn't so sure that that was such a great idea. The less people that know about the money, the better. Besides, what if Bianca had a good idea where the money could be found, and she chose not to say anything?

As a last-minute decision, Sierra decided not to mention the money. Her best bet would be to try and get Bianca to offer some possible locations without even knowing it. Sierra stood at the front door and took a deep breath. A light gust of wind passed by and caused the metal chimes hanging from the edge of the roof to jingle. The somewhat musical tone of the hollow cylinders bumping into each other momentarily held Sierra's attention hostage.

She always wondered why people would have such things hanging up on their porches. To her, they looked tacky. But now, listening to the sound of one, in the situation that she was in, opened her mind to their true purpose. They were meant to soothe and relax. Not understanding how, but none the less feeling refreshed, Sierra knocked on the door. She wasn't left to wait long before a soft voice called from the inside.

"Just a minute."

Sierra adjusted her weight from one foot to the other and glanced up at the wind chime again. Its design was just like many other ones she had seen, only with one difference. The wind chime was nothing more than 5 small, hollow, metal cylinders attached to 5 pieces of string that became one as they reached the roof. In the center of the 5 cylinders were two flat metal circles keeping them from coming into contact with one another unless the wind was blowing. There was one string going through the centers of each circle. None of that, however, is what caused the wind chime to look slightly unique.

It was the metal piece hanging just below the two circles and out of the reach of the swinging cylinders that really caught her eye. Sierra squinted at it to get a better look. The piece was no bigger than 2 ½ inches in diameter and it was shaped like a heart. The design that was carved into it is what made it stand out though. Sierra cocked her head to the side and tried looking at it from a different angle. She wasn't able to make out what it was before the opening of the front door drew her attention. When the door swung completely open, Sierra found herself standing face to face with a smiling Bianca Burby.

Sierra was caught off guard by how pretty she was. Bianca Burby was a dark-skinned woman with strong facial features. Her petite frame was covered by an orange sundress. She only stood about 5"2 and weighed maybe 120lbs. Sierra wondered what could possibly have caused the Police Chief to separate from her.

"It's a golf course." Bianca said, before even asking who Sierra was.

"Excuse me?" Sierra stated, confused as to what Bianca was talking about.

Bianca used her head to point in the direction of the wind chime. "I saw you looking at it through the peephole. Everybody wonders what the design inside of the heart is."

Sierra looked up at it again. Now that she knew what she should see, she was able to see it. While Sierra was admiring the delicate hand that went into cutting out the design, Bianca was looking her up and down. When her eyes came to rest on the badge on her hip, she knew that this was not just a normal visitor.

"So," Bianca said, folding her arms across her chest. "What brings you by?"

Sierra quickly snapped back to the task at hand.

Extending her hand, she apologized for her rudeness.

"I'm sorry. My name is Detective Sierra Martin." She told her. "If you don't mind, I would like to ask you a few questions about your late husband, Police Chief Robert Burby."

Bianca had grown weary of answering questions about Robert. Sighing loudly to show her unwillingness to go over this again, she said, "He was a two-timing bastard who only cared about himself and he ended up getting just what he deserved."

Sierra was shocked by the level of detachment Bianca had to the whole thing. Even though they were separated, she still shouldn't be glad that he was gone, and even if she was, she still should be in some type of mourning for her son. Sierra fidgeted nervously. She wasn't ready to encounter this type of attitude. She was expecting a grieving mother and widow. Not sure how to proceed, Sierra simply decided to keep her talking and maybe something would come up.

"You say he was cheating on you?" Sierra asked, pulling out a pen and a pad as if she were going to write something down.

Bianca saw the notepad and guessed that the things she was saying was about to be on the record.

"Well," she answered, unfolding her arms. "I don't have any proof that he was sleeping around, but his actions told me that he was."

Sierra glanced up from her notepad.

"Mrs. Burby," she said. "Do you mind if we go inside and talk about this?"

Now, it was Bianca's turn to get nervous. One of the detectives who had previously questioned her insinuated that she might've had something to do with

Robert's murder. Of course, she didn't, but she knew firsthand how the police could sometimes twist the facts to make them fit any scenario that they came up with. Hell, she was married to the Chief of Police and he was probably as crooked as they could get.

Bianca didn't want to invite Sierra into her home, but she also didn't want it to appear as if she had something to hide. Reluctantly, she motioned for Sierra to follow her in.

Entering the home, Sierra realized that the inside was just as old looking as the outside. The two couches that sat along the walls in the living room could easily have been 25 years old. The cloth appeared to be knitted together over cushions that had the form of the couch. The three different shades of brown that made up the color contrast didn't look right to her neither. Propped up against the far wall, immediately in front of the door, was an entertainment center. Only, this entertainment center housed no TV, nor radio.

Bianca was using it as a make-shift library shelf. Stacked in every compartment of it were books. Sierra quickly scanned some of the titles. There was no one particular subject that dominated the majority of the books. Bianca liked a little bit of everything. There was one book, however, that stood out because of its unique designs and symbols on the cover. Sierra instantly recognized the book as one of the books that she owned. It was titled, 'The Secret Codes of the Essenes'. Sierra wondered if Bianca helped Burby come up with the codes he used, or if he simply got the idea from one of her books.

Bianca motioned towards one of the couches.

"Please." She said. "Have a seat."

Sierra accepted the offer and sat down. Bianca sat down on the other couch. There was an awkward silence as both women waited on the other woman to speak up first. Sierra decided to say something.

"So," she said, penetrating the quiet. "You said that you couldn't prove that your husband was cheating, but you suspected it. What made you suspect him of cheating?"

Bianca laughed out loud.

"Let's just say that a woman knows these kinds of things." She told her.

"Ummm. Could you be a little more specific?"

Bianca turned her head towards the ceiling as if she were trying to hold back a few tears. Sierra wondered how this woman's moods could change so swiftly. Bianca chuckled under her breath then placed her tongue on her top lip.

"I gave my all to that man." She began. "I gave that man 12 years of my life and look how he repaid me. When his own family turned their backs on him, I was there, telling him that everything would be just fine. When he went outside of our marriage and got that young girl pregnant, I forgave him and pretended like we adopted

Robert so that his cheating, pedophile ass wouldn't get locked up."

Sierra's eyes got wide. "Robert wasn't your son?" She asked.

Bianca looked at her with pain in her eyes. "Honey." She replied. "The doctors told me a long time ago that I would never be able to conceive a child."

She waved her hand.

"Something about my uterus isn't right." She continued. "That's part of the reason why I forgave his sorry ass. I knew that he wanted something that I would never be able to give him. Every time I looked at that boy, my heart broke though."

Bianca wiped her eye. A tear had formed.

"I endured all of that. I endured all of that in the name of love, and as soon as that bastard came into a little money, he forgot all about me and thought he was a bachelor again."

Sierra's ears tuned in when she mentioned money.

"Does she already know?" She thought.

"Wait a second." Sierra said, interrupting her. "Burby came into a little money. What do you mean?"

Bianca looked at her quizzically. "Oh, you're young." She said. "Well, this happened back before you got on the force, probably. Do you remember hearing about a man named Luis Wilkinson getting gunned down while in police custody?"

Sierra thought back to the recording she seen.

"Remember it?" She thought. "I witnessed it."

Instead of giving up too much information, she simply nodded her head.

"A lot of people speculated that Robert had something to do with that." Bianca continued. "But I don't have to speculate. I was there. I know firsthand that he had something to do with it. The exact same day that Robert arrested that man in connection with the murder, 3 thugs came out to our house in Alvin. Robert made me go in the back while he talked with them, but it doesn't take a rocket scientist to guess how the conversation went."

Sierra thought back to the tape she watched. Sticks and his men had come to the house before Wilkinson was arrested, so she must be referring to a visit by Infamous and his goons.

Trying to offer an explanation for the visit, Sierra said, "So they offered to pay Burby to look the other way while they got revenge for Infamous son."

Bianca made a half-smile. "You got it, sistah."

Sierra pretended to jot down a few notes. Everything she was finding out was good, but she still didn't have any insight into where the money was. Seeing how Bianca already knew about the cash, she decided to ask straight out.

"So, what did Burby do with the money?"

"He fucked it off." Bianca replied.

"Fucked it off? How could he fuck off all of that money?"

Bianca slapped her knee and laughed out loud again. "You think $500,000 is hard to spend? Well, I got news for you honey. When you start gambling, wasting money on young prostitutes to satisfy your sick desires, and buying entire 18-hole golf courses, $500,000 will go faster than you think."

Sierra was really getting confused now. Apparently, Burby didn't tell his wife how much money he really had. She was glad that she didn't mention an actual amount.

"Can you believe that?" Bianca asked. "A freaking golf course? This man actually had the nerve to try and right all of his wrongs by buying me a golf course for our 11th Anniversary, and I don't even know how to play golf."

Sierra thought about the wind chime. "Burby must've really liked golf." She said, pointing with her pen in the direction of the wind chime.

Bianca followed the pen with her eyes. "Yes." She answered, realizing what Sierra was pointing at. "He gave me that wind chime when he told me about the golf course."

Bianca rolled her eyes. "You know how a person can buy you a gift that's really meant for them instead of you? It was something like that. When I complained about how selfish the gift was, he kept promising me that if only I would go out and see the golf course with him, I would forgive him, and we would live happily ever after."

Bianca smacked her teeth. "As if a round of golf could really make up for all of the wrong, he did to me. Honey, I'll tell you one thing. I would rather live up here in my mother's old house, all by my lonesome, than to ever forgive that man for wasting the best years of my life."

Both women turned their heads when they heard the phone ringing.

Rising to her feet, Bianca said, "Excuse me, Detective."

Sierra smiled. "Take your time, ma'am."

When Bianca was gone out of the living room, it took all Sierra had not to shout for joy. If she was right, the biggest mistake Bianca could've made was to not go by that golf course on their Anniversary night. Piecing together the puzzle as best she could, Sierra prayed that she finally figured it out. Burby did not buy Bianca the golf course as an anniversary gift. Burby bought the golf course to help him conceal the real gift.

Sierra speculated that the $20 million was buried somewhere on the grounds of that golf course and judging by it being a present for their 11th Anniversary, Sierra was willing to bet that the money could be found somewhere on the 11th hole. It made perfect sense to her. Keeping in line with how Burby used the Essenes code of writing, known as Dyscletia, she wasn't surprised that the number

11 would be the number 11 backwards as well as forwards.

Sierra had to admit, she admired Burby's forethought. He really put together an interesting way of winning his wife back. Sierra sort of felt sorry for Bianca, but sometimes life was hard. She seemed like an extremely strong woman, so Sierra knew that she would survive.

"Maybe I'll anonymously give her some of my cut." She told herself.

Sierra wanted to exit the house right then, but she knew that she should at least wait until Bianca returned. It would be suspicious if she was gone when she returned from the back. Sierra didn't have to wait long. Only about two minutes passed before Bianca emerged.

"I'm sorry." She said, making her way over to the front door. "I really need to cut this conversation short. I lost track of time until I just now looked at my clock. I should be getting ready for work now."

Sierra stood to her feet as Bianca was ending the questioning for her.

"I understand completely."

Sierra walked past Bianca and headed towards her car.

Stopping in the middle of the yard, Sierra turned around and said, "One more thing, Mrs. Burby. What is the name of that golf course your husband bought you?"

Bianca rubbed her chin trying to recall the name of it.

"Bayou... Bayou... Bayou" she mumbled. "Oh yeah." She said, slapping her forehead. "It's called Bayou Golf Course. It sits off of 25th Ave N."

Sierra knew where that was. "That's in Texas City, isn't it?"

"Yeah." Bianca answered. "Off the Loop."

Sierra thanked her for her time and drove off. Talking to herself, Sierra said, "The money has been right under our nose the entire time."

Sierra picked up her cell phone. She had a number for her contact that she was instructed to only use when she located the money. Sierra thought it over. Where else could the money be? It had to be buried somewhere on hole 11. It had to be. Feeling confident, she dialed the number. After only two rings, the familiar voice answered.

"You found it?" They asked excitedly.

"Meet me at the Bayou Golf Course off of the Loop in Texas City." Sierra answered. "Oh, and bring the two of us something to dig with."

Chapter Thirteen

Shock sat down on the edge of the bed and rested his forearms on his thighs.

Staring devilishly at the woman he had tied up and gagged, he growled, "Like a fly caught in the spiders web."

Shonda laid stretched out on the floor with her hands tied behind her back and her feet tied tightly together. She had no idea who the man with the raspy voice was, but she prayed that Squeak would hurry up and come home. The man already said that he was waiting on her boyfriend to return, but she had no idea of knowing how long he would wait. Something about his emotionless glare told Shonda that he would kill her in cold blood and not think twice about it. She knew that her only hope was Squeak. He would know how to handle the situation.

Shock stood to his feet and slowly waved his gun from side to side, pointing it along the length of Shonda's frame. He enjoyed placing fear in the hearts of his victims. All too often he had to kill his prey swiftly and flee before being found out. It was an extremely rare pleasure to be able to indulge in his fetish of death. Gazing at his catch through the eyes of the predator, he noted how much beauty she had. Her dark skin, defined features, and womanly curves made her very attractive to him.

"Such a shame to have to end the life of something so exquisite." He mumbled loud enough for Shonda to hear.

Shock chuckled when she shivered.

"Please hurry up." Shonda thought, pleading with Squeak with her mind power.

Squeak couldn't hear her thoughts, but he just so happened to be turning onto Anderson street at that very moment.

"So, you gone call me later, huh?" Adriana asked, trying to be sure that she would hear from Squeak again.

He thought back to the escapades he just indulged in.

"Adriana." He said, rubbing her thigh. "I would be a fool not to keep in touch with you."

Adriana smiled. She had somewhat low self-esteem and she desperately needed the reassurance of a second fuck. In a female's world, one-night stands were never good. Even if the woman wasn't interested in the man, she wanted him to pursue the second fuck anyway. If he didn't, she felt like her sex wasn't good, and without good sex, a woman couldn't keep a man.

"I'm glad you feel that way." She replied, feeling all giddy inside.

Squeak was watching her as she drove. It surprised him that he could make a woman he just met, so happy. He had no idea that sex could be so powerful. While he was watching her expressions in amazement, she pulled up outside of his house. Squeak caught a glimpse of the maroon Pontiac Sunbird parked behind the Cavalier. He instantly knew that something was wrong. There was no way that Shonda would allow someone inside of their house. Squeak took his hand off of Adriana's thigh and patted on his waistline.

Adriana could tell that his whole attitude changed.

"What's wrong?" She asked, thinking that he was nervous because his girlfriend was at home.

"Fuck." Squeak growled, when he rubbed on his waistline for the fourth time.

The way he cursed stunned Adriana. "Fuck what, baby?" She asked, trying to calm him down by squeezing his shoulder.

"Fuck I don't have my pistol." He answered, more to himself than to her.

"Pistol?!" She repeated. "Why do you need a pistol?"

Squeak opened the car door. "Look," he said, before he climbed out. "You need to just drive off and I'll call you later."

But Ant..." she called after him, but he shut the door with no further explanation.

He had no idea what to expect, and no idea how he could help, but he did know that his sister was inside of that house and she more than likely needed him.

Running to the front door, Squeak didn't even waste time with the lock and the doorknob. Adriana watched in wonder as Squeak rammed his shoulder into the door and burst into the house. She couldn't help but to be curious as to what was going on. He told her to just leave, but she didn't know if she should leave, call the police, or what. The single gunshot she heard only moments after Squeak entered the home answered her question of what to do. She backed out of the driveway to get out of harm's way. As she drove off, she debated calling the police.

Shock was standing in the middle of the living room when Squeak burst in. The single shot he released into the wall right next to him, stopped Squeak in his tracks. Squeak wanted to rush the man with the gun, but he knew he needed to wait for the right time.

"Where's Shonda?" Squeak demanded, scanning the room for a sign of his sister.

"Shonda." Shock repeated, pronouncing each syllable. "So that's her name?"

He licked his lips.

"So that would make you, Squeak."

When the man's voice reached Squeaks ears, he thought he recognized it from somewhere. Something told him that he knew him.

"How do you know me?" Squeak asked, trying to buy some time so he could figure out how to disarm the man with the gun without being shot.

"I know you from your girlfriend." Shock replied, making sure to keep his pistol aimed directly at Squeaks torso.

At the mention of Shonda, Squeak instantly began to worry again. His heart was beating so fast and so hard in his chest that he thought it was trying to escape. He knew that he would never be able to forgive himself if something happened to his big sister. Squeak cursed Adriana and Sierra under his breath. While he was off satisfying his flesh, his sister was being overtaken by a man who was no doubt working for Sticks.

Hearing Squeak mumble, but not understanding his words, Shock asked, "Is something wrong, Squeak?"

"Where's my sister?"

"Sister?" Shock thought.

He glanced towards the room. Squeak saw Shock look away and he took a step closer to him. In an instant he debated if he should rush him or not. The gun was still pointed at him, but the gunman wasn't looking in his direction. Squeak decided to go for it. Just when he was about to rush the man, he turned back to face Squeak.

"She's your sister?"

Squeak silently scolded himself for not taking the opportunity when it presented itself. Cutting his loses, he took the man's actions to indicate that Shonda was still alive.

"Yes." Squeak answered. "She's my sister. Now tell me what you want with us. Tell me why you're here."

Shock just stared at him. Squeak noticed his expression changed. Doing his best to read it, Squeak thought that it registered as pain.

"Everybody but me." Shock whispered.

Squeak just stood there. Most people were shocked by the revelation that he and Shonda were brother and sister, but he couldn't understand why that mattered to the intruder. Then, just as quickly as his expression changed from that of a cold-blooded killer, it transformed right back.

"Lay face down." Shock instructed him.

Squeak felt his chances slipping away to get him and Shonda out of this alive.

Hesitant to lay down, he said, "You never answered my question?"

Shock glared at Squeak with a stare that could cut through iron. Hearing that the two of his hostages were brother and sister brought memories of the family that he lost to the fore front of his mind. It upset him that these two could still be in contact with their loved ones and he was so heartlessly snatched from his.

Shock took one step closer to Squeak. "You have exactly 3 seconds to lay face down or you and your sister die."

Squeak scanned his eyes.

"One." Shock said, counting off.

Squeak could tell that he meant business. He was a killer himself, so he knew when a killer was prepared to kill over disobedience. By the time Shock was finished with the number two, Squeak was laying on the floor with his hands behind his back. Shock cautiously made his way over to him. He knew that Squeak was probably planning some type of heroic maneuver and it was his job to keep him from having the chance.

Shock withdrew the handcuffs from his back pocket and knelt down next to Squeak. Squeak heard the handcuffs and knew that he needed to think fast. All hope would be lost if he allowed this intruder to incapacitate him. As Squeak debated within himself on how to act, Shock pressed the barrel of his gun to the back of his head.

"If you move," Shock told him. "I won't hesitate to shoot you."

Squeak felt defeated. He knew that there was nothing he could do. This man made only one mistake and Squeak was left kicking himself for not utilizing the moment. Shonda struggled against her restraints as she listened helplessly to the exchange going on in the living room. When she heard the click of the handcuffs, she knew that they probably wouldn't survive. As thoughts of death entered into her mind, Shonda kicked frantically trying to free herself.

Shock finally felt like he had the situation under control. He could now enjoy his prey like he wanted to, and when he became bored with them, he could kill them at his own leisure.

Shock helped Squeak to his feet and followed him into the back room with his pistol against his neck. When Squeak entered the room, he was hit with two emotions at the same time. He was ecstatic to see his sister still alive, but it hurt him to see her tied up and gagged.

"Shonda!" He called out when he saw her.

"Mmmm-mmm." She mumbled against the gag.

Shock shoved Squeak down hard and he landed next to his sister. Shonda was struggling against the sock that was stuffed in her mouth to talk, but nothing understandable was coming out.

"Shhh." Squeak urged her. "It's gone be alright. I'm going to get us out of this. Ok?"

Squeak looked Shonda directly in her eyes and tried his hardest to appear confident. He didn't want her to know how worried he actually was. Trying her best to have faith in her brother, Shonda shook her head to let him know that she understood.

"Awww." Shock mocked. "Isn't that cute?"

Then he laughed as he stepped over the pair and went inside of the walk-in closet. He wondered if anything Squeak owned could double as another costume for him. If he had some authentic Villain gear, he would be able to play the wolf in sheep's clothing more convincingly. Shock knew that his hostages would be trying to get away, but he was sure that they wouldn't escape.

Taking his time, Shock scanned the items in the closet. Squeak watched Shock disappear into the closet and saw what very well might be his last chance to get them out of there alive.

"Look." Squeak whispered. "I'm going to try to untie your feet so we can get out of here."

Shonda nodded her agreement.

The two of them adjusted their bodies until Squeak's hands were next to Shonda's feet. Working against the clock, Squeak picked and tugged at the various knots. Shonda prayed that he hurry up. If Squeak could only get her feet untied, they could make a run for it. They may not get far, but then again, they were sure to die if they stayed there.

Shock tied the rope on her legs and feet extremely tight like he was some sort of former boy scout or something. Squeak was becoming slightly frustrated with the professional knots, but he refused to give up. To give up would be to die.

In the midst of Shock searching the closet, he felt around on the top shelf. He couldn't see what all was up there, but when his hand slid across cold steel, he knew that he encountered a gun.

Pulling it off of the shelf, Shock was impressed. The pistol he found was a .380 with a silencer attached to it.

"Nice." He said, admiring the weapon. "This will look good in my collection."

Shock made sure that the safety was on, slid the gun in his pocket, and continued to search around on the top shelf. Hoping to find another gun, he rubbed around until his hand came across a picture frame lying face down.

Curiosity caused him to pick it up and examine it.

The photograph had to be old, because it was in black and white. The frame was a simple solid black frame, too. The photograph was a picture of what Shock assumed was Squeak and Shonda's family. The family was inside of a living room seated on a couch. In front of them, sitting Indian style on the floor, was a young boy and a young girl. Sitting in the woman's lap was another little boy. All of the kids seemed close to the same age.

Shock's best guess was they were about 4 or 5.

....

Adriana had decided to call Sierra about the situation with Ant, but for some reason she wasn't answering her phone. She called over and over again, but every time she got the same result. The voicemail. Not being able to get through to Sierra, Adriana eventually decided to call Rose. He was sitting in his car in front of his house when he his phone rang.

"Detective Derrick Rose." He said, trying to stay professional, even though he was dying on the inside.

Adriana was borderline hysterical.

"Rose!" She said into the phone. "You don't know me, but I'm Sierra's sister-in-law. My name is Adriana. I got your number from her. She said ya'll were partners."

"Ok." Rose responded. "Is there something wrong with Sierra?"

"I don't know." She told him. "I'm calling about, Ant."

"Ant?" Rose asked. "Who is Ant?"

"Ant is my boyfriend." She replied. "Well, technically he's not my boyfriend because I'm married. He's more like a friend."

Rose was getting confused. "So, what seems to be the problem?" He asked, trying to get to the point.

"The point is…" she answered. "I just dropped him off at home and somebody shot at him."

Rose was attentive now.

"Who shot at him?"

"Ummm." She replied. "I'm not sure, but I know they drive either a maroon Pontiac Sunbird or a black Chevy Cavalier."

Rose sat straight up in his seat. There was no way she could be talking about the car he was just following, could she.

"Pontiac Sunbird? Where's the Pontiac now?"

"It's still at Ant's house over on Anderson." She replied.

Rose threw his car into drive and pulled off.

"You did the right thing by calling me." He said. "I'll take it from here. You just go home and stay out of the area."

They hung up with each other.

Something deep down told Rose that this Pontiac was the same Pontiac that he was just following. He couldn't believe his luck. He considered calling for backup, but then he decided against it.

"Not this time." He said, speeding toward Anderson street. "This one is personal."

....

"I... almost... got it." Squeak whispered, as he felt the knots beginning to give.

"Mmmm." Shonda mumbled her encouragement.

It only took a few more tugs on the rope before Shonda had enough room to wiggle her legs free from the restraints. Both Shonda and Squeak knew that all they needed was their legs and feet free in order to make a run for it. When Squeak felt Shonda pull her legs loose from the rope, he started trying to get to his feet.

Shonda followed suit. Their relief level rose when they made it to their knees. They could almost taste freedom. Before they could make it to their feet, however, they were frozen in place by the voice of their attacker emerging from the closet.

In a low voice, Shock called, "Squeak... Shonda."

Shonda was afraid to look back. Squeak knew that he had to. The sight he saw was not what he expected. There, standing in the door of the closet, was Shock. In one hand he was holding his gun, and in the other hand he was holding an old picture of Tune, Laina, Shonda, Squeak, and Richard. What fucked Squeak up the most were the tears streaming down Shock's face. Squeak didn't know how to respond. He thought for sure that Shock was going to kill them for trying to escape.

Squeak watched in amazement as Shock slowly put his gun into his pocket.

"What are you doing?" Squeak thought.

Then, he watched as Shock's free hand began to shake as he rose it up to his face.

Gently wiping the tears away, he whispered, "I remember."

Shonda slowly turned around and saw the same sight that Squeak saw.

"Remember what?" Squeak asked, slightly afraid of the response.

Shock turned his head to the left and rubbed a long black scar that ran along his neck. Squeak had not noticed it until just then.

Shock's lips quivered. "I... I... I remember how I got this."

Shock swallowed hard. His consciousness had blocked all memories of that faithful day out of his mind.

"I got this protecting mama." Shock said. "I was protecting mama from daddy and he shot me. I... I stabbed him in the leg, and he shot me."

Shock rubbed the scar. "Do you remember? Do you remember when daddy shot me?"

Both Squeak and Shonda almost fell over. That scar was why his voice was so raspy. They stared at Shock, and his new revelation sent waves of recognition bombarding both of their brains. They looked at each other in disbelief, then back at Shock.

Everyone was silent for about one full minute. Then, Squeak broke the silence with three words that reverberated in everyone's ears.

"Richard... you're alive!"

Chapter Fourteen

The candy blue H3 used its huge size to blaze through traffic. The average vehicle didn't stand a chance in a head-on collision and the average driver was well aware of that. So was Sticks, and he was using that to his advantage. The cars in front of him were parting like the red sea supposedly parted for Moses. On any other day, he would've been basking in the power, but not today. Today he was on a mission. Sticks had two stops to make.

The war in the streets was getting out of hand. He very rarely got his own hands dirty anymore, but desperate times call for desperate measures. Sticks thought that he had successfully gotten rid of the rat that infested his organization, but now he thought differently. If Archie was the only snitch, how could Detective Rose find out about Shock if Archie was dead?

That left only two other alternatives. Either Archie wasn't the leak, or Archie wasn't the only leak. If it was one thing that Sticks couldn't stand, it was disloyalty, and he decided to cleanse his organization himself. Besides, if Shock was being followed, he couldn't go on any missions right now anyway.

Sticks puffed on his apple flavored mini-blunt. Looking down on his lap, he noticed the sunlight entering his truck through the windshield and reflecting off of his chrome Desert Eagle. Sticks didn't kill often, but when he did, he did it with style.

As he approached the next stop sign, he read the street name out loud.

"14th St."

He came to a complete stop and surveyed the block. There were cars parked in driveways, but only a few children playing in the yards along the street. Making a right turn, Sticks told himself that this was probably as good as things would get. If he was waiting on the area to be completely void of movement and life, he would probably never act, and not acting was not an option.

Sticks casually pulled up to a small brown house and killed the ignition. Staring at the residence through the driver's side window, Sticks hit the blunt one last time and then smothered the cherry in the ashtray.

"Here goes nothing." He said to himself, as he tucked the Desert Eagle into his waistband and hopped out the H3.

Sticks kept his head on the swivel as he made his way up to the front door. The initial looks that his vehicle drew had died down. No one was still watching him. Sticks pulled out one of his credit cards and stepped up to the door. Early on in his career as a criminal, Sticks use to burglarize houses. At the time, it was the best hustle he could come up with. It was one of the easiest too. He often came away empty handed, but sometimes he would find large amounts of cash and high-class jewelry that he could sell to people in the streets. Burglarizing homes made him an expert at opening locked doors.

When he made it to the front door, he jimmied it open so fast, that anyone who was looking would assume he used a key. The brown skinned woman sitting on the couch watching TV, looked over at the tall skinny man entering her home.

Jumping to her feet, she shouted, "What the hell are you doing?"

Sticks closed the door behind him and revealed his weapon.

"If you scream again," he said coolly, and with a blank expression. "I'll kill you."

The woman, who was none other than Loretta Gilmore, threw her arms straight up in the air as if to surrender. Sticks knew that Infamous ex-wife lived alone, so he didn't bother to search the premises. He came to do a job, and he was staying fully focused on the task.

Crossing the room with his pistol pointed at Loretta, he instructed her to sit back down on the couch. Without hesitating, Loretta complied.

"Now," Sticks said. "We are going to play a little game."

He stood directly in front of Loretta and lowered his gun.

"I'm going to ask you some questions." He continued. "You're going to answer those questions."

Sticks leaned over and grabbed Loretta's chin, making her look him in the eyes.

"If you refuse to answer me… you die. If you lie to me… you die. If I so much as think you're lying to me… you die."

He released her face.

"Do we understand each other?"

Loretta nodded her head. While the man was talking, she recognized who he was. He was the man that Archie worked for. The man responsible for her son's death. Loretta knew that he had no problem with killing her, so it would be in her best interest to just go along with whatever he said.

"Good." Sticks said, in response to her willingness to cooperate. "First question. How did you know Archie?"

Loretta figured he would ask about that. She heard about what happened to Archie and she thought that his murder had something to do with her. After all, he was killed shortly after leaving her home. She fidgeted in her seat.

"Were the two of you, lovers?" Sticks asked.

Loretta was shocked by the question.

"Lovers?" She repeated. "Heavens no! Archie and my son were friends. After Korey got killed, Archie came by my house to console me. He was one of the only people who came around and said that they knew my son, so I could tell that him and Korey must have been good friends. He used to just come by to check up on me from time to time."

Sticks considered her answer. It made sense. Back before Sticks knew that Korey was the son of Infamous, he worked for him as a dope runner. Sticks had a lot of youngsters on his team and Korey was just one amongst many. He didn't trust someone that young to do the job by themselves, so he paired him up with Archie. Archie was a little older and had been down with the Hooligans for a while, so Sticks put him over Korey. It was Archie's job to teach him the ropes and make sure he did the job right. Apparently, he had become attached to the kid.

Sticks rubbed his chin.

"So... it was his loyalty to Korey that eventually led him to tell you how your son died?" He asked.

Once again, the question threw Loretta for a loop.

"Is that why Archie got killed?" She asked, disgusted. "Because you thought he told me about what you did to my son?"

Loretta gasped in shocked horror as her mind tried to wrap around what she just heard. She couldn't believe that Archie died because of that. He never mentioned to her how Korey was killed. His only connection to her was his attempt to try and ease her grief. Remorse for Archie flooded into her heart.

"Oh my God." She mumbled, as she placed her hands over her chest. "Please don't tell me you killed him because of that."

Sticks studied her expressions. They seemed genuine enough.

"You mean to tell me that Archie wasn't how you got your information?" Sticks asked, becoming confused.

"No!" Loretta shouted, as the tears began to flow.

The memory of her son and the knowledge that her sons only friend got murdered for nothing was too much for her.

In between sobs, she said, "Demetrius told me what happened to our son. Not Archie."

"Infamous?" Sticks questioned. "How did Infamous know?"

Loretta wiped her eyes. "I don't know." She answered. "He just came by one day and told me that the man who got charged with the murder of Korey didn't do it."

Sticks thought about how he ordered the hit on Archie. One of his loyal soldiers became a victim of a misunderstanding. A casualty of war. A part of him wanted to mourn Archie, but another part of him knew that he had business to take care of. There was a more important issue at hand than the death of Archie. Sticks had to now figure out how Infamous found out that he had something to do with his son's death. Things were getting complicated.

Sticks rose his Desert Eagle and pointed it at Lorette. She took a deep breath. Sticks contemplated shooting her. He had every intention of murdering her when he showed up, but that was because he thought she told Infamous about what happened. Now, he wasn't so sure that she did anything worthy of death.

Loretta closed her eyes and waited on the gunshot that she felt was imminent. After a few seconds of silence, she heard the door open. She opened her eyes to see Sticks exiting the house. She finally released the breath she was holding. He let her live. Loretta sat perfectly still until she heard Sticks truck crank up and drive away.

Once she felt safe, she got up and ran over to the phone. Loretta took a couple of deep breaths as she fumbled with the phone trying to dial the number. She was shaking like a leaf from the encounter with Sticks. Loretta hated guns and she hated everything that came along with them. That was one of the main reasons she divorced Demetrius. She didn't like being the wife of a gang lord. It was entirely too dangerous. His gangster lifestyle came back to haunt her anyway. It claimed the life of her only son, and now it almost got her killed.

Gaining her composure as best she could, Loretta placed the phone to her ear and listened to it ring. She stood there sniffling and shaking slightly. After about 3 rings, someone picked up.

"Hello." They answered.

Loretta burst into tears again.

"Demetrius! You gotta do something." She cried into the phone.

Infamous could recognize his ex-wife's voice anywhere. Even though they weren't together, they kept in touch. When he heard her crying, he knew that something was wrong.

"Loretta." He called into the receiver. "What happened?"

She tried taking a few more deep breaths so she could talk.

"What happened?" She shouted. "What happened is I almost got killed because of you!"

"What?!"

He was still very protective of Loretta, and hearing her say she almost got killed, made him instantly enraged.

"Sticks just left from over here." She informed him. "He had a fucking gun to my head! A fucking gun, Demetrius!"

Infamous went silent. Sticks himself had pulled a gun on his ex-wife. He had gone too far now. As if killing his son wasn't enough. He was now terrorizing his ex-wife.

Loretta grew tired of waiting for Infamous to respond.

"Demetrius! I said he put a gun to my head! Did you hear me?"

Infamous slammed a fat fist down on his desk as hard as he could. "I'll kill him!" He declared, with nothing but malice in his voice. "I'll kill him! I'll kill his wife! I'll kill his children! I'm going to burn that motherfuckers house to ground!"

Infamous yelled with so much force, everyone inside of the barber shop could hear him.

....

Sierra sat at the entrance to the Bayou Golf Course and held her cell phone in her hand. Her contact should've been there by now.

"What's taking you so long?" She wondered.

Sierra wanted to call back and find out where they were at, but she didn't want to hound them. Sitting on the hood of her car, she decided to continue to wait.

"Fuck it." She said to herself. "I'll just play solitaire until they show up."

When she turned her phone on, she noticed that she had four missed calls from her sister-in-law, Adriana. She wondered how she missed the calls. Then, she remembered she turned the ringer off when she went to go question Bianca. Whatever Adriana wanted had to have been important for her to call four times in a row. Sierra started dialing her number to see what it was that she wanted, but before she could press the button to actually make the call, she noticed a blue Eclipse pulling up next to her car.

She cancelled the call and hopped off the hood. Sierra watched as the woman inside of the car popped the trunk and climbed out. Without speaking, she made her way over to the trunk and withdrew two shovels.

Holding them up, she said, "Let's go get that money."

Sierra walked over to her and grabbed one of the shovels.

"I was wondering how long it was gone take you to get here."

"Well," she replied. "Now that I'm here, let's go see what Burby has for us on hole #11."

....

Shonda and Squeak continued to stare at Shock in total disbelief. Was it possible that he could actually be Richard? Could he really be the younger brother that they thought died? True, neither one of them had any memories of a funeral, but they witnessed Richard get shot with their own eyes. Squeak looked at the scar on Shock's neck again. He tried to remember which side of Richard's neck got struck by the bullet.

Shock looked down at them and wondered why they weren't smiling.

"What's wrong?" He asked. "Don't you believe me?"

They just stared. It was entirely too much to take in. Shock held up the photograph.

"I have a picture of this exact same woman in my apartment." He said, pointing to Laina. "She's my birth mother. It's the only thing the foster home let me keep."

Shock took a step closer to them and both Squeak and Shonda flinched. Shock was 100% convinced because of the photograph. Shonda and Squeak wanted to believe it, but that feat would take some major reprogramming. To them, Richard died when they were kids.

"Look." Shock said, trying to think of a way to convince them that he was their brother. "If I'm lying, why would I do this?"

He pulled out the keys to the handcuffs and reached for Squeak. Shock spent his entire life dreaming about the family that he lost. Never in a million years did he think that he would ever be reunited with them, but now that fate stepped in on his behalf, he was willing to do anything to get his family back. Shock was about to put the key into the lock when he heard a car pull up outside. Dropping the keys to the floor, he ran to investigate.

Shonda and Squeak looked at the keys.

Shonda went for them.

Shock rushed into the living room and peeked out the window.

"Fuck." He growled, when he noticed Detective Rose's Crown Victoria parked out front.

He pulled his gun out of his pocket and debated his next move.

Rose looked at the license plate number on the Pontiac. It matched the car he was following earlier. He wondered whose house he invaded, and what for. He could see that the front door was wide open. That indicated some type of illegal forced entry. Something was definitely going down inside of that house.

Rose got ready to get out of his car when he thought twice. The last time he went after an armed man alone, his partner got killed. He went over his options. He didn't have a partner with him this time. Besides, it was only one, armed man. He could handle that. Also, what if the owners of the home got killed while he was waiting on backup? Rose pulled his weapon out and stepped out into the hot air. His decision was made.

Shock backed away from the window and was watching the cop's movements from an angle. He figured Rose just drove around until he saw his car again. Shock thought back to moments ago when he was forced to flee from the pig. Lifting his weapon, Shock's mind instantly went back into predator mode. It didn't take much for him to zone out in anticipation of a kill.

"Remember what I told you?" Shock whispered under his breath. "The hunter has unknowingly become the hunted."

Shock smiled.

His smile soon faded when he heard the familiar sound of a pistol being cocked behind him. Squeak and Shonda had completely freed themselves and Squeak grabbed the gun he kept stashed under the mattress.

Looking out the window, Squeak asked, "Who is that?"

Shock didn't turn around. He didn't know if Squeak believed he was their brother or not, so he was hesitant to make any sudden moves.

"That's a detective." Shock said, doing his best not to move. "Will you kill me and let the pig live?"

Squeak said nothing. He simply reached inside of Shock's pocket and withdrew his .380.

"Kill you?" Squeak repeated, placing a hand on Shock's shoulder. "Tell lil bro the motto, sis."

Shock turned his head to face the pair.

They were both smiling.

Shonda placed her hand on Shock's other shoulder. "Shiiiit. Blood is **Thicker Than Water**. All day every day."

Rose held his weapon out in front of him and closed the gap between him and the door. He licked his lips as he strained his ears to hear what was going on inside of the house.

"Heeeelllppp." He heard a woman screech.

The call for assistance caused him to spring into action. He jogged towards the door and saw a woman laying on her side about 10 feet inside the residence. Thinking that she was wounded, Rose rushed inside the house. As soon as he made it over the threshold of the door, he saw something move out the corner of his eye. Realizing his mistake, he tried to aim his pistol in the direction of the object, but it was too late.

When Shock and Squeak saw Rose step completely inside the living room, they both began firing all 3 guns. Rose body jerked as the multiple shells connected with his flesh. Shonda covered her ears as the shots combined with the hellacious screams of Rose, to create a symphony of a painful execution. As Rose dropped his weapon and stumbled to the floor, his entire life flashed before his eyes. The playback of his existence came to rest on the night that Tameka got killed.

"Not again." He thought, as bullets penetrated his torso, legs, and arms.

The pain became so intense that Rose could no longer feel it. Shock and Squeak walked over to Rose and watched his body twitch. Rose coughed up blood and stared up at his assailants with horror in his eyes. He thought that death was making him delusional. Standing over him, side by side with guns drawn, was the hitman for the Villains and the Hooligan he saw with Sticks on Burby's recording.

"It can't be." He thought.

Shonda jumped up. "Come on Squeak. Come on Richard. We gotta go."

Shock and Squeak looked at Shonda and then back at Rose.

"Southlane Villains. Big Squeak." Squeak stated.

"Dramaside Hooligans. Killer Shock." Shock said.

Then, the both of them emptied the remainder of their ammunition into the torso of Detective Rose.

Rose would've thought, how did these two get together?

He also would've wondered, if both of them was sleeping with his wife?

Rose probably would've also pondered why he so ignorantly set himself up to be ambushed again by the same motherfuckers.

Truth be told, Detective Rose would've thought, wondered, and pondered about a million different things with this new development in his case, if it wasn't for one minor detail. Once the heart stops beating, and after the air leaves the lungs, the brain no longer thinks, wonders, or ponders.

Chapter Fifteen

The trio, Squeak, Shonda, and Shock knew that it wouldn't be long before more police arrived. The sound of all of those gunshots was sure to make one of the neighbors call the authorities. Squeak and Shonda rushed around the house trying to grab what they could. The slain cop stretched out in the middle of the living room told them that they would never be able to return home again.

"Hurry up." Shock urged them. "If we get caught inside of this house, we're finished."

Squeak's main concern was unloading the contents of his safe. He wasn't about to let the police confiscate the money he worked so hard to acquire. He hadn't counted it in so long that he had no idea how much he actually had. As he removed the money from the safe, and relocated it to a travel suitcase, he could tell by just looking at it that it was a whole lot more then he thought it was.

Shonda, on the other hand, was grabbing drugs and clothes. In her mind, the time finally came for her and Squeak to leave everything in Texas City behind and just start over somewhere else. Her main concern was getting things that had sentimental value or that could link her and Squeak back to the house.

Shonda wanted to make sure that once they skipped town, nothing from their past would try to hunt them down. Shock searched the body of Detective Rose. He took his badge, wallet, shades, and gun.

"Who knows when I might need to dress up like a cop." He thought.

Squeak finished loading up the money.

"Come on, sis." He said to Shonda, standing up. "We're out of time."

Shonda stood in the middle of the room with her suitcase full of items in her hand. She didn't want to get caught, but at the same time, she didn't want to forget anything neither. Shonda swung her head from side to side scanning the room. Squeak knew that they already waited too long. Not wasting any more time, he grabbed Shonda by her free hand and tugged.

"Come on, sis."

"But... but." Shonda stammered out as Squeak pulled her out of the room by her hand.

"But nothing. We gotta get out of here."

Shock looked up from kneeling over Rose body when Squeak and Shonda entered the living room.

"Ya'll ready?" He asked, rising to his feet.

Squeak glanced down at Rose.

"Yeah." He answered.

"Good." Shock replied, filling his pockets with the Detective's possessions. "I got somewhere that we can go. Just follow me in ya'll car."

Shonda nodded.

Shock led the way out of the house. He knew that the neighbors were more than likely watching, but that was the least of his worries. Shock jogged over to his Pontiac and climbed in. Shonda and Squeak followed his lead by jumping into their Cavalier.

Mrs. Johnson, the elderly white woman that lived next door, was standing in her doorway witnessing their escape. While she watched, she was relaying their every move to the Texas City Police. She told them everything. From their physical descriptions, to the make and model of their vehicles, and she even recited the license plate numbers of both cars.

Mrs. Johnson heard the very first shot when it was fired, but she wasn't sure that it was a gun shot. Later on, when she heard the rapid succession of shots caused by all 3 guns, she knew without a doubt that something was extremely wrong next door. That's when she picked up her phone and went to investigate. The operator told her that some officers were on their way and to stay inside of her home.

As the two cars turned off the block, she knew that the police would show up too late to catch them. All she could hope for was that the information she provided would aid the officers in locating the two men and one woman. Mrs. Johnson wondered what happened to the man that pulled up in the Crown Victoria. The fact that he didn't come back out of the house made her think that he was the victim of all of those shots. Common sense told her that if he did get struck by all of the bullets that she heard, there was no way he could've survived.

It wasn't long after the two cars sped away before Mrs. Johnson heard the howl of police sirens and the wails of the ambulance. When she saw them turn onto the block, she wondered how much of a difference the ambulance could make.

Once Shock made it a comfortable distance from the crime scene, he slowed down. He didn't want to risk getting pulled over for reckless driving or speeding. In the car right behind him, Shonda and Squeak were trying to figure out their next move. In a short period of time, their entire lives had been turned upside down. Not only had they almost been killed, but they found out that their attacker was their younger brother. A younger brother who they grew up believing to be dead. And to make matters worse, he worked for the people that Squeak was at war with. Plus, they just lost their home, the police were no doubt looking for them for the murder of a cop, and the only place they could turn to was to this brother that they weren't even 100% sure they could trust.

Shonda looked nervously at Squeak.

"So." She said. "What are we going to do?"

The question was an extremely serious question. Squeak rubbed his mouth and thought before he answered. He knew that his ways of handling this situation were limited. It was like being backed into a corner. Squeak had so much going through his mind that his brain felt like a super computers data processor. He cut his eyes at Shonda. Squeak wished he had more time to consider all of his options. Unfortunately, he knew that time was a luxury he did not have.

He would have to pick a route and pick it fast. Squeak wondered if he could trust Richard or not. True, they were family, and true he murdered the cop with him, but what did that really prove? Squeak was sure that Richard wanted to get away from that cop just as much as he did.

"But," Squeak thought, "he could've killed us both and been done with it."

He looked over at Shonda again.

"So, what do we do?" She asked.

Squeak watched Shock turn on his blinker as they approached the Rancho Santa-Maria Apartments. Making his decision, he turned his blinker on too.

"We gone trust Richard." He finally told her, following the maroon Pontiac into the parking lot of the apartments.

Shonda trusted her brother's decision. She just prayed that he knew what he was doing. Shock found his regular parking space and pulled in. Squeak parked next to him. As the trio exited the vehicles, Shock led the way to his apartment.

"This way." Shock told them, walking as fast as he could.

He knew that they didn't have much time before the authorities tracked them to their new location. They needed to get underground, and fast. Both Shonda and Squeak were still a little nervous, but they were trying to play it by ear. As they made their way to Shock's unit, they noted what type of neighborhood they were in. Squeak concluded that his younger brother was somewhere low on the totem pole in the ranks of the Hooligans. The area he stayed in was completely drug infested. That theory raised some serious questions, though. Like, what was he doing inside of his house with his sister tied up? Squeak figured he'd ask him when the opportunity presented itself.

Shonda looked around at all of the street people and frowned up. It wasn't that she felt like she was better than anybody. It was just that seeing them brought up a lot of unwanted memories. For the majority of her life, she lived in areas like that, and she never once enjoyed it. She was ecstatic when Squeak decided to rent out the house on Anderson street. Shonda knew that Squeak had no problem with living right in the heart of the hood. His whole long-term goal of moving away from all of the madness was a direct result of his sister's constant complaint of the neighborhoods they lived in.

Most everything Squeak did that could be considered positive was because of his sister. Shonda ate that up, too. She enjoyed being the most important person in his life. He was by far the most important person in her life.

Shock led them to his front door and unlocked it. "Don't expect nothing extravagant. I live pretty modest."

Squeak and Shonda looked at each other with expressions that said, "We know you live modest. Just look at the apartment complex you stay in."

Shock opened the door and told them to make themselves at home. He had been holding his piss for a while now. Squeak and Shonda entered the efficiency apartment and took a look around. It seemed like their younger brother never cleaned up. The sink was filled with dirty dishes and the counter tops were covered with bags that once contained meals bought from the various fast food places in Texas City.

Shonda ventured into the bedroom to see how it looked. She only took one step into the room before she stopped. A wave of grief washed over her and she covered her mouth with her right hand. Hugging herself with her left arm, she tried to fight off the tears building up in her eyes, but she couldn't. Squeak turned his attention from the health hazard Shock called a kitchen and placed his gaze upon Shonda. At first glance, he thought he was tripping.

"Is she... crying?" He thought.

He watched as Shonda's body heaved slightly and the overhead light reflected off the wetness of her cheek. Squeak wondered what she could've seen that stopped her in her tracks and so completely changed her mood. Slowly making his way over to her, Squeak hugged her from behind.

"Sis." He said, with concern in his voice. "What's wrong?"

Up until just then, Shonda was still undecided if Shock was indeed Richard or not. After a lifetime of believing that he was dead, accepting the fact that he was still alive was proving somewhat impossible. The only reason she trusted him this far was because Squeak told her to, and right or wrong, she trusted Squeak. Now, all doubt left her mind. It all made sense. The scar on Shock's neck. The fact that he mentioned getting that scar by trying to protect their mother.

Shonda remember all too well the night that their father shot Richard, and now, on top of that evidence, she found something that clenched it for her. Squeak gave Shonda a little squeeze to let her know that he was there with her and whatever it was, she'd be alright.

He glanced around the room and asked her again. "What is it, sis?"

Before she could respond, Squeak saw for himself what it was. He realized then that Shock wasn't lying. There, over on the nightstand next to the bed, was a picture of the late Laina Tune. As the realization of what that photograph meant sunk in, both Shonda and Squeak got emotional. Shock had been standing in the mirror rubbing his fingers across the long black scar on his neck. His entire life he wondered where it came from. The foster people would never tell him. Now, in one extremely strange day, the memories all came flooding back.

He remembered the fight his parents had. He recalled stabbing his father in the leg, and he could even remember feeling the bullet penetrate his neck. The pain didn't last long though. The shock of being shot in the throat left him unconscious. Before today, he could remember nothing clearly that happened before the day he entered foster care. Only bits and pieces. Everything that he knew about his real family was told to him. Now, he could remember being taken from his family because of the incident.

Shock closed his eyes and thought hard. He could see a woman with a briefcase and caring eyes coming to visit him in the hospital. For a long time after the shooting he couldn't talk, so the woman simply asked him a series of yes or no questions.

"Do you like living at home?" She asked.

Richard fought the pain and shook his head. "No."

The woman jotted something down in her notepad.

"Are you afraid that your father will try to hurt you again?"

Richard was never really afraid of his father, but then again, his father never shot him before. He thought about the question.

"Maybe," he thought, "if I tell her that my father will hurt me, she'll help mommy."

Richard nodded his head, "Yes."

Then, the woman with the caring eyes smiled and rubbed his head gently.

"Don't worry." She told him. "You won't have to worry about your father hurting you ever again."

That night, Richard went to bed knowing that he helped his family. He did a good thing.

Shock snapped back and realized what he actually had done. The woman with the caring eyes must've been with Child Protective Services. When Shock answered yes to that last question, he gave the woman a reason to take him away from his family. He brought it on himself. Shock felt sick. He adjusted the sink so that the water coming from the faucet was warm. He splashed a little water on his face.

"You gotta hold it together." He coaxed himself. "There's too much going on for you to get all emotional right now."

Splashing water on his face one more time to help regain his composure, Shock turned the water off and went to stand over the toilet. Pulling out his penis, he noticed something strange on the tip of it.

"What the fuck?" He mumbled, bending over and pointing it up to get a better look.

With his free hand, Shock tore off a few sheets of toilet paper. Wiping the tip of his member and holding the paper up to his face, he frowned. It looked like a glob of clear gel. Shock squeezed his penis and watched in wonder as more of the gel-like substance came out. He wiped it off with toilet paper. When he squeezed it a second time, nothing came out. Confused, Shock shrugged his shoulders and dropped the toilet paper into the toilet. Then, he aimed his penis and prepared to piss.

Shock had been holding his urine for so long, he cocked his head back in anticipation of the much needed release. As soon as the urine began to flow, Shock's toes curled up and he gritted his teeth.

"Shit!" He growled, as the sensation of razors passing through his pee-hole sent a pain through him that he never felt before.

Luckily, it didn't last the entire time that he was urinating. When Shock was finished relieving himself, he shook the last few droplets of piss from the tip of his tool.

"What was that all about?" He asked himself, referring to the gel and the sensation of razors.

Shock flushed the toilet and concluded that he didn't get all of his cum out when he had sex with Rebecca earlier that day. Trying to put his mind back on the task at hand, Shock walked out of the bathroom and into his bedroom. Squeak was standing in front of his closet with his eyes wide and his mouth open. Shock grinned. He knew that Squeak was no doubt in awe of his arsenal. Shock figured that Squeak was probably one of the various dope dealers working for the Villains. He couldn't wait to reveal that he long ago surpassed the job of common street thug. He was a professional. A real live hitman for hire. Shock knew that he no doubt killed some people that Squeak, and Shonda were close to, but he expected they would forgive him because he was family.

Squeak had been staring at the weapons and different wardrobes in the closet ever since he discovered them. When he saw the outfits, he thought back to when he saw Shock taking the badge and identification from the cop they just killed. He was in awe of the number of guns that his little brother owned. In Shock's closet, he saw hand pistols, A.K.'s, assault rifles, S.K.S.'s, and revolvers. Squeak wondered where Shock kept the atomic bomb stashed. Cocking his head and eyeing Shock suspiciously, Squeak asked the question that was nagging the hell out of him.

"You work for Sticks, right?" He asked.

Shock knew that they would have to eventually go over that.

"Yes." Shock answered.

Squeak turned to face Shock.

"What is it that you actually do for him?" Squeak questioned him, folding his arms.

Shock looked at Shonda, who was sitting on the edge of the bed holding the picture he had of their mother.

"Look." Shock replied, trying to break the news to them gently. "I know that ya'll are Villains and that ya'll work for Infamous. So naturally, up until now, we've been on opposite sides of the fence. So, before I answer, I just want the two of you to know that if I've ever crossed you unknowingly, I'm sorry. It was never my intention to hurt my family."

Squeak and Shonda thought back on all of the Hooligans that they either shot or shot at over the years. They figured that nothing Shock could say would be worse than the job they had.

Sensing Shock's apprehension, and acting on a bit of his own, Squeak stepped up closer to him and said, "I feel where you are coming from lil bro."

Shock liked being referred to as 'lil bro'.

"Honestly." Squeak continued, "I'm sure that we've both done some things that this new revelation of our relation to one another makes us wish we could take back, but the truth is, we can't. The best we can do is just agree that no matter what we've done in the past, we won't let it affect us getting to know each other as family right now in the present and down the road in the future."

Shock appreciated how Squeak came at him. Hearing him mention the future meant he had plans of trying to put together the pieces of their shattered family. Shock also liked the agreement of immunity for past deeds. He knew that their past couldn't be worse than his, so it was good that they mentioned it first. Shock took a deep breath. There was really no easy way to say it, so he decided to just say it.

"I'm the hitman for Sticks." He revealed. "I kill people for money."

Squeak thought that he heard him wrong.

"What?!" Shonda asked.

Squeak knew that her outburst was confirmation that he heard correctly. He turned his attention back to the vast array of firearms in Shock's closet. He was so shocked by the guns that he totally overlooked the obvious. In the midst of the weapons and outfits, Shock had a dreadlocks wig. Squeak thought back to the description they had of the man who killed Jesse. Then Squeak laid his eyes on the all red unit as if for the first time. He could hear Tao's voice ringing in his ears when he had described Suko's killer.

"He was flamed up and he had a real funny voice."

Shock watched Squeak's face as he absorbed the new knowledge. He knew that Squeak was more than likely tallying up the deaths that could now be traced back to him. He couldn't help but wonder how many of them were personally close to Squeak and Shonda. Shock hoped not many. Somewhat nervous about the response he was going to get, Shock rubbed his hands along the side of his legs. As Squeak put all the pieces of the puzzle together, he concluded that Sticks must've sent Shock after him and Shonda.

"So," Shock said, breaking the silence. "Don't just stand there. Say something."

Squeak thought about how parallel their lives had run. Killing must have just been in their blood. Not knowing what else to say, Squeak decided to reveal what his job within the Villains was.

"Well, what can I say?" Squeak stated. "You and I are more alike than you think."

Shock looked at him quizzically.

"What do you mean by that?"

Squeak glanced at Shonda and then back at Shock.

"I'm the hitman for Infamous." He told him. "I kill people for money, too."

Shock took a step back.

"You're a hitman, too?" He asked, with surprise and relief both registering in his voice.

The day just kept getting stranger and stranger.

....

Sticks had only one more stop to make after he left from Loretta's house. He wished his new stop wasn't necessary, but it was. Sticks pressed a few buttons on the navigation system inside of his H3. A few days ago, he instructed one of his men to install a tracking device onto his wife Silvia's car. He noticed her acting a little strange for a couple of months now, and he wasn't sure why. Pride wouldn't allow him to admit it at first, but he was sure that she was having an affair. He knew that Silvia was getting fed up with the gangster lifestyle that he led, but he didn't know what else he could do. His entire family had grown accustomed to living the good life. Even his wife. She enjoyed spending money just as much as he enjoyed making it.

Sticks told himself that Silvia wouldn't leave him because she couldn't find another man like him, but she didn't have to leave him to go outside of their marriage for pleasure. As Sticks drove down the street, he watched on the monitor as satellites orbiting the earth, located his wife's vehicle and transferred the information to him. A small map of the area she was in came up and a red dot appeared on the screen.

The red dot represented the tracking device attached to the underside of Silvia's car. She told Sticks that she was going to go to her homegirls house because she was afraid of being at home alone in the midst of the war that was going on. Sticks hung his head momentarily but raised it again to put his eyes back on the road. The car was stationary, but it wasn't at her homegirls house. Sticks figured that she was at the other man's house.

His imagination went wild with thoughts of how the mystery guy was enjoying his wife. Sticks gripped the steering wheel tight and clenched his jaw. The mental picture of Silvia allowing someone to insert his foreign instrument inside of what was supposed to be his native soil was sickening. The thrust, the moans, the pleasure, the pain. The dishonor, the disloyalty, the disrespect, the degradation. The wet hold, the hard pole, the...

"Aaauuuggghhh!" Sticks growled.

Half of him wanted to cry and the other half wanted to kill. He gently picked up his Desert Eagle from the passenger seat. Sticks looked at the red dot on the navigation monitor display and kissed the chrome pistol. It was cold, much like his wife's heart had to be in order for her to go through with an affair.

Whispering to himself, but talking to his two sons in his mind, he said, "Don't worry. I can be your mother and your father."

....

Rebecca felt herself get weak in the knees and light-headed long before she hung up the phone, but even when she did, the feeling did not leave her. She sat down on the couch and placed the palm of her hand over her forehead. Becoming short of breath, she leaned backed on the sofa and inhaled deeply. Her entire body was rocking, and tears were pouring out of the wells of her eyes as if there was no end to her bodies supply of the liquid induced by immense hurt.

"It's all my fault." She told herself.

Rebecca just got off the phone with the police. They told her that her husband, Detective Rose, was just involved in a shooting. Normally, in situations like that, the police wouldn't release too much information over the phone, but since they knew Rebecca personally, they decided to bend the rules a little bit. They told her that Rose didn't have a pulse when they arrived, and he wasn't breathing. The last they saw of him; he was being rushed to Mainland Medical Center Hospital.

Workers were doing everything in their power to revive him. It didn't look good though. They could tell from the amount of blood loss that Rose had been shot numerous times, but they had no way of knowing yet just how many times he was hit, and if that wasn't enough to completely destroy her, the alleged attacker was. The police knew from a witness that their suspect drove either a black Chevy Cavalier or a maroon Pontiac Sunbird.

Rebecca knew which one it was, instantly. She just watched Rose follow the man off of their block. Rebecca knew that Shock was a thug, but she had no idea he was capable of murder. Rebecca buried her face into her hands. All she wanted to do was get back at Derrick for sleeping with Sierra. She didn't want him to die.

"Lord." She mumbled in between sobs. "Please... please." Rebecca began to sniffle because her nose was trying to run.

"Please, Lord." She begged, with her face contorted with so much remorse that there was no doubting the sincerity of her words. "Please don't let Derrick die because of my sins. Please don't let him..." her words trailed off as she slid off of the couch and curled up into a little ball on the floor.

"Just... just bring him back, God. I promise I'll be good."

Rebecca wanted to go to the hospital, but she was afraid of what she might see. She didn't know if she could handle the sight of Rose hooked up to machines, or worse. She couldn't even handle thinking about the "or worse".

....

Sticks was about 11 blocks from his wife's location when his cell phone rung. He watched it ring 3 times before he finally answered it.

"Hello." He spoke into the mouthpiece.

'Boss." One of his soldiers responded. "We have a problem."

Sticks looked at the pistol in his lap. "What kind of problem?"

The soldier knew Sticks wasn't going to like the latest development, so he hesitated.

Sticks waited.

Finally, the soldier spoke. "Shock just murdered some cop over on Anderson St."

Sticks almost dropped the phone. He just spoke with Shock earlier. Detective Rose was following him, but Sticks told him directly to leave the situation alone.

"How do you know that?" Sticks questioned, praying that he made a mistake.

"It's all over the news." The soldier replied. "They didn't use his name, but they have his description and the description of his car. It won't be long before they find out who he is."

"Damn it!" Sticks cursed.

He told Shock not to make a move, but not only did he disobey a direct order, he pulled off an extremely sloppy job. Sticks knew that his soldier didn't know the whole story, but he did. Detective Rose was already on to the connection between him and Shock, and if Rose knew, other officers knew. Now, because of Shock's irresponsible decision making, he was now going to be implemented in the death of a cop as well.

'Boss." The soldier called into the phone. "What do you want us to do?"

Sticks already knew what had to be done.

"I want you to stand down for now." He told him. "Let me try to figure this thing out first. Stay on alert, though. We may need to take care of Shock. We can not allow his mistakes to take down the organization."

"Yes sir." The soldier replied, and then they hung up.

Sticks tossed the phone into the passenger seat, then dug around in the middle console for another apple flavored mini-blunt. He needed something to calm his nerves. Once he had the weed lit, he hit the blunt extra hard. The THC rushing into his lungs was a much needed reward. Ever since the day Abdul got killed, his entire empire had been spiraling out of control. He knew that there was no way Infamous could've predicted all of this, but all of the backlash from the street war was turning out to be in his favor. He was winning, and Sticks didn't like that one bit.

Looking down at the red dot, he thought about continuing on his mission to go confront his wife and her lover. It would indeed bring immediate satisfaction, but it would also bring immediate consequences. Using his brain to override his raw emotion, Sticks pressed a single button and the map of the area that his wife was in disappeared.

"There will be a next time." He whispered, turning away from the direction in which he was headed.

Sticks had a whole new objective now.

....

Shonda, Squeak, and Shock spent as much time as they could catching up, before they forced their minds to focus back in on the task at hand. Shonda turned the TV on to the news and all 3 were watching quietly. Their physical descriptions, as well as the descriptions of their cars were all over the news. Things were worse than they suspected.

"That bitch!" Shonda shouted, when she saw where all of the cop's information was coming from.

Shock looked at her with an inquisitive stare. Shonda pointed at the old white lady being interviewed by the reporter.

"That's Mrs. Johnson." She informed him. "I used to help her old ass carry her groceries inside of her house, and this is how that bitch chooses to repay me."

She tapped Squeak on the shoulder.

"Squeak. Can we go back and kill that hoe?"

Squeak didn't take his eyes off the screen.

"Shhh." He instructed her.

Squeak was giving the broadcast his undivided attention. Mrs. Johnson told the police everything. She even mentioned what color suitcases they had. Squeak knew that they needed to know what the police knew if they were going to act accordingly.

RING! RING! RING!

Shonda and Squeak turned to face Shock. Shock withdrew his cell phone from his pocket and held up a finger. Walking to the opposite end of the room, he answered the call.

"What's up, Hooligan?" He answered.

Sticks wasted no time expressing his disapproval of Shock's actions.

"What the fuck do you think you're doing?" He spat into the phone. "I thought I told you to lose Rose, not kill him."

Shock expected this type of response.

"I had no choice." He told him. "He had me cornered inside of a house."

Sticks remembered that his soldier told him that the shooting occurred at a house on Anderson.

"Whose house were you at? Don't tell me you left more than one witness."

Shock looked up at Shonda and Squeak. There was no way he could tell his boss that he had the hitman for the Villains, and he let him live. He tried to dodge the question.

"The only witness was the next-door neighbor." He lied.

Sticks was confused.

"What about the people that lived there?"

"Ummm." Shock said, struggling to find an explanation. "I took care of them, boss. Don't worry about that."

"Don't worry?" Sticks shot back at him.

There was no mention of other victims, so he knew that Shock was hiding something.

"What do you mean, don't worry?" Sticks continued. "First, you fuck up and get made by Rose. Then, you fuck up and get cornered by Rose. Then, you fuck up and get caught killing Rose. That shit was sloppy, Shock. That shit was real fucking sloppy, and now... you have the audacity to tell me not to worry."

Shock looked at the phone that he held. Who did Sticks think he was talking to like that?

"Sticks." Shock said, trying hard to keep his composure. "I understand you're upset, but don't let that..."

Sticks cut him off. "Upset isn't the word, Shock. Do you realize that everything you've done will eventually fall back on me? ME?! I'm suddenly compromised because of YOUR fuck ups!"

Shock always had a bad temper, and even his boss could push him too far. Sticks cursed him out one too many times.

"My fuck up's?" Shock yelled. "You better watch your mouth when you talk to me. All that tough guy shit doesn't move me one inch."

Shonda and Squeak snapped their heads when they heard Shock yell.

"Who the FUCK do you think you are?" Sticks continued. "I'm the god damn boss! The BOSS! I'll talk to you any way I god damn please."

"The boss?" Shock repeated, pacing the room. "You the boss, right? You the boss? Well, fuck the boss! How about that? Fuck the boss. Fuck the boss. Fuck the boss. How 'bout you suck my dick, boss? You like that? You can suck my dick."

Spit was flying out of Shock's mouth as he spoke and the veins in his neck began to bulge. Squeak stood to his feet and watched his brother transform. He could tell from the term, boss, that he was on the phone with Sticks.

"You the boss? Well I'm the motherfucking killer." Shock pointed out. "I'm the motherfucking killer."

Shock grabbed his dick. "So, like I said, nigga, FUCK YOU! Suck my dick!"

Shock threw the phone into the wall. The battery separated from it and the phone shattered into several pieces.

"What was that all about?" Squeak asked, trying to figure out what was going on.

Shock marched into the closet and picked up his A.K. 47.

"He wanna cross me?" He said to himself, licking his lips. "Let the motherfucker cross me, then. I do this shit for real. You nigga's just playing gangster."

....

Sticks cursed when the phone went dead. He was fuming. He couldn't believe the level of disrespect that Shock just showed him. First his wife, and now his assassin. Sticks wondered if there were any loyal members of his team left. To think, he rescued Shock when he was nothing more than a runaway foster child. He bought him some new clothes, put him up in an apartment, and gave him a way to make money. He single-handedly made Shock the man he was today. Sticks found him dirty, hungry, and without guidance, and he cleaned him up, fed him, and taught him how to survive in the streets.

He showed him how to harness his anger, hate, and disdain for the world and translate those emotions into a means of generating income. He provided Shock with an outlet for his rage and he made him rich in the process. Sticks squeezed the phone so tight that his hand began to hurt.

"For all of my troubles." He said, glaring menacingly through the windshield. "This is the thanks I get. You came to me like an animal, and I made you a man, but just like an untrustworthy Pitbull... you turned on me; and everyone knows what happens to a dog that bites the hand that feeds him."

Sticks began dialing a number into his cell phone.

Putting the phone up to his ear, he waited for someone to answer.

While he waited, he said, "They get put to sleep."

Chapter Sixteen

Squeak's cell phone was ringing off the hook, but he chose to ignore it.

"Shock." He said firmly, putting his hands out in front of him. "Put down the gun."

Shonda was standing behind Squeak holding on to the back of his shirt out of fear. That phone call that Shock received sent him over the edge. Ever since he chunked his phone, he had been waving his A.K. around talking about killing anybody that tried to bring it to him.

He said that Shonda and Squeak didn't have anything to be afraid of because he wasn't threatening them. They just met Shock though. They had no idea what he was capable of. Shock placed his back against the wall next to his window and leaned over to peak out.

"I can't put down the gun, bro." He told, Squeak. "They on their way over here, and I guarantee that they'll have guns."

"Who is they?" Squeak asked, becoming frustrated. "And why will they have guns?"

Shock looked at him crazy.

"Are you serious?" He asked. "That man I just cursed out was Sticks. There's no way in hell he's gonna accept that."

Shock peeked out the window again.

"As we speak, there's probably 10 to 20 Hooligans on their way over here, and when they get here, there will be no time to talk."

Shonda came from behind Squeak.

"What?!" She shouted. "And you wanna wait on them to show up? Oh hell no."

Shonda picked up her suitcase.

"We should be getting up out of here as soon as possible."

Shock walked away from the window.

"And run???" He asked, as if that wasn't even an option.

Shock pointed at the weapons in his closet.

"We can take 'em."

Shonda looked to Squeak. He knew that it was going to fall on him to make the decision. Squeak knew that trying to go to war like this wouldn't be smart. Even if they had enough fire power to win, which he thought that they did, it was still a lose-lose situation.

"Shock." Squeak said. "I feel where you're coming from."

Shonda slapped his arm. He was supposed to be talking him out of it, not encouraging him. Squeak ignored her and kept on talking.

"From what I see, we got more than enough guns and ammunition to take on 100 motherfuckers."

Shock smiled.

"But…" Squeak added. "Even if we completely slaughter all of them, we still lose."

Shock was confused. "How do we still lose if we kill them?

Squeak tapped on the side of his head with his index finger. "Think about it, bro. The Hooligans aren't the only people looking for us. We just murdered a cop. A detective at that. Right now, every cop in all of Texas City is looking for us. If we have a shoot-out, it would be like shooting off flares and exposing our location."

Shock lowered the A.K. He hadn't thought about it like that.

Squeak saw that he was getting through to him.

"Our best option is to ditch those cars and get the hell out of dodge. We not running from no man that bleed like we do. We're running from the electric chair."

Shonda stepped up again.

"So please, Richard. Let's get the fuck out of here."

Shock snapped back to reality. His initial plan was to get underground anyway. The argument with Sticks got him sidetracked. He needed to stop allowing his anger to control him. Or better yet, he needed to stop allowing other people to control him by way of his anger.

"You're right." Shock said, setting the gun down. "I'm trippin'."

Squeak picked it up and put it on the bed.

"Don't sweat it, bro." He told him. "He just ran you hot. It happens. Just hurry up and pack some stuff up so we can get to a safehouse."

With no further conversation, Shock went to the closet and knelt down in front of his safe. Squeaks phone began to ring again. Having finally resolved the situation, he pulled the phone out of his pocket. When he saw who was calling, he cursed.

"Fuck." He said, before reluctantly answering. "Hello."

"Squeak." Infamous replied. "I'm watching the news. Are you and Shonda ok?"

Squeak was happy to hear from infamous.

"Boss. If you're watching the news, you know I'm in one hell of a predicament right now. Me and Shonda are alright, but we need a place to lay low for a while."

Infamous was more than happy to help. Squeak did so much for him over the years that he was like family.

"I own some property out on the Westside." Infamous told him. "There's 3 empty houses over on Fulton St. They are all side by side and painted blue and white. One of them has a garage. The garage is never locked. The police are looking for your car, so park it inside the garage and don't move. When you get there, call me. I'll send someone over to help."

"Thanks, boss." Squeak said.

"Oh, and Squeak." Infamous added. "Who is that with you?"

Squeak thought about Shock. He couldn't tell Infamous the truth. There was no way he could explain that he was hiding out with the hitman for the Hooligans. Nothing he could say would make Infamous understand that.

"He's a friend, boss." Squeak lied. "I'll explain later tonight once we get to the safe house."

With that, they hung up. Shonda was standing close to Squeak trying to hear both ends of the conversation, but she couldn't.

"What did he say?" She asked.

Squeak smiled. "If we can make it to the Westside without getting caught, we're good."

Squeak knew that he could count on infamous to help him. They had a pretty close relationship when Squeak started running the streets. Infamous took him under his wing like a son. Squeak explained to Shonda the details about the safehouse while Shock finished packing. In one suitcase, he loaded up all of his money, and in another he packed all of his different outfits. Then, last but not least, he tossed all of his guns and knives onto the bed with the A.K. and wrapped them up in the blanket.

Tossing the tied part of the blanket over his shoulder like an oversized purse, Shock picked up both suitcases and said, "Let's go."

Squeak and Shonda grabbed their suitcases.

"We only need to take one car this time." Squeak suggested, leading the way out of the apartment. "It'll make travel easier."

"Let's take your car." Shock said. "My car is low on gas, and I doubt ya'll wanna stop at a convenience store and fill up."

Squeak agreed as he walked out the front door.

Shonda was behind him and Shock was behind her. On the way walking down the stairs, Squeak passed up a dark-skinned woman with big breast and real thick thighs. She looked at the trio oddly.

"Shock, baby." She said. "Are you moving out?"

Shock didn't want to stop and hold a conversation.

"Something like that." He said, as he kept walking.

Regina fell in line behind him and followed him down the stairs.

"Don't tell me you were gone leave without saying goodbye."

Shock sighed and rolled his eyes. Ever since he paid her for sex a little while ago, she been hounding him.

"That's what I get for putting that dick on her as good as I did." He thought.

"It ain't like that." Shock told her, trying to shake her. "I'm just really in a rush right now. I don't have time to talk."

Regina was persistent though. She continued to follow him.

"Ummm." She said, biting her lip. "I have something real important that I need to tell you."

"I'm listening." Shock said, as they entered the parking lot.

"Well. Don't be mad, but I may have given you a S.T.D."

Shock stopped in his tracks and turned around.

"What?!?" He thought back to the strange episode in the bathroom a while ago.

Regina threw her hands up. "My boyfriend gave it to me. It's not my fault."

Shock's anger kicked in. He forgot just that quick about controlling his temper as a means of controlling himself. All in one move, Shock dropped his suitcases and the guns and grabbed Regina by her shirt so she couldn't run.

"Baby, I'm sorry." She told him, using her hands to cover her face.

"Bitch." Shock yelled, as he drew his hand all the way back.

Regina braced herself as much as she could. Shock swung his hand around and slapped her with all of his might. The blow was so loud, Shonda and Squeak turned around to investigate. What they saw was Shock holding Regina in place with one hand and beating her mercilessly with the other.

"Start the car." Squeak said to Shonda.

The woman was screaming bloody murder. Shock upgraded from slaps to punches, and the woman already had a busted lip. Squeak grabbed Shock and forced him to release his victim.

"What the fuck are you doing?" He asked. "We need to be getting out of here."

Shock struggled against Squeak's grasp. Regina turned around and ran towards her apartment.

"You're fucking crazy." She screamed back.

"That bitch gave me a S.T.D.!" Shock revealed.

"So what?" Squeak replied, refusing to let go. "Did you already forget that we on the run? You wanna spend the rest of your life in prison behind that shit?"

The reference to prison helped calm Shock down. He realized that he did it again.

"Damn." Shock cursed. "My bad, bro. That bitch just got my dick feeling like I'm passing razors when I piss."

Squeak couldn't help but to laugh.

"Stop fucking these females naked head." He told him, releasing him.

Shonda honked the horn of the Cavalier. She already loaded up her and Squeak's things and she was sitting in the driver's seat with the car running.

"Come on." Squeak said, picking up the blanket full of guns to help lighten Shock's load.

Shock picked up the two suitcases and headed towards the car. When they made it to the car, Shock was on the side facing the street. What he saw made his heart drop.

"Get in the car!" He yelled to Squeak, rushing to get inside the vehicle himself.

Squeak looked behind him to see what had spooked Shock. Pulling up to the Rancho Santa-Maria apartments was about 6 cars, all painted blue, and all filled up with Hooligans.

"Damn." Squeak thought. "They must really respect my lil brother gangster. They came super deep."

Squeak and Shock jumped in the backseat of the car.

"Drive, sis! Drive!" Shock shouted.

Shonda looked at the caravan of Hooligans.

"Shit." She said, throwing the car in reverse.

To her left was the street and the enemy. To her right was the alley that ran behind the apartments. Shonda swung the car in the direction of the alley and peeled out. In her rearview mirror she could see men hanging out of the windows of the cars and aiming pistols in their direction.

"GET DOWN!!!" She warned, just as the first shots rang out.

The bullets made 'ping' noises as they came into contact with the body of the Cavalier. Shonda made a hard, right turn when she reached the alley and sped off behind the apartment complex toward the street that ran alongside it.

"DO SOMETHING!" She screeched, as the Hooligans turned into the alley behind them.

She didn't need to tell them. Shock and Squeak both were already untying the blanket trying to get to the weapons concealed within it. The Cavalier kicked up small rocks and dust particles as its wheels propelled the vehicle 50 miles per hour. Shonda held the wheel with both hands and kept remarkable control of the car. She held her head ducked down so low that she could barely see over the wheel. She knew that she needed to just drive long enough for Squeak and Shock to return fire, and they would survive.

All the residents of the apartment complex and the nearby neighborhood instinctively dropped to the ground as the sound of gunshots seemed to go on forever. In the backseat of the Cavalier, Shock reached one of the weapons first. Grabbing his trusty A.K., he smiled. He was waiting for the perfect opportunity to utilize its power. Still crouching down below the windshield, Shock pressed the button to lower the back doors window.

Squeak, who was more of a hand pistol type of dude, grabbed his .380 and a 9mm. Seeing him grab the 9mm, Shock yelled over the sound of the bullets.

"Just take the safety off! All of my guns are ready to shoot with one in the chamber."

Squeak released the safety and started rolling down the window on his side. Shonda made it to the street and yoked the car to the left. There was a huge pothole at the end of the alley, so when she hit it, the entire car hopped. The thrust caused Shock, who was climbing out the window, to fall back into his seat.

The asphalt gave Shonda better traction and she took full advantage of the fact by flooring it. The Cavaliers 4-liter engine howled. Once the car got back stabilized, Shock stuck his torso out the window again. The street was wider than the alley, so the Hooligan that was behind the man in front came from behind him and pulled up alongside him. Now, instead of two gunmen, there was four. Shock wasn't worried though. He could hear the bullets from their guns whizzing by his head and it only amped him up.

"Let's get it!" He shouted at his attackers as he applied pressure to the trigger of the A.K.

BLAAK! BLAAK! BLAAK!

The noise that the A.K. made was invigorating. Squeak hung his torso out the other window.

"GO FOR THE DRIVER!" He yelled to Shock, as he joined the shoot-out with shots of his own.

In the short amount of time that Squeak knew Shock, he somewhat figured him out. Squeak knew that Shock would be more than likely trying to turn the vehicles into swiss cheese. That's probably why he grabbed the A.K.

Squeak had other plans. To hell with the vehicle and the shooters. If they could take out the person driving the cars, the other two factors would be immobilized by default. Every shot Squeak fired was aimed directly at the driver. Shock, on the other hand, continued to go for the people shooting at him. He wanted the body count.

Shonda wanted to make evasive maneuvers, but she saw her brothers hanging out the windows. As she blew past other motorist, she tried to use them as obstacles to hinder the Hooligans. They would always swerve easily around them though. Lucky for her, traffic was light. Had this highspeed chase been going on during rush hour, a collision would've been imminent.

The two cars immediately behind the trio was an all blue Dodge F150 truck and a sky-blue Chevy Impala. Shock was letting rounds off in the direction of both vehicles. He was swinging the A.K. back and forth, refusing to ease up on the trigger. His wild antics, reminiscent of a Rambo movie, finally paid off when he saw the man hanging out of the passenger side window of the Impala jerk back violently as one of the shells from his A.K. tore into his chest.

The man dropped his weapon as his arms flung out to his sides. Trying to recover from the shot, the man lurched forward and clutched his wound. Shock didn't know if he was dying, or if the shock of being hit knocked him off balance, and really, he didn't care. He watched gleefully as the man slumped over. When the Impala swerved, probably trying to save the man, his entire body slid out of the window and hit the pavement rolling.

The car behind the Impala bounced up as it ran the dude over. No one in the caravan of Hooligans stopped to check on him. Squeak saw what happened and grimaced. That was a horrible way to die. Hitting a moving target while being a moving target yourself was proving to be harder than expected. He struck the windshield of the F150 several times, but he failed to hit the driver.

BANG! BANG! CLICK! CLICK! CLICK!

"Damn." Squeak cursed.

He was out of bullets. Squeak slid back into the backseat and tossed the two pistols he had on the floor. He needed another weapon. Shonda saw Squeak re-enter the car and saw her chance.

"Grab Shock!" She yelled.

Squeak looked up. He had no idea what Shonda was telling him to grab Shock for, but he obeyed none the less. Extending his body over the blanket, he wrapped on to Shock's legs. Shock looked down quizzically. Shonda gripped the steering wheel tight as she neared the next intersection, hit the brake, and turned the wheel hard to the right onto Hwy 146.

The tires squealed as the car was forced to do something it wasn't designed to do. The gunman hanging out of the F150 noticed the pause in the trio's gun fire and capitalized on it. He fired off 3 quick shots at the discombobulated Shock.

"Auugghh!" Shock growled, as one of the bullets tore into his left shoulder.

His body jerked from the sudden change in direction of the Cavalier, and his body rocked from the force of the hot lead. The A.K. he was holding almost fell, but Shock mustered enough strength to hold on to it. He wasn't about to let his baby go. Squeak heard Shock growl and felt him lurch back and forth. His instincts told him something was wrong. As Shonda completed the turn, Squeak pulled Shock back inside the car.

"I'm hit." Shock said, dropping the A.K. down on the blanket.

"What?" Shonda shouted, trying to stabilize the car. "What happened? Is he ok?"

Squeak quickly scanned Shock's body looking for wounds. Shock helped him find it by placing his hand over his shoulder. Noticing the entry wound, Squeak became afraid that he might lose his little brother again.

Using his free hand to grab another pistol, Shock said, "I'm alright. Don't worry about it."

Fighting off the pain as best he could, Shock attempted to lean out the window again and continue shooting.

"Don't worry about it." Squeak said, as he picked up the A.K. that Shock dropped. "I got 'em."

If it's one thing that Squeak just absolutely abhorred, it was when a person tried to hurt his family. Seeing Shock grimace in pain, infuriated him. He wasn't the type to lose his cool though. He was a very meticulous individual. Squeak knew that this fiasco had gone on long enough. Gripping the A.K. tightly, Squeak lunged back out of the window and aimed. Bullets ricocheted off the hood right next to his face.

The Hooligans hit one of them and they were desperately trying to get the other one. Squeak didn't let it faze him. The sound of gunshots coming in his direction startled him. He looked over his shoulder and saw Shock's good arm extended out the other window. He was firing a revolver. Squeak couldn't help but to smile. His little brother was a damn fool for real.

Getting back to the task at hand, Squeak aimed at the windshield of the truck and let loose.

BLAAK! BLAAK! BLAAK!

The man driving the F150 swung his head from left to right trying to dodge the gun spray. Squeak held down on the trigger. Shonda peered through the rearview mirror as the driver of the truck began to lose control of the vehicle. She didn't know if he was hit or if he was just blinded by the damaged windshield. Either way, he swung the truck hard to the left and then back to the right.

His judgement of how much pressure to apply to the steering wheel was off. He swung the truck right into the Impala. The sound of metal colliding with metal echoed for blocks. Squeak continued to shoot as the two cars tried frantically not to total out. It was nothing they could do though. Their unexpected drop in speed caused the cars behind them to crash into their bumpers.

Tires squealed, glass shattered, metal crunched, and Squeak still continued to shoot. Soon, all six cars that were pursuing them was piled up in a horrific wreck that extended from one side of the street all the way to the opposite side of the street. Before Squeak retreated back into the Cavalier, he shot one last round at the two bodies that were discharged from the vehicles.

"That's what I'm talking about!" Shock yelled happily, as he watched the aftermath through the back windshield.

Squeak slid back into the backseat. Maintaining a level head, he instructed Shonda to hurry up and get them to the safehouse on Fulton St.

"What about Richard?" She asked, turning off the road that the wreck was on.

Shock spoke up while clutching his wound.

"We'll worry about me when we get there. I'll be alright."

....

Rebecca finally built up enough courage to drive herself up to the hospital. She was still afraid of what she might find there but running from reality would not change reality. She made it to Mainland Medical Center Hospital 3 minutes ago, but she was still sitting inside of her car. Rebecca was trying hard to make herself get out of the car.

"Come on, Rebecca." She said, wiping the tears off of her face. "Derrick needs you."

Rebecca took one last deep breath and exited the vehicle. It was a struggle, but she literally had to will her legs to move.

"Just walk, Rebecca. Just walk."

Once she started in the direction of the front door, she would not allow herself to stop walking. To her left and right she saw a few police cruisers.

"Derrick's coworkers must've shown up for support." She thought.

As she got close to the glass doors, they automatically slid open. Rebecca was rushed by two uniformed officers as soon as she stepped inside the building.

"Mrs. Rose." One of them said. "I'm so sorry."

Rebecca tried to speak, but her voice got caught in her throat. So instead of verbalizing her response, she simply raised her hands to let them know that they didn't need to apologize. The two officers looked nervously at one another.

"Ummm." One of them said. "Do you want us to show you to the O.R.?"

Rebecca's heart jumped.

"The O.R.?" She asked, praying that she didn't hear him wrong. "You mean he's…"

Rebecca couldn't even finish her sentence. For the first time since she received that fateful phone call informing her that Derrick was gunned down in the line of duty, Rebecca experienced a feeling of hope.

Wiping her face with the palms of her hands, she asked, "Is he alive?"

The tall, dark skinned officer talking to her said, "You don't know?"

He thought for sure that Detective Rose wife was updated on his condition. Then again, she just made it to the hospital. How could she know?

"Come on." He said to Rebecca, leading her to the O.R.

The other officer stayed put.

"So…" Rebecca said, urging the officer to let her know what was going on. "You said he's in the operating room. Is he alive?"

"Well. I'm not a doctor, but I can tell you what the word that's been going around is. They say that Rose was dead on arrival, but somehow, the E.M.S. workers were able to get his heart to start beating again. Now, while that is a good sign, they weren't able to get him to regain his consciousness."

They made it to the elevator and the officer pressed the button to retrieve the next available one.

"You have to understand." He continued. "Rose lost an awful lot of blood. Any time the body goes through that kind of shock, it naturally shuts down as a defense mechanism. Right now, the doctors are trying to remove all of the bullets from his body, patch him up, and keep his heart pumping all at the same time."

The elevator door slid open.

"So, he's alive?" Rebecca asked again, stepping into the elevator.

The officer followed her in and pressed 5. The operating room was on the fifth floor.

"Last I heard, he was." He told her, as the door shut.

Rebecca hugged herself and buried her chin into her breast. Whispering in a low voice, she thanked the Most High God for answering her prayer. She remembered how she petitioned Him not too long ago. Rebecca wasn't a religious woman, but she told herself that if God brought Derrick through this ok, she would definitely do her best to establish some sort of relationship with Him. The remainder of the elevator ride, and the walk to the O.R., the two were silent.

Officer Ronald "Pookie" Hall, the Officer that was walking with Rebecca, knew that this must be an extremely tough time for her. He knew that his wife would be totally hysterical if his life was hanging in the balance like the Detectives was. The situation really brought home the danger that they all faced daily. All of the cops on the force were thinking about their own mortality, whether they wanted to or not. Detective Rose wasn't everyone's favorite cop, but in times like these, they all pulled together.

As Officer Hall and Rebecca neared the O.R., Rebecca decided to try some more of that prayer. All of her life she heard stories of how prayer caused so many various phenomena, but she never been one to believe the hype. She always chalked up the occurrences to coincidence rather than divine intervention. Rebecca grew up thinking that if there was a Supreme Being watching over everything that took place within the universe, one human in the midst of countless planets, stars, and galaxies was way too insignificant to warrant that Supreme Being's attention.

Now, in the face of a problem that was too big for her to handle on her own, she began to wish that all of the stories were true. If they were true, then she had help from someone that could actually make a difference. She just hoped that He would answer another one of her prayers. He already brought Derrick back to life, but now she needed him to regain consciousness.

Rebecca wasn't sure how prayer was supposed to work. Did God only answer one request per crisis? If so, she should've been more specific when she called on Him back at her house. The two of them made it to the O.R. and stood just outside of the door. A couple of years back, there use to be a window that allowed people in the hallway to look into the operating room and see what was happening. The board at the hospital made the decision to remove the window after members of the patient's family began constantly beating on the window and shouting at the doctors to work harder.

The noise became too distracting to the doctors. At the present moment, Rebecca wished that it was still there. On the one hand, she wanted to know what was going on with Derrick, but on the other hand, she didn't. At least if the window was still there, the decision to peer inside would've already been made. She would've had no choice but to gaze in and see for herself what was going on.

Rebecca stood there for a moment and weighed her options. Then, taking a deep breath, she reached for the door. Before her hand made it to the knob, someone on the inside turned it and opened the door. Rebecca stepped back and watched as a light skinned Doctor in green scrubs came out. He stood about 5"9 and was handsome looking.

"Terrance." Officer Hall said, approaching the doctor. "This is Rebecca, Detective Rose wife."

The doctor looked over at Rebecca.

"How's my husband?" She asked.

"Mrs. Rose." He answered. "We're taking real good care of your husband and we're doing everything in our power to help him."

"Yeah." Officer Hall stepped in. "Terrance here knows Rose, and he's personally seeing to it that whatever can be done, is being done."

Rebecca looked at the man strange. She didn't know who he was. How did Derrick know him?

"You know my husband?"

"Well." He replied, feeling slightly put on the spot. "It's not that I know him personally, but I know of him. See, for the past few days my baby sister has been working on a case with him and she's mentioned him a couple of times."

Rebecca's mind thought about who he could be talking about. Then it hit her.

"Are you talking about Sierra?" She asked, hating to even speak the woman's name.

"Yeah." He answered. "Sierra's my sister."

Rebecca instantly thought back to how that little homewrecker was the cause of all of this. If she wouldn't have seduced Derrick, she wouldn't have slept with Shock, and if she wouldn't have slept with Shock, Shock wouldn't have shot Derrick. Every single molecule in Rebecca's body wanted to go off on Terrance right then and there, but she restrained herself. Not because it wouldn't be proper, but because she didn't want it to come out that she had an affair with her husband's attacker, and that was the reason he was shot. Instead of opening the door for everything to come flooding out, she directed the conversation to the condition of Derrick.

"Is Derrick going to be ok?" She asked.

For the next few minutes, Doctor Terrance Martin filled Rebecca in on everything he knew about Detective Rose. Rose had been shot a total of 13 times. Three bullets struck his left arm, two bullets struck him in the right arm, two hit him in his left leg, one hit him in his right leg, three bullets penetrated his chest, and two bullets struck him in the stomach.

The way things were looking, Rose was more than likely going to lose a lung. Two of the bullets that entered his torso caused one of his lungs to collapse. For the most part though, they were able to keep Rose alive. When the doctor got to that part, Rebecca cut him off.

"Wait a minute." She said. "What do you mean... 'for the most part'?"

Dr. Terrance rubbed his hands together.

"You have to understand, Mrs. Rose." He said, choosing his words carefully. "Your husband was clinically dead for a total of seven minutes before the E.M.S. workers were able to revive him. That type of stress on the human body is very extreme. Even though we were able to get his heart to beat on its own again, getting his brain to function properly is something medical science isn't advanced enough to do yet."

Rebecca felt the hope she once had slipping away.

"A brain deprived of oxygen for that long a time period has the potential to be severely damaged." Dr. Terrance continued. "We're doing all we can, but..."

He let his sentence trail off.

"But what?" Rebecca asked, wishing he would just say what it was that he was trying to say. "What are you saying?"

Terrance looked nervously from Rebecca to Officer Hall. He never enjoyed being the one to deliver the bad news to the family of his patients. No matter how many times he went through the process, it never got any easier. In fact, it sometimes got harder.

Dr. Terrance took a deep breath.

"Mrs. Rose." He said, figuring he should just go ahead and get it over with. "Derrick Rose is brain dead."

Rebecca's knees buckled. Both the Doctor and the Officer rushed to her side when they saw her falling to the floor. Everybody else that was on the fifth floor at that particular time turned to look when they heard the scream.

"NOOOOOOOO!!!!!"

....

"We gotta switch cars." Shonda said, doing her best to stay on the back streets. "This bitch here done got way too hot."

Squeak considered what she said and decided that she was right. The poor Cavalier had so many bullet holes in it, he wondered how it was still drivable. The back windshield alone had about six holes in it.

"She's right." Shock spoke up, unzipping one of his suitcases. "Ugh."

His wound began to throb.

Grabbing the suitcase from him, Squeak said, "Here. Let me get it. What are you looking for?"

Shock leaned back in his seat.

"Do you know what a dent puller is?" He asked, trying to conceal the fact that his wound was hurting like hell.

"Know what it is?" Squeak repeated sarcastically.

He opened the suitcase and retrieved the dent puller.

"Damn lil bro. What don't you have in here?"

Shock laughed.

"Since you know what it is, do you know what to do with it?"

Squeak smirked, reached in the suitcase to find a screwdriver, and then said to Shonda, "Pull into the next apartment complex that we come to."

Shonda looked into the rearview mirror at her two younger brothers. She could already tell that they were going to playfully compete to see who was the most hood. Lucky for all of them, they were only about two blocks away from Lakeview Apartments. As soon she got closer and began to turn into the parking lot, Squeak began giving instructions on what to do.

"Go all the way to the back."

Then, to both of them, he said, "Look. This how we gone do it."

Squeak explained the plan while Shonda made her way to the back side of the parking lot. Pulling up into an empty space, Squeak was the only one to climb out. With the dent puller in hand and the screwdriver in his pocket, he quickly, walked from car to car, checking to see if any one of them was unlocked. The atmosphere was perfect because there were no witnesses that he might've had to deal with.

Better still, it only took him a total of three tries before he hit the jackpot. A gray two-door Regal opened right up for him. Squeak wasted no time climbing in.

When Shonda noticed that Squeak had found one, she said, "Come on, bro."

Her and Shock grabbed one suitcase a piece and headed towards the Regal. Squeak was busy screwing one end of the dent puller into the ignition of the car when Shonda and Shock opened the passenger side door. He didn't even look up as they tossed the suitcases into the backseat and went back to the Cavalier for another load.

After Squeak screwed the screw completely into the ignition, he waited patiently for Shonda and Shock to finish transferring everything from one vehicle to the next.

On their last trip, Shock climbed into the backseat. "Aiight bro. Hit it."

Squeak gripped the opposite end of the dent puller and yanked on it hard. The force of the ignition being pulled out of its slot made a loud noise.

BANG...BANG...BANG!

It finally gave on the third tug. Squeak quickly inserted the screwdriver into the hole where the ignition once was and used it to crank up the car. As the engine roared to life, Squeak backed out of the parking space and drove off. When he left the parking lot and turned on to the street, he drove the car as if he had every right in the world to be behind the wheel.

"We're good now." He told them. "Just sit back and chill. It shouldn't take us no more than another 5 or 10 minutes to make it to the safehouse."

"Good." Shock replied. "Because my fuckin' arm is killing me."

Shonda turned around in her seat.

"Don't worry bro. You gone be alright. We lost you once already when we were kids. We're not about to lose you again."

Shock smiled in spite of the pain.

Chapter Seventeen

Sierra raised the shovel above her head and cried out in frustration. She was tired, sweaty, and covered in sand. Her and the woman with her spent the last 2 hours digging around in the two sand traps on hole number 11 at the Bayou Golf Course.

"Damn it!" Sierra exclaimed, hurling the shovel to the side.

Both women had their hair matted to their faces and they were exhausted. After their grueling endeavor of back breaking manual labor, they had come up empty handed. The woman pushed her shovel to the side and allowed her fatigue to take over. No longer caring about the filth, she plopped down on one of the piles of sand she displaced. They both thought for sure that they would find the $20 million buried within one of the sand traps, but they didn't. After all, the sand traps were the only place that made sense.

They weighed all of their options. It was pretty safe to assume that Burby didn't tell anybody about the money. Why would he? No one could possibly be trusted with the whereabouts of $20 million. Money has the power to turn friend against friend, mother against daughter, and father against son. A man as crooked as Burby understood that more than anybody. Sierra used that logic to conclude that Burby buried the money on his own. If he would've dug up any of the actual green grass on the course, it would still be evident. The sand, however, could be easily dug up, replaced, and then smoothed over.

Plus, one of the essential objectives of the game of golf is to avoid the sand traps at all cost. So, Burby could be pretty certain that his buried treasure would be able to remain buried, virtually undisturbed, for as long as he chose to leave it there. The only problem with that theory was that they dug up both the sand traps on hole number 11 and hadn't found any money.

Sierra wanted to cry. She ran her sand covered hands through her hair and looked back and forth across the gold course. Deep down, she was trying to will herself to see something of significance.

"Think, Sierra." The woman said to her, knowing that Sierra was close to giving up. "There has to be something we overlooked."

Sierra dropped down in the dirt next to the woman.

Hanging her head, she said, "I don't know. Everything pointed to this golf course and this particular hole."

Sierra opened her arms wide.

"Everything!" She reiterated.

"The timing of when Burby bought it, the reason Burby bought it, and even how he told his ex-wife that everything would be ok if she just came out to see the damn thing."

The woman thought it over.

"Well maybe he moved it and it's not buried on the golf course anymore?" she offered.

Sierra spit out a few grains of sand that entered her mouth.

"That wouldn't make sense." She said, trying not to sound too judgmental. "This was the perfect spot to hide it. The only way I could see Burby moving it from this golf course would be if he was skipping town and going to go live overseas somewhere, but we have no indication that he was planning anything like that."

The woman scratched her head. She wanted to be of more assistance, but she couldn't. She told Sierra everything she knew about the money. The rest had to be figured out by the amateur detective.

"Maybe," the woman said, offering one last possibility. "Maybe the money is here, just not on this particular hole. I mean hell, there's 17 other holes to choose from."

Sierra looked up at the woman as if she just made the most intelligent observation in the world. The woman nervously studied the wide-eyed expression that now graced Sierra's face.

"Ummm. What did I say wrong?" She asked, expecting a backlash for her most recent comment.

Sierra stood to her feet and gazed out at all of the yet to be explored area.

"You didn't say anything wrong." She assured her. "In fact, you said something downright brilliant."

Sierra wondered why she hadn't thought of it herself. True, the golf course was a gift for Burby and Bianca's 11th Anniversary, and the number 11 could be read the same way backwards as it could forward, but that didn't mean hole 11 was the only hole that Burby could use to hide the money. Sierra felt her enthusiasm returning. She still had a chance to come away from this thing extremely wealthy.

Stepping out of the sand and onto the grass, Sierra exclaimed, "The money has to be on one of the other holes. It has to be."

When she bent over to pick up her shovel, something behind her clicked. The noise sounded oddly familiar.

"What the fuck is this?" A man behind her asked. "And what money has to be here?"

The two women watched as a figure emerged from behind the trees that lined the golf course. Sierra's eyes focused in on the big chrome gun the man was holding. The woman that was with her focused in on something totally different.

Staring in horror, she stammered out, "K... K... Kenneth. What are you doing here?"

Sticks looked at the badge attached to the hip of the woman with his wife.

"What am I doing here?" Sticks repeated. "I was just about to ask you the same thing, Silvia. What are you doing here?"

Sierra and Silvia exchanged nervous glances. Sierra was more confused than Silvia though. She recognized the man from one of the recordings that Burby had. He was the leader of the Hooligans. Sierra wondered how Silvia knew him as Kenneth. She only knew him as Sticks. Sierra figured she could worry about that later. The more important issue was how she was going to get her sidearm off of the golf cart that she and Silvia used to get out to hole 11. She silently cursed herself for leaving it. In her defense though, she had no way of knowing Sticks would show up and hold them both at gun point.

Silvia climbed to her feet.

"It's not what you think, baby." She said, extending her arms out in front of her.

Sticks thought about the reason he was there. She was right to say that it wasn't what he thought. He thought that his wife was cheating on him. Finding her digging around on a golf course with a female police officer was not what he expected at all.

Silvia cut her eyes at Sierra.

"She made me come out here." Silvia told him, trying to save herself.

Sierra looked at Silvia with surprise on her face.

"What?" She exclaimed.

Silvia turned to face Sierra.

"Don't front now, cop. You threatened to take away my babies if I didn't help you find Burby's money."

Sierra's jaw dropped. What the hell was Silvia doing, and why did she call Sticks, baby?

"I didn't threaten you." Sierra shot back. "You found me and asked for my help."

"Lier!" Silvia shouted.

Sticks watched in wonder as the two women began to argue. He had no idea what money they were talking about, so he let them argue for a while in the hopes that they would give him some insight into what was actually going on. Silvia knew that she couldn't allow the truth to come out. Sticks would kill her if he knew. She decided that in order to save herself, she would have to sacrifice Sierra.

Sierra was racking her brain to try and figure out what exactly was going on. She didn't know if Silvia was trying to confuse Sticks to hopefully get them out of this mess, or if she was really doing everything in her power to cut her throat. She was leaning toward actual betrayal. Sticks listened to the women bicker for a few moments longer before he had enough. Their game of going back and forth was getting him nowhere. Sticks pointed his pistol at the trees and let off a single shot.

BANG!

The many birds that were resting in the branches of the nearby trees all took flight at the sound of the shot. The two women both ducked and looked at Sticks.

"Ladies." He said, in a calm voice. "Your arguing is not productive. So, what I want to know is why there's a cop, digging up dirt on a golf course, and talking about money that the late Police Chief buried here. Not only that, I would also like to know why this cop has elicited the assistance of my fucking wife."

Sierra's ears twitched when Sticks referred to Silvia as his wife. Her brain instantly started putting it all together.

"Silvia is your wife?" Sierra asked, not really desiring an answer.

She now understood why Silvia wanted to protect Shock. By protecting Shock, she would've been protecting Sticks, and by protecting Sticks, she would've bought herself a little more time. The fact that she was married to Sticks also explained how she knew about the money in the first place. Silvia could tell that Sierra was now beginning to see the big picture.

Slowly trying to climb out of the sand trap and approach Sticks, Silvia said, "I'm so glad you came, baby. Now we can get rid of this cop together, find the money Burby stashed, and get the hell out of here."

Sierra now knew that Silvia wasn't running any kind of game. She was trying her hardest to get her killed.

"Don't trust her, Sticks." Sierra called out. "She tried to get you murdered."

Sticks pointed the pistol at Silvia and stopped her in her tracks.

"What is she talking about?"

Silvia shook her head. "She's lying, daddy. She's just trying to save her own skin."

"No!" Sierra shouted. "She's the one lying. Think about it, Sticks. Have you ever wondered what caused this war between you and Infamous to start in the first place? Aren't you the least bit curious as to how Infamous found out that you had something to do with the death of his son?"

Silvia glared at Sierra.

"SHUT-UP!" She screamed.

Sierra ignored her and continued to expose her.

"She told Infamous what you did. Your wife. Your own wife turned on you."

Sticks thought back to his visit with Loretta. She told him that Infamous informed her as to what happened. He glared at Silvia.

"B... b ... baby." Silvia stuttered. "You don't believe her, do you?"

Sticks considered the possibility. Silvia was aware of what happened, but that didn't mean she told Infamous. Sierra waited to see how Sticks would respond to what she just told him. He appeared to be a bit undecided. Sierra thought about what she could say or do to convince him.

Her mind floated back to the first night she met Silvia. It was a few days before the very first murder. Sierra was sitting around her house smoking on a personal blunt. There was a program about creatures of the sea on the Discovery Channel. Sierra puffed on the blunt and then ashed the top of it in the ashtray she had on the cushion next to her. She was enjoying the time to relax after a long day of driving around in her cruiser making her rounds.

She never was big on arresting people, so she just pulled over a couple of people for traffic violations. The work itself wasn't strenuous, but it was so boring that it left her fatigued. Sierra liked watching shows about wildlife ever since she was a little girl. She was deep into the segment on sharks when a knock on the door distracted her.

Setting her blunt down in the ashtray, she climbed off the sofa and went to answer the door. Opening it, she was surprised to see a tall, slim, light brown skinned woman standing there.

"I don't mean to bother you." She said. "But do you mind giving me a moment of your time?"

Sierra looked the lady up and down. It was at least 9:00pm and she never seen the woman before in her life. Sierra noticed the woman was clutching an oversized purse. All Sierra was wearing was an extra-large t-shirt, a pair of gray gym shorts, and no weapon. She couldn't help but to be a little nervous.

"Ummm." Sierra replied, looking the woman up and down. "Who are you, and what do you want?"

The woman glanced up and down the block. Sierra got the impression that she wasn't supposed to be there.

"My name is Silvia." The woman answered. "And I have a proposition for you."

"What kind of proposition?" Sierra asked, placing her hands on her hips.

The woman grabbed the zipper of her purse. Sierra watched, ready to slam the door in her face, as she opened it up.

"A proposition." The lady responded, opening the purse wide so that Sierra could see the contents. "A proposition that will ultimately make you a very rich woman."

Sierra's eyes got wide. If she was a cartoon character, her pupils would've changed into big green dollar signs. Inside of the purse, the woman that she now knew as Silvia, had stacks and stacks of 100-dollar bills. Sierra was speechless. She just stood there with her mouth open, googling the money. Her reaction let Silvia know that she chose the right person to go to.

She closed the purse.

"Can I come in?"

Sierra, still mesmerized by the money, was more than happy to invite her in. For the next 10 minutes or so, Silvia filled Sierra in on exactly what she needed her to do. Sierra listened to every word. The woman was talking about giving her $20,000 right then and there for allegiance, and $2 million when they found some money that the Chief of Police supposedly had stashed away.

At first, Sierra was skeptical. Why did the woman need her? Silvia explained that she needed someone with police connections to assist her in finding the money. When Sierra asked how she even knew about the money, Silvia told her that she had proof that the leader of the Hooligans paid him a large amount of money to cover up a crime for him. Sierra asked to see the proof. Without hesitating, Silvia pulled out her cell phone and showed Sierra a videoclip that she saved on it. What Sierra saw, plus the offering of $20,000, was enough to convince her that Silvia was telling the truth.

By the time Silvia left that night, Sierra was $20,000 richer and she was racking her brain trying to come up with a way to find the rest of the money, and just when she was thinking she wouldn't be able to uphold her end of the bargain, the war between the Villains and the Hooligans jumped off. It dawned on her almost immediately that Silvia must have been the one that started the whole thing. After all, it was in the aftermath of the war that Sierra was able to make all of her progress.

Sierra's daydream/recollection didn't take long to play out in real time. The whole scenario came and went in what may have been 5 seconds. When she began to focus again on the here and now, Silvia was still trying to inch closer to Sticks and deceive him. Sierra wasn't the smartest person in the world, but she had enough game about herself to know that if Silvia was keeping her actions a secret from Sticks, she obviously had plans on giving him the shaft too when it was all said and done.

"Sticks." Sierra called out before Silvia had a chance to close the gap between her and Sticks.

Both of them turned to face Sierra. "If you don't believe me, why not just check her cell phone and see the videoclip she sent to Infamous."

Sticks looked at Silvia. If a human ever had the look of a deer caught in the headlights, Silvia did just then. She thought about what she showed Sierra to convince her to help her. Taking a step backwards, Silvia cursed herself for not getting rid of that recording. Sticks noticed Silvia nervously stepping back and aimed his gun at her torso.

"What is the cop talking about, Silvia?" He asked, walking up to her.

She extended her arms out in front of herself and shook her head.

"Sh... she's... she's just trying to confuse you, baby. She wants to turn you against me."

Sticks still wasn't sure what was really going on, so he didn't trust either one of the women. He didn't trust the cop simply because of her occupation, and he didn't trust his wife, simply because she was obviously working with the cop.

Sticks held out an open palm.

"Give me the phone."

Silvia grabbed the cell phone through her pants pocket and held on to it.

"Honey, she's manipulating you." Silvia said, in a final attempt to keep him from checking her phone.

Her hesitation let Sticks know that at least some of the cop's words were true. He wondered if Silvia had actually been the one to turn the police on to Shock. He wasn't worried about Shock though. He had sent his soldiers to take care of that.

Becoming upset with his wife's incriminating actions, he quickly stepped up to her and pressed the barrel of his chrome Desert Eagle to the side of her head. Sierra licked her lips. Her instincts were telling her that if she would have any chance of getting out of this alive, her only opportunity was coming up.

"Silvia." Sticks said, glaring directly into her eyes. "I'm beginning to think that you're the one who's been manipulating me."

He reached into her pocket and pulled out the phone.

"So, if you continue to speak," he added, tapping her head with his gun. "I'll shoot you."

Silvia's lips quivered. She knew firsthand that her husband was a killer.

"But Kenneth." She pled, beginning to cry.

Sticks rolled his eyes. "I just told you…" He said, letting his words trail off.

Sierra watched as Sticks slapped Silvia in her face with the gun.

"Uuunngghh!" She cried out, as she stumbled backwards and fell into the sand trap.

Sticks pointed the pistol at her. "I said, shut… up."

Silvia grabbed the side of her face and stared up at Sticks with fear in her eyes. Her head was throbbing, and her heart was beating fast. When Sticks started going through her phone looking for the recording, she knew that it was only a matter of time before he found what he was looking for, and when he found it…

The thought of what he would do caused Silvia to shudder. She looked over at Sierra for some kind of help.

Sierra mouthed the words, "Go to hell!"

Ironically, Silvia knew that in a few moments, she might literally do just that. Sticks pressed a series of buttons on the phone and flipped through the list of titles that Silvia had come up with to label the individual video clips. Most of them were pretty generic. Things pertaining to their two sons, and holidays. At first glance, nothing stood out to him as odd. He didn't want to watch each clip, but he was prepared to.

Making it to the end of the list, Sticks began to scroll back up to the top. It looked like he was going to have to view them one by one. Halfway to the top, he stopped. He noticed something that he didn't notice before.

"The boys first Christmas."

He read the title out loud, quizzically.

"First Christmas." He thought.

Sticks peered over the phone at Silvia. She was still sitting in the sand massaging her face. The cop was still standing next to the sand trap. Sticks thought back to when he bought the phone for his wife. She only had it since 2014. Their two sons were born November 8, 2012, so their first Christmas was in 2012. Silvia didn't even have the phone for their first Christmas. She didn't even have the phone for their second Christmas either.

Sticks rubbed his thumb over the cell phones keypad. Then, he pressed the button to view, 'The boys first Christmas'. The view was coming in from a funny angle. It didn't take him long to figure out what it was a recording of though. He remembered that day like it was a yesterday.

One of his drug runners, a new kid named Korey, just somehow lost 18 ounces of Sticks dope. Sticks had Shock and Abdul bring the kid by his home in Amburn Oaks. His kids were asleep, and his wife was sitting on the living room couch with him when his soldiers arrived. It was apparent that Silvia was holding the phone next to her thigh while she was recording.

He couldn't figure out why she was recording though. He disciplined his foot soldiers in front of her before, so he figured she just liked to watch. Now, he was thinking she just needed something to incriminate him with. The video clip began after everyone was there. Sticks was looking at himself standing in front of Korey, with Shock and Abdul standing on Korey's left and right sides.

"How the fuck do you lose half a bird?" Sticks shouted, throwing his hands in the air.

Korey guarded his face thinking that Sticks was about to strike him.

"I told you, boss. Alexis came banging on the door hollering about the jump out boys was coming down the alley, so I panicked. I panicked and ran."

Sticks put his hand on his forehead.

"Come on, kid." He began as if the whole thing was unbelievable. "Alexis is a smoker. Why did you believe her?"

Korey was afraid. He knew that he messed up bad.

"I... I... I just panicked." He answered.

Sticks shook his head.

"So, you panicked, ran off, left my dope behind, and somebody just walked inside of the house and took it? Is that what you're telling me?"

Korey nodded his head.

Sticks turned sideways and placed his hands on his hips. Everybody in the room stood silent. Then, with surprising quickness, Sticks backhanded Korey with all of his might. Korey cried out in pain as well as fear and fell to the floor.

"I'm sorry, Sticks." He apologized.

"Sorry?" Sticks repeated. "Sorry doesn't get me my drugs back!"

He kicked Korey in the side.

"Sorry doesn't get me my money!"

He kicked him again.

"Sorry doesn't do shit!"

Sticks kicked him a few more times until Korey was balled up into the fetal position struggling to breathe. Sticks adjusted his clothes. They became a bit disheveled in the onslaught of blows.

"Get him out of my sight." Sticks instructed, Shock and Abdul.

The two bent over and picked up a coughing Korey. As they drug him towards the door, the kid found his courage.

"You gone get yours, Sticks." He threatened in between coughs. "You can't do me like this. You don't know who my father is."

Shock and Abdul stopped.

Sticks laughed.

"Your father." He replied. "As if I give a fuck who your father is."

"You do give a fuck." Korey told him. "That's why you made a truce with him. You knew that my father was going to kill your bitch ass."

Everybody froze. Sticks let what the kid said roll around in his head for a few moments.

"Yeah." Korey continued, seeing that Sticks realized who his father was. "Let's see how tough you are when Infamous comes after you."

Sticks couldn't believe how disrespectful the kid was being. He walked up to Korey. Shock was holding one arm and Abdul was holding the other.

"You got the nerve to come into my house," Sticks began, speaking slowly and evenly. "And threaten me."

He looked around.

"In front of my men. In front of my wife."

Sticks grabbed a fist full of Korey's shirt.

"Plus, you threaten me with a piece of shit like, Infamous."

Korey opened his mouth to defend his father's name, but Sticks slapped him again before he could get the words out, and this time, Shock and Abdul continued to hold him while Sticks beat him.

Sierra licked her lips. Her options were running out. Sticks and his gun stood between her and her gun.

"Maybe I can hit him with the shovel?" She thought, looking at the possible weapon that laid at her feet.

Slowly, doing her best not to be noticed, Sierra bent down and grabbed the shovel. Before she could make a move, Silvia, knowing that she had to do something quick too, picked up a handful of sand and tossed it at Sticks face. The grains of dirt hit Sticks before he had a chance to block or close his eyes.

"Shit." He exclaimed, dropping the phone to the ground and trying desperately to get the sand off of his face.

Both women saw their chance to do something while Sticks was temporarily blinded. Silvia made a beeline for Sierra's gun. Sierra only had a second to react. Figuring that Silvia would make it to the gun before she would, she tossed the shovel at Sticks and ran full speed towards the trees that lined the golf course. As soon as she felt like she had a little cover, she dug her cell phone out of her pocket.

Behind her, she heard 3 gunshots ring out. She didn't know who was shooting at who, who got hit, or if anyone was dead, and really, she didn't care. The only thing that mattered to her was making it off of that golf course alive. At first, she dialed the police station, but thought twice before she made the actual call. Instead, she erased that number and called Rose. She didn't want to have to explain to her coworkers what was going on out there, but she might possibly be able to explain things to Rose.

Sierra kept running full speed as she listened to the phone ring.

"Please pick up." She begged, as she swerved in, out, and around tree trunks.

When Rose didn't answer, she cursed. Becoming tired, but not wanting to stop running, she tried his number one last time. When he didn't answer, she gave up trying. In the distance, she heard what sounded like the motor of a golf cart. Sierra knew that she wouldn't be able to make it back to her car before the person on the golf cart found her.

She had to think fast. Turning her head from side to side as she ran, she noticed a small pond dug out just past the tree line. Growing out of the water, maybe two feet above the water line, were several clusters of grass. Not seeing any other option, Sierra turned and ran towards the pond. When she made it to the water's edge, she stopped and looked behind her.

The golf cart sounded closer, but it wasn't visible through the trees. Moving slow, trying not to make too many ripples in the water, Sierra stepped one foot into the pond. The water was ice cold, but she forced herself to ignore the frigid feeling. Sierra slowly dipped her entire body into the water. Along the edge, it was only about four feet deep.

Crouching down until only her head was above the water, Sierra made her way to the nearest grass cluster. Closing her eyes to keep bugs and insects out of them, she buried her head in between the blades, praying that they were enough to hide her from view. Sierra did her best to keep her breathing shallow. The low temperature of the water caused her body to shiver slightly, but she didn't think it was enough to disturb the surface too much. As she sat there in hiding, she recited every prayer that her father ever taught her.

....

"We're here." Squeak informed Shonda and Shock as he turned onto Fulton St.

Both of them could hear the relief in his voice and both of them concurred with that emotion. They couldn't help but to be tense in the wake of everything that already happened that day. They had the police looking for them, Sticks looking for them, and if Infamous was to find out who it was riding around with them, then Infamous would no doubt be out to get them too.

Squeak wanted to get out of Texas City as soon as possible. An assassin's best friend was the shadows and the dark places. Once he was forced into the light, he could no longer move in stealth again like his profession called for. The only thing left for him to do would be to disappear, becoming nothing more than a character in the local folklore.

Squeak studied the houses as he crept up the block. He realized that Infamous sent them to the perfect spot. Outside of the 3 houses that belonged to Infamous, there were only 4 more homes on the entire block, and every single one of them had a 'for sale' sign posted in the front yard. The seclusion was more than welcome. It was damn near required. Squeak pulled into the center house. It was the one with the garage. Pulling up pretty close to the garage door, Squeak instructed Shonda to get out and lift it up.

Shonda complied.

Before long, they had the stolen vehicle safely tucked away in the garage, and they were tending to Shock's wound. Surprisingly, the entire house was fully furnished. It had everything in it needed for habitation, except for food. Squeak walked into the backroom to call Infamous, and Shonda helped Shock out of his shirt.

"Ungh." Shock grunted, as the fabric peeled away from his open wound.

"Ssss. I'm sorry, bro." Shonda apologized.

Shock shook it off.

"Don't worry about it, sis. I'm cool."

Once Shock was naked from the waste up, Shonda examined the gunshot wound.

"You got lucky, boy." She observed, looking at the back of his shoulder. "The bullet went straight through."

Shock cocked his head trying to see the exit wound.

"I thought I was going to have to dig the bullet out."

Shock forced a chuckle. He was glad that he didn't have to burst her bubble. Little did she know, there was no way he was about to get a bullet dug out of his shoulder. He saw that done on television enough to know that it hurt like hell. The kind of hurt his pride wouldn't let him feel because he wasn't sure how he would respond to it. He was a killer. How would it look if he was to be reduced to hollering like a bitch?

Walking away to find the bathroom, Shonda said, "Let me go see if I can find something to clean and wrap the wound with."

The safehouse was two-stories, so Shonda used the excuse of searching for medical supplies as a means to do a little exploring. She had no reason to think that they weren't there alone, but still she needed to satisfy her curiosity and gain some type of familiarity with her surroundings.

Shock watched as Shonda climbed the stairs. Finding himself suddenly alone, Shock took a seat on the living room sofa and leaned back. He looked at his wound. He couldn't believe that Sticks actually tried to have him killed. The closes thing to a father he ever known wanted him dead, and all behind a no-good cop. It didn't make sense to him. To assist himself in his contemplations, he forced himself to go into meditation. Within moments, he was deep in thought.

In the back room, Squeak was hanging up with Infamous. He filled him in on what happened with the cop, the shoot-out with the Hooligans, and the identity of their companion. He stretched the truth just a little bit, though. He told his boss that the man with him was a friend that he knew since childhood. He told him that the dude helped him on various jobs, he just never introduced the two because he wanted to stay low key.

Squeak said Shock's name was Rich. When asked about the cop, he told him that his only guess was that somehow, he was made. Squeak didn't want to tell him the truth. It would've destroyed his lie about who Shock was if he would've told him about the break-in and that first shot into the wall that probably prompted the visit by the police. The only explanation for the shoot-out was half fact and half fiction. Squeak said that he knew the police would now be looking for Rich, too. So naturally, he had to go underground with him and Shonda. The only problem was that Rich lived on the same side of town as all of the Hooligans.

So, in the midst of getting Rich packed, they ran into a fleet of Hooligans. The rest of that story was unfolding on the news as they spoke. The main thing that all of the reporters kept saying was that the war between the two gangs was more intense than ever. Squeak wasn't sure if Infamous believed all of his tall tales, but he sure hoped that he did. If he didn't, they were all in major trouble.

Squeak didn't like lying to Infamous, but he felt as if he had no other choice. He took a deep breath and headed back towards the living room. This whole thing was spiraling out of control. He bought them a little more time, but Squeak knew that eventually they would have to make a move. Once that move was made, he knew that neither one of them would ever be able to look back.

Squeak entered the living room and saw Shock sitting perfectly still on the couch, with his head facing the sky, and his eyes closed. Standing out like beacons of turmoil, suffering, pain, and anguish, were the two bullet wounds that Richard obtained defending the ones he loved. The long black scar, testifying to the never selfish loyalty that he had long ago, and the fresh, open, slightly oozing wound, testifying to the never selfish loyalty that he still possessed.

Squeak always wondered what would've happened if he stood up to their father instead of Richard. After all, he was the big brother. It was his job to protect both Richard and Shonda. Right then and there, Squeak made a promise to himself. He swore on the grave of his mother Laina that he would kill anybody that threatened the life of either Shonda or Richard ever again, and it didn't make a difference to him who it was.

Chapter Eighteen

Sierra pulled her body from the ice-cold pond and crawled away from the water's edge. She concealed herself below the surface for as long as her body would allow. She knew that if she would've stayed under any longer, she would've run the risk of suffering from hypothermia. Her body shook as a light breeze blew across her soaking wet frame. She wasn't complaining though, she was just happy to still be alive.

She still had no idea what the 3 shots that she heard meant, but simple logic told her that either Silvia or Sticks laid dead on hole 11. When the police and the media got wind of what happened, the entire Bayou Golf Course would turn into a circus. Sierra started walking in the direction of her car. If the police turned the golf course into a crime scene, and the media came around in search of a good story, her chances of finding the $20 million were drastically reduced.

As she walked, water dripping from her body, Sierra debated on how she should handle the situation. It would take an extremely long time for her to single-handedly dig up every single sand trap on all 18 holes. Time that she didn't have. Plus, she was soaking wet, cold, and tired. Finding the money that night began looking more and more like an impossibility.

Sierra shook her head. After everything that she been through, she was still walking away empty handed.

"If Silvia was the one to survive." She said to herself. "I'm going to kill her myself."

Sierra retrieved her cell phone from her pocket. In her haste to escape the two people with the guns, she submerged herself beneath the surface with the phone still in her pocket. She looked at the screen. It was completely blank. Sierra banged it up against the palm of her hand and pressed every button on the keypad.

Nothing happened.

The water had totally ruined the cell phones circuits. Sierra planned on calling Adriana. She called Sierra's cell phone so many times while her and Silvia were digging up the sand traps, Sierra turned her ringer off. She figured she didn't want to do anything except talk about her new friend, Ant. Sierra was trying to get paid. She didn't have time to compare notes about Ant.

Sierra pressed the buttons a few more times before finally giving up. She had to accept that she wouldn't be making any more calls from that phone. When she dropped the phone back into her pocket, a strong gust of wind blew past her, chilling her to her core.

Sierra shook.

It seemed as if the wind blowing up against her wet clothes was colder than the actual water was. She stopped walking and looked around. Reassuring herself that there wasn't another person in sight, Sierra unbuttoned her white dress shirt and peeled it off. Her skin was wet too, but her clothes were drenched. She was still cold, but the low temperature tingled her nipples pleasantly.

Sierra started walking again, doing her best to ring out the shirt as good as possible. She had a lot of ground to cover and she wished she had one of those golf carts to ride back to her car in. If she remembered correctly, there was at least one on each hole. All she really had to do was make it to hole 10 and then she would be good.

Sierra crossed through the tree line and waved her shirt as she walked, trying to dry it off some. Sierra told herself that if she ever saw Silvia or Sticks again, it would be on.

"Fuck Silvia." She grumbled, when she thought about how the woman had just completely switched up on her.

She had been running around like a chicken with its head cut off ever since she met the lady, and this is where the relationship ended up. Sierra looked at herself and shook her head.

"The lengths people will go through for financial stability." She said.

When Sierra emerged on the other side of the tree line, she noticed that she ran faster and farther then she first suspected. She already made it to hole 10. She scanned across the greens and saw what she was looking for. Over next to the tee off spot was a golf cart parked next to an all green sign. Realizing that she wouldn't have to walk all the way back, Sierra got excited.

She took off jogging in the direction of the cart. Her breasts were bouncing up and down, barely contained by the one size too small white bra that she was wearing. Sierra could practically feel the warm bath water that she was going to soak in as soon as she made it home. She wanted to light some candles, put some bubble bath in the water, and sit back and relax with a fat ass blunt. Sierra reached the golf cart quick, motivated by thoughts of the sanctity and safety of her home. Tossing her shirt onto the seat of the golf cart, Sierra climbed in.

All of the golf carts were the same. They ran off of electricity stored up in the battery. On the right side of the steering wheel, on the part of the cart that could only be called the dashboard, there was a little black knob. Sierra grabbed the knob, pressed it in, and turned it to the right. She felt the cart wobble slightly when the motor started up. The low, monotonous hum of it was oddly soothing to Sierra.

Just as she was about to put the cart in forward, something made her look up. Immediately to the right of the cart was the big green sign. Sierra noted that there was one of these on each hole. She just didn't pay too much attention to them. They let you know what hold you were on, gave you a brief description of it, and it had an illustration of it drawn on the left-hand side.

Sierra squinted her eyes at the sign. She cocked her head to look at it from a different angle. Something about it made the illustration stand out to her. It felt familiar for some reason.

"You're tripping, girl." She said to herself, taking her eyes off the sign. "You probably remember it from when you and Silvia passed by it earlier."

Putting her mind back on relaxing at home, Sierra put the car in forward and applied pressure to the pedal. She only drove maybe 10 feet before it hit her. Sierra removed her foot from the pedal and stepped on the brake. She hopped out of the cart and turned to face the sign.

"How could I be so blind?" She asked herself.

The key to the puzzle had been right there the entire time. She was just so caught up in making it to hole number 11, she missed the obvious. Sierra thought back to the wind chime she saw hanging up at Bianca's house. The odd design on the heart dangling from it was not just some random picture of a golf course. It was an exact replica of the illustration posted on hole 10.

That was it. Burby bought the wind chime and he had the attachment made to mark which hole the money was buried on. It was like the "x" on a treasure map. Sierra quickly scanned the hole. There was only one sand trap and it wasn't that big. Sierra felt the fire begin to burn within her again.

"Could the $20 million really be that close?" She wondered, staring at the lone sand trap.

She couldn't leave the golf course until she knew for sure. Sierra jumped back in the cart and drove as fast as she could, but she couldn't help but wonder if this would be another dead end. If so, it would be the third one. Sierra thought it over. Arriving at the edge of the sand trap, she decided the prospect of becoming a millionaire outweighed the fear of being disappointed by a longshot. Sierra climbed out the cart and realized that she didn't even have a shovel.

She thought about driving back out to hole 11, but she decided against it. Neither one of the other two sand traps were deep, they were just wide. Assuming that this one wasn't deep neither, Sierra stepped in and started digging around with her hands. It didn't even matter to her that she wasn't wearing a shirt. In fact, the task at hand was easier with only her bra on. As she searched, the sand clung to her body because it was still a little wet. She didn't mind though.

Sierra knew that if she was successful this time, the entire $20 million would be hers. She wouldn't be committed to share it with anyone. Sierra, with determination in her movements, speedily scooped dirt with both of her hands and tossed it to the side. Most of it was landing on the grass, but some of it piled up along the edges of the trap.

The deepest part was dead center, so Sierra figured if the money was anywhere, it would be there. She grunted as she dug up sand with her bare hands. Something about the whole ordeal made her picture herself as a dog in her mind's eye. As if she were frantically attempting to bury or dig up a bone.

"Come on, Sierra." She urged herself, as the muscles in her arms started registering fatigue.

Sierra stopped digging and fell over on her hands and knees. Her breathing became heavy. She inhaled deeply and exhaled hard. The act of digging up the other sand traps, fleeing for her life, hiding in ice cold water, and now digging up a third sand trap by hand, had her biceps feeling like they were on fire. As she tried to catch her breath, her body begged her to give up and go home. Her brain, which was filled up with thoughts of exotic beaches and luxurious living, pleaded with her to keep going.

In between breaths, she said, "$20 million. $20 million."

The drive to find riches overwhelmed the desire to quit. Forcing herself to push through the pain, Sierra started scooping out sand with her hands again.

"Ugh." She grunted, as the sand seemed to get heavier.

She knew that it was only her muscles getting weaker, not the sand getting heavier. Feeling almost zapped of all of her strength, Sierra buried her hands into the dirt for another scoop. When she did, she heard and felt her nails scrape up against something. Sierra held her breath as she wiped the sand off of the object she had encountered. Her heart skipped a beat as she noticed something silver just below the level of sand she dug down to.

"Could it be?" She thought.

Only about 3 inches of the silver object was visible, so there was no way of knowing exactly what it was. Not unless she continued to dig; and continued to dig is what she did. Sierra worked excitedly at uncovering the rest of the object. Actually, having a particular spot to focus her dig on helped. She just removed the dirt from around the object. It didn't take her long to get it completely uncovered, and when she did, Sierra knew without a doubt that she had finally found what she was looking for.

The silver object was a briefcase. Sierra was willing to bet that the briefcase contained money. She used her hands to unearth the handle, then she tugged at it until it slid from its place in the sand. Directly beneath it, Sierra noticed another briefcase that was identical to the first one. She looked at the one still buried and then at the one in her hand. Sierra was confident that the money was inside of the briefcase, so she figured $20 million was too much to fit inside of one briefcase.

She tossed the briefcase that she was holding out of the sand trap and over next to the golf cart. Then, she worked to retrieve the second briefcase. To her surprise, there was another silver briefcase underneath that one, so she tossed it to the side and went for the third one. It didn't take long for her to get all of the briefcases out of the sand. There ended up being four of them in all.

A little quick math and Sierra concluded that there was probably $5 million in each one. How it was distributed didn't really matter to her though. As long as it added up to anywhere close to $20 million, she would be good. All of the briefcases were locked with a keyhole style lock. Not having time to bother with picking it right then, Sierra just tossed them onto the golf cart and sped towards the entrance of the Bayou Golf Course and her car. Her shirt dried somewhat, but she still opted to leave it off.

She was so filthy that the only remedy for her would be a nice long bath. Sierra made it to her car and knew instantly what happened back on hole number 11. Still parked next to her car was a candy blue H3. There was no blue Eclipse anywhere in sight.

"Silvia must've made it to my gun before Sticks could recover his sight." She told herself.

That meant that he was still stretched out on hole 11. It seemed slightly ironic that one of the most feared gang lords in Texas City would be taken out like that. It wasn't his enemies, the streets, or the police that finally got him. It was the closes person to him. The woman that was supposed to be his soulmate. His better half, his rib, his Eve.

Sierra shook her head.

"His own backstabbing ass wife, killed him."

Sierra told herself that she would be glad when all of this was nothing more than a distant memory. Now that she finally got the money, she would be on the first thing smoking out of Texas City.

Sierra pulled up next to her car.

"That... bitch!" She exclaimed, in total disbelief.

Her doors windows were all busted out. She looked at them and glared. Silvia had done that out of spite and nothing else. Sierra's mind instantly started conjuring up ways to get even. It wasn't enough that Silvia tried to get her killed, she vandalized her vehicle too. Sierra glanced at the briefcases next to her in the golf cart.

"To hell with it." She thought, calming down. "I'll just buy a whole new car."

The idea of getting a new car fresh off the lot made her smile. Sierra told herself that with $20 million, she wouldn't have to worry about anything else ever again. Feeling like she couldn't be touched, Sierra cut off the golf cart and went through the motions of loading up her cargo into her Dodge Neon.

"At least the bitch didn't slash my tires or burst out my headlights."

The sun was beginning to set, and not having taillights would've gotten her pulled over for sure. Considering the events of the day, her coworkers were high on her list of people she didn't want to see. Rose often talked about walking on that gray line between legal and illegal. Sierra knew that she crossed over long ago. It wasn't that she wasn't a good person, or that she didn't enjoy her job, it was just that $20 million was the kind of financial stability that a pension couldn't provide.

As she made her way home, deep down she felt bad for deceiving Rose. With all they been through, she become attached. She took a deep breath. There was no way that she could look back though. It was only a matter of time before the whole story got told; and when it did, she would have to be in a faraway country with absolutely no extradition laws.

True, she hadn't done anything too bad, but it was her city issued firearm that killed Sticks. If she were to explain what really happened, she would risk losing the money. Sierra told herself that her best option would be to skip town. That way, there would be no questions, no accusers, no unknown enemies, and no way for her to lose her money.

Sierra spent the remainder of the drive back home convincing herself that she did the right thing. It wasn't easy, but it proved not to be impossible either. By the time Sierra pulled up to her house and carried all four briefcases inside, she made up her mind about where she wanted to go. She remembered reading somewhere about a small island in the Indian Ocean known as Komodo Island. It was the perfect place for her. Komodo Island is one Island out of over 17,000 Island that make up Indonesia. The largest lizard on earth, the Komodo Dragon, is named after the Island because it is heavily inhabited by them. There are only about 2,000 people on the Island and those people are the descendants of convicts who were exiled there. From the pictures she seen, Komodo Island was probably one of the closes places to paradise on earth if someone were looking for isolation from the rest of the world.

Looking down at her phone, Sierra noticed that someone had left her 15 messages on her answering machine.

"Damn Adriana." She said. "I'm gone get at you girl."

Sierra figured her sister-in-law was just worried because she wasn't answering her cell phone. She had more important things on her agenda. Such as opening those briefcases. Sierra learned how to pick locks a long time ago. Her and her homegirls used to do it in jewelry stores all the time. They would walk in about five deep, four of them would distract the employees, while the fifth one would unlock one of the display cases and grabbed what she could get. They would always rotate who actually had to commit the theft.

Sierra walked into the bathroom, found a bobby pen, and went back into the living room. The four briefcases were all sitting on the floor next to the couch. Sierra plopped down on the sofa and sat one of the briefcases down on her lap.

"Let's see what you got." She said, inserting the bobby pen into the keyhole.

Sierra fidgeted with it for a while but couldn't get it open.

"Either I've lost my touch, or you're a tricky lock."

She wasn't about to give up that easy though. She just tried harder. While she was picking the lock, her home phone started to ring again. Sierra ignored it. She didn't need the distraction. It rung a few times and then went to the answering machine. She was happy about the silence.

The noise was frustrating her because she couldn't get to her money.

"Ok, Sierra." She said, trying to regulate her breathing. "Just take your time and work your magic."

She slowed down and concentrated on what she was trying to do. When the phone started ringing again, Sierra jumped. Before she had time to curse out the ringing phone, her unexpected movement turned the bobby pen and she heard the lock click. Sierra looked back down at the briefcase in her lap. The sound of the phone became drowned out by the multitude of thoughts that were now dancing around in her head.

"Did I just hear what I thought I heard?" She wondered.

Slowly, as if any sudden movements would ruin her chances of getting to the contents of the briefcase, Sierra reached out and placed her thumbs on the latches. Licking her lips, and closing her eyes, she flipped them open. Even with her eyes closed she could feel the briefcase open up just a little. Butterflies bombarded her belly as she realized the briefcase was unlocked. Taking three deep breaths, she opened her eyes and lifted the top all the way up.

Sierra's bottom jaw hung open and she stared without blinking into the briefcase. The amount of money she saw made the $20,000 that Silvia gave her look like chump change. Inside of the briefcase, stacked up in neat piles, was what Sierra believed to be $5 million in cash. Sierra jumped up and down laughing and shouting for joy.

She hit the jackpot. Sierra fell down to her knees and started tossing stacks of hundreds up into the air.

Some landed on her computer desk, some landed back on her, and some landed on her glass table next to her bible. One of the stacks landed on top of her remote control, and it caused the TV to spring to life. Sierra continued to laugh as she glanced up at the picture that came up on the screen. Her laughter slowly died down as she realized it was a live news broadcast on. The number in the top right-hand corner of the screen told her that the TV wasn't even on a news channel. That meant the breaking news had to be important.

Sierra reached for the remote control and turned up the volume. She recognized the reporter as Mindy Ray from the Channel 10 News.

"... becoming one of the most tragic and complex stories I've ever had to cover. As if the shoot-out and six car pileup that left 5 dead and 6 more wounded wasn't enough, I've just received word that the shooting victim from earlier over on Anderson St. was none other than Detective Derrick Rose."

Sierra thought she heard her wrong. Did she just say that Rose got shot?

"An anonymous caller has identified one of the shooters as a man who calls himself, Ant. The woman, who asked to remain anonymous, said that she dropped Ant off at the residence moments before the shooting. She even told us..."

Sierra knew they were talking about Adriana. That must've been the real reason why she had been blowing up her phone. It wasn't to gossip about how good the sex with Ant was. It was to tell her that Ant had shot Rose.

But why?

What could've possibly happened while she was gone? Mindy Ray put a finger up to the earpiece attached to her ear. Her expression was one of surprise as well as a little joy as she listened to someone on the other end of the connection.

"This just in." She said, looking up at the camera and holding the microphone tightly. "We have the names of two of the suspected shooters. The man called Ant's real name is Anthony Tune Jr. His sister, who fled the scene with him, has been identified as LaShonda Tune. Police are..."

Sierra got lightheaded. She could now see everything clearer. That's why Ant looked so familiar. Ant was Squeak. The same Squeak that killed Wilkinson, Abdul, Burby, and countless others. The same Squeak that they were looking for. The same Squeak that... that...

Sierra felt sick. It was the same Squeak that she just had sex with. Sierra jumped up and wobbled. The new development left her dizzy. It was all too much to take in at once. The phone started ringing again. Sierra thought about Adriana, Squeak, Silvia, Sticks, and Rose. She ran into the bathroom and dropped to her knees in front of the toilet. All she been through finally caught up to her.

Sierra began to throw up, and she didn't finish until it felt like all of her insides had been emptied into the toilet.

Chapter Nineteen

Dr. Terrance stepped into Rose's room. As he suspected, his wife, Rebecca was still sitting in the chair next to his bed. He and his colleagues managed to stabilize Rose's condition, but they had no choice but to hook him up to life support. Seeing the Detective with multiple tubes inserted into his body was a far cry from the man he'd somewhat known through his sister's stories. The Detective Rose that Sierra talked about was as close to invincible as a human being could get.

Dr. Terrance wished he could do more for the man. He felt genuine sadness when he looked at Rebecca. Ever since Derrick left the operating room and got assigned to a bed, Rebecca had been seated next to his bedside faithfully. Dr. Terrance watched for a moment as the woman sat with her body folded over and her face in her lap. Her cries of distress were no longer able to be heard down every hallway, but the sporadic way that her back rose and fell told him that she was still sobbing.

Following hospital policy and procedure, Dr. Terrance informed her about all of her options since she was Rose's wife. As with anyone that is classified as being brain dead, the immediate family has to consider pulling the plug. Rebecca hollered like a banshee when he mentioned pulling the plug. In his experience, most people did. They were never really prepared to let a loved one go as long as there was a chance that they could somehow pull through.

Rebecca began to quote newspaper articles she read about men and women that were vegetables for years, and then, for no apparent reason, woke up and made a full recovery. She said that Derrick was a fighter. He was a fighter that deserved the chance to fight. She wouldn't be able to live with herself if she gave up on him so fast.

Dr. Terrance didn't press the issue. The only reason he mentioned it was because he had to. He never advised families to give up so soon neither. The chance for a miraculous recovery was slim, but it was there. He had grown up with a preacher for a father. He didn't just hear about miracles on Sunday. He heard about them all throughout the week. Actually, it was part of his motivation to become a doctor.

The stories about Jesus healing the sick, making the lame to walk again, causing the blind to see, and raising people from the dead, sounded like a superhero to Terrance when he was young. A man that could walk on water and not sink, speak to a storm and have it obey him, and command evil spirits to exit a person, had to be more than just a mere man. He was more powerful then Superman, Batman, and Spiderman all rolled up into one.

Even death could not stop Jesus. The man had no weaknesses. No Achilles heel. He had no kryptonite. So, when most of the other kids wanted to be the Incredible Hulk or someone like that, Terrance wanted to be Jesus. As he got older and realized the deeper spiritual meaning behind the stories about Jesus, his desire to be like him matured also. There was no way for him to become the sinless Son of God, but he could mimic some of Jesus's works with medical science. It was in times like these though, that Terrance knew it had to be an act of the real superhero, and not just a wannabe, to heal the person that was sick.

Dr. Terrance walked towards Rebecca. She heard his footsteps on the tile floor and looked up. Her face testified to her grief. Her eyes were bloodshot red, and her cheeks were moist from the tears. Although she was only awake for a few hours, but the stress of crying her heart out made the skin under her eyes puffy and black.

"Hey." Terrance said softly, placing one hand on Rebecca's shoulder. "How are you holding up?"

Rebecca wiped her face off with the palms of her hands and sniffled. Without answering his question, she looked over at Rose.

"I can't lose him." She said, shaking her head. "Not like this."

Dr. Terrance kneeled down beside her so he could get on eye level with her.

"What did we talk about?" He asked, taking her hands into his. "With God, all things are possible."

Rebecca closed her eyes and nodded her head. Dr. Terrance kept talking.

"Remember the widow woman's son that Elijah raised from the dead? Remember I told you about a man named Lazarus who was dead for four days and Jesus spoke but a word, and the breath of life returned into him? Do not let go of your faith, Rebecca. Continue to petition God on your husbands' behalf. Now, I can't promise that God will heal him. It is not in me to know the will of God in this particular matter, but I can promise that God is able to revive him."

Rebecca sat quietly as Dr. Terrance spoke and she found comfort in his words. She felt like God had placed him in her path to let her know that He indeed heard her prayers. Rebecca was amazed because she hadn't even mentioned the fact that she prayed, and Dr. Terrance just began talking to her about the Bible and God.

Somehow, everything he was saying was soothing to her. Rebecca opened her eyes and looked at her hands resting inside of Dr. Terrance's hands. For the first time since she met him, Rebecca noticed a wedding band on his left hand. She looked him in the eyes.

"You're married?" She asked, quizzically.

He hadn't mentioned his wife. The question sort of caught him off guard.

"Ummm. Something like that." He answered.

Rebecca sat up straight. That wasn't the kind of response she was expecting.

"Something like that?" She repeated. "What is that supposed to mean?"

Dr. Terrance instantly began to think about his wife, Adriana. He loved his wife to death, but things hadn't been the same between them for some time now. At one point, they had a storybook marriage. Everything was going fine. At least he thought it was. That is, until his sister called him and burst his bubble. Sierra told him that Adriana had been cheating on him, but she refused to say how she knew. He had been become suspicious of her actions, but he still didn't want to accept the truth.

So, him and Sierra got into an argument. She accused him of having his nose wide open and he accused her of being envious of his relationship. Sierra promised him that she would never mention it again and hung up in his face. Since then, they made up, but Dr. Terrance never could bring himself to confront Adriana. He knew that adultery was a reason to divorce and not be held accountable before God, but he also knew that from the beginning it was not so.

God only allowed man to get a divorce over adultery because of the hardness of man's heart. From the beginning it was until death do you part, with no if, ands, or buts, about it. Dr. Terrance was trying his hardest to live up to that, but even though he forgave her, he couldn't force himself to look at her the same way. Once he found out that she had given herself to another man, he lost almost all of his sexual attraction for her.

Adriana would always do little things to get a rise out of him, like buying sexy lingerie, but nothing really worked. Rebecca noticed that her question sent Dr. Terrance to some faraway place.

"I'm sorry." She apologized. "You don't have to talk about it if you don't want to."

Dr. Terrance stood up.

"No need to apologize." He assured her. "As a matter of fact, I think the both of us could use a little something to take our mind off of the stress."

He checked his watch.

"I'll tell you what. If you agree to go grab a bite to eat with me in the cafeteria, then I'll tell you all about it."

Rebecca looked at Rose.

"I... I don't know." She said, not wanting to leave his side.

Dr. Terrance pulled her up from the chair by her hands.

"He'll be ok." He promised. "If anything changes, that machine that he's hooked up to will alert the staff immediately."

Dr. Terrance held her hand and led her out of the room. Rebecca went reluctantly, looking behind her at the virtually lifeless Detective Derrick Rose.

....

"What about one of the countries in Africa?" Shock asked.

Squeak and Shonda thought about it. They were all sitting around the living room of the safehouse trying to figure out where they should go. It was a unanimous decision to leave Texas City and never look back. Altogether they estimated they had close to $2 million in cash. That was more than enough for the 3 of them to go start a new life somewhere else. All they needed to do was agree on a destination.

While searching the house, Shonda got lucky and found a whole first aid kit in the upstairs bathroom.

She cleaned out Shock's wound and wrapped it up in a bandage. All they had to do now was figure out where they wanted to go and then go. One thing Squeak knew was that they were running out of time. The sun had set, and the darkness was all he was waiting on.

"Don't everybody over there in Africa got Aids?" Shonda asked.

Squeak shook his head.

"That's what they want you to think." He told her. "In reality, a good part of Africa is actually developed country. They got schools, hospitals, buildings, and stores, cars, you name it. They have everything luxury we have over here in America. They just paint that negative picture of Africa to facilitate the exploitation of the continent."

Shonda frowned up.

"But still." She said. "That sounds good and all, but I don't want to go to no Africa."

She was used to seeing the images of Africa on TV. The starving children with fly's swarming around their heads and nothing more than a spoonful of rice to eat.

"I'd rather go to some exotic islands somewhere with clear skies and blue waters." She continued.

Squeak shrugged his shoulders.

"Like where?"

Shonda stood up.

"When I was looking for that first aid kit, I did a little quick search of the upstairs. One of the rooms up there is like a mini library. I flipped through a couple of the books and I came across a National Geographic magazine called '50 of The World's Last Great Places'. It had a lot of good ideas in there."

Squeak stood up, too.

"Well, let's go check it out. Because the way I see it, we need to be on our way out of Texas City within the next couple of hours."

Shonda led the way towards the stairs. Shock reached down and picked up one of his guns.

"Ya'll go ahead." He called to them. "I'm going to reload the guns. You gotta stay ready to keep from getting ready. Ya dig?"

"Alright." Squeak said, as him and Shonda climbed the stairs.

Once they made it to the top, Shonda turned and went left. There was a bathroom immediately in front of the top of the stairs, a bedroom to the right, and two bedrooms to the left. Shonda led squeak left, to the one at the very end of the hallway. When they entered the room, he could see what she meant by mini library.

The only furniture inside the room was a study desk positioned directly in the center of it. The desk even had a lamp attached to it for reading in the dark. Along each wall was a wooden book rack with 6 shelves on each one. Squeak was surprised to see that every single shelf on every rack was packed with books.

"What the hell does Infamous do here?" Squeak asked, looking around the room in amazement.

"You tell me." Shonda replied, just as confused as Squeak was.

Squeak scratched his head. They really didn't have time to ponder why Infamous needed a library.

"Where's this book?" Squeak asked, trying to get back on track.

"Oh yeah." Shonda walked over to the study desk.

"It's right here."

The magazine was already opened to the destination spot that stood out the most to Shonda. Squeak read destination spot number 29 out loud.

"Komodo Island. Land of real-life dragons."

Shonda smiled and pointed at the picture of the place.

"Now that is as close to paradise as we're going to get. And in a place like that, no one will ever find us."

Shock's shoulder wasn't throbbing as much since he had gone through his meditation technique. Besides, he sometimes fed off of pain. The slight burn that he felt from reloading the guns was more invigorating then it was a hinderance. Shock treated all of his weapons like beloved children rather than inanimate objects.

From the very first time he shot a pistol he had fallen instantly in love. The way that the hot lead sent his enemies scurrying away like rodents mesmerized him. All of his life he had been one of the have nots. He was treated like a subhuman all because his parents didn't want him, and his voice was marked by a violent episode that he never quite remembered nor understood.

His gun, however, was able to get him the respect that he could never quite get on his own, and for that, he swore that he would always be eternally grateful. Shock sat in solitude reloading all of the guns that they emptied in their shoot-out with his ex-family. He couldn't help but to feel a little hollow inside because the Hooligans and Sticks had been the only real family relationship he ever experienced, but Shonda and Squeak were his blood relatives.

The same blood relatives that he dreamed about his entire life. Truly, his loyalty should lie with them. After all, they weren't torn apart because of any turmoil amongst themselves. It was a sick and twisted father that caused them to grow up on opposite sides of the track, and ultimately, it was a sick and twisted father that embedded within them all the killer instincts that eventually played catalyst to their storybook reunion. Shock knew that he could live with his decision to side with his brother and sister. After all, it was the right thing to do.

Meanwhile, unbeknownst to Shonda, Squeak, and Shock, Infamous sent 3 of his Villains over to the safehouse to check up on Shonda and Squeak and drop off some supplies that they might need. A gray Cadillac turned onto Fulton St. and pulled into the driveway of the safehouse. Three men, all flamed up in red exited the vehicle and approached the front door. The first man was on the phone with Infamous.

"Yeah, we here boss." He informed him, as he knocked on the door.

"Ok." Infamous said. "Call me back after you get a chance to talk to Squeak and Shonda."

"Will do, boss."

Shock heard noises coming from outside the front of the house, so he stood up to go investigate. The closer he got, the more certain he was that he heard voices. Moving quietly, Shock peeked out of the peephole.

He watched in horror as one of the men outside on the porch retrieved a key from their pocket. Shock also saw Tao attempt to hang up the phone as his partner opened the front door. When the door swung open, Tao instantly recognized the man standing there with his shirt off and his shoulder wrapped up.

"You!" He said, with a mixture of anger, pain, and surprise in his voice.

It didn't take Shock but a moment to recognize the man as well. It was the same half black, half Vietnamese, man from the mall. Shock saw Tao reach for his gun, so he slammed the door in his face and ran towards the guns he had spread out in front of the couch.

"SQUEAK! SHONDA! GET DOWN HERE!" He shouted, as he dove headfirst and grabbed the first pistol his hand came into contact with.

Tao, and the two men with him pulled out their guns. In his haste to kick the door in, Tao dropped his phone but didn't cut it off.

"What's going on over there?" Infamous asked.

He got no response. He simply listened in horror as gunfire erupted on the other end of the line.

As soon as Tao kicked the front door open, Shock was rolling over onto his back. He let off two quick shots to Tao's one shot. The Villains fell back to either side of the door to avoid the shots.

"SQUEAK!" Shock yelled again.

He knew that there was only so much he could do with one arm immobilized. Tao heard Infamous screaming into the phone and picked it up. Shock scrabbled behind the couch letting off random shots to keep his attackers at bay.

"Boss!" Tao shouted. "It's the dude that murdered Suko. He's working with Squeak."

Infamous was silent. It couldn't be. Squeak was as loyal as they came.

"Send back up!" Tao shouted. "Send them now!" Then he hung up the phone.

Bullets were knocking off pieces of wood right next to his head and focusing on the phone might get him killed. Shonda and Squeak heard the shots and came rushing down the stairs. Had Sticks somehow found them?

Shock saw them coming to his aid.

"It's your people." He said.

Squeak couldn't believe it. Infamous must have saw right through his lies earlier.

"Shit!" He exclaimed, running down the stairs.

He rushed past the door when he made it to the bottom and pushed it closed. Shonda followed him as he sped towards the guns. He grabbed a pistol and Shonda grabbed one.

"How many of 'em is it?" Squeak asked, ducking behind the couch next to Shock.

"I saw 3." Shock answered. "But I'm not sure. There may be others."

BAM!

The door flung back open, but no one stood in front of it.

"Is that how you do it, Squeak?" Tao shouted. "You switch sides and ride with the enemy? You a flip-flop now?"

One of the Villains reached in and let off two rounds. They didn't land anywhere near the trio.

"What are we gonna do?" Shonda asked, firing two shots at the door.

"I don't know." Squeak replied, "But whatever it is, we gotta do it fast. It won't be long before we have to deal with just as many Villains as we did Hooligans."

Shock grunted as he got on all fours.

"Hold 'em off right there." He instructed.

Before Squeak could ask him what he was doing, Shock crawled toward the back. The gunshot wound to his shoulder had flared up and now could be classified as excruciating pain. He gritted his teeth and fought through the pain. Squeak let off two more shots.

"You don't know what's going on, Tao!" He shouted.

"Don't know what's going on?" Tao repeated.

He forced a laugh.

"You're a fucking flip-flop. That's what's going on. That motherfucker killed my brother. Now you're riding with him?"

Tao motioned with his head for one of the Villains with him to go in. The dude was somewhat afraid, but he had to obey the order. He took a deep breath and spun around, placing his body directly in front of the doorway. Holding his weapon in both hands, he shot at the couch as he slowly stepped forward. The second Villain prepared to go in after him. Shonda, not knowing that they entered the home, popped up to shoot. When they made eye contact, they both fired their weapons.

The Villain missed his mark.

Shonda did not.

The man cried out in pain and fell backwards. Shonda shot one more time, striking the man directly in his face. The Villain behind him caught him and quickly drug him out of harm's way. Shonda dropped back down with her back up against the couch.

"I got one, Squeak." She squealed with joy. "I got one."

Squeak smiled at her enthusiasm. Tao looked at the limp body of his Villain and shook his head. That was exactly why he didn't want to go in first. He knew all too well how dangerous Squeak and Shonda could be. Shock had gone out the back door and crept around the side of the house. When he peeked around the corner, he saw the mixed breed still standing at his post by the door. The other Villain was laying his apparently dead companion down in the grass.

"Perfect." Shock thought.

He came from around the corner and let off two shots in the direction of Tao. Both shots hit him in the torso. As he stumbled back and fell, Shock fired at the other Villain and the other Villain turned to fire back.

From the inside, Squeak heard the shots, heard Tao cry out, and he knew what was happening. He jumped up and rushed the door. When he got there, he saw two Villains lying motionless and Tao grimacing in pain. Squeak wasted no time delivering the kill shot to his forehead. He looked to his left.

"Shock!!!" He yelled.

Shock was laying stretched out with another bullet wound in his stomach. Shonda followed Squeak out the door.

"Richard!" She screamed.

They both rushed to the side of Shock to see if he was ok.

Chapter Twenty

Silvia had driven as fast as she could to her homegirls house and picked up her two sons. She couldn't believe that she actually murdered Kenneth. Sure, she was sick and tired of being the gangster's wife, but her plan to start her life over again blew up in her face. She thought she could incite the gang war as a distraction for her husband while she hunted down the $20 million and then skip town. Everything went wrong. She didn't have the money, but she did have more than enough reasons to have to skip town.

"Why are you crying, mommy?" DeShawn asked, as Silvia emptied the safe in her bedroom into several pillowcases.

Silvia looked at him.

"Mommy is ok." She lied. "We just have to pack up a few things. Like I told you, we're just going on a little trip."

She wiped her face and went back to transferring the money from the safe to the pillowcases. Silvia knew it was only about $500,000, but it would have to do. The rest of her husband's money was scattered around the town at various drug houses.

"Where's daddy?" DeShawn asked.

Silvia couldn't even look him in the eye.

"Daddy's waiting for us at the airport. Now, you and your brother go pack up some of your favorite toys."

The boys ran off in the direction of their room, chanting, "We're going on a triiip! We're going on a triiip!"

Silvia finished sacking up all of the money and went to pack up a few clothes. She knew that she didn't have time to pack much. Sierra probably had the cops on their way to her house at that very moment. Afraid of going to jail for killing her husband, Silvia tossed maybe 3 outfits into a suitcase and jogged out of the house and toward her car. After she placed the suitcase and the pillowcases into the passenger seat, she shut the door and ran back inside.

"DeShawn! DeAnte!" She called out, approaching their room. "Are you ready?"

When she stepped into their room, the boys were sitting on the floor playing. They hadn't packed a thing. Silvia placed her hand on her forehead. She couldn't waste any more time getting them ready.

"Come on." She said, grabbing both of their hands. "We have to go."

As she pulled them out of the room, they struggled against her tug.

"Nooo, mommy." They protested. "We wanna take our toys."

Silvia looked down.

"Look." She said, not releasing them. "I'll buy you all new toys when we get there ok."

The boys looked at each other. They liked the sound of that. DeShawn and DeAnte broke free from their mother's grip and sprinted towards the front door.

"Yaaaa!" They screeched. "We're getting new toys."

Silvia placed her hands on her hips and blew her hair out of her face. She was still covered in sand, but she didn't care. She could bathe at any one of the million hotels outside of Texas City. Silvia ran down the stairs and stopped in the doorway. She looked back at the home she was leaving behind one last time. This was not how she intended for things to be. A part of her wished she could go back in time. She would've never schemed to get that $20 million and she would've never sent that recording to Infamous, but in real life, you could never go backwards. Time machines only existed in science fiction films.

You could only move forward. Silvia took a deep breath, closed the door behind her, and helped her two sons into the backseat of her Eclipse. Climbing into the driver's side, she instructed DeShawn and DeAnte to buckle their seatbelts as she pulled out of the driveway of her past and headed towards an uncertain future.

....

Sierra blew through her house like a tornado, grabbing only the things that held some type of sentimental value. There was no way of knowing how much time she had to get out of town, so she assumed she had zero. Not wanting to procrastinate in the shower, Sierra simply wiped herself off with a towel and dawned her police officers' uniform. She didn't know what she was going to encounter, but she figured a police officer had a better chance than a civilian.

Sierra was extremely grateful that she hadn't lost her badge in all of the excitement of the day. She pinned it to the chest of her uniform proudly and grabbed two of the briefcases full of money. Sierra was only able to get one of them opened, but she told herself that $5 million was more than enough to carry her to her destination. Once she safely made it to Komodo Island, she would have all the time in the world to pick the other 3 locks.

Sierra carried the briefcases out to her car and placed them in the trunk. Then, she hurried back into the house and grabbed the remaining two. All she removed from the one she successfully opened was $2,000. The rest would be better off hidden. Once Sierra loaded up the money, her sentimental value trinkets, and a few articles of clothing, she was ready to go.

She decided to not contact anyone until she was situated in paradise. True, her family would worry about her, but she would just have to figure out a way to let them know that she was ok. Sierra was a little apprehensive about leaving everything behind, but she got used to the idea days ago. She didn't expect it to be like this, but at least she had the money.

She really felt sorry for Rose. He was a strong man though. If anybody could pull through, he could. She just hoped he wouldn't look at her differently once he found out what she had done. She never intended for him to get hurt. She really didn't. Sierra rolled down her cars windows so you couldn't tell that they were busted out and she pulled off into the night.

She already cleaned the majority of the glass off of the seats, but there were still a few scattered shards on the floorboard. There were several different ways to get out of Texas City, but Sierra chose the route that she felt would be less congested with traffic. She headed in the direction of Hwy 3. Using Hwy 3, she could easily get out of Texas City. Once she made it out of Texas City, her options would be endless.

....

"Be still!" Silvia called to the two boys in the back.

It was nearing their usual bedtime, but for some reason they were both hyper as hell. DeShawn and DeAnte giggled at their mother's frustration. This wasn't the first time they went on a trip in the car. They both knew all too well that they couldn't get a whooping while their mommy was driving. Silvia put her eyes back on the road.

"Calm down." She told herself. "You're upset with the situation, not with them."

Silvia hated to take out her anger and frustration on her sons. She realized that it was the events of the day that had her wired up, not them. They would be alright when they found a nice hotel room outside city limits. Silvia racked her brain trying to come up with the best route to take to get out of town. She weighed her options.

Interstate Hwy 45 was her closes option, but she had seen on Facebook that the police put up roadblocks on I45 and they were checking all vehicles trying to leave Texas City. The City was on a small lockdown because of that cop getting shot. She considered using Hwy 3 or Hwy 146 as well. Hwy 146 would get her out of the city too, but Hwy 3 was closer. In the end, she settled on Hwy 3. It was her best option.

Silvia made a right turn when she exited the Amburn Oaks subdivision and drove in the direction of Hwy 3. Her travel time was only about 10 minutes before she turned onto her road to freedom. Her heart skipped a beat when she noticed a roadblock up ahead. There was a line of maybe 3 cars in front of her.

"Shit." She grumbled.

DeShawn and DeAnte looked at each other.

"Ooohhh. Mommy, you said a bad word." DeAnte accused, smiling mischievously.

Silvia ignored him.

"Ok, Silvia. Think." She urged herself.

She knew that she would look suspicious if she pulled out of line and tried to turn around. There were two patrol cars up ahead, with two wooden partitions blocking both lanes of traffic. You couldn't leave Texas City or enter Texas City without going through them first. Silvia stuck her head out of the window to try and see what was going on.

She noticed that the two officers had photographs in their hands. Silvia knew it had something to do with those people that shot that police office. As long as they weren't looking for her, she should be fine. All she needed to do was stay calm.

....

Sierra watched as the car in front of her spoke with the officers operating the roadblock. She expected this from watching the news. Reports indicated that the shooters they were looking for had suitcases when they fled. The police suspected that they were trying to flee the city, so they set up roadblocks at all of the exits out of town. Sierra knew that her uniform would help her make it past the cops. In her sideview mirror, she saw a woman hanging out of her cars window trying to see what the hold-up was all about.

"Wait a minute." Sierra said under her breath, squinting to get a better look.

"No... fucking... way!" Sierra turned all the way around in her seat and struggled to see past the car that was in between her and the woman.

"Is that... Silvia?" She asked herself, thinking that her luck was too good to be true.

"That IS Silvia!" She exclaimed, when she was sure of the woman's identity.

Silvia was trying to get out of town.

"So." Sierra said, turning back around in her seat. "You think you can try to get me killed, murder your gangbanging husband, and then get away scot free?"

She shook her head.

"Not if I can help it."

The car that was in front of Sierra passed through the roadblock and Sierra pulled up. Silvia noticed the line moving and felt the butterflies in her stomach begin to act up. She had her story ready, but she wasn't sure if the police would believe it or not. She planned on telling them that she didn't feel safe with those killers on the loose, so she was going to stay with her mother in League City until everything calmed down.

Silvia sat there for about 2 minutes before the officer speaking with the motorist backed away from the vehicle and whispered something to the other officer that was with him. Then, they both looked back at her. Fear spread through her body so completely and so quickly that she was trembling before her consciousness even knew it should be afraid.

She instinctively looked in her rearview mirror. There were already cars pulled in behind her. They were so close to her bumper; she couldn't even maneuver her car to turn around. As one of the officers walked past the vehicle in front of her, and approached her car, Silvia felt like a rat caught in a trap.

She watched as the officer still at the roadblock let the lead car pass. The car drove just passed the wooden partitions and then stopped. A woman in a police uniform stepped out and waved at her. Just as the officer made it to her window, she recognized who the woman was.

It was Sierra!

"Can I please see your driver's license and insurance ma'am?" The officer asked, peering inside of her car.

Shaking, and not knowing what to do, Silvia swallowed hard and reached for her glovebox to get her insurance.

Satisfied that she had gotten the revenge she was looking for; Sierra climbed back into her car and drove off.

"Komodo Island." She said triumphantly. "Here I come."

Silvia opened her glovebox and saw the gun she took from Sierra. The same gun she killed Kenneth with. She totally forgot that it was in there. The officer saw it too. He swiftly removed his weapon and aimed it at Silvia.

"Put your hands on the steering wheel!" He shouted.

Silvia complied.

"She's got a gun!" The officer called to the other cop.

Her sons in the backseat started crying.

"Mommy!" They called, afraid of the cops' weapon.

Silvia panicked. She wasn't about to spend the rest of her life in prison. Silvia gripped the wheel tight and looked at her two terrified sons in the backseat.

"Hold on." She told them.

"Don't do it, lady." The officer warned, anticipating her next move. "Don't you fucking do it."

Silvia was no longer listening. She screamed at the top of her lungs and smashed down on the gas pedal, hoping she could push the car in front of her out of the way. Her Eclipse smashed into the rear of the other car. The officer had no choice but to open fire.

BANG! BANG! BANG! BANG!

All fours bullets hit their mark. Silvia jerked from the force of the shells. Sierra heard the shots but kept on driving. The only thing Silvia heard was the screams of her now orphaned sons, and the horn of her car when she slumped over onto the wheel.

Chapter Twenty-One

Squeak dropped down next to Shock.

"Lil bro." He called out to him, with panic and concern in his voice.

Shock grunted as he used his wounded arm to apply pressure to the spot where the Villains bullet had penetrated his abdomen.

"Is he ok?" Shonda asked.

"Yeah. Yeah." Shock answered, using his good arm to lift up to his feet.

Squeak helped him.

"I don't know." Squeak said. "You've already been shot once. Maybe we need to get you to a hospital."

Shock looked Squeak directly in his eyes.

"Are you crazy?" He asked, pulling away from Squeak's grasp. "If I go to the hospital, I got to jail. Fuck that shit. Ungh! Let's just get out of here before it's too late."

Shock walked towards the body of Tao. He was hurting like hell, but he refused to admit it. He knew that if they stayed to try and treat his new wound, either more Villains would show up, or the police would. Shock was a gangster, but he knew the reality was they couldn't survive another shoot-out.

Squeak and Shonda watched Shock, not sure how to react. On one hand, they knew they needed to get the hell out of there, but on the other, they also knew that Shock needed help. Shock dropped down next to Tao and rummaged through his pockets.

"What are ya'll waiting for?" He questioned, looking up at Shonda and Squeak. "I told you I'm ok. Go load up the car with the supplies while I move this Cadillac out the way."

"Fuck it." Squeak thought.

The sooner they got to safety, the sooner they could tend to Shock.

"Come on." He told Shonda, sprinting back inside the house.

Shock watched them disappear through the doorway. Knowing that they were no longer analyzing his every move, he allowed his face to contort into an expression of agony.

Through clenched teeth, he growled, "Augh!"

The bullet that went in and out of his shoulder was a mosquito bite compared to his gut shot. Every time he inhaled and exhaled, it felt as if some evil little creature inside of his belly was striking a lighter and holding it up to his intestines. Shock forced himself to finish his search for the keys to the Cadillac. They weren't hard to find.

Tao had them in his front left pocket. Shock retrieved the keys and glanced at Tao's gun lying next to his head. He couldn't help but to notice the hole that Squeak left in it. Shock smiled at his brother's ruthlessness as he scooped up the weapon. He dropped his own firearm when he had been shot. Shock struggled to get back on his feet.

"I'm losing a lot of blood." He thought, as the stress of standing up left him feeling light-headed.

Shock shook it off and limped over to the Cadillac. Opening the driver's side door, he slumped down hard into the seat. Exhaling heavily, Shock closed his eyes and leaned back. It felt unusually relaxing to be off of his feet.

"I'm... I'm just gonna rest." He mumbled. "Just for a second."

Almost immediately, Shock started slipping away into a dream world. The sleep was so inviting. He noticed the feeling of pain and anguish beginning to subside. Slowly, the reality of what was going on started to fade into a fantasy of bright lights and fluffy clouds.

Shock smiled.

He never experienced a feeling of euphoria like this before. Nothing seemed to matter anymore. Not his past, not his wounds, not his fears... not anything. He concluded the emotion he was experiencing must be joy. He liked joy. It felt good. Shock inhaled but the breath got lodged in his throat. The sudden lack of oxygen rocked his body. Shock's eyes flew open and he began to cough.

Cough. Cough. Cough.

"Nnnnn." He groaned, as the joy left, and the pain returned with a vengeance.

Shock looked around. He saw the pistol on his lap, the 3 dead bodies in the yard, and the garage door rising. Shock remembered what was going on. He hurried to crank up the car. Squeak lifted the garage door up high enough for the Regal to pass underneath, then he watched Shock back the Cadillac out of the driveway. He was still worried about his little brother, but he knew that Shock was a soldier. He would be alright. They just had to hurry.

As Shock turned the Cadillac onto the street, he started coughing again. This time a little more violently then before. Shock covered his mouth with his fist.

Cough. Cough. Cough. Cough.

"Hurry up." He silently urged Shonda and Squeak, as he watched them back out of the garage.

He wasn't sure how much more he could take. He needed to get to a stable position and let Shonda patch him up again. Shock placed his hand back on the wheel. Surprise crossed his face. There were a few drops of blood where his mouth encountered his fist.

Shock had a lot of blood on him, but this particular blood seemed new. Using a clean part of his arm, he dabbed at his mouth.

"Shit." Shock exclaimed.

He had started to cough up blood.

"I can't let them see me like this." Shock decided. "They'll get too worried."

Shonda backed the Regal they had stolen down the driveway and pulled up next to the Cadillac so Shock could hop in. To her surprise, Shock waved for her to follow him, and then pulled off. Shonda got in behind him as he sped off.

"What is he doing?" Shonda asked.

Squeak scratched his head. "Maybe he knows a quick way out of town." He offered.

Shonda turned left behind Shock.

"That doesn't make sense." She said. "He could've gotten in with us and just told me which way to go."

Squeak couldn't dispute her logic. Something was up. They followed Shock for about 3 more blocks before Shonda told Squeak to call him on his cell phone. Shock blew through a stop sign. He was frantically trying to get out of Texas City. His body was begging for more of that sleep he tasted back at the safehouse, but something told him that that just might be the sleep he would never be able to awaken from. He drove fast, struggling to stay focused.

Shock knew that the closes route out of town was Highway 3, so he headed in that direction with determination. He figured it was the best road to take also. Highway 3 was a two-lane street on a side of town that not many people used to enter and exit Texas City. They could probably slide out undetected.

Ring. Ring. Ring.

Shock looked down at his thigh when he heard his cell phone begin to ring. He wondered who it could be. Shock dug the phone out of his pocket.

"Yeah." He answered, recognizing the number as Squeak's phone.

They exchanged numbers back at the safehouse. It was a good thing too, because if he wouldn't have known the number, he wouldn't have answered it.

"Shock." Squeak said. "Where are you going?"

Shock glanced in his rearview.

"Towards Highway 3." He said. "It's the best way out of town."

Squeak looked at the next street sign that they passed. They were within blocks of Highway 3.

"Alright." Squeak told him. "But check this out. I think it would be better if we were all in the same car. We don't wanna risk getting split up."

Shock considered what he said. He didn't want them to know how bad off he was, but he was no longer sure how long he could control the vehicle under his own strength. He was becoming weaker every second.

Shock spit out more blood.

"Ok." He finally agreed.

He could drive no more. Shock got off the gas and pulled over onto the side of the road. As Shonda tried to pull up next to him, they all heard police sirens in the area. Looking around for the direction of the noise, they all saw what had to be at least 6 police cruisers turn onto the street behind them.

"Fuck!" Shock yelled into the phone. "Go! Go! Go!"

Shonda smashed the gas, pulled out in front of Shock, and Shock peeled out behind her. The lead police cruiser was caught off guard by the actions of the Regal and the Cadillac two blocks in front of him. They were responding to a shooting that just occurred on Highway 3. Were those two vehicles somehow involved?

"Maybe they're trying to get out of the way." He thought.

His suspicions rose when he saw both cars turn onto Highway 3. Shonda made a left turn and got the surprise of her life. Not only was there a caravan of police cars now chasing them, there was also a police roadblock up ahead. Shonda saw a line of about 6 cars at a standstill. At the front of the line, she saw two police officers standing in the left-hand lane of the highway. From the way all of the motorists were hanging out of their windows, Shonda could tell something was wrong.

"Tell Richard to just follow me." She instructed Squeak.

As he was relaying the message, Shonda turned the wheel and swung the Regal onto the wrong side of the road.

"Hang on." She said, as she forced the car to go as fast as it could.

Shock floored the Cadillac right behind her. The two cops saw them approaching fast and reached for their weapons. They couldn't get to them in time. In a desperate attempt to stay alive, both officers' dove into the ditch that ran alongside the Highway. The cars lined up at the roadblock watched in awe as the two cars sped by them. Shock followed Shonda as she plowed through the two wooden partitions. They both broke into pieces as the vehicle mowed them down. In his rearview mirror, Shock watched the police cruisers turn onto the street.

"What the hell?" The lead cop said, when he assessed what was going on.

For some reason, those two cars had broken through the roadblock. He got on his C.B. and called in the chase. He was definitely not going to let them get away. Five of the six police cruisers got in hot pursuit of the Regal and the Cadillac. One of them stayed behind to assist the officers in the ditch.

Shock dropped the phone and grabbed the wheel with both hands.

COUGH! COUGH!

Blood oozed out of his mouth.

"Shipt." He mumbled.

It was becoming difficult for him to speak with all of the blood on his tongue.

"Ibbm... not... gone... mabe bit."

COUGH! COUGH!

Shock felt his body get cold. He blinked several times trying to clear his vision, but it was slowly blurring. Squeak turned around in his seat and saw Shock swerving slightly.

"Shock." He called into the phone. "What's wrong?"

He didn't get an answer.

"SHOCK!" He yelled.

Shonda looked in the rearview.

"What's he doing?" She asked, suddenly feeling afraid for her brother.

Shock heard Squeak screaming his name into the phone. He looked at his newfound family in the car ahead of him and felt the tears coming. Shock knew that there was only one way for them to get away. He would have to sacrifice himself. Shock lifted the phone to the side of his face. He spit out a glob of blood to allow him a second of uninhibited speech.

"Squeak." He called.

Squeak was happy to hear his voice.

"Shock." He replied. "Is everything alright?"

Shock grimaced.

"Listen bro." He answered, not wasting any time. "I'm not gone make it. You and Sho..."

Squeak cut him off.

"Don't talk like that, bro. You'll be fine."

Shock began to cough again. Squeak heard him.

"Ya'll just keep driving." Shock told him, ignoring his last comment. "I'm gone make sure ya'll get away. Just... keep... driving. No matter what."

A sharp pain flashed through Shock's stomach and the phone fell into his lap.

"What are you talking about, Richard?" Squeak shouted.

Shonda looked at Squeak and then back at the road. She was flying down the two-lane highway at 95mph. The two deep ditches on either side of the road meant that any mistakes behind the wheel would equal death or something extremely close to it.

"What's going on?" Shonda asked, struggling to keep the car straight.

The extreme speeds were causing the Regal to shake. Squeak kept looking out the back windshield.

"I think he's going to do something crazy." Squeak informed her, not taking his eyes off of Shock.

Shock looked in his rearview mirror and saw the police gaining on them. He knew that he would have to act fast. Shock strained to raise the phone up to his face again.

"Squeak." He called.

"Yeah, bro." Squeak answered.

"Remember the motto you taught me?" Shock asked, allowing the tears to flow freely now.

Squeak thought back. He remembered telling Shock the motto right before they murdered the cop together.

Slowly, Squeak said, "Yeah, bro. Blood is... **Thicker Than Water**."

Shock sniffled.

"Tell Shonda." He said, fighting the emotional and physical pain.

COUGH! COUGH!

"Tell Shonda I said that I love ya'll."

Squeak's eyes got wide.

"RICHARD, NOOO!" He screamed.

The line went dead. Shock tossed the cell phone into the backseat.

"Aiight, cops." He said. "Let's see how bad you want 'em."

Shock took his foot off the gas pedal. Then, he turned the wheel to the left and hit the brake. The cops watched as the driver of the Cadillac turned his car sideways to block both lanes of the road. Not wanting to crash, they all smashed on their brakes.

"Stop the car!" Squeak yelled.

Shock hopped out of the Cadillac with his wounded arm holding his gut, and his good arm holding the gun that he took from Tao. The police jumped out of their vehicles and drew their weapons. Shock left off a few rounds in their direction and limped to the back of the car and popped open the gas tank.

Squeak jumped from the Regal with the A.K. in hand.

"RICHARD!!!" He screamed, running full speed back towards Shock, and shooting in the direction of the cops.

It was a long distance on foot. Shock watched Squeak running towards him, and he listened to the cops demanding that he drop his weapon. With a bloody hand and a heavy heart, Shock unscrewed the gas cap and tossed it to the side. Then, helping his family like he did when he was 5 years old; he put the barrel of his gun into the hole, and closed his eyes.

"DROP YOUR WEAPON!" The cop screamed.

"RICHARD!" Squeak screamed.

BOOOOOOOOOM!

Everyone watched in horror as the Cadillac exploded into a ball of fire. The blast knocked Shock back 15 feet. When he landed, his flesh skidded across the pavement and peeled off in chunks, but he didn't feel a thing. He died almost instantly.

"NOOOO!!" Squeak cried, dropping to his knees.

Shonda rushed to his side crying. She witnessed the entire thing too. Placing her hand on Squeak's shoulder, she urged him to his feet.

"Oh my God." She said, watching as the flames licked at the night sky and the smoke rose towards the heavens.

"He... he... he sacrificed himself for us." Squeak said, reluctantly back pedaling towards the Regal.

Neither him nor Shonda wanted to just leave, but they both knew that Shock was gone, and to stay there would be to make his sacrifice meaningless. Both Shonda and Squeak cried as they ran back to their vehicle. They lost their little brother again, and this time, he wouldn't be miraculously coming back.

Feeling slightly lost, confused, upset, and afraid, they got back inside of the Regal and sped off. Behind them was a roadblock of fire, preventing the authorities from following. A roadblock that their brother had given his life to provide them with. They both tired hard not to look behind them as the flames got smaller and smaller in the rearview. The car was silent except for the familiar sounds of grief, pain, mourning, and loss.

Squeak wiped his face off.

"Shonda." He whispered, staring straight ahead.

Shonda sniffled.

"Yeah?" She asked.

Squeak swallowed hard.

"Richard... wanted me to tell you that he loved you."

Shonda's lips quivered. Then she looked up towards the heavens as she drove.

"I love you too, Richard."

She whispered under her breath.

"I love you too."

The End

To Be Continued In Another Book

EPILOGUE

Seven Days After The Escape

Seven days after Squeak, Shonda, and Sierra fled from the gang war that was taking place on the streets of Texas City, Tx., a red Chevy Impala could be seen pulling into the parking lot of the On Point Barber Shop. The Villains standing guard at the front door of the establishment didn't even reach for their weapons. They were all well aware of the identity of the driver.

The man's name was Hall. Officer Ronald "Pookie" Hall to be exact. He was on the payroll of the TCPD, but he been in Infamous' pocket for years, and since Infamous paid him more than his police salary, it wasn't hard to guess where his real loyalty was at.

Parking in an open spot, Officer Hall climbed out of the vehicle. From the looks of him, you wouldn't even know he was a cop. Hall was wearing an all red Sean John denim unit, with a red Sean Jean ball cap cocked slightly to the right and tilted forward just a little. He said nothing as he walked past the Villains at the door and entered the shop.

As usual, the place was packed with people trying to get haircuts. Hall made his way to the back and knocked on the door that led to Infamous office.

"Come in." Infamous called, watching Hall on the surveillance camera.

Hall obeyed.

Once inside, he closed the door behind him and approached Infamous desk. Infamous was sitting behind his desk, smoking a cigar and watching TV.

Without looking up at Hall, Infamous asked, "So what's the verdict?"

Hall shook his head.

"No, no, and no." Hall replied.

Infamous was not discouraged. He simply dug around in one of the drawers of his desk. Finding what he was looking for, he pulled out a magazine titled, 50 Of The World's Last Great Places. Opening it up, Infamous took a black marker and drew a huge 'x' over destination spots number 1, 2, and 3.

Infamous found the magazine removed from the shelves back at the safehouse. Something told him that Squeak and Shonda fled to one of the locations mentioned in the book, and if he had to check up on all 50 locations to find them, so be it. Infamous wrote the next 3 spots down on a piece of paper and handed it to Hall.

"Find them!" He ordered.

"Don't worry, boss." Hall said. "We'll get them."

....

Judge Susan Criss lightly banged her gavel.

"Quiet please." She said, over the emotional sobs of the family in her courtroom. "I have made my decision."

Everyone got quiet and listened.

"It is obvious to me." She began. "That these two young boys come from a family that is prone to violence. Their father was a drug lord who got gunned down by their mother, and their mother ended up being gunned down by police, right before their eyes, as she attempted to escape prosecution. In cases such as these, I would normally readily recommend that the children be placed in Foster Care. However, seeing as how there are living relatives with no criminal history willing to take them in, I have decided to grant custody of both DeShawn and DeAnte Wayne to their deceased mothers' sister, Ms. Wilma Cartwright".

………………..

Adriana stood in the doorway to her home and watched as her husband, Dr. Terrance Martin drove away. She could tell that something about him was different, but she couldn't quite put her finger on it. He had been somewhat distant for a while now, but he was always distant and depressed. Lately, he had become distant but happy. That didn't sit right with her.

As Terrance drove, he thought about Rebecca. They had become real good friends in the past few days. They both enjoyed each other's company because they both were very understanding about the situations they faced. Dr. Terrance couldn't help but to wish his wife was as dedicated to him as Rebecca was to Rose. She was standing by his side through thick and thin.

Dr. Terrance pulled over in front of the house and blew his horn. Within moments, Rebecca came jogging out. She looked so pretty to Dr. Terrance in her light green sun dress. The longer he knew her, the more she seemed like the perfect woman. Rebecca climbed in and sat her purse down on her lap. Dr. Terrance could tell that she was a little jittery.

"What's wrong?" He asked.

Rebecca ran her fingers through her hair.

"Are you sure this is ok?" She asked. "I mean, I don't want it to seem like I'm going out on dates while my husband lays up in that hospital bed."

Dr. Terrance grabbed her hand.

"It's not even like that, Rebecca." He assured her. "We're just friends. Friends go out all the time. Besides, Rose would want you to do something to clear your mind."

Rebecca looked him in his eyes.

"Well." She said, forcing a smile. "I guess you're right."

Dr. Terrance released her hand and pulled off.

"Of course, I'm right." He told her.

....

Sierra laid stretched out in her hotel room on a bed covered with one hundred-dollar bills. Everything about the Komodo Island was more beautiful and exotic then she had imagined. Giggling and squirming around just to hear the money crinkle, Sierra hit the blunt she was holding.

She called her family members one by one from a stopover in Florida to let them know that she was alright. She didn't want to book a direct flight, so she bounced around from place to place and ended up at her destination 4 days ago. Sierra couldn't believe she pulled it off. After opening all four briefcases, she attempted to count it all, but gave up at only $250,000.

Her next order of business was to purchase some land, get a house built, and make her new life. Sierra grabbed a handful of money and chunked it across the room.

"I'm fucking rich!" She exclaimed, laughing at the top of her lungs.

....

Squeak woke up and reached for Shonda. Feeling only a blanket and no body, he pulled the cover back. Shonda was gone.

"Maybe she went out to go stand on the beach." He thought.

Squeak had to admit that Shonda picked one hell of a spot for them to go to. Everything about the Komodo Island was perfect. The air, the water, the food, the seclusion, and even the people. No one got in your business. Everyone was just there to have a good time.

Squeak rolled over to go back to sleep, but he heard someone coughing in the bathroom.

"Shonda?" He wondered.

Climbing out of bed to go investigate, Squeak was praying that the sudden change in environment didn't get his sister sick. He knew all too well about people going to strange lands and catching deadly viruses. Making it to the bathroom, he opened the door. Shonda was down on her knees in front of the toilet, coughing up the last few bits of her stomach's contents.

She looked like hell.

"Damn, sis." Squeak said. "You been throwing up in the morning for the past few days now. Do you think you're coming down with something?"

Shonda looked up menacingly.

"Hell no!" She replied. "You did this to me." She accused, as she spit into the commode.

Squeak was shocked.

"Me?!" He repeated. "What did I do?"

Shonda lifted her head up and removed her hair from her face.

Looking Squeak directly in his eyes, she said, "I think I might be pregnant."

Special Thanks

First, I would like to thank you, dear reader, for reading my novel, Thicker Than Water, and I hope that you enjoyed reading it as much I enjoyed writing it. Because you have taken the time to dedicate some of your life to reading my book, the two of us will forever be connected and I will forever be in your debt.

I would also like to thank my loving and supportive wife, Raquel Daniels. Without you, this would not have been possible. Special thanks are also due to my children. Heru Aamir Amen-Ra Daniels, Samiah Jayde Daniels, and Gabriel Augusto Cantu III.

Special thanks to my father, Rev. James E. Daniels and my mother Judy A. Colvin. I would also be remiss if I did not make mention of my wonderful family. LaShelle Long, Bobby Robinson, Eddie Daniels, Damon Robinson, Joe Daniels, Joshua Daniels, Jason Daniels, and Hope Daniels.

Special thanks to the artist who created the cover art for my book, Mikey. Last but definitely not least, special thanks to all of my fans. Without you there is no me.

Also, go out and purchase my debut novel, which is already available in stores.

Suicide Note

Be on the lookout for other novels coming soon from Matthew Daniels aka TheRealBookWorm.

Thicker Than Water pt.2

Secret Identity

B.I.E. Manifesto of a Black Identity Extremist

Scapegoat

www.ingramcontent.com/pod-product-compliance
Lightning Source LLC
Chambersburg PA
CBHW021839010726
47493CB00005B/1469